FADE TO BLACK

NOIR STORIES OF DRIFTERS, GRIFTERS & UNLOVABLE LOSERS

Robert White

Close To The Bone Publishing

Copyright © 2024 by Robert White

First published in Great Britain in 2024 by Close To The Bone

ISBN 979-8-32508-527-7

All rights reserved. No part of the book may be produced in any form or by any electronic or mechanical means, including information storage and retrieval systems, without permission in writing from the publisher, except by a reviewer who may use brief quotations in a book review.

Close To The Bone
an imprint of Gritfiction Ltd
Northampton
Northamptonshire
NN4
www.close2thebone.co.uk

The characters and events in this book are fictitious. Any similarity to real persons, living or dead, is coincidental and not intended by the author.

Cover Photo & Interior Design by Craig Douglas
First Printing, 2024

Contents

Author Foreword	i
Marigold's Diner	1
Roy Boone's Return	27
Missed Call	51
The Soul Food King of Indianapolis	53
Ravi Floating in Light	71
If Only Julia	89
Kiss of Death	117
Fish Out of Water	127
A Perfect Stranger	143
I Remember	161
Gone Fishing	181
Kettle Blowing	197
A Civilized Man	211
Home for the Funeral	221
Easy Money	227
Barn Find	239

The One Who Saves You	251
Boosting for the Devil	261
The Defecator	281
Wrong Place, Wrong Time	287
Last Supper in New Zenith	291
Revenge of the Judas Goat	307
Notes on Stories	319
About the Author	321

Author Foreword

I put these 23 stories under the subhead "noir" instead of "crime," "hardboiled," or "revenge," all or any of which would have sufficed under the generic rubric "mystery." It's not that easy to exclude any one of those terms when there's a mixed bag like this. "Noir," however, seems to be the one term critics like to argue about most. In this instance, darkness—mental, physical, or moral—is at the core of every story, whether murder, crime, or depravity is involved.

The one arguable ingredient excluded was the private-eye story, which has firmed up its borders too well owing to the necessity of the "detective" protagonist, although not to the degree of, say, the locked-room mystery. Once atmosphere enters the discussion of "noir" versus "crime," it gets stickier. I believe noir offers the reader that satisfying experience of what's to come, and it's always ominous, more so than other kinds of mystery fiction just as the grim opening scenes of *Bladerunner* propel the viewer toward that familiar sense of noir. Is it the same as Walter Neff dictating his murder confession in the privacy of his darkened office in *Double Indemnity*? Probably not—but, then, Raymond Chandler was the co-writer of that noir classic.

What I love about noir fiction are the many possibilities of character portrayal from the embittered through the revenge-minded to the betrayed, with or without sardonic humor. If you factor in a wicked, if poetic, justice in the denouement, and add a hefty dose of aberrant psychology, then stir in some unpredictable lowlifes (a popular US Midwest term that cuts a wide swath through much of humanity), you have the right ingredients for a stew of gritty noir fiction.

I hope readers of *Fade to Black* will be pleased with the darkest of these tales and that they do not resist those that might skirt the edges of noir fiction with less mayhem or mystery.

My sincere thanks to Craig Douglas for his outstanding magazine and his line of books that do not leave any lover of dark mystery fiction behind.

Robert T. White

Ashtabula, Ohio, USA

Marigold's Diner

Scott Suddeth drove five miles over the speed limit with nothing more on his mind than putting miles between him and that colossal fuckup at the casino back there. Suddeth had years of experience keeping his feelings to himself. Neither man wanted to say anything much after Vegas.

"Sorry, man," Jason said when they'd split up at the motel at first light. Both were lucky to get out of there after the custodian double-crossed them and ratted out the heist. "I thought the guy was solid." Jason's helter-skelter, jailbird tatts were a map of the Southwest's prison system. Scott asked him where he was heading to lie low.

"Arizona," Scott replied. "I got a shitty camper in Kingman."

"The guy" was Jason's contact in the casino they planned to hit, a custodian who could get them an access key to the counting room. Instead, he almost got them twenty years in Ely State for attempted armed robbery. The Nevada Gaming Board had the best CCTV system in the country. They had crack agents on 24/7 call in their enforcement division and, if needed, could assemble a multiagency task force big enough to invade Canada in less time than it took Jason's contact to score his fentanyl.

When the custodian failed to arrive for his shift, they tracked him to his apartment. He sat on his ratty couch huddled under a blanket, blubbering from dope sickness. Scott restrained Jason from beating him to a pulp, which turned out to be a good thing because not only could their inside man not go through with it but he blabbed to a co-worker, who promptly informed management. Had Suddeth stepped into the casino that night, his next few steps would have been between a dozen FBI agents and Clark County's SWAT team.

After that, no casino would need facial recognition software to nail him because he had reconned the small casino in a backwater street off Fremont a half-dozen times for the layout, observing shift changes while dropping a few bucks at the blackjack tables. BOLOs and mug shots of both men would be in every podunk desert town between Nevada and Arizona by noon.

The chamber of commerce sign on Highway 93 announced Pioche ahead with its historical attractions: Boot Hill, Million-Dollar Court House, Thompson Opera House to sidetrack the vacationer—or escapee from Vegas, in his case. He'd just passed Caliente, which dangled natural lures like Echo Canyon and Cathedral Gorge to attract traffic. Scott planned to hook a right turn at Panaca and take Highway 56 into Utah. Having a trio of states looking for him, including Arizona to the south, might increase the odds of a jurisdictional snafu. Scott Suddeth had a gift for statistics and probabilities since youth and liked any improvement in the odds after last night.

At the Utah junction turnoff, the horseshoe warning light signaled low pressure tire. The odds of that happening weren't factored into his exit. Fate stepped in as fate always had before in his life. In this instance, a flattened rattlesnake on the highway had decomposed in the desert sun at exactly the right angle to plant one of its formidable fangs in the tiny space between the sipe and the tire block to leak air in his Civic's left front wheel.

Decision time. Pull off to the shoulder and put on the spare or return to Caliente to avoid a passing state trooper checking him out. In a town of fewer than a thousand residents where he'd stick out like a dog's balls, he decided to pull off at the first convenient stop. Once in Utah, he'd blend in with all the RVs and campers. That settled it: Utah.

Suddeth didn't believe in luck, good or bad. What happened to his heist or his tire didn't mean an unlucky streak commenced. Even seasoned gamblers fell for the Monte Carlo fallacy, believing that, if you flipped a coin and it landed heads five times, then tails would come up next. The universe doesn't change for gamblers; mathematical odds restored themselves to fifty-fifty like water finding equilibrium.

Suddeth was state-raised, did time in juvie facilities, several foster homes, and one nasty county jail in New Mexico but never served time in a real prison. He loathed a state pen as a vampire feared sunlight and wouldn't drive past a prison. At 27, he was wary as a fox for opportunities to get in and out of sticky situations fast. Ever since he hit the road at eighteen, he never stayed long anywhere, ate at diners across the country.

The weathered billboard proclaimed: "Marigold's Diner. Your Last Chance For Gas and Our Heavenly Hamburgers." His steering wheel fought him harder with every mile; his grip on the wheel tightened which whitened his knuckles to diamond points like a boxer's hands.

He swung off and drove around the canopy, past the self-service pumps near the concrete block diner with its triple array of plate glass windows facing the dusty lot. He pulled next to a battered pickup with a load of pallets in the bed beside a Harley Fat Boy with ape-hanger bars.

Observing through the glass, he saw a woman in a robin's-egg-blue uniform wiping down the counter in front of a biker with a braided, salt-and-pepper beard, which jutted up and down as he spoke.

Scott had seen worse eateries in his travels. A white-bearded man in farmer's denims ate with gusto in a booth.

He never looked up. Scott took a seat midway down the counter, too far to hear what the biker said to the waitress, although the words came out in a low rumble. She was intent on rubbing a spot midway between his can of Budweiser and the counter's edge.

When Suddeth upped the ante from break-ins to gunpointing people, he'd developed a keen sense of situational awareness. If anything appeared out-of-kilter to a baseline normal, he did a quiet turnaround and disappeared. He could spot an undercover cop or a set-up in a heartbeat.

The biker never gave him a glance. He was intent on his seduction, although one glance at the girl's set mouth would tell any man she wasn't buying. He reached for the one menu in the rusty chrome holder. It was stained, full of misspellings. Nothing but the standard roadside fare of a greasy spoon: mystery-meat specials, burgers, fries, and beverages. A large man moved behind the serving window. His belly stretched the apron like a pregnant woman's maternity blouse.

The biker reached out a hand to cover hers. She pulled it back the way kids do in the game of slap-hand. Abandoning the washcloth and the biker still talking, she came down to take his order.

"What'll-you-have?" She flashed a pinched-off smile as soon as she uttered her routine line.

Pale like most native residents who endure scorching temperatures by staying inside, she wore her chestnut hair parted in the center with bangs over her eyebrows. Jason would have dismissed her as another "hatchet-faced bitch" in Vegas—except she was out here working in a hole-in-the-wall diner. Up close, he understood the biker's attention. She wore an oversized uniform that disguised her breasts, well out of proportion to her slender physique.

"I'll have a couple of your Heavenly Hamburgers and

coffee."

Being bullied in institutions taught him to spot someone being pressured. He wasn't sure why he wanted to relax her. He wasn't in the habit of picking up strays, especially when things went sour.

"What?"

"You know, the sign."

"I don't know what you mean."

The biker at the end laughed, a sound like coyotes yipping. Cupping a hand to his mouth, he hollered to the man in the kitchen: "Hank! Guy out here wants a couple of your finest Heavenly Hamburgers."

She slipped away as soon as Hank came around the corner wiping his hands in an apron.

"You makin' a joke, fella?"

"I'm trying to order food," Scott said.

"Fuckin' satanic you ask me," the biker growled. "Them hamburgers." He added a snort to his repertoire of yips.

"He means the Marigold sign, Hank." Her voice barely rose above a whisper.

Hank gave Suddeth a derisive look and returned to the kitchen without saying another word.

"I just started here," she said to Scott.

"I'll have a couple hamburgers and coffee," Scott repeated.

She wrote on her pad, peeled away the check, and placed it on the counter. She dinged the bell.

Hank bellowed from behind the serving window: "You ain't got to ring the got-damned bell, Jessica. I'm standin' right friggin' here!"

She blushed. Her skin so pale that Scott watched twin crimson stripes rise up her neck to bloom in her cheeks.

"Come back here, Jess, honey," the biker said. "We

ain't done talkin' about the weather."

The old man in the booth got up and stood waiting in front of the cash register. Jessica rang him up and counted out his change. He folded the bills into his wallet and stopped by his booth on the way to the exit to place two quarters next to his plate.

"Thanks, Clyde."

"See you tomorrow, Jess."

The biker staring at the transaction. "Big tipper," he mocked.

Before his mother led him by the hand to the fire station in Omaha where they'd been living for only a couple weeks, she whipped him around by the arm as though they were a mother-son dance routine. She dropped to her haunches and looked him in the eye.

"I don't know who your father is," she said. "I think he's a biker. Goodbye!"

She rose to her feet, pivoted, and walked away so quickly that he'd have had to run to catch up to her. He never thought of doing it. Even then, he knew she wanted him out of her life. By the time he was twelve and living in his fourth foster home, his interest in psychology drove him to the local public library where he asked for manuals like the outdated *DSM* volumes. He studied them under the sneering gaze of the old female librarian, who checked to make sure he wasn't defacing them. He came to the conclusion his mother exhibited that rare form of bipolar disorder in that she suffered from bouts of hypomania without the attendant depressive cycles.

"Who is Marigold?"

"What? Who?"

He'd caught her in a reverie, obviously unpleasant from the squint in her eyes, a dull sheen. He thought of a drowning victim swimming to the surface.

"Marigold," he repeated.

"Somebody before Hank bought the place, I guess."

Her fingertips danced on the counter top.

"Ain't no Marigold," the biker said, interjecting himself into the conversation.

He hoisted his bulk off the stool and sauntered toward Scott, casually but aggressively like two dogs meeting in the road.

He expected a response but Suddeth stared ahead. He knew bikers, worked with some of them from time to time. He didn't despise bikers because he might have been fathered by one.

Scott dismissed him as a threat when he entered the place. The shiny boots, clean Levi's, leather vest with Mongols patch—all said he was about the outlaw image. Scott was a veteran of diners. He'd observed a thousand males put on displays like male birds wooing females with their colors. Like men who exchange love letters with strange women in prison, there's something about a vulnerable, captive person that draws them to the opposite sex.

"You got a name, dude?"

"Yes, I do," Suddeth replied. He edged his butt over the seat to plant his feet fast if necessary.

"What is it?"

"None of your business."

"Well, Mister None-of-Your-Business, here's a tip for you. That's Hank's girl. You don't want to flirt with her and make Hank upset, now do you?"

"Is that what you were doing? Keeping her safe—for Hank?"

The toothpick in the biker's mouth switched deftly to the other side. Scott rested his right hand loosely on his thigh, palm up—a man with nothing in his hand. He wanted to show submission when he was measuring the distance between his hand and that toothpick for a strike. One to ram the toothpick into the man's throat, the other to rake down the face, gouge eyes, in the "eagle's claw" technique.

"Better watch yourself, buddy," the biker huffed. Suddeth kept his eyes on him as he moved off to pay his check. He'd been knocked out in a street fight once before by a biker who used the look-away-and-sucker-punch on him.

She brought his coffee and gave him a genuine smile this time, making amends, although Scott never blamed her for any of it. If she'd brought his hot coffee sooner, he'd have had that as a better weapon to throw into the biker's face.

The last thing he needed was a dustup in this shithole diner.

Her expression told him she was used to being mistreated. The thought made his gorge rise. Years ago, he had to make the choice between being a wolf or a sheep.

"My name's Scott," he said, extending a hand across the counter.

She hesitated, her body relaxed. She shook his hand once, quickly, and released it.

"I'm still waiting to hear about Marigold."

"I'm new here. I moved up with my son from Vegas a month ago."

No wedding ring but he'd known and picked up many married women who conveniently pocketed the ring at work.

"Odd place to look for work, if you don't mind me saying it," he replied. "Vegas hires all the time."

He sipped his coffee, waiting to see if she'd respond. Hank came barreling around the corner again, eavesdropping from the kitchen. The odor of cigarette smoke clung to him in the wash of his arrival.

"Jessica, If you ain't too busy with these two hundred customers out here, why don't you start prepping for the evening rush."

To Hank, he said: "You have an evening rush? Seriously?"

"Maybe you ought to finish up your coffee, and git on out of here."

"I'm waiting on my hamburgers."

Hank scowled. They watched his broad back leaving for the kitchen.

"I'm in for it now," she whispered.

"What will he do?"

"Mostly dirty jobs, stuff that don't need doing."

"Quit."

"I can't... My little boy needs me."

She left and returned with a paper sack and handed it to him.

"Here are your hamburgers."

"I was planning to eat them here," he said. "But that's fine."

He put a twenty on the counter while she wrote out the check.

"Your change," she said.

"Keep it, Jessica. So long."

"Goodbye... Scott."

At the door, he turned around. "You remembered."

"Good luck wherever you're going."

"Don't count on luck," he said and immediately wished he hadn't. It sounded like a rebuke. She wore her vulnerability like a cape. The world was full of women like her. They hoped the world would treat them well, especially if they had a purchase on beauty. But that never lasted, and once men entered the picture as they inevitably did, they found themselves on the down elevator wondering how it happened so fast.

He tossed the bag on the seat and replaced the leaky tire in minutes. He'd done it faster. When crime became his occupation, not just for the thrill, he wrote himself a list of rules to follow. One was to keep his vehicles in tip-top shape. Let the body rot, it blended into traffic better. Camouflage on the road. In the minutes and first hours after a heist, he was a gazelle on the savanna running under the watchful gaze of hyenas on the lookout for any limp. Like a cowboy in the Old West, his horse wasn't just his transportation; it was his livelihood. Moreover, it was the one thing he counted on to keep him out of jail.

He replaced the tire lever in the trunk and was coming around to get in when a glint from the harsh, reflected sunlight on the ground caught his eye. Tiny grains sparkled in the sandy soil at his feet. He licked his fingertip, bent down and stuck a few grains to it. No doubt about it, that bastard of a biker. He stood up and scraped his sneaker across the ground beneath the gas cap. More grains popped to the surface.

The only question now that mattered was how much. Sugar won't dissolve in gas; it was heavier and sat at the bottom of the tank. Suddeth knew he could drive a short ways before it stalled out, but he couldn't risk more than a few miles.

Empty desert all around, nothing but sand and rocks speckled with bur-sage, cat claw cactus, and mesquite. The empty space yawned at him, indifferent to his problem. He did a quick mental calculation and started the engine. Parking behind the dumpster, he shut off the engine. Two vehicles, a new silver Ford F-150 and an older model Toyota, were parked near the back door. The beat-up, red Toyota obviously Jessica's.

Taking his go-bag from the trunk, he put on a jacket

for the cold desert night ahead, replaced his sneakers with Doc Martens, grabbed three bottled waters, energy bars for food, and an empty 32-ounce for urination. The sack of burgers went into the dumpster. He figured Hank would do something disgusting with his food.

The last item was tig-welded into a secret compartment built in the spare tire well. He set the five-shot, heavy-frame revolver chambered in .44 magnum rounds on his lap, pulled the seat lever as far back as it would go and settled in for his vigil. His view of the highway was partially obscured by the dumpster but he would be invisible to anyone leaving or approaching the diner in the black night. Suddeth never expected to use a big-bore gun in a shootout. He didn't want to field-strip and lubricate it weekly. In an ambush, that gun was far better than the niners thugs used. Some men he partnered with or had to trust over the years were more dangerous than law enforcement, who were required to give warnings before they shot you. It would fire if pressed into a body, bipedal or not, and fire repeatedly.

Being confined in his crappy vehicle for hours didn't bother him; prison taught you how to wait inside a cage or else you'd never survive a long sentence. Sleeping was one way. He nodded off in minutes, barely beneath the surface, another skill he'd taught himself years ago. Suddeth rarely dreamed, and if he did, it was always in the murky black-and-white world of his boyhood at the mercy of the forces of randomness. He always woke up easily and alert.

The sound of big motorcycle engines whining down the highway woke him. Alert in seconds, he pulled the lever to the upright position and listened to the riders cycling through their lower gears with bigger sound waves cascading against the concrete blocks and thick desert night air. Scott couldn't see from his vantage but he knew they pulled up to the front of the diner and were lining up their iron horses in a row according to their positions: ride leader first and every member according to his place in the gang's hierarchy.

The back door opened. Jessica came out with a large garbage bag in each hand. Her head down, she didn't see his car until she'd tossed the bags in and closed the lid. He set the revolver on the passenger seat.

"It's me, Scott," he said, rolling down the window, and calling in a friendly voice to avoid startling her.

"What—what are you doing out here?"

She cast a look over her shoulder, ready to flee.

"I'm not here for trouble, Jessica." He was afraid she'd have run away with sparks flying from her shoes if he tried to exit the car.

"That biker this afternoon—remember? I think he put sugar into my gas tank." It was a reasonable lie because it had happened once before, forcing him to clean out the fuel injector.

"Ah, I thought one of the dispensers was really low when I refilled them," she said.

"I need your help. I'm willing to pay."

"I don't know," she replied. Again, the uncertain, backward glance to the diner. "Those biker friends of Hank's are here. He lets them stay past closing. He makes me stay late. It might be hours."

"That's fine. I can catch up on my sleep."

"I can call you a cab. It might be a while before they come out this far."

"I'd rather give you the money than some Uber driver," he said. "Look, I just want to park it here and have it towed in the morning."

He stepped out of his vehicle calmly like a man approaching a stray cat. Taking out his wallet, he held out a wad of bills. "Maybe you and your boy can use some money."

The light bulb above the door in the back of the building was a 100-watt bulb but didn't shed enough light this far to let him see her eyes or glean much from her expression. He hoped she hesitated because she was looking at the money in his outstretched hand.

"Two hundred dollars," he said quietly.

"Why so much?"

"I'm in trouble," he said. "Something back in Vegas." All that psychology he'd studied told him she was the kind who took in strays and didn't think about the consequences. Like his mother.

"I can use it to pay a real babysitter," she said, as though deciding aloud.

Still wary, she let his hand brush against hers with the money; now suddenly it was in her hand as though it had passed to her without effort. He breathed easier, knowing this was progress.

"I'll catch few winks. Just tap on the window. I'll wake up."

He thought she was still standing there looking at him until he heard the back door open and a rectangle of light bloomed in the blackness. The tough part lay ahead: convincing her to let him stay at her place. Every barracks, sheriff's station, and motel office between here and Las Vegas already had his face coming over the FAX machine.

She came out at two in the morning. Minutes earlier, the throttling of big Harley engines had shattered the quiet of the night air.

She didn't come to wake him, however. Instead, she got into her car. The cone of light shed by the backdoor bulb showed her unsteady on her feet. She dropped her keys, bent down to the gravel on wobbly legs to retrieve them. She drove off weaving. Scott cursed her, himself for being gulled by her soft-spoken, shy-girl act. His history of pickups in diners like the Marigold told him she was just another hookup looking for after-work sex. Married, single—it didn't matter. For money, they did what he asked and never thought about who was at home waiting.

She crossed the centerline three times and swerved twice to avoid the shoulder.

Home turned out to be a two-story apartment that would have embarrassed Soviet architecture in the 1980's—an ugly, L-shaped building two miles from the diner in the middle of nowhere. Nothing but a rusted, barbed-wire fence and balls of tumbleweed banked against it. Tiny windows spaced at intervals, no balconies to distinguish one apartment from the other.

Jessica parked in front of the metal steps leading to the second floor and got out before he parked his stuttering Honda. He ran after her, hissing, "Jessica, hold up!"

She ignored him, stumbling twice. At the top of the steps, he caught her hard by the triceps.

So unsteady, she swung into his chest and nearly collapsed. Her breath reeked of fumes. The dim lighting reflected the glazed look in her eyes. They darted side to side, unfocused. She spoke in a slurred jumble.

"Give me your key. Is this your apartment? Jessica!"

Her head lolled or nodded—he couldn't tell. He reached into her uniform pocket and drew out the keys. One had the apartment number. He opened the door and came back for her. She didn't resist him. He pulled her inside and set her on the couch. She moaned and slumped.

"God damn it, Jessica! Wake up!"

He grabbed her chin in his fist. Her eyes wouldn't focus. He gave her a hard slap across the face. He was about to repeat it when he felt a presence behind him. A small boy in PJs was rubbing his eyes and looking at him.

"Mommy," he said.

"Everything's OK, kid. Go back to sleep. Go on now. Your mother's fine."

The boy did as he was told.

When he turned back to Jessica, she had passed out. He picked her up and carried her down the hall to the bedroom she shared with the boy. He was already in his small mattress on the floor against the opposite wall. He laid her in bed, took off her shoes off and loosened her uniform. She was so blitzed that he could have stripped her nude.

Having had his fill of sleep, Suddeth lay on the couch in the tiny apartment and waited for dawn.

In the morning, he called a tow truck service in Caliente to have his Honda towed to a station to have the tank drained and refilled and the fuel filter replaced. He grabbed his go-bag from the car and waited for the tow truck. He gave the driver instructions, got the address of the service station he worked for, and gave the man a generous tip.

His stake intended for the casino heist was dwindling. An unbroken rule was to hold enough back for emergencies.

Jessica was still asleep; her drunken snores reverberated into the living room. The boy came out and stood there staring at him. Scott realized for the first time he was a Down syndrome child. Thinking of his mother in there sleeping off a drunk infuriated him. She'd left the kid alone all night. Some mother, the pig.

He watched the local television news channels and played the radio in the kitchenette for any news about him. Las Vegas hampered bad news in the media because it affected tourism. Still, something might have made the news. He had to be on law enforcement's radar.

Around noon, he made the boy a PB & J sandwich and gave him a box of fruit juice to drink because the milk in the carton had soured.

"What's your name?"

He made a mushy-voweled response. He guessed *Joshua*.

"Joshua, I'm a friend of your Mom's, OK? She has an upset tummy right now, so I'll stay here to make sure you're both all right. Is that OK with you?"

"O'ay wi'me."

"Good. Now, go play in your room for a while. I'll give Mommy some medicine."

"O'ay."

The air in her bedroom had a fruity reek. What Suddeth wanted to do was slap the bitch in there silly.

"Jessica," he said, shaking her by the shoulder. "Get up. Your boy's awake. He needs you."

She slurred gibberish at him and then bolted upright. Her uniform top had loosened more in the night. He remembered how disheveled she appeared under the lighting last night. She ripped at the collar and popped buttons in some kind of wild-eyed frenzy, as though she were caught in a waking nightmare. She sat against the bed board in a stupor. One of her breasts exposed. Then she turned to look at him, as though trying to remember who he was.

Scrambling out of bed, she shoved him aside and staggered out of the room. Suddeth found her cradling the ceramic bowl with her arms and heaving into it. Streams of brackish vomit were ejected from her throat and splattered against the cover and rim of the bowl. In seconds, the stink of her vomit wafted into the hallway and left its effluvial reek all the way to the kitchenette.

"What were you thinking, drinking like that with your kid alone?"

Her head swiveled toward him and her eyes rolled back. She fainted.

Scott ran to her, picked her up in a heap, and placed her in the shower. He let the cold water hit her full force. She screamed once. He shut the valve and stripped off her fouled uniform. He pulled her socks and panties off and adjusted the spray to lukewarm. He soaped her body, avoiding her breasts and pubic areas. Then he picked her up and laid her on the narrow floor between the sink and shower and chafed her skin with towels. She moaned and cried out.

This wasn't a typical bout of drunkenness followed by waking in a booze fog. She was barely conscious after his manhandling.

Calling her a doctor meant a welfare check by cops and a visit from Child Services.

"No strays," Scott said to himself, leaving her lying and groaning on the bathroom floor. He was going to check on the boy when a triple knock at the door stopped him. He fetched his gun from the go-bag, walked to the door with finger on the trigger and the gun resting against his backside.

The peephole showed a rough-looking, older woman with a cigarette in her mouth standing outside the door. No one with her.

He cracked the door. "Who are you?"

"I'm Myra. Jess asked me to check on the boy if she got home late."

"It's afternoon."

"I got a life, too, ya know."

She was anywhere from forty to sixty. Scraggy wisps of dyed hair made a zigzag on the crown of her head where the roots were exposed. Her face crosshatched with wrinkles, the cigarette arcing to her mouth as though she needed it to breathe.

"You can't smoke in here," he said.

"Jess lets me smoke."

"I'm her cousin from Arizona," he replied. "I don't."

She muttered something, then stubbed out the cigarette against the door frame.

She told him she lived in the apartment below, and checked up on Joshua but apparently kept no set hours. She tried to go past him into the apartment, but he blocked her.

"Jessica's in the shower right now. Come back later."

"Tell her she owes me for Tuesday, you got that, cousin from Arizona?"

She lit up before she was halfway down the metal stairway.

Jessica didn't come around until nearly three that afternoon. He'd heard from the gas station that his car wouldn't be ready until the next day. He left instructions for it to be towed back to the apartment where he'd pay the driver's fee and the station's bill at the same time. He sweetened the proposal with an extra fifty bucks off the books for the service manager and promised a twenty over the bill for the tow-truck driver.

"They drugged me," she said, sitting up on the couch, still groggy.

"How?"

"Billy, Carl, and T.J. Billy's the one who hassled you at the diner."

His first impression about her had been right, but he didn't trust his own judgment.

"Hank gave me a soda. I didn't have anything else."

"Did they make him do it?"

"He's afraid of them guys. He acts like he's one of them but he's shit-scared when they come around."

"Did he—"

"Did he rape me, too? Is that what you want to know?"

"Easy, Jessica. I'm not here to judge."

"Why are you here then? What are you doing in my

apartment? Get the fuck out!"

She got up and stumbled down the hall. He heard her sobbing and Joshua crying, trying to comfort her.

Decision time: get out of this sordid mess before it sucked him into it. He'd already squelched through enough emotional mud with this mother and child he barely knew. What did she expect from him anyway?

When she came out of her bedroom hours later, he was watching the news. He didn't say anything. She looked ghostly pale with her dark brown eyes sunken into her face, her mouth a tight slit.

She walked past him to the cupboard for a sleeve of crackers and poured herself a glass of water. When she passed him, she said: "I need to put something on my stomach."

"You don't owe me an explanation. This is your place. Look, I can make the boy some food until you feel better."

"I'll feed my son. Be gone when I come out of the bedroom. You men, you're all the same, all alike—"

He leaped from the couch and grabbed her hard by the shoulders and shook her.

"We are not all alike! I'm not like those animals!" He didn't understand his own rage.

Like a dam bursting under too much pressure, she broke down. She told him, a stranger, what she'd never have told anyone, including that wretched woman from downstairs. She was a Jehova's Witness, like her husband who brought her out West to join a community. He abandoned her and the boy soon after. When it came to the gang rape, she said she remembered being in the kitchen with Hank's beefy red face handing her the soda can and looking at her in "a weird way." She was used to his grabby hands but that look was different. Then she remembered her uniform being rucked up around her thighs, hands pulling at her, then nothing. She said she was "gone."

"Gone?"

"My mind took me somewhere else," she said quietly. Tears streamed down her face in the same tracks as the ones that dried. He held her and let her cry.

"That's the whole catastrophe of my life so far," she said. "And it ain't over yet."

Suddeth cleaned her apartment, washed out the bathroom, and opened the windows to air out the place. By ten that evening, the sounds of mother and son talking together had stopped and he heard breathing coming from their room.

He decided without actually thinking it. Rummaging in the boy's toy box, he found water balloons, an empty pickle jar from the wastebasket, and a thick athletic sock from the clothes bushel in the corner of the dining room. Her cupboards were nearly empty except for a few cans of vegetables and tuna. He took a can of tuna, grabbed his bag and her car keys; then he headed for the parking lot.

He siphoned gas into the jar from her tank and placed it on the seat next to his bag. He drove to the diner, killed his lights and slowed to a crawl; he noted the Harleys out front, and parked behind the dumpster.

With his infrared pen light, he checked the items he needed: gun, nylon twist ties, length of rubber tubing. He carried odds and ends like tubing, which had more uses than the average person thought of besides siphoning gas. It made a handy tourniquet to stanch an open wound or a garrote for that rare occasion when he might need to choke someone out. He even carried cattail cobs for starting a fire, thickening a stew on the run, or using the pollen for stuffing into a jacket for extra warmth. He'd have eaten them at a pinch.

With his pen light, he checked his watch. One-thirty-two in the morning.

Running below the window levels, he heard laughter and talking inside. He touched the mufflers: all three cold. He inserted the gas-filled balloons into the exhaust.

Racing around back with his homemade sap of a tuna can inside the sock, his gun snugged into the back of his belt, Suddeth entered the storage room to the kitchen. He knew how to move in the dark without knocking into things.

All four were boozing it up. The pungent aroma of weed filtered back to him. The familiar, obscene-laden language of rough men. He'd heard talk like it all his adult life, heard about heads broken and faces smashed in, enemies hurt, people cheated, women fucked—heard it so many times in so many places that it meant nothing anymore.

Drinking meant pissing. No opportunity in the dining area. Smoking weed induced hunger. A better chance that way. Sooner or later, Hank would be sent to the back for grub. He found a place to hide behind a stack of cartons containing industrial-sized cans of vegetables. He sat down to wait with more patience than a cop on surveillance.

An hour passed before he heard someone coming. The shuffling gait said: Hank, the fattest of them.

Rising, he crept toward the sound. Hank's shoes and trousers to the knees, obscured by the open door of the big freezer.

Scott moved across the cement floor around the food tables. Stopping a couple feet behind Hank, he whispered his name.

The big man jumped and dropped the package of frozen burgers. Scott brought his sap down on Hank's head with one tight, fierce swing. Hank stutter-stepped backwards into the freezer and nearly toppled it. He slumped to the floor.

Scott stood over him. "Here's one more from

Jessica." He split Hank's forehead open, creating a scimitar-shaped gash of a wound. Hank jerked on the floor like a fish hauled on deck. His lips parted. A ropy drool streamed out.

Tucking the sap in his back pocket, he brought out his gun and entered the dining room like a customer returning from the lavatory. The smallest biker sat astride a chair facing the booth with his two comrades leaning against the back, both smoking and laughing at some anecdote.

He was still talking but his two companions spotted him at the same time. Both sat upright like marionettes jerked by one wire. Before they could scramble out of the booth, Scott pointed the barrel at the back of the little biker's head.

"Carl, Carl! Shut up! Stop talking! Look behind you, for fuck's sake!"

"What the fuck are you—Whoah, hey, what the fuck—"

"Shut up, Carl," Scott said. "Stand up, all three of you."

"What are you doing here, you crazy motherfucker?"

To Billy: "You tub of shit. You feel like fucking up my car now?'

Carl, still astride the chair, said: "Billy, he's the same guy—"

The other biker, T.J., said nothing during the exchange. He smoked his blunt and stared calmly at Suddeth. That told Scott who the alpha male of the dog pack was. Smaller than Billy, but without the gut, he had muscled forearms and big hands.

"Stand by the counter. If I say it again, I'll shoot. Who wants to be first?"

Billy and Carl muttered curses but stood up and moved to the counter. T.J., watchful as a cat, went last.

"All of you, hands on the counter, spread your legs."

They assumed the position. Billy growled, "Lights are on, asshole. Some trooper goes by and sees us standing here—"

He flicked Billy's ear lobe with the barrel, cutting off his speech. He kicked all three pairs of legs wider apart.

"You ain't no cop, motherfucker," Carl said.

"What now partner?" T.J. asked, his voice as calm as before.

Suddeth hit Billy over the head with the gun butt hard enough to fracture his skull. He shifted to Carl, who half-turned and took the force of the butt on the bridge of his nose, blinding him, and sending a red geyser into the air between them. Before he fell backward in a sprawl, T.J. lunged with his boot knife and stuck the blade between Scott's ribs. Expecting something from him, Suddeth had partially twisted out of range but still took three inches into his side.

T.J. was on him in a split-second, bear-hugging him down to the floor. Scott's back and shoulders slammed into the legs of chairs and sent them flying. He held the gun but couldn't raise it for a shot.

Then, sensing he had victory over the smaller man, T.J. reared up to hammer Scott's face with his fist. Suddeth jammed the gun into the biker's body and fired until the click of dry-firing was the only other sound besides Carl's snake-like slithering on his back into chairs, upending tables. Suddeth rose to a sitting position, his side a blow torch of agony, and watched the little biker stagger to his feet and lurch toward the kitchen.

His vision blurry, he swung the pistol around in a 180-degree arc to ward off any further attacks, but Billy and T.J. were both prone, out of the fight.

Scott walked to the back door, alert for an ambush from Carl. He started pulling the car keys from his pocket until he realized two of his fingers were broken, sticking away from his hand at crazy angles. He didn't recall it happening.

The car lurched, stalled, stalled again, and finally caught. He did a donut in the soft ground behind the dumpster and fishtailed his way to the road. He gave Jessica's car as much speed as it would handle, but the engine was in lousy condition and had no acceleration.

The motorcycle engine started before he was two hundred yards up the highway. It gained steadily in the rearview mirror—that is, until it erupted into a halo of flames from the exhaust like some kind of trick motorcycle in a circus.

The rider swerved back and forth, panicking, unable to get the bike under control. Scott watched in the side mirror as it veered sideways with a fantail of yellow-red-blue flames in its wake. The crash in the desert terrain at that distance was a giant match appearing in the darkness.

A second flash appeared seconds later. Scott didn't know how many were chasing him. He came close to fainting before he reached Jessica's. When she opened the door to him, her hands shot to her mouth in horror. Minutes later, he sat on the toilet seat watching her clean his wound with a bottle of antiseptic.

"You'll need stitches," she said.

"I just cleaned this toilet," he said. "Now look at it."

The blood that dripped from his side soaked his Levi's down his pant leg to pool around the edge of the toilet.

"You'll be lucky if you don't get sepsis."

He said: "Billy the Kid once squeezed a pint of pus out of a gunshot wound." Talking tough. She wasn't impressed.

The sky lightened from matte-black to cobalt blue in the false dawn. She helped him down the stairs with her son following behind in his pajamas.

"We should wait for my car," he said to her again. "This junker of yours won't make it."

"We'll make it," she insisted. She'd taken the keys from his hand. "I'm driving. Make sure Josh is buckled in back!"

Myra came out of her apartment to watch them. Jessica ignored her questions.

Jessica didn't turn her head to look at the smoldering remains of the two Harleys, one in a ditch and the other twenty yards out in the desert. She didn't even turn to look at Marigold's Diner when they passed it with its lone boobytrapped bike standing out front—a horse without a rider.

"You made it, Jessica," Suddeth said, breaking the silence. "You're free now."

She quoted the bible in response: "Behold, I shall send you out as sheep in the midst of wolves."

Scott wondered which she thought he was, sheep or wolf. In the back, Joshua read his book, occasionally sounding out words. Scott Suddeth, never one to pick up strays, thought about fate as he stared through the windshield at the thunderheads building up over Iron Mountain.

Roy Boone's Return

It was inevitable. The two trashiest families in town with all their brood would find their way to one another. Intermarriages between the Clancy and Boone clans were as common as dirt and as old as water, as the Northtown saying goes. If you see a Boone smiling from the *Herald-Tribune*'s "Who's Engaged?" section, you'll probably see a photo of a Clancy grimacing as he's shoved into the back of a cruiser or a different Boone doing the perp walk in front of the Justice Building; in fact, both occurred on the same day. If you live here, you became used to seeing a Boone's or a Clancy's name in the *Trib* tagged with the phrase so-and-so "is no stranger to the police…" right next to the photo.

I won't say your average Boone-Clancy marriage lasted any longer or shorter than your average citizen's, but I will say that, when one of them had a marriage end, no one in town was surprised if it ended violently. A coroner's signature on an autopsy report was more likely to grace a Boone or Clancy certificate than a justice of the peace's. The saying "a Boone (or "a Clancy") divorce" became another familiar Northtown saying.

What no one saw coming in this disturbing mashup of genetics was Roy Boone. His mother Rosalee was a Clancy who died in a car crash with her drunken husband behind the wheel. Roy, however, was an anomaly. For one thing, he was handsome as the devil, smart enough to graduate college, and athletic. Boone males were normally known as much for their beer bellies as their low IQs and tendency to violence. Roy was lean, wiry, a basketball star voted prom king. When he failed to get into OSU's med school, he obtained a license as a chiropractor.

"Doctor" Roy, as his family insisted the papers call him whenever he attended one of their clan weddings, was often seen with an attractive woman by his side. Most of our local beauties were willing to turn a blind eye to his notorious family. One relationship even reached the level of engagement, but it didn't last long. She was from Akron and rumor had it she was related to the Goodriches. The intermingling of families must have proved too much when they actually got to meet some of the Boone clan and saw the threat of white-trash blood looming, up close and personal. A Boone get-together was basically a drunken, hillbilly dustup and in this case put the kibosh on the couple's nuptials.

Roy had it made, the family boasted, when his practice took off. Everyone thought he'd managed to escape the curse of both clans. He had an expensive house with a four-car garage in Vireo Estates, Northtown's only gated community. Passing his driveway, I scoped an Audi, a Jag Spyder, and a Range Rover—and the best part, townsfolk agreed, was that Roy didn't crow about his success.

When I first interviewed Roy, I was in Sports where all *Tribune* probationers started out. As a veteran reporter told me, "You can be dumb as a box of rocks and still do sports-writing. It's all clichés." Roy had just been named "all-state," and I might have been a bit too cocky in my tone, remembering all those braindead jocks from my own high-school days. Most of those guys were stuck in dead-end jobs around Northtown getting drunk reliving their glory days. Roy picked up on my tone right away but didn't hold it against me. He was a gentleman, all courtesy and politeness. More impressively, his responses to my inane questions ("What does the future of basketball hold for Roy Boone?") were thoughtful and realistic. ("I'm not nearly good enough for the NBA, but maybe a small college somewhere.")

Some townsfolk might have resented his fortune, mocking him as "the King of Northtown," although he didn't flaunt his success outside owning an expensive home with vehicles lined up and down the length of his curved driveway bordered with brilliant red hibiscus plants with blooms the size of grapefruits.

Roy's rise to prosperity took years; his fall, however, was as rapid as if he'd grabbed hold of a manhole cover and stepped off a fire escape. It began with accusations of inappropriate touching of one high-school volleyball player who had come to his clinic for treatment. Then her classmate, a soccer player he'd also treated, came forward. Then it turned into an avalanche of accusations and unfounded rumors on social media. I'm ashamed to say my own paper investigated some of these stories as if media in that age group were anything but a stewpot of half-baked rumors. By that time, I was the *Trib*'s "crime beat" reporter. While the police were investigating, the first lawsuit was already filed.

Worse always comes to worse, as people like to say, and Roy was formally arrested for sexual assault. His lawyer argued for change of venue because, he exclaimed, the town "was poisoned against my client's family." The presiding judge denied the motion and the trial went forward. It lasted two weeks; the verdict was evenly split. The city attorney's office filed again and a second trial rendered a ten-against, two-for Not Guilty. When the holdouts wouldn't budge, the judge declared a mistrial. The prosecuting attorney refused to file a third time, citing "witness problems." In other words, the two girls' testimony was unraveling.

Even without a criminal conviction, the civil trial proved the death knell of his good luck. He was found guilty by a seven-to-five majority and was ordered to pay a huge judgment. His assets—house, cars, and bank account—were seized or frozen pending an appeals court decision. By then, Roy was bankrupt. He found himself evicted and had to move in with a cousin on the east side of town. Then he disappeared. His clinic was torn down when the hospital bought the land for extra parking space. No one in years could recall seeing Roy in Northtown again, not even his combined families and all their prolific breeders.

Boone's name came up seven years after the civil trial. At first, it was just barroom gossip. It was shortly after the town's first unsolved murder in anyone's memory, and I was all over it, bugging Northtown's PD's public relations officer daily for updates. People naturally began to speculate who the murderer of a respected local citizen could be.

There was reason to speculate. The gossip mongers said Boone might have held a grudge against both the town and Steven Gleason. Gleason had been a juror on his civil trial. Roy's name easily got tossed into those casual speculations all around Northtown. People like to hear about sordid catastrophes. The police, however, weren't naming suspects. Word got out that a whole bunch of Boones and Clancys were on that list of "persons of interest" for one reason or another.

Three months passed, Gleason's murder faded from interest but it wasn't forgotten. When a second person was found murdered who had a connection to Roy Boone, gossip ran amok. Bobby Joe Tennant was no taxpaying, solid citizen like Gleason. His death could have been explained by his past record of drug convictions going back to high school. He died of blunt force trauma, according to the ME's report. The blows could have come from an ordinary carpenter's hammer. Someone got behind him and delivered three blows to his head.

I managed to get a peek at the preliminary report owing to my job and tried to decipher the pathologist's handwriting and arrows aimed at parts of the victim in that boilerplate drawing of a male's nude body.

"Doc, what's that say? Your handwriting's atrocious even for a doctor. And what do those squiggly lines coming out of his head indicate?"

He snatched the page from me. "Jesus, are you stupid or what—'Brain matter extruding from both nostrils,'—" Doc Frieland read out.

"Je-sus is right."

"Those blows were delivered with some force," Doc said, nodding. He sounded gleeful.

The police rounded up the town's drug freaks, meth cooks, and pushers, interviewed others in county lockup and even paid a visit to some local felons doing hard time for drug-related crimes in the state pen in Youngstown.

Nothing, nada, zip.

The story cooled and I went back to my usual round of small-time stuff: the B & Es, the domestic violence calls, the drunken brawls on Bridge Street, possession of drug paraphernalia, possession with intent to sell, et cetera et cetera—*ad nauseam*. In other words, all the lowlife activity a rust-belt city like mine gets up to when the factories close and the marriages dissolve like sugar in water.

In my ambitious little heart, I yearned for the Big Story. For months, I went out on my own time to do some amateur sleuthing, conducting witness interviews while doing my normal routine of writing up sob-story articles my idiot fellow citizens told me when they forgot about the baby or toddler in the car while shopping at Walmart or when they stood in front of the fire-blackened ruin that used to be their home, scratching their asses and wondering how it could have happened. Our fire department hands out smoke alarms like candy corn at Halloween every year to no avail. I must have written "We-couldn't-get-the-dogs-out-in-time" a dozen times. Often it was Granny forgotten in the back bedroom.

Drinking is an honorable journalist's occupational hazard. I started hanging out more often at the Wyandotte Club on Bridge Street and that's where I finally overheard a useful tidbit. "Black" Bart Massey, deputy sheriff and former jock at my high school never said two words to me back then unless it was when he shoved me against the locker and threatened to knock out my teeth because I'd bumped into him. Massey prowled the bars for women, a real whoredog, but he likes to brag, so when I heard him mention to Petey Maki a couple bar stools over that Ray Jarvi was "trying to find Roy Boone," my ears perked up.

"Why's he looking for Roy after all these years?" Pete asked him.

"Ray's former girlfriend Corrine asked him to."

Raimo Jarvi is Northtown's only private investigator. I know him from my contacts with the same law enforcement people. Ray was severely burned in a tent fire when he was a kid and his face carried bad scars from it. People in town say Ray opened up his practice after the lawsuit was settled "because he ain't got nothing better to do all day but sit around and listen to Bart Massey brag about the women he's been with."

As usual, gossip gets part or most of it all wrong. Ray Jarvi solved a couple big cases two or three years ago and stepped on some important feet doing it.

The next day, I paid *Raimo Jarvi Investigations* a visit.

"Let me help you find him."

"I don't need your help."

"I can put my paper at your service, you know, like, setting up a tip line—"

"I told you I'm not looking for Roy Boone," Jarvi replied.

"That's not what a little birdie told me in the Wyandotte."

"Bart talks way too much. Don't let the door hit you in the ass."

A few productive minutes in the *Tribune*'s library riffling through old copies of the Society pages and I found her: Corinne Mohan Lesperance. Even her name sounded rich. Not his ex, though, because they were never married. She was the almost-wife. Writing those godawful Society pieces, I used to put my brain on the desk while I composed. Hers must have been published just before my transfer. My promotion to "Crime" didn't come a day too soon.

No law prevented me from contacting Jarvi's client. I paid her a visit that same day.

"How'd you find me?"

Her first question after I explained who I was and after my pitch on what I could do for her.

"I'm not a private cop like Ray Jarvi," I said, "but you still have a distant relative here."

Her facial muscles twitched, creating a moue. "My cousin Alyce Blymire. It figures. She introduced me to Roy at her engagement party at the country club."

"Look, I won't get in Jarvi's way," I said. "He won't even know I'm around."

I made a sign of zipping my lips shut and finished up with the Boy Scout salute. Truth was, I could not have cared less whether Jarvi knew I was horning in on his case.

"It doesn't matter," Corinne said. "It's not a secret."

"If you don't mind, and I know it's none of my business, I'm curious why you care whether Roy is back in Northtown. After all, he didn't—"

"—marry me?" Corinne finished. "You're right. It's none of your business. Roy didn't deserve having his reputation trashed. Those girls lied at the trial. I'll say this much. I have a picture of returning Roy's ring in my head that still haunts me. I'm a happily married woman now with kids. But I let my family bulldoze me. This is one small thing I can do for him."

So where to look for one of Northtown's once favorite, now disgraced, sons?

If Roy was working through a "hit list," I had to discover why Bobby Tennant was a target. Did he sell drugs to Roy? Did he rip him off in a deal? Hardly a killing matter but who knows when it comes to rage that boils for years and finally boils over? I've seen my share of Northtowners who got killed for some pretty silly reasons.

I dug through Bobby's past and every time I discovered Ray Jarvi had already gotten there ahead of me. After a few beers at the Wyandotte, I swallowed my pride and called Jarvi's office.

"If we pool our time and resources," I pleaded, "we can learn more, sooner."

"I'm not interested in collaborating with you or furthering your career. Get your Pulitzer without my help."

"C'mon, Jarvi, be reasonable—"

Click.

Not even 'goodbye,' the scar-faced creep—

I was determined to find Roy Boone before Jarvi, and my goal was to get to him with the blood still wet on his hands. *We'll see who laughs last, Mister Gumshoe.*

I had this much going already: Tennant said he was a pal of Roy's, but those who knew Bobby back then called it bullshit. "Roy never had much use for Bobby at all," a former girlfriend told me. "He told Bobby this one time I remember if he sold drugs to any of his friends, Roy was gonna find him and stomp the yellow shit clean out of him. His exact words, man... Boy, was Bobby pissed off!"

"Did Bobby do anything about it? I mean, did he

ever confront Roy?"

"Oh hell no," she said. "Bobby was full of more shit than a Yuletide turkey, always braggin', always actin' tough, sayin' he knows all Northtown's big shots 'cuz he sells 'em drugs. But it was all talk, ya know."

Still, I reasoned, Bobby could have sold drugs to someone Roy cared about and despite the passage of years, Roy could be collecting some late payback. I spent hours going half-blind in the microfiche room checking out drug-related deaths between the dates of Roy's trial and the time he disappeared, none of it digitized for lack of money. Seven deaths, all young people between 22 and 30. Not one among those deceased had any connection to Roy or to his family.

I used an old ruse that Ray Jarvi might have liked. I called both girls at the center of Roy's catastrophe. I wheedled my way past their mothers with a smidgeon of scuttlebutt I'd heard on the streets myself. I hinted a decision on Roy's estate by the final Court of Appeals in Columbus was "forthcoming"—not a complete lie, of course. Judgment Day is forthcoming as far as that goes. I was grateful to the Me-Too movement for lubricating the wheels of Justice with a heavy dollop of greed on the part of accusers of past sexual harassment or assault.

Both Kristy Lynne Whitmire and Donna de Lobo were as easy to crack open as rotten pistachios. Neither girl admitted it openly but the subtext was easy to read. Both were coerced. I knew their testimonies on the stand from the transcripts, and I also had access to the tape of their original reports to the PD. Coached by whom and to what purpose remained the big mystery, but I was getting closer to my Pulitzer. Roy Boone had an enemy he might not have known he had; this enemy knew how to bring him down like a house of cards. Old Doc Frieland still gets a charge out of telling the story of a local surgeon whose thirty-year practice was ruined overnight because it was claimed by gossip mongers he'd looked at the reverse of an X-ray and cut off the wrong leg of a diabetic patient.

I spent a lot of my own money gathering information about the two girls. For one thing, Donna and Kristy were classmates in high school, but there was a huge class difference. Donna's father was a groundskeeper at the country club, whereas John Whitmire was a long-time county commissioner. Kristy was exactly the right girl to bring about the destruction of Boone's reputation. I learned she was on the homecoming court having missed being voted queen by two votes from the Boone twins, Becky and Lucy, that went to another girl because they refused to go along with the fix to get Kristy the majority of votes from her class. Donna told me Kristy was so furious when she heard the girls had been swayed "by their Uncle Roy" to vote against her. The reason was that Kristy's father blackballed Roy when he applied for membership in the country club and cast the single vote the bylaws required for blocking an applicant's bid for membership.

I spent a small fortune buying access to dozens of people, present and former politicians, friends of the Whitmires. I spoke to the surviving Boone twin. Becky was a casualty of Ohio's ongoing opioid scourge "dead and gone two years now," Lucy told me through the plexiglass when I finally obtained permission to see her. Lucy was completing a three-year bid in the Ohio Women's Reformatory in Marysville outside Columbus. I'd seen her graduation photo. A girl with a fox face and striking blue-gray eyes; the ombré hair was popular with blondes back then.

Most of her privileges had been revoked for fighting, but the warden granted me a fifteen-minute interview after claiming I was working a cold case "with another law-enforcement professional." Behind that scarred plastic window was a hard-faced woman sporting a buzzcut all around except for a long hank of hair that fell over her forehead. I glimpsed part of a neck tattoo, maybe a Chinese glyph, and those eyes of her school photo had been replaced by a pair of the coldest eyes I'd ever had fixed on me.

"Why did you vote against Kristy?"

Lucy barked a laugh, if that's what it was, and set the phone down for a moment as if pondering the depth of that question.

"You drove all the way down here just to ask me about that cunt?"

"Your uncle lost his business, his house and life savings over it. I thought you might be interested in helping me find out the truth of what happened."

"The truth? Becky and me, we cornered that bitch outside the mall when we heard she accused him of molesting her. You don't mess with a Boone and get away with shit like that."

"What did she say?"

Lucy gave me that look again. "She said her sister made her do it."

"Made—why? What did she have against your uncle?"

"They was dating, he broke up with her, she was pissed off. That hoity-toity family of hers didn't want no white-trash messin' up their bloodlines."

My heart sank. I was sure Lucy was confusing Corinne Lesperance, Roy's fiancée from that time, with the older sister of Kristy Whitmire, who still lived in town, but who was never mentioned in the same breath with Boone despite all the people I'd interviewed.

"Lucy, who told you this? I need to confirm it."

"How the fuck should I know, man, and who gives a shit now?"

A guard approached her.

"Time's up," Lucy said, glancing up at her escort. "Don't forget to put money in my commissary account like you said."

"I won't."

"You do, motherfucker, I won't forget you."

She gave me a fierce look back as she was led away, hobbling in leg irons and belly chain.

On the drive north on Interstate 71, I jettisoned a planned trip to St. Croix for which I'd been scrimping and saving for two long years. I planned to drain every dollar in my savings account to prove or disprove what I'd just heard from Lucy Boone.

I almost did—spend every dollar, that is. Northtown's full of junkies who'd sell their grandmothers into sexual slavery for dope money. Lucky for me, plenty of Northtown lawyers will knock their grandmothers to the sidewalk if they saw her standing on a quarter. The lawyers cost me much more than the fiends, but in the end, I had enough information.

Kristy Whitmire's sister Anita Rose dated Roy on the sly during senior year of high school. They kept their relationship a secret from friends, as difficult as that is to do in the world of teens. It might have been made easier because of Anita's parents who, like the Lesperances much later, dreaded an intimate affiliation with a family so notorious. I picked up this much scuttlebutt: something bad happened at a party she attended back in high school. One male I was told to see was Jimmy Connelly, the football team's captain. He went on to graduate from West Point and returned to the Academy after his tours in Iraq and Afghanistan.

Over the phone, I begged him to tell me what he knew or remembered about that party. He was reluctant but I let the prospect of a tell-all newspaper article naming names fester in his imagination. Finally he agreed to meet me in the lobby of the Thayer Hotel near the Academy. He would not name names, he said.

I was barreling along the Dewey Thruway with my heart racing faster than my car. *This was it, do or die…*

"Seven of us," Major James Connelly said after we shook hands in the lobby. "We'd just beaten Geneva High for the conference title. Nicky's father said we could have the basement—he even stocked the fridge with booze. He told Nicky we could party all night 'without adult interference.'"

Adult interference—he couldn't keep the bitterness of a bad memory out of the words.

"Where was Roy?"

"Roy never showed up, which was strange. He was all-city safety the year before. Might have made school history with a two-sport, all-state nomination that season. Things would have been so… different."

"So no one knew Roy was dating Anita?"

"It didn't seem possible. The Whitmires would never have approved. Don't get me wrong. Roy was nothing like the trash in his family. We all liked him."

He looked at me with a twisted smile below his neat moustache. "Roy never spoke about his family. I mean he never bad-mouthed anyone."

"How could you guys could take advantage of a girl like that?"

Me, the moral conscience of Northtown.

"We were supposed to lie to our girlfriends. It was meant to be a celebration for us guys on the team—no girlfriends. We were going to get drunk, have some laughs. Things got out of hand."

"How 'out of hand'?"

"The weed, somebody bought dope from Bobby Tennant," Connelly said. "It was laced with something. One of the guys passed them around, called them 'bazookas.'"

Crime reporting teaches you about dope. "Banano" and "basuco" meant marijuana doctored with cocaine. "Bazooka" packs more wallop—crack mixed with weed.

"No one tried to stop it?"

"Easy to say. Ever try to stop a stampede of male bulls by waving your arms and asking nicely? It doesn't work."

"What did Roy do when he found out?"

"Never said anything to me or the rest of the guys. He just quit the team. We got our asses handed to us in the district playoffs."

"What about Anita?"

"I heard they broke up. That's all I know."

Connelly lost his composure, his ramrod posture wilted for a moment and he fidgeted against the plush leather. "If you do write anything, I'll hold you to your promise to keep my name out of it."

"My word is my bond," I said.

His look said he doubted that. He checked his wristwatch. "I've got a lecture to prepare in twenty minutes."

Then he dropped a bomb on me.

"Your friend with the facial scars said there weren't going to be any repercussions when we spoke. I hope I can count on you for the same discretion."

He left me sitting there with egg on my face. *Jarvi, you miserable rat...*

I had a queasy feeling in my stomach. I was disgusted I'd been bested once again. I had to talk to Anita Whitmire, and I would have sacrificed an arm to do it. Preferably Jarvi's.

Knock me over with a feather—people still say that. Anita Whitmire was in the phonebook under her married name, Calaforte, and agreed to meet me without hesitation.

Anita Rose Calaforte impressed me immediately as a

gracious, lovely, and well-bred woman.

"I use my husband's name although we've been divorced five years," she said with a gorgeous smile. "You're right on time."

Ten minutes after admitting me into her house, a three-story refurbished Victorian overlooking the gulf where the Northtown River splits the town in two, I'd expected to see some cracks in the façade but this wasn't the same girl Connelly had spoken of and my imagination had painted as a damaged woman evolved from the girl at the party in Gleason's basement. I chided myself for naivete or stupidity. What did I expect—a big red letter tattooed across her forehead?

"Ms. Calaforte, I was wondering if—"

"Anita, please. Would you like something stronger than green tea, Mister—"

"No, no, tea is fine. Thank you."

She almost winked as she gestured toward the colorful display of liqueur bottles on the tea cart.

"Most of the gals in my reading circle like a little pick-me-up after our discussion of whichever whodunit we're discussing that week. You wouldn't believe how passionate we can get about our favorite mysteries."

"Anita, I was wondering if any legal action was ever taken against those boys who—those boys from high school. The ones on the football team."

"You needn't tiptoe up to it nor be so delicate about my sensibilities, I assure you," Anita replied. "I had years of therapy because of it and no, I do still carry a burden of guilt."

"I understand," I said. "Survivor's guilt. You were a victim."

"No, you don't understand," she replied and fixed me with a look that seemed to come from another place. "I initiated it."

"In-initiated it?"

The cup slopped in my lap. I couldn't take my eyes off her face when she said that. The effect of the spilled tea on my groin area went from wet to scalding hot in an instant. I resisted the urge to stand up and fling off my belt, undo my pants.

"I was high as well as those boys, most of whom were my friends. The dope had quite a kick and made me feel *uninhibited*."

"You weren't thinking of Roy. How he might… feel?"

"I was angry at Roy for standing me up. Then I grabbed the boy nearest me and started kissing him. I suppose I wanted Roy to hear about it in school. Make him jealous. Not to put too fine a point on it, that boy and I found a utility closet or something. The next thing I know I'm performing fellatio on him… I should have expected there'd be a line outside the door…"

Her voice, so self-assured up to that point, drifted up the scale in a quavering tremolo note and left her sentence unfinished.

She looked at me, composed again.

I burned with shame. My overheated imagination created a whole different scenario: a young girl, eyes glazed from the drug, gobs of jissom in her hair… something akin to a *YouPorn* video.

"I'm sorry," I said.

"Don't be. It was a long time ago. The scandal hurt my father and probably destroyed his political ambitions for good. Our name was mud in this town. I'm practically a recluse in this house."

I left as soon as I could. I was filled with anguish for her. I'd come to her with my paltry ambition for a story. I hoped Jarvi would leave her in peace. With that inflated sense of virtue, I went to see Jarvi the next day.

"She's still grieving. For God's sake, leave her alone! The woman has suffered enough for one mistake in her youth. She has no idea who's behind the two murders. Being connected to Roy makes her more likely to be the next victim."

He smirked at me. I actually balled my fist.

"You're assuming a lot," Jarvi said. "Why don't you try being a real reporter and get the facts."

"What do you mean, Jarvi? Anita Calaforte's a survivor, not a suspect—"

"You said you wanted to join forces with me. Be here tonight at seven-thirty."

Without any further explanation, he escorted me out of his office.

I showed up early, anxious to hear what he had to say.

"We'll talk when we're settled into the surveillance," Jarvi replied.

"Always the gumshoe, but I have questions and I want answers."

Jarvi drove a beige Honda Accord and parked half-a-block from her house. He put Zeiss binoculars to his face and ignored my questions. Around eight-fifteen, the lights in Anita's big house started going on, first the downstairs, then the rooms upstairs. The house was a cubicle of blazing light in the pitch-black of a country evening.

"It's a good sign," Jarvi said, more to himself than to me. "She gets plastered to the gills when she puts on the lights."

"Plastered? What are you saying? That woman drinks green tea and hosts a reading club."

Jarvi said nothing. He fended off my questions. He

refused to talk about the case and I had no choice but to wait for him to open up. At eleven-oh-four, we heard a car start up.

"It's her," he said. "She can't help herself. She has to look."

"Look? Look *where*, Jarvi, and look at *what*, you tightlipped, two-bit Sam Spade—"

"I've lost her twice before because I can't get too close. She stays on back roads until she hits the township line. Let's hope she's too buzzed to notice we're following."

To me, it sounded like harassment. I contemplated getting out of the car but that little reporter's instinct in my head said: *Wait, this guy has been two steps ahead of me all the time. He must know something...*

She took a byzantine route back to Five Points, a jumble of intersecting roads and highways going in all directions.

"She's got great instincts for an amateur," he said. "She knows how to look for a tail. I'm still hoping her urge to see him is greater than her fear of being seen."

"Being seen—you mean Roy. She's meeting Roy Boone. Damn it, Ray, all you had to do was tell me that in the first place!"

We closed the distance as she turned off Greene Road and blended into the sparse traffic on Highway 193 in Kingsville.

"Is Roy hiding out in Kingsville? That town's a flyspeck. Someone will recognize him."

"You'll see."

She turned off the highway and drove in the direction of Conneaut Creek.

"Jarvi, there's nothing out here but barbed-wire fences and lobo wolves. Roy can't be waiting for her out here."

"You think?" That smirk again.

"I'll be damned," I said. "Roy Boone has returned to Northtown."

"He never left," Jarvi said cryptically.

"What? What are you talking about—he never left?"

"Someone on the football squad found out Anita was dating Roy. He was pissed off because she had dumped him for Roy. He wasn't from as prominent a family as the Whitmires, so my source told me, but it must have stung to be replaced by a Boone. He organized the party with Nick Gleason, the linebacker. Bobby Joe Tennant sold the drugs. Word went out on the school grapevine that Roy planned to two-time Anita at a party that weekend."

Jarvi looked at me. Even in the dim lighting of the car, he possessed a feral look; his scars seemed to soak up the light and absorb shadow, as if he wore a mask. "Her name doesn't matter," he said. "She's completely innocent. Some of the 'boys' who were present are some of Northtown's more respectable citizens."

I was close—but no cigar. Jarvi had put all the pieces together.

"There! Up ahead, she just turned off." Jarvi pointed.

He killed his lights as we came within five hundred yards of her vehicle.

"How do you know that's her? We might be following the wrong car all this time."

"See the right taillight? I put a strip of duct tape there so I won't lose her in traffic."

"A real gumshoe, eh? You know, I always thought being a private detective was—"

"Shut up," Jarvi said. "I have to think."

She took a road that might have been made by four-wheelers. The ruts tossed me around and my head smacked the head rest a couple times. She was three hundred yards ahead and we were driving blind again.

Then her big Caddy stopped abruptly at an angle and she cut the lights. Jarvi stopped at once and cut his engine.

"Don't make a sound," he said.

I don't know how long we sat there. I heard night sounds all around—the night breeze rattling leaves, insects galore, small animals out there moving in the dark among the cattails. The pungent odor of swamp rot hit me in the face.

"We walk from here," Jarvi said. He disabled the overhead light and removed a heavyweight flashlight from under his seat. "Let's go."

The quarter moon gave no light to see by. Only the rough track beneath our feet indicated we were moving at all.

I made out the rough outline of a building ahead of us.

"She's inside," Jarvi whispered.

Jarvi was beside me and the next thing I knew he was gone. I had never experienced a darkness like this. I feared turning an ankle with every step or running smack into one of those stunted trees bordering the path.

Jarvi, you crazy bastard... the thought he could be taking me on a snipe hunt and abandoning me out here in country as revenge for my mixing in his business occurred. I had no choice but to keep putting one foot ahead of the other, worried about coyotes or black bears or whatever else occupied the natural habitat out here.

I made my way to the building stopping every few seconds to listen.

Nothing but a cement-block structure, abandoned decades ago. When my eyes adjusted to the interior, I guessed from the rails and hooks dangling overhead it functioned as some farmer's slaughterhouse. Tips of branches grown through the broken windows were tapping against the panes as the breeze funneled through. Weeds and vines had taken over the exterior but inside was eerily still.

I'd come this far, I wasn't turning back now. Deeper in, cloying odors of dust and mildew wafted about. I had an urge to sneeze.

A beam of light at the far end of the building. I walked across the broken foundation floor where chunks of concrete loomed up to trip me. Avoiding one, a coil of rusted iron snagged my ankle and I did a belly flop. I got up with a shard of broken glass sticking into the palm of my hand.

I'd had enough—

"Jarvi! Jarvi!"

"Here!"

His beam swung my way like a miniature lighthouse before rotating back to fix on whatever he was pinning with his beam. A large lump sprawled at Jarvi's feet and moaned. The hair on my neck prickled with fear. I pressed my wounded hand against my chest to stanch the blood and moved toward Jarvi's position.

Hearing me approach, he swung the light under his chin, a goofy Halloween trick, illuminating his face with its maze of livid scarring.

"Take a look," he said.

He shone the beam on Anita curled on the filthy floor, her legs tucked under her arms.

"My God, what did you do?"

"Nothing," he said. "She's just drunk. I found her like this."

"Where is Roy?"

I had a sickening feeling Roy Boone would come charging out of the darkness with a baseball bat or a machete. My terror had no brakes just then.

"Right over there," Jarvi said. His beam picked out a fifty-five-gallon steel drum with the neck ring and lid removed, both lying beside the barrel.

"Have a look. It's what you wanted, newspaper man."

My stomach churned as I stepped over to peer down into the mouth of the barrel.

"This should help," Jarvi said.

He aimed his beam into the maw of the barrel and I glimpsed ankle bones inside a shoe. Roy Boone's shriveled and desiccated corpse lay tucked like a homunculus into the bottom where time and rot had settled the remains.

I stepped away and bent over to throw up into the dark... *You bastard, Jarvi.*

"She visits him," Jarvi said quietly. "She can't help herself. Been doing it for years. Ever since she killed him."

"Why?"

It took me a while to get the word out. I was still wiping ropy strings of drool from my chin.

"Find a shrink and ask... OK, seen enough? We have a long night at the sheriff's station. I hope you've got a change of shirt handy."

More words than I'd heard him speak all night.

"Fuck you."

I was sick. Sick at heart. Sick of myself. Sick of human beings and their ideas of love and hate.

"What about... her?"

"Leave her," Jarvi said. "It's the last time she's going to be alone with him in this lifetime."

***

I see Ray Jarvi from time to time on Bridge Street. He nods at me, I nod at him. We don't speak. My paper went berserk in World-War-Three-sized type on the front page when the whole story came out over the next several days. The rumormongers in town had a field day with the ghoulish details. The story of Anita Whitmire and Roy Boone will be transformed from a sordid, small-town catastrophe into a wild urban legend in a generation or two. Long after people forget the two murder victims.

Want to know the irony of it? My editor refused to let me write it.

"You're too involved in the story," he explained. "You have no objectivity."

He did allow me to write a sidebar to the main article, which provided a little satisfaction.

Jarvi garnered ink and might get some business out of it, but he's a lousy self-promoter. He refused all requests for interviews, including those from the big Cleveland stations. He threatened a *Plain Dealer* reporter for harassing him. Thinking of that night, I still see her, the bones inside that shoe—and gooseflesh pops up and I start hyperventilating.

A small, sad detail came to light months later, thanks to Bart Massey in the Wyandotte: the forensics unit discovered a bent playing card at the bottom of the barrel when they extricated his remains. The King of Spades. Anita's final insult, a last taunt after she unloaded her .45 into him. Some slugs were recovered but the mummified condition of the body made it impossible for Doc Frieland to say how many times he was shot.

There's enough irony for everyone in the story of Roy Boone's demise. On the day Anita was sent to Marysville to commence a generous fifteen-to-life sentence for Roy's murder (thanks to daddy's high-powered lawyers), Lucy Boone was released from the Ohio Reformatory. I wonder if the two women caught a glimpse of each other in that dismal place. I can imagine Lucy fixing those icy, steel-blue eyes on Anita as they pass by.

Missed Call

Another missed call. His lawyer, worth every billable hour but why so urgent and this time of night? His collision with the old guy destroyed his custom-made bike, which resulted in a measly speeding fine. Big deal. Over, done. Let's all move on, people.

His cell phone, again. Chicks like the babe in the kitchen mixing him a dirty martini were impressed by classical music ringtones.

Still woozy from the first drink she mixed, he watched her buttock shift the dress.

"Who was that?"

"Nobody, babe. My lawyer again. Did I tell you back in the club about that old fool stepping into the crosswalk? Wrecked my Italian Pantera, remember?"

She approached him smiling. He wobbled toward her, reaching out for the crystal flute—another chick magnet: expensive crystalware. Instead of the drink, she handed him her cell. He glimpsed his own selfie of the cracked helmet with his caption from the day of the accident on that corner in Haight Ashbury: "Boo-Hoo," he wrote. *Witty.* But her face was stern, dark eyes narrowed to slits.

His limbs jellied. He didn't think he could stand up.

She opened her other hand; something glittery winked: a butterfly knife.

"My father," she said.

"Wait," he said. The word stuck in his esophagus.

"We have a long night ahead, *babe*," she crooned.

The Soul Food King of Indianapolis

I learned my father died by reading about it in the *Tribune Star*. My name was there as the "surviving son." My mother's name seemed an afterthought. She was referred to blandly as the "first wife" who had pre-deceased him. No mention of his second marriage. No memorial service—just the obligatory conclusion requesting donations. In his case, to the American Heart Association. Appropriate since a coronary thrombosis was noted as the cause of death.

My father would not have cared about making the Terre Haute paper. He would have been pleased to see that he garnered a paragraph in the *IndyStar* as the "Soul Food King."

I was in high school when my father broke the news to my mother he wanted a divorce. She didn't want it, but she didn't fight it. I moved with her back to Terre Haute. He was generous in the settlement: my mother got the house, a big alimony check. He also paid for both my bachelor's degree and my McKinney School of Law degree.

All the years I spent in Indianapolis just five miles from downtown where he built his first soul-food franchise. I never saw him, although the odds were good he'd be at one store or another. By then, he'd sold his Burger Kings in South Bend and his KFC in Valparaiso. His plan was to put a fast-food franchise in every black community between Gary and Indianapolis. His Gary store took off just as the pandemic hit, and he lost his West 37th-Street property in the bankruptcy order. He had to scrap plans for three others.

He was a demon for work. I imagined him adding to his normal ninety-hour work week with even more hours. His weight ballooned from 245 to 285 when he died. He was a heart attack waiting to happen. My mother spoke of his "betrayal" twice: first, when we packed up and headed back to Terre Haute, where I was born, and where she first met my father when he came out of his tiny office and spotted the wheat-blonde, high-school girl standing at the counter gazing at the overhead menu.

My last words to him comprised that unoriginal, three-word phrase everyone knows—the first word is *Go* and the third word is *yourself*. The final time my mother spoke about him was in her living room while she lay dying in a hospice rental bed, cored like an apple by her cancer; all she said was an embittered "I hope he's happy now."

I wish I hadn't said it. A dying woman has the right to go into the beyond with whatever peace of mind one can muster in those awful moments. I held her hand and said: "He'll never be happy." It was true. My father chased money. He was never happy, never still. Up at three and out the door every morning. Back at nine or ten, frazzled, exhausted— only to repeat the ritual the next day.

I wasn't thinking about his second marriage to the woman my grandmother in Terre Haute euphemistically called "a stage dancer." My grandfather's words for Jasmine were harsher, unrepeatable except for the "whore" he concluded his tirade with. She grew up in Gary as the third-youngest of eight children sired by a steelworker in Indiana Harbor who lost his job when the steel mills closed. Her parents had no marriage certificate, a common means of boosting welfare benefits for "single" mothers. Her real name was Renée Yakeshia Noble.

I had two days before my oral exam for the bar. I was confident that my contract brief would carry me over the line if any flaw in my tort brief were insurmountable. Being a dozen miles from his second house on North Meridien, I had no compelling reason to go there. I didn't know Jasmine, and I suspected she wouldn't be interested in meeting me, either.

The lawyer who managed my father's probate gave me an appointment that afternoon.

Jonathan Griggs offered me coffee, which I declined. I asked the most important questions on my mind first.

"Wow, counselor, you sure you're not heading for a career in criminal law?"

"Wills and Estates," I replied. "I don't mean to be abrupt. I apologize if it sounded that way."

"No, no, I understand. I mean, Big Jim didn't tell me much about his... prior life, but I assumed things between your mother and him weren't amicable, if I may use that lawyer's term we all love."

"Was his death suspicious in any way?"

He looked hard at me, reached into his drawer, and came out with a business card.

"This is Detective Forbes. Call him. He'll give you whatever he can."

"Is the will above suspicion?"

"The will is absolutely above suspicion."

My question must have rankled.

"I didn't mean—"

"Forget it," he said with a wave of his hand. "Your father stipulated you were to get a single dollar bill. That was his wife's suggestion, by the way. Not mine. I told him that was purely symbolic and irrelevant."

This time I waved away his concerns. "I have no intention of contesting the will."

He shrugged his shoulders and looked at me through his bifocals. "Then I'm unsure exactly why you wanted to see me."

"Can you tell me what he was worth?"

"That's confidential."

I had a rough idea. I held up three fingers, signifying three millions. "More than this?"

Another noncommittal shrug. "Look, your father worked like a dog after the pandemic to rebuild and recoup his losses. Lots of people are millionaires on paper. It doesn't mean much. For what it's worth, I advised him against buying that house on North Meridien. What he paid in property taxes you could buy a good house south of Thirty-eighth."

"I appreciate your time, Mister Griggs."

"Good luck with the bar exam. Most people think of lawyers as just another biblical plague between boils and locusts. There's always room for more good ones."

His secretary came into the office and signaled him in some private way I didn't catch.

He slapped his forehead playfully. "God, I'm getting old. Your father gave me a letter for you. He said if you didn't come for it in person, I was to burn it."

The last thing I wanted was some sentimental tripe from "Big Jim" from beyond the grave, some whiny apology for ruining my mother's life. I tucked it into a side pocket.

Spending my college years north of that demarcation line in neighborhoods named Rocky Ripple, Meridien-Kessler, and Woodstock made me oblivious to the poverty and crime below West Thirty-eighth where my father's soul-food store was. Indianapolis isn't Chicago and it won't get the title of Murder Capital, but Indianapolis has the same problems, rust-belt Midwest capital notwithstanding.

I was tempted to check out one of his franchises after I left Griggs' law office. I expected to see Black teenagers scrambling behind the counter, taking orders, working as fry cooks and counter servers. The online reviews were unkind: "Chicken ain't just rubbery it tastes like shit," wrote one. "Greasy fried chicken tastes like ass, lousy side dishes like the sticky mashed potatoes you can hold up on a fork." Another: "Fuk dis shit. Go to Mickey D's yo. Even the political activists took a shot: "Dude owner ain't black. Don't patronize the white man. Power to the people!" This one would have been a beak in my father's heart, he was so proud of his specialty concoctions: "Took one bite, tossed the SuperSoul straight into the dumpster out back!"

Other reviews were either rife with obscenities or contained messages in code. One poor writer actually praised the quality of the food; he or she was heaped with scorn by the next five reviewers.

My father's scheme regarding soul food was merely to add collard greens and chitlins to a typical burger-and-chicken franchise. His menu claimed to reinvigorate the authenticity of Black Southern cooking. In fact, Soul Food Kitchen noted in an asterisk at the bottom of the menu that it would swap kale or spinach for the greens "as needed"; my father believed that, if he slathered everything in a thick gravy to disguise the taste, it would pass muster. When I was a kid, and he had the KFC store, he spent hours in the kitchen on weekends trying to duplicate the Colonel's chicken recipe. When my mother finally refused another bite of one of his experiments, that left me as the family's "official taste tester." He used dollops of gumbo filé and his own mix of Creole seasoning and sweet apple cider. Frankly, it could have been crushed crackers with peanut butter for all the customer's taste buds knew.

Opening the letter in my car, four blank pieces of paper fell into my lap along with a house key and a password—at least, that's what I assumed it was: Xibabla2020^$$$.

My father's business sense was comparable to a shark's with bloody chum in the water. As for his imagination in other areas, you could circumscribe it inside a shot glass with a fat crayon. *Xibalba* was easy, according to *Wikipedia*: a "place of fright," the Mayan word for their underworld ruled by their death gods.

I had no desire to get wrapped up in his bullshit, whatever it was.

I called the precinct number and asked for Detective Forbes.

"Forbes."

I gave my name and asked if could set aside a few minutes for me.

"Where are you?"

"In the parking lot out back."

"Ten minutes. Ask the desk sergeant for a pass."

The detectives' bullpen looked like a TV set for a crime drama. "Officer, my father's lawyer told me you were lead investigator."

"That's right."

Det. Forbes, nattily dressed, wore a hound's tooth sport coat despite the warmth.

"Officer, was his death in any way suspicious?"

"Pathologist ruled thrombosis. We had no reason to say otherwise."

Polite, reserved, unforthcoming with details, he folded his hands on a desk he shared with another detective. A Black family portrait faced off with a white family at each corner.

"My father was overweight but not in ill health."

"His wife found him at the bottom of the cellar stairs. 'Blue in the face and ice-cold,' she said. We verified her absence from the house at the time of death."

"How can you be sure of the time? Isn't rigor mortis

an approximation?"

"She was having sex with another man at the time. He confirmed it."

"I see."

"Look, I don't want to sully your father's memory. My job is to make sure any unattended death is not the result of foul play. Sometimes, we find out things the family might not want to know."

"I was estranged from my father. I hadn't spoken to him in ten years."

He cast a quick eye down to his wristwatch.

"Your father and his wife—"

"Second wife," I corrected.

"Second wife. They were into some kinky stuff."

"How kinky?"

"Open marriage, according to her. Hang on, I'll get the murder book. You can't look at it whether you're a lawyer or a wanna-be lawyer, got it?"

He stepped away and returned in half a minute with a thick three-ring binder.

Grabbing it in the middle the way you might a misbehaving puppy by the scruff of its neck, he flipped it to a section. I sat back in the chair, my eyes unable to avert from the lurid glossies.

"The long and short," Forbes resumed, "your father gave his approval. We found lubricants and, let's say, rubber devices, in the upstairs closet. Lots of videos on the laptop. Nothing you'd want to share at the memorial service. The ME said no drugs in his system other than amounts of cyclic guanosine monophosphate, phosphodiesterase—I'm not reading the rest of this shit."

"Viagra," I guessed.

"That and Cialis, same thing, different day. Rows of prescription bottles on the bathroom counter he took like

Pez candies. That didn't help the old ticker."

"He was still in his fifties."

"He worked twelve—, fifteen-hour days. Longer on weekends, they told me. Traveled between here and Elkhart. The wife said he planned to open a soul-food store."

I looked at the cop's face to see if it held a hint of mockery.

"The man was overworked," he continued. "We didn't just take his wife's word for it. Everybody from bank managers to staff said the same thing."

I used to joke to my friends who'd ask me about my dad: "Look up *workaholic* in the dictionary. You'll see a photo of him next to the word."

He checked his watch more obviously this time. "We gave his investigation everything, we held nothing back. I personally took fifty-two pieces of evidence out of that house."

"It's legal in this state to request autopsies if you're next of kin. That qualifies me. Why not save me the trouble and let me peek at those glossies you tried to cover up a moment ago?"

"You're gonna make trouble, aren't you?"

"Not if you show me the photos."

He handed over a dozen. "Take a look and hand them back."

I riffled through them, lingering over a couple where the damage from the fall was worse.

"So how come the injuries wasn't listed as a cause of death?"

"The medical examiner said, 'contributing factors.' Nothing lethal in his tumble. He cracked some ribs against the railing. If his heart hadn't given out, he might have had a serious concussion. As it was, he was deader than Julius Caesar before he hit that first step."

"Your bedside manner, Detective, is wondrous to behold. I hope they don't let you do too many death notices."

"I suit my words to the circumstances. Anything else I can help you with today, sir?"

I tapped the murder book with an index finger. "What about his computer?"

"We had his password," Forbes sighed. "His wife gave it to us. Full cooperation. We dumped both cell phones. Nothing. *Nada.* Zero. Zilch-point-shit. No word searches on 'How-to-kill-someone-and-make-it-look-like-a-heart-attack.'"

"What about the kinky stuff?" I felt like a voyeur in asking it, nauseated to be invading my father's most personal moments.

"Plenty of videos of the two of them. Sometimes a third party. We tracked down every man and woman who partied in their bedroom."

Then he stunned me: "You know what a pirate is?"

"A... a pirate? You mean, like, 'Yo, ho-ho-ho, and a bottle of rum' pirate'?"

"Not one pirate," Forbes said. "A whole convention of them. They meet annually. They do things."

He meant cosplay like reenactment actors of battles, only these were purely hedonistic pirates.

I imagined the hilarity that provoked around the station once my father's secret life was exposed. Cops running around, growling, "*Arrrgh*, matey..."

"Your stepmom seemed to be the inspiration for it. Your dad went along with it. I don't think his heart was in it—sorry, no pun intended. Your ten minutes are up."

"Thanks for your time, Detective."

"No secrets in a murder investigation, man. That's just how it is."

Curiosity, nothing more, compelled me to drive past his house twenty miles up Meridien sandwiched between an office complex and Ye Olde Country Inn & Suites, a notch above the Bates motels and Crazy 8 places surrounding the innerbelt.

A long, winding driveway, unmanicured lawn, minus the distinctive topiary of the elegant mansions closer to my old stomping grounds in Broad Ripple Village. No trendy bars or monster houses out this far, but easily in the hundreds of thousands of dollars' range if you were keen to establish your *bona fides* with a North Meridien address.

No car in the driveway. I wondered whether Jasmine was unable to occupy it formally until probate cleared. I parked under the *porte cochère*. The side lawns near the hedges were overgrown with onion grass. Blue grape hyacinth grew unkempt in a raised flower bed. Forsythia bushes, long neglected, created their own impasse in the back of the house. My father wouldn't have wasted five minutes planting flowers, so it had to be the prior owner.

Maybe I was struck by the irony of being a day from admission to the bar, yet I was as good as breaking in to a man's house—if it weren't for the fact that I had a key. The nearest neighbor was several hundred yards off, which fact gave me courage to try out the key. The wooden front door was blistered and flaked. The brass lock, however, was shiny and opened easily. I stepped inside the foyer, smelled must with a hint of citrus—a woman's perfume. My father's cologne was a frontal assault on the nasal cavity.

Boxes were piled near the front picture window with designations: KITCHEN, UPSTAIRS BACK BEDROOM, DEN. One jumped out at me for the sheer oddity of it: PIRATE ROOM.

I took a slow inspection of the downstairs and upstairs. Someone had recently cooked in the kitchen but left the dishes undone with a crust of congealed grease on dinner plates. The master bedroom upstairs was the only furnished room. The quilt and duvet struck me as feminine, not my father's taste. No pirate room. No computer in sight to apply the password.

The cops still had my father's laptop, so there didn't seem to be a purpose in having his password. I went to the pile of boxes and found three labeled PIRATE ROOM.

Costumes, capes, hats with feathers, swords that might have come from a seasonal Halloween shop. Bundles of brochures advertising "Pirates at Play." Apparently these pirates traveled between Bloomington and tiny Mishawaka near the Michigan border.

Pirates in Indianapolis. *What the hell.*

The brochures explained some of it, although not speaking much to my dead father's belated interest in cosplay and how that connected to his open marriage. Part of me could see a wife-swapping adventure, a bunch of keys tossed into a heap on someone's coffee table; partners chosen with keys. It seemed quaint, a seventies thing, whereas an open marriage smacked of contemporary times. It didn't compute with my father's personality.

These modern-day Indiana pirates dressed elaborately—well-heeled in the depictions of the colored brochures, far from the seedy desperation of an historical pirate's reality. The men, mostly bearded, looked more like the caricatures of the Three Musketeers from my collection of *Classics Illustrated* in boyhood. Elaborately trimmed and coiffed, man-buns or long flowing hair, they looked too clean and post-hippie-esque to be dangerous. I wasn't surprised that they talked in pirate lingo, albeit a strictly Hollywood version, nor that they engaged in swordplay—that, too, noted as "comedy sword-fighting at its best." Musicians were part of the fantasy at these conventions, which blocked out time for singing songs and drinking rum.

The women, like the men, were dressed in period garb, sported loop earrings like males, and revealed hair styles that resembled a modern woman's contrived just-stepped-out-of-the-shower look; some involved extensions and hair weaves. The page-boy cuts might have been authentic, but I was no expert.

It didn't make suspicious; it made me sad. My father's age would have put him at the tail end of the age spectrum in the photos. A twenties- and thirties thing mostly. I knew from my grandparents' fury that Jasmine was at least twenty years younger.

I retraced my steps, even checked the attic: no room where pirates cavorted.

On a shelf in the basement, mostly a fieldstone dugout, there were lanterns placed in a row. That seemed unusual enough to send me back down there. No one really intended to hide it from a more than a casual search. A door behind a pantry I'd missed the first time.

Shoving it aside, I opened it to a spacious room, clean, remodeled, and nothing like the rest of the basement. Pine fence-board walls. Tasteful prints of nudes and couples locked in coitus on every wall. Mattresses sans box springs or headboards set on a mosaic tile floor separated by night tables. Sheets folded at the foot of mattresses. The most obvious item was the camera on a tripod at the foot of one mattress.

I hit Play, stomach in knots. The secrecy of this room told me Det. Forbes and his cops might have missed it.

Three-way sex, mostly Jasmine and another woman engaged with a well-hung male. No costumes or pirate acting—just pornographic sex. Plenty of it. Throughout most, my father was a spectator on the sidelines, perhaps a masturbating voyeur. Jasmine was the star of every show.

I decided to fast-forward through it. The others on the mattresses became twitching mannequins, whereas Jasmine was a singular blur of action, topping or bottoming for her partners. The frenetic doggie-style of the men was the only time they matched her velocity. She serviced men and women equally, a sexual dynamo. Jasmine was no great beauty; however, I understood my father's—most men's— animal attraction to her: short, even squat in size, her caramel-colored skin and round, pleasant face would not have made her the top draw in a strip club like the one she danced in back in Gary. But her voluptuous, heaving breasts bouncing above her shaved pudenda made her the queen of the highlight reels. Lonely college boys would draw out their wallets the instant she took the stage for her set. They'd think of her at night as they fondled themselves in their dorm room beds. If my father thought his money would compensate for flaccidity or age, he obviously discovered otherwise. He bore the maddening burden of the willingly cuckolded husband as best he could.

Underworld... sewerage—

I don't know why my mind made the connection, but I knew there had to be a reason why he left me the house key and a password. Down on hands and knees, I searched along the baseboards. Behind one mattress facing the back wall was a pair of parallel hairline cuts ninety degrees to the floor. With nothing handy to use, I kicked that section of board until it splintered, knocking it off plumb. With my fingers, I pried it loose and set it on the floor. A laptop covered in bubble wrap with cable wires running behind the boards to a height of five feet, ending in the corner. I removed the computer and followed the wires to a gang box that looked recently installed. At the end was a trail camera hidden behind a board aimed directly at the bed. Someone replaced the board so that the lens was pointed through a sepia print on the wall of a pair of lesbians engaged in scissoring with the camera eye disguised behind the hirsute pubic ruffs of their joined legs, a lush, rococo effect. You'd have to stand directly in front of it to see the camera eye.

I booted up the computer and put in the password. I had to go through a dozen variations of my father's name until I put in "BigJim" as the username.

More sex. Just two people. But now exclusively Jasmine and a male lover—a thin white male around thirty who wore a ponytail. I recognized him as one of the minstrel entertainers from a brochure. I watched the two of them make love, not in the frenzied way of the ménage à trois I'd witnessed before. This was slow, languorous lovemaking, with a lot of kissing absent in the pirate hookups. The pixel resolution was twice as good as the camera work. The audio clear, each whispered or spoken word crisp.

I started to fast-forward when I realized my father had hid this from his wife but wanted me to find it.

Two of the ugliest words in English are *fuck* and *kill*. Both were used frequently by the lovers, especially Jasmine.

"…kill him. Sick of him."

She had to remove his organ from her mouth to express that baleful sentiment.

I heard another woman's name mentioned, which I took to be the name of his wife or lover, one who was deeply in love with Jasmine and didn't at all mind sharing her man without her.

They talked about my father as though he were an odious object, a form of unsightly caries that had to be removed. They discussed finding a hit man if the cocktail of Viagra she ground up and put into his drinks didn't show results "soon": "The fool is watching me. He knows something is about to happen."

She crooned endearments around his member,

laughing, stretching it—slapping her cheek with it and exclaiming, "Look, Kim Kardashian."

What was clear was her adoration of the man she was with. His contribution to the conversation was minimal, mostly groans and gestures to enhance her performance.

Often her fellatio interfered with my hearing what she said. One remark emerged painfully clearly when she bragged about talking my father out of leaving me the house.

His eyes closed, enjoying the attention, he said at one point "Put Roundup in his coffee. That should do it."

Jasmine said, "I've made up my mind. Tomorrow." As though in sync with her mental decision, her fist pumped gobs of his ejaculate into the air while he arched his back in bliss. The time stamp on the video said it was the day before he was discovered at the bottom of the stairs.

Nauseated, I was sickened by the thought my father's last thoughts were about me. It hit me harder than Jasmine's betrayal. I popped out the SD card of stored data inside the camera.

The front door opened and closed just as I replaced the pantry shelving.

"Who's there?" A female voice. Hers, minus the soft touches.

I shouted up the cellarway: "I had a key to get in."

"Get your fuckin' ass up the stairs, motherfucker." Said without much heat.

At the top of the steps, she stood there looking down on me. My face burned.

"I'm just…"

"You just what, motherfucker? You here to steal, huh?"

"No, no, nothing like that. I'm—I was just at the probate lawyers and he gave me a key."

"Griggs gave you a key? Wait'll I see that

cocksucker."

My father, when he cursed—which was rare—often blushed. His modest Methodist background showed in the color rising slowly up his neck. My mother, a slender woman who always appeared borderline anorectic, never cursed. My grandparents were strict Lutherans of the old-school Finnish variety. The only time my mother got physical with me was to insert a bar of soap in my mouth after a Little League game when I went O-for-4 at the plate and cursed mildly on the ride home. Even then, I heard her sob in her bed for having done it. On video tape, Jasmine was articulate, well-spoken in her vocabulary. The lapse into street argot was strictly for my benefit, a charade to hide behind.

"You're his kid."

"I am. Thanks for not shooting me."

"See? No gun."

She opened her hands to expose a wicked-looking folding knife with a serrated blade. "What'chu you doin' in my house, bitch?"

I introduced myself. She stood there, assessing me with an auger stare.

"I had a key," I repeated.

"Yeah, Griggs is gonna hear about that, sure as shit. Now answer my motherfuckin' question. What are you doing in my house?"

"Actually, he didn't give me the key."

Her eyebrows arched, waiting for me to explain. "Say what?"

"I came here because my father intended me to find evidence you planned to kill him, you and your ponytailed boyfriend. You fed him so much Viagra it showed up in the autopsy. Then you shoved him down the stairs."

"Fuck you, you fuckin' lyin' bitch!"

"I've got it all on this," I said, holding the SD card in

my hand for her to see. "Detective Forbes has seen you having sex a dozen times. Maybe that was your intention. But seeing you plot a murder will get my father's case reopened."

She came at me with the knife out, aiming for my groin. I deflected it with a forearm that sent the knife skittering across the floor. My skin felt molten where she cut me. Teeth bared back like a wolf, hands extended like claws, she lunged at me again. Her long red fingernails raked the flesh of my cheek.

"Kill you, motherfucker!"

Out of the corner of my eye, I saw him—her ponytailed lover. He stepped out from the kitchen where he'd been hiding and jerked a short-barreled gun at me just as Jasmine attacked again. Jasmine's head snapped backwards, as though she were leaning into the barrel when he fired the shot.

He fired at me as I bolted past to the front door. Too much adrenalin coursed through my bloodstream for me to feel anything,

I heard him cry out just as I flung open the door: "Baby! Baby! Oh no! Oh no!"

I risked a glance back. On his knees, caressing her hair and face, moaning and rocking, he cradled her head in his arms. A worm of blood trickled from one corner of her mouth.

Fumbling with the key, I dropped it, cursed, sobbed, found it, started the engine.

Red eye floaters gathered in front of my vision like a ragged curtain about to unfurl.

Back in town, I parked in front of the precinct. A woman writing traffic tickets gave me the fisheye.

I walked up to the desk and asked for Detective Forbes. I set the SD card on the counter.

The desk sergeant's mouth opened and closed like a

guppy's. He reminded me of a soprano's pear-shaped O. He pointed at the bloody footprints behind me. That's when I dropped to the floor in a dead faint.

Det. Forbes visited me in the hospital the day after he served a warrant on Jasmine's boyfriend for complicity in first-degree murder. The bullet nicked the brachial artery, and I nearly bled out. When my law school dean asked me to reschedule the oral exam for the bar, I declined. I decided the world didn't need one more lawyer.

Ravi Floating in Light

The final hour of Ravi's double shift crawled to a close. He could swear his tight-fisted uncle had somehow rigged the clock's hands with molasses to slow them when it came to the last hour. He could also swear someone had thrown grit into his eyes owing to the painful itch.

He was sick to death of working in this shitty, motel-*cum*-restaurant—basically a cinder-block crash pad for long-haul truckers and trysting couples. The restaurant itself was an L-shaped dining room with a small kitchen that belied its jaunty tropical vibe with a menu that hadn't changed from its staple of hamburgers, hot dogs, and fries or the "Captain's Delight," meaning a frozen square of fish that was either pollock, haddock, or whitefish depending on the day of the week, frozen clams, and a dollop of cocktail sauce. Ravi supervised the cleaning rooms, hired the maids, ran errands, and manned the lobby desk when they were short-staffed, which was almost every weekend. He'd do anything and everything for his Uncle Ajay, the owner along with Aunt Chandana; they did the sponsorship paperwork and assisted with his work visa.

"I plucked you out of Dharavi," Ajay reminded him every chance he got. "You'd be starving in Mumbai with the rest of our family if not for me."

Ravi had no choice but to express his undying gratitude and smile. If he fell short at times on the feeling behind his gratitude, it was owing to his providing inexpensive labor to the running of the motel. Ravi wasn't short on ambition. He didn't intend to remain a servant forever. He knew how to bide time until he could gain his freedom in America with the proper credentials to show

Naturalization & Immigration why he shouldn't be deported.

Meanwhile, it was a daily litany of: "Someone throw up in the bathroom?" *Ravi, take care of that right away!* "The night-shift desk clerk fail to show?" *Ravi, you're on duty tonight.* "The fry cook call in sick again?" *Ravi, I need you on the grill right away...*

Exhausting, mind-numbing, 12- to 15-hour shifts, six days a week with every other Sunday off.

Ravi fell asleep with his clothes on, dreading that 5:30 a.m. wake-up call. Aunt Chandana glowered at him whenever he passed the cubbyhole office where she kept the books. Her long gray hair braided in a thick rope hanging down her back. If he asked for an advance on his pay to send back to his father in Dharavi, Mumbai's biggest and oldest ghetto, she glared at him with her deep-set, brown eyes as if he'd asked her for one of her kidneys.

Talking to Uncle Ajay yielded no better results. Catching him during the week was difficult because he was often irritated. On the rare occasions Ravi found him in a good mood, he'd throw an arm over Ravi's shoulders, break into slangy Mumbai dialect, and wax nostalgic for "our motherland," although he hadn't returned home since he left for the USA as a teenager. The general message was the same if Ravi did manage to broach the subject, whether in English or Hindi: *Sorry, sorry. Too busy right now... we'll talk later.*

This time, Ravi caught Uncle Ajay leaning over Auntie's shoulder while she tallied numbers. Seeing a smile emerge on Ajay's face, Ravi shucked the apron he'd balled in his fist and leaned the industrial broom against the doorway to seize his moment. Noticing Ravi approach, Uncle Kumar's smile disappeared like an ice cube in hot water. Aunt Chandana's scowl a split-second later stopped him in his tracks.

"Uncle, Auntie, I'd like to talk to you both about my

working fewer hours—"

"Can't you see Auntie and I are going over the week's accounts?"

"You promised my father I could begin attending college."

"Yes, yes. As soon as the business settles down, I told you. Yes, I do remember what I promised my younger brother. But later, Ravi, not now. Please go away."

"But—"

"Not now!"

The door slammed in Ravi's face.

He stood listening to Auntie Chandana's angry, singsong English through the door. Then silence, the two of them sardine-packed into a cubicle the size of a broom closet. An amusing sit-com scene in a family TV show—but Ravi was not amused by the thought. His heart surged with anger. Every word of his prepared speech to Uncle Ajay had skipped out of his brain like so many drops on a hot grill.

Ravi understood his fate: that green card he was once so thrilled to possess was nothing more than an indentured-servant document. Uncle Ajay wasn't his sponsor as much as he was Ravi's slave master. Ravi was handcuffed to his uncle's business and always would be. If he tried to leave his employment, it was only a matter of time before he'd be saying hello to a pair of Immigration and Customs Enforcement agents and saying goodbye, America. His dream of becoming a civil engineer would go straight into the rubbish bin. Like a fish hooked with his uncle's grip on the fishing rod, he could flap his gills, wriggle until he lost his strength and accept his fate. Ravi thought of those untouchables back home, the cremation handlers of the Ganges. As a boy, he'd seen a leg sticking out of a burning *ghat* when he and his father attended Diwali, the ceremony of lights.

Growing into manhood, Ravi scoffed at the religion of his youth. *Moksha, nirvana*, Hinduism, Buddhism—all of it was meant to suppress or deny human aspiration, not lead to enlightenment. He did, however, believe in the Japanese *satori*, that moment of sudden understanding. A Dom could not touch a higher-caste person until that person's death. Those funeral Doms at the burning ceremonies helped others escape the cycle of rebirth and death through the purity of fire.

Ravi knew he must escape his own confinement or grow old and worn out in his relatives' service until, like a battered spouse, it was too late to leave and he was too afraid to take the risk. That night, lying in the tiny room at the end of the motel where he slept, he understood how. He had a grimly pleasant image of Auntie Chandana joining her husband's funeral pyre just as in the days of the British Raj.

The following morning, dawn barely lightening the sheers over the single window, he got up, showered, shaved, and dressed for work. He was scheduled to work the grill as "sous-chef," Uncle Ajay's pompous term for an array of multitasking duties in the kitchen from grilling through dishwashing to bussing tables.

Ravi's mood was light. He hummed *Fakira*, a popular tune from a recent Bollywood film. Oblivious to the kitchen bustle, the daily dance of chefs, servers, busboys, and cooks all performing their ballet of just missing collisions with one another at the last possible second, he stayed busy assisting wherever the work flow began to sag.

Jamal, one of the bus boys, laughed. "Ravi, he must be in love. Look at him so happy."

Soon a chorus of good-natured jeers and quips greeted him every time he appeared beside someone. "What up, Ravi, that true? You in love?"

Felix, the head chef, normally as taciturn in the

morning as a doorknob, picked up the chant: "Ravi got a girlfriend" and "Look, ya'all, Ravi blushing!"

Ravi smiled and took it from all directions, laughing, shaking his head, acting embarrassed. It wouldn't do to call attention to himself now that he had embarked on a dangerous, solo journey.

Hykeem, the new waiter, and Jamal were the last two to join in on the fun. Ravi had interviewed both in Aunt's small office a week earlier. Both were tatted up in gang insignia. Hykeem bore a puckered bullet wound in his forearm; he had gold incisors that reminded Ravi of a spitting cobra when he smiled.

Donzell the busboy said, "It's that night clerk, the chick with the purple skunk stripe."

"Yeah," Jamal, said, "She looks like Billie Eilish."

Chants of *Billie! Billie!* erupted for the next two minutes. Ravi smiled throughout and kept working. Nothing would make him lose composure. He'd happily play the fool if that's what it took, but his heart thumped with fear. His boyish imagination once held images of the five angry gods. It wasn't Kali or Shiva that popped into mind but Hanuman, Lord Rama's devotee, who takes fierce umbrage at anyone who plots misdeeds.

The day after his uncle picked him up from Customs at the airport, chatting away about his "new duties," Ravi had no idea what a con job Uncle was feeding him. Uncle Ajay made it sound like a few hours of easy work, the rest his own time free to see the sights and go anywhere he chose. He wanted to embrace this big, wonderful country just as his uncle had and make a success of himself—until he discovered in just a few days what list of exhausting and tedious jobs lay unspoken behind his uncle's pleasant nattering during that ride. Uncle Ajay had given him a "friendly" warning on the ride to the motel, too.

"Don't get too friendly with the staff."
"Why, Uncle?"
"Trust me, it doesn't pay to be nice to people."

Ravi didn't understand. He believed all his life that Americans were a warm and generous people, friendly to a fault, but his uncle's sharp tone precluded any further discussion. He didn't want to appear rude to a family elder and his own benefactor hours after arriving. Ravi, however, never forgot the words.

Among the photos and civic acclamations cluttering the walls of the tiny office was a certificate from a county agency lauding Mister Ajay Kumar for Hiring Second-Chancers. Ravi learned that "Second-Chancers" was a euphemism for hiring convicted felons.

His uncle went beyond the certificate's extolling—but not out of the goodness of his heart. Uncle Ajay didn't just hire people with misdemeanor records for check fraud or shoplifting; he hired killers, drug dealers, and hardcore ex-cons with multiple assault convictions from the state's maximum-security penitentiary. While that might sound noble, Ravi soon understood the mechanics of his uncle's generosity in hiring practices: he paid many of his ex-felons under the table. One woman, whose neck was tattooed with grim visages that reminded him of Kali's garland of skulls, was an arsonist. From kitchen scuttlebutt, he'd picked up an assortment of prison slang and even a little information about their crimes.

But Ravi had steeled his heart and wasn't turning back now. He had to be careful in his approach to the arsonist. Her name was Donita Ramirez. She was a chain smoker, often used weed with staff behind the dumpster, and had the vilest vocabulary of any human being he knew. Obscenities and profanities in a clipped slang poured in a torrent of filth from her mouth whenever she was high or upset about something.

Ravi was already mentally calling her "Kali."

***

"Better be right about the money."

Ravi found it hard to stare into her eyes—big, mocha-brown pupils, bloodshot streaks in the corners. They seemed to take in his entire being, not just his face.

She blew twin streams of smoke from her nostrils his way. Ravi wanted to gag on the smoke. Up close, Donita was formidable enough with her crazy eyes and myriad tattoos, never mind the dragon exhaust from her nose. They stood side by side in the alleyway near the dumpster, the only place his uncle permitted cigarette breaks by staff.

"Ka—Donita, look. I've seen the insurance papers in the office. Twenty-five thousand as soon as the company cuts the check. Easy money for starting a fire."

"Somebody tried to double-cross me once. It didn't go so good for him."

Ravi didn't want to know the details. He tried not to look intimidated. He googled everything there was on her, read every conviction and newspaper article digitized. One husband burned to death while he lay in a drunken stupor. A laundry list of criminal offenses that ranged from spousal abuse to petty theft. She'd been fired from two jobs as a nursing home aide because of complaints—no charges filed because the Coronavirus was sweeping the nation then and everything was out of kilter. She did her prison, refused to attend a parole board hearing scheduled for her. He'd overheard Hykeem and Jamal talk about her once; she had a family left behind in the prison, a woman who was her "wife," with whom she kept in contact and a "daughter," who was a femme convict the couple "adopted."

The jury balked at her lawyer's "battered woman syndrome" defense at trial because there was nothing about Donita Ramirez that suggested any man would have had an easy time thumping her around the family home, in this case a rusted-out trailer—which, Ravi discovered to no surprise, was another common denominator in the woman's past. "Kali" left behind two burned-out trailers in her wake. Newspaper articles mentioned "arson suspected"; and once again, no charges filed. She'd even tried to collect on the trailer after torching her husband.

Ravi was confident his Kali would never find out about the true insurance payout: $150,000 on Uncle Ajay, $100,000 on Auntie Chandana. Ravi grimaced—his uncle remained a cheapskate when it came to marital equality. But the business was insured for a million-dollars.

Ravi spent his meager portion of free time in his efficiency. Uncle Ajay charged him "a modest rental fee," another shock to Ravi upon his arrival. His window faced a deserted DIY lot with a barbed-wire fence littered with shreds of one-way plastic bags, discarded needles, and food wrappers. He'd seen homeless people camping and wandering about out there at night. Sometimes the wind carried a foul smell whenever too many people used the same spot for a toilet. Several motel workers went out there to score dope.

Before working up enough nerve to contact his Kali, Ravi had made a risky, mid-day recon into the office in a search for those insurance papers. His ruse was bringing lunch on a tray when he discovered that both relatives were preoccupied outside at the other end of the motel with a roofing contractor. Slipping inside with a duplicate key, he held his breath while going through files in the double-drawer cabinet, one ear cocked to the hallway outside.

He located what he needed in minutes, thanks to his

aunt's meticulous filing system. He put on the medallion of the bandicoot rat his father had given him on his last birthday, which sat at the bottom of his clothes drawer. The rat, often depicted with the elephant-headed god Ganesha, symbolizes the god's determination to overcome all obstacles to get what he wants. Setting his disdain for superstition aside, Ravi discovered a different side to himself, one his doting father wouldn't recognize—but then, he doubted his father would recognize the two-faced, grasping hypocrites his older brother and sister-in-law had become in America.

Ravi was on duty from noon to midnight. The Giggler, as he dubbed her from those irksome wake-up calls, would immediately call his uncle if he were a minute late, although she herself rarely was on time, constantly showing up an hour late, sometimes half-stoned, when it was her turn to relieve him.

Today, she barely acknowledged him. Ravi planned to make copies of the "borrowed" papers from the small xerox machine behind the desk. He felt as if his breathing was constricted. As a boy, he had watched an Ajgar, a python, climb a date palm tree after a bird's nest, its thick muscle of a body flexing, bunching, and loosening as it shimmied in slow-motion up to the nest. The Giggler wore earbuds, fixed him with a vacant stare, and resumed texting, both thumbs bobbing like twin hammers on a single revolver.

"You're early," she said, startling him, as if he had violated some unspoken rule.

He glanced at the empty coffee pot for guests, the plethora of stick-it notes adorning the plastic chassis of the computer. She slathered notes everywhere but didn't seem to remember that her job was to perform what the notes said. Ravi was used to the mess, including the raft of phoned-in messages spiked beside the keyboard. For once, he was relieved—everything looked normal.

"I didn't get time" was her blanket excuse. *No doubt,* Ravi thought, *because you spent the entire night phoning, texting, Snapchatting, and posting selfies to Facebook and Instagram.*

"That's all right," Ravi interrupted her. "I'll take care of it."

He had the papers tucked under his arm in a file folder. Later, when it was quiet, he'd sneak off to the office and replace them in their proper folders.

Aunt and Uncle rounded the corner heading his way, both looking in his direction and not liking what they saw, if expressions mattered.

"Uncle, Aunt Chandana, greetings."

His uncle frowned. "Ravi, can I count on you?"

"Of course, Uncle. Always."

"Then why do I find the things I ask you to do undone?"

His uncle looked at him with such a plaintive, disappointed frown on his jowly face that Ravi's mind reeled. For a moment, he thought his piracy had been discovered, all was lost. Maybe he'd be reported to the police if his uncle inferred his nephew's true intentions behind the theft of those insurance papers—what other reason could there be? Ravi saw his life swept away in a tsunami of anguish and grief…

"I called the meat wholesaler just now," Uncle Ajay said. "You didn't call in next week's order like I asked you, did you?"

"I'm sorry, Uncle. I forgot… *what with all the two-dozen other jobs you asked me to do 'in my spare time.'"*

Uncle and Aunt exchanged an identical, sour look. *Such a disappointment after all they had done for him.* Ravi knew the look by heart.

"You make a stick to beat your own back by not doing things in a timely manner. Procrastination is the thief of time, Ravi! Do things at the time you are asked to do them."

"I'll do better," Ravi said. "I promise." *You wait and see how much better, Uncle...*

His face burned with a mix of relief, rage, and shame.

This is the last time you'll lecture me, Uncle Tightwad and Auntie Cheapskate.

Ravi mentally added a few choice expressions to describe them and their lineage from his time in the kitchen, picking up lingo. His aunt made a snorting noise through her nostrils. They both turned away and resumed whatever the conversation in Hindi had been prior to coming upon their wastrel of a nephew.

He felt a weight lifting from his shoulders.

Safe, I'm safe...

Seconds earlier, his mind had been a pinwheel; now it was as empty and litter-strewn as the vacant lot from his window. He was aware of the melodious notes wafting about his ears, an angelic voice coming through the sound system. The Giggler always swore at the canned music, rushed to turn it off the moment she arrived on duty, and plugged in her own music, full of defiance, teenaged angst, betrayals of lovers, male and female, and issues with drugs.

The Giggler's parti-colored hair, scrambled imagery adorning her twin tattoo sleeves confused Ravi but, over time, he was able to discern the interlocking hearts, unicorns, and female warriors astride horses or brandishing swords. Her social life was a dog's breakfast of complications and seemed light years from the tender voice piping its soft lament into his consciousness. He recognized the singer who remained popular at home. He keyed in to the words—a lost love.

"I cried my last tear last night over you," she sang through the tinny sound system.

"I hear you, Miss Lisa Stansfield," Ravi mumbled, looking at the indifferent Giggler, absorbed in her cell phone.

***

Ravi looked at the big cop in the small room. The man looked put together in masonry chunks and a rumpled suit stuck over the loose bits. He also looked as if he wanted to break Ravi over his knee.

"You understand why I put a hold on the insurance payout?"

"Yes, sir, I do."

"The fire marshal's investigator found saddle burns. That's arson, pure and simple."

"I see."

"Do you?"

If Ravi ever thought Aunt Chandana's black looks were intimidating, he realized she could take lessons from the detective. *Dude's big enough to eat apples off my head…*

Jamal's influence on his vocabulary still working despite the eight weeks since the fire and everybody gone from the hulk of a smoking ruin.

"We're still looking for one of your uncle's employees," the cop said, reaching over to fetch a paper from his file. "She's an ex-con, name of Ramirez. Donetta Ramirez."

"Donita," Ravi corrected. "Her name's Donita."

"So this woman, Ravi. You haven't seen her since the day of the fire?"

"No, sir. As I said to you before, I gave the other officers a lengthy statement after my uncle and aunt—"

A little catch in the breath here for effect won't hurt, Ravi thought.

"—my dear relatives were burned to death in that tragic fire. I might have spoken to her once or twice the whole time I worked for my uncle.

"What kind of talking did you two do?"

"Just greetings. You know, 'Hi there, what's up?'—that kind of thing. I barely know what she looked like."

Whoops, too far, Ravi realized.

"Oh, you'd recall her all right. Check out her mug shot."

He shoved a pair of 8 x 10s across the table. Donita's mugshots holding the placard with her booking data, facing center, then left. "Nice glam shots, wouldn't you say?"

Ravi furrowed his brow, studied the photos. "She seems a—formidable-looking woman, Officer."

"That's one way to describe her," the detective said. "Prison shrink's report says she's a bona fide sociopath, notes her as BPD. Know what that means?"

"Borderline Personality Disorder," Ravi replied.

Why am I being a clever clogs for this cop? He's aching to get me to admit something. He suspects. He doesn't know…

"I don't recall seeing her after the fire," Ravi said, moving the photos aside.

Kali's big all-seeing eyes continued to stare back at him even from a distance.

"That don't make you wonder? I mean, this woman went down for arson?"

"Many of my uncle's employees were… *transitory*, Officer. Some worked a few weeks and disappeared. He was constantly hiring people."

"Hiring killers and convicts like our tattooed beauty here."

"Are you suggesting that my uncle and aunt got what they deserved because of my uncle's efforts to help out disadvantaged people—some with criminal records that made it difficult for them to get hired anywhere?"

Ravi couldn't get the indignant tone to work right. The cop stared at him, unimpressed.

Shut up, wanker! his inner voice demanded—but he couldn't help himself.

"My uncle gave them a second chance! Is it because they're Indian-Americans you find it difficult to believe they had good intentions toward everyone?"

The cop's face darkened to the color of mulberry.

"I'm not saying that at all," he fumed. "Don't go putting words into my mouth."

Ravi kept his face blank.

He'd heard American cops were obsessed by politically correct etiquette.

"Your father is the beneficiary of their insurance policies," the cop said matter-of-factly. New forms were submitted just a week before the fire. Your uncle would have died intestate."

Turning tack now, he wants to throw me off...

"I didn't know that, Officer."

Ravi's voice modulated just enough to show indifference.

"Two-hundred-fifty thousand. The business worth a million. That's a lot of reasons for murder and arson."

"My father misses his brother and sister-in-law far more than any compensation."

Ravi avoided looking at his watch. The interrogation was going into a third hour. He'd kept his nerve, replied evenly, answered all the cop's questions carefully and avoided adding information. He refused to rise to the bait when the officer tossed out Donita's name as a potential suspect.

Another hour later, the questions-and-answers

devolving into pure repetition, Ravi was told he could go — "for now." The cop told him to expect "a follow-up interview."

Ravi thanked him and said he would oblige any request if it would help bring "the perpetrator to justice."

"But no second thoughts on the polygraph?"

"It's inadmissible. I have a legal right to refuse."

That warranted a hostile stare. The cop shifted his bulk in a chair more suitable for church bingo.

Outside, Ravi let go of the breath he was holding, suspecting he was still on CCTV. He maintained a slow pace to the Honda. His father wired him the cash through an ETF transfer that allowed Ravi to buy the used car so that he could meet his father at the airport in three days. His last paycheck was frozen like the rest of his uncle's business while it remained in probate.

Ravi figured they would have to get a lawyer to take their case on commission pending a successful lawsuit.

Ravi fingered the chain at his neck, smiling at the image of the bandicoot rat on the medallion. His childish image of America from the slums—sandy beaches, tanned, gorgeous girls, palm trees, Bel-Air mansions—all of that evaporated in his time at the motel. Ganesha had smiled on him for his cunning and his enterprise. Ravi had slept guilt-free every night since the fire.

He played online chess until ten o'clock. He drank a bottled water before climbing into his uncomfortable bed.

So many unpleasant things finally coming to an end.

Ravi hated this cold, Midwestern city. Once the lawsuit was settled, he would head for California and flash his roll—*another Jamalism*. His limbs felt heavy; he seemed to be floating above his bed one moment and then plunging through it to the bedsprings the next.

Odd taste in my mouth, too... and then fell into a black

vortex.

The hard slap to his face woke him from his deep sleep.

"I put too much in your bottled water."

The voice hovered from above, familiar and ominous at the same time. Each word separate as a dust mote before coming together in a rush. A husky voice but not a man's.

From a far-back corner of his mind, it clicked into place like a tow-truck's spring-loaded lock. *Donita—Kali.*

"You awake now, sleepyhead?"

Another stinging slap to his cheek. Ravi's eyes bugged, settled on the blocky face. Then her eyes, those cold eyes despite the warm color like the black gaze of a shark as a seal swims into view.

"My money. Where is it? I came for my money."

"I don't have it, Kali!"

"Who?"

"Donita! I haven't got any to give you right now—"

Slap, slap, slap.

Like a small-caliber gun going off. For a dazed moment, Ravi thought he actually had been shot.

"The insurance… hasn't paid… need more time…"

"Are you fucking me over, Ravi?"

"No, no, no…I swear!"

"You remember our first conversation behind the dumpster? What I said to you?"

"Yes, yes. I remember."

Blood-flecked spit bubbles oozed from the corners of his mouth and he swallowed blood and a chip of one of his teeth. An olfactory memory of that alley conversation speared him. He recalled vividly a whiff of something pungent, something unpleasant coming off her not like the smell of unwashed clothes. More like a chemical smell, the smell of madness.

"I come for my money, motherfucker," Donita repeated. "I been watching you at night."

"Watching?"

"I been sleeping out in the fields, out in a sleeping bag. Cold at night—"

Her voice lilted upward. She seemed lost in a reverie of nights outside in the dark and cold. Nights spent thinking about him…

Ravi tracked her eyes, the pupils swallowed up in a deeper blackness. Murky light in the room made it difficult to see. Whatever she'd doped his water bottle with was still coursing through his system. His limbs were leaden; he couldn't move without enormous effort.

"Remember, Donita. Remember I said we'd have to wait for the insurance payout when the coast was clear."

"Clear…"

At last, a morsel of logic seemed to penetrate. Ravi felt his slide toward the abyss halted.

"Once the cop's investigation ends, we can collect. Both of us."

"Pay me now, motherfucker."

"I can't!"

She swiveled her head around, like an insect, as if to see him better. Ravi saw the neck tattoo he'd missed among the helter-skelter of ink—a coiled serpent.

A boyhood memory of visiting a temple in the holy city of Varanasi hit him like a fist. Clutching his father's hand, he stepped from brilliant light into the shadowy murk of the interior to be confronted by the massive statue of Shiva the Destroyer with his serpent wrapped around his neck—

Another blow.

Wet.

What—what is this?

Ravi lifted his head from the pillow to see the glint of a filleting blade wink in the light as it arced above her head and then plunged, quivering, into the meat beneath his breastbone.

It plunged in and out of his chest, as if attached to a marionette wire, in and out, again and again, blood flying everywhere—onto their faces, speckling the bedsheets, comets of bright blood flecking the ceiling.

Ravi turned his head away from the slaughter. Vision coalesced into a red beam with black dots floating in it like vultures circling aloft finding the scent. All sound disappeared, his moans and cries, her slavering, incoherent rant. A whirring noise that began as an insect chirring in the fields ended in a tornadic rush of air being squeezed through his lungs.

Then the room disappeared.

At last, Ravi knew exactly where he was—knew where he had been all that long-ago time when his father showed him the muddy-brown river for the first time.

There I am. That's me, atop a burning raft of blood.

If Only Julia

Slapping a magnet to hold my goodbye note to the fridge felt satisfying as hell. As the hours went by and the miles from my house increased, I felt less happy with my decision to walk out of my marriage to Julia and my career teaching economics at the community college in Toledo. I was approaching Oklahoma City by then, and according to the dashboard clock, it was three in the morning—the time medieval mystics called the Dark Night of the Soul. The time when your life has collapsed around your ankles like unread books and you finally realized it.

Three days ago, everything was in place, normal, another notch in the belt toward inevitable oblivion. I'd canceled my six p.m. class in Macroeconomics. I didn't recognize the car in the driveway when I pulled in. The man on top of Julia in our bed wasn't recognizable to me, either. He looked young. Maybe a dozen years younger and a couple inches longer.

Trying not to replay that scene on my long, dark drive through the night was impossible. What I said, what she said sitting on the other side of the bed with sheets wrapped modestly around her, which struck me oddly inappropriate after what I'd witnessed—combined with his hasty retreat, clothes scooped from the floor and bundled in his arms. I regretted not kicking him in the balls as he sidled past me to the door. What saved him from that, more than my neutered persona or physical cowardice, was his youth. My wife, the cradle-robber. I was more sickened by the humiliation than by the rage bubbling in my esophagus. The walloping thud in my temples from the migraine won out, resulting in my tirade chopped short, as I bolted for the toilet to heave up the bile in my stomach.

The next day was all grim silence. We avoided each other and didn't speak for the few seconds we were in each other's company in the kitchen heading for our respective jobs. The following day was the same except for her futile attempt to "talk about it." I ignored her. I'd never so much as called her an unkind name in the ten years of our marriage or the eight months of our courtship preceding it. Now I wondered what it would be like to smash her face into the wall and watch the blood spurt between her fingers.

Leaving seemed the best of all bad options. I'd been bored with teaching anyway. On the other hand, I wasn't yearning to try out a new life as a fry cook in Wyoming. The status quo of my life numbed me to life-changing decisions. Julia's simple beauty, her ash blonde hair, oval face, and blue eyes knocked me out of the doldrums damming up in my neocortex at that time. My discontent collapsed like a citadel under siege from our first date on through our courtship to our marriage six months later. Then a headache made me cancel class.

By sundown, the landscape around me looked as barren as I felt inside. Nothing to see from the windshield but rusted-barbed wire fencing, a few cattle or horses grazing, abandoned farms and orchards. A still life of oil derricks and wind-bent scrub trees.

For the last fifty miles, even that much disappeared leaving nothing but highway mile-marker signs. I knew Oklahoma City was up ahead because of the last junction sign I'd glanced at in my zombie-like state. The sudden surge in big-rig traffic snapped me out of my lethargy and the replays of Julia's Bedroom Fornication. I needed gas. I needed food and coffee.

I didn't even bring a map with me or my cell phone, being my way to tell her I was beyond reach and we'd communicate through lawyers from there on out. With a couple hundred and my credit cards to finance the "escape," she'd understand how deep was the wound — or not. I hit Interstate 75 South out of town and didn't look back. Nothing like an embittered imagination to accompany me on a momentous trip because images of her cavorting in bed with her secret lover tumbled out of my mind like circus clowns out of a Volkswagen.

Three eighteen-wheelers a half-mile ahead pulled off an exit ramp. I decided to follow. I could use the coffee if I planned to keep going to—wherever I was going. I'd taken highways on a whim and drifted westward until I saw the first Oklahoma sign. The sensory deprivation of hours inside my vehicle with my only companions the two sides of my warring personality arguing with each other over Julia as either my soulmate or that treacherous woman was boring me to a leaden indifference.

My idea of food quality at a truck stop comes down to a mental image of an unshaven short-order cook in a grease-spattered apron banging a big wooden spoon against a swill bucket. A dozen trucks in front of a roadside diner won't convince me otherwise. Regarding the number of big trucks in the lot at that time of night was another sign of America's low culinary standards. The place was either undeniably popular or else everybody pulled off the road because of a global catastrophe happening right then.

The chatty girl who led me to a booth informed me it wasn't a meteor heading Earth's way but the simple coincidence of geography.

"Righ' cheer," she said, handing me the menu, "is the Dallas Junction Complex. Don't ask me why they call it that."

The plastic menu confirmed it. I saw an inset map of blue lines indicating Interstates 35, 40, and 44 conjoining like three deep veins in a thrombosis scan. I tried to be pleasant as I thanked her.

"Lots of truckers here tonight despite the hour."

"Lots of meth deals goin' on out in the parking lot," she replied in a chirpy voice, which was more information than I wanted. I glanced down at the menu while she hovered, apparently unneeded elsewhere in the spacious dining room. The reek of grease told me my estimation of truck stops wasn't about to be overturned that night. Then I spotted several unusual items in the dinner fare section.

"What's bhindi with makki di roti?"

"That don't mean nothin'," she replied. "It's just okra in tomato sauce and flat bread made from corn meal."

"Chole puri?"

"Spicy chick peas served with puffy fried wheat bread."

"Is this customary Oklahoma dining fare?"

"Hunh?"

"Do people in Oklahoma usually eat—"

"Oh, lawdie, no. That's cuz we get lots of Indian truck drivers since the pandemic. You know, them guys in the red whatchamacallems, towels."

"Turbans."

"Yeah, right."

She took my order of a steak and eggs and walked off. I watched her go, trying to promote some lust into my gaze as a small revenge on Julia. Young, attractive, her long pony tail swinging in rhythm to her hips, I envied her instead, the mindless *sangfroid* of youth and health, the bulk of life's inevitable betrayals and disappointment still looming in the wings.

It took me a minute to absorb the fact that Sikhs were in the long-haul trucker industry. That was news. I took it in as part of my new re-education into life going forward.

All I knew from a long-ago class in world religions was that Sikhs were compelled to earn an honest living and that they were required to keep certain items on their person at all times like a wooden comb in their turbans and a small sword, symbolically denoting their status as warriors for God.

I could have used a Sikh sword on the steak she brought me with my eggs and potatoes. The coffee was the predictable, watered-down variety you get everywhere. Only the liquid filth served in the vending machines back at school was worse, and not by that much.

Road weariness from the long night, the itchy burn of my eyes, and my stomach bloat reminded me that, however revolting the meal, I had to acknowledge that I'd never seen a meal served so fast that it seemed my ponytailed server had merely walked into the kitchen empty-handed and turned around two minutes later with the platter of food. Pushing the chewy steak around in my mouth, I was unwilling to hit the highway again. I dreaded asking Sherri, according to my server's plastic nametag, for advice about where to aim my car next. It was unseemly and showed me for the weak, indecisive man I was, as though my lackluster role in the *Cuckold Sees His Wife at Play* back in the bedroom three nights ago needed confirming. Mentally I was still going in circles even if my Wrangler held true to its southwesterly vector despite my confusion.

When Sherri came around again, I ordered a lassi, vaguely recalling it was something like a yogurt smoothie with mango or peach. I promised myself to have a direction by the time I finished dessert and hoped the cooling drink would dampen the fire in my stomach.

Three big men, all looking like truckers, took the booth in front of mine. Overhearing is an awkwardness I try to avoid but the proximity of booths, the lack of customers at that time of night made that impossible. Their voices, aggravated by smoking and solitude on the road, were too loud to ignore. I perused the menu Sherri didn't pick up to avoid the appearance of eavesdropping.

They must have been communicating over their CBs before arriving at the diner because they spoke in clipped monotones, as though knowing what each one was going to say. At first, their conversation was laced with jargon about disengaging shift linkages and determining a cab's pivot axis. Their voices lowered immediately, however, when two new topics emerged, which I only partially understood. The first concerned a "package."

One trucker seemed especially irritated the "handoff" wasn't happening on time. He kept referring to a Joe or a Beth—maybe a couple meant to take delivery? Given the sloppy colloquialisms of American speech, the "they" they referred to could have been a single individual. How many people did it take to receive the package? Unless it's a grand piano delivered in the middle of the night, one should do.

Sherri's casual remark about drug deals in the parking lot popped into my head. This nexus of intersecting highways and the prospect of money could easily make that a temptation.

The trucker whose back was to me kept growling about the lateness of the pickup until his companions told him to relax. The one sitting by the window, either Russ or Rusty, told him to "zip it," and tapped his own ear for emphasis. The two men facing me looked right at me. Rusty or Russ swiveled his had around; his eyes bored into me while I studied that menu like a monk examining a page of the *Book of Kells*.

"He ain't listening," he said to the others.

Five minutes passed before their conversation resumed its normal pitch. Sherri brought them coffee and took their orders. She knew a couple of them from the light banter. Their spaghetti-and-meatballs, fried chicken steak and gravy with extra rolls and salads would have fed half the population of Burkina Faso. Sherri was barely out of earshot before her anatomical dimensions were discussed, dissected, approved of or quibbled over. "Damn girl's ass looks like a upside-down heart," said the one I now knew to be Russell.

I tuned them out after that, forced to half-listen from the sheer volume of their chat until the words *Mongols* and *Cossacks* brought me to full attention. For a split-second, I ludicrously thought the truckers had elevated their conversation to talk of history—something to do with ancient Eurasian battles. Then Russell said something about the arriving Bandidos, and I realized they were talking biker gangs. I concentrated on the bottom of my lassi glass; it was evident they were talking about that notorious shootout at a family restaurant in Waco, Texas some years back that left nine bikers dead.

Those greedy truckers sitting around a table stuffing their faces with starchy foods until their hearts are the size of a canned ham yapping about a prospective drug deal with biker scum.

If you'd asked me two days ago what business of mine it was, I would have told you I didn't give a shit if half the country mainlined fentanyl-laced heroin. As long as those drug-addled losers kept to their side of the road, I believed people should be allowed to choose their own damnation.

If only Julia had remained faithful, that tectonic shift in my thinking would have remained the same. But the Earth had reversed its polarity. My moral compass went with it. Toledo used to be a decent, middle-class city. In recent years, it had become a filthy, polluted, rats' nest of drug overdoses, gang shootings, and prostitution by the baby-faced killers from Detroit who used Toledo as a launch pad for sex trafficking teenaged girls and boys in Ohio and across the

Midwest.

My face flushed, and I bristled at the casual way those men discussed their side business as though it were just another meal in a diner along the route. Almost on cue, a song came over the speaker system, the 60's tune by the Stones—"Sympathy for the Devil." I had no sympathy for the devil left.

I paid my check, left Sherri a $20 tip, which caused her eyes to widen. She stuttered a thanks, turned the bill over to see if a short man in a top hat might not be on the back instead of Alexander Hamilton. Before heading out the door in search of my destiny after being forced to wallow in the sordid tales of those truck-driving men, who didn't give a damn about adding to the putrid catastrophes of suffering they contributed to with their "packages," I stopped at their booth. They ceased talking. None of their expressions looked friendly. Russell stood up, glaring.

"'th'fuck you want, man? You got a problem?"

"Your eighty-thousand-dollar salaries aren't enough you have to do . . . deals?"

The trucker opposite him reached out and gripped him by his leather vest. "Leave it be, Russ," he ordered. To me: "Keep going, mister, or you're gonna get more'n that meal you just ate tonight."

I walked out, still fuming.

Why was I so helpless? Again, life threw me a challenge and I waffled like the coward I was, content to make a mealy-mouthed comment to a trio of dope-dealing truckers just as I had no other ammunition than a volley of words to boot that guy in the ass as he slunk off after climbing on my wife. Helpless, a useless, bloviating windbag—that's what many of my students thought of me and said so on their semesterly evaluations of my performance.

There was something I could do—

I could grab their dope before their biker pals showed up and turn it over to the cops. For once in my life, I wanted to act, not talk.

Opening the gate of my Jeep, I removed the tire iron for loosening lug nuts. The beveled edge might not be enough to pop open an 18-wheeler's cab door, but I was going to try.

Which semi, however? If this were noontime instead of four-thirty in the morning, I'd spend an hour looking for the right one. Even at this time of night, there were a couple dozen Kenworths, Freightliners, and Macks in the back lot. Most of these 80,000-pound behemoths rumbled, idling to keep the big diesel engines warm while the drivers ate in the diner or snoozed in the sleeper cab or compressors running for perishable cargo in the trailer. All that engine noise provided cover to saunter past the rows of tractor-trailers, yet what did I expect? They'd mark one out for me with a big red X marks the drug semi? Hopeless—until I came to a woman's name in elegant script on the side of one cab: *JoBeth*. The name I'd confused inside.

I hopped onto the truck step attached to the rocker panel and peered inside to be sure it was empty. I couldn't get in tight enough to put enough pressure on the bar even if the door itself wasn't so heavy-duty as it looked. Just standing there was enough to get me charged with attempted break-in. I was about to give it up, hop down to the pavement when the light shifted inside the cab. Unless the world turned a degree differently on is axis, the movement came from inside, not outside.

With my face pressed to the glass, I saw a pair of sneakers. They emerged from the sleeping quarter behind the driver's seat. I stared again, uncertain whether it was a trick of the light or something I'd actually seen.

The tennis shoes appeared again—small feet, either a small boy's or a woman's. They kicked uselessly at the long, curved shifter in the center of the cab's floorboard between the seats. A strangled, gurgling sound—definitely a woman's voice.

Jumping down, I looked around to check if I'd been seen. Was she traveling with one of the drivers? But why out here while they're inside eating food? The obvious answer hit me a second later: *She's confined in that narrow cubicle... a captive.*

Which realization opened up a tangled web of colliding thoughts in my head. One thing I knew: I was out of my depth. So much for ratting out dope-hustling truckers. This was kidnapping, whatever else was involved.

I needed a better look before reporting it to the police. Rounding the front to the passenger side window, I climbed up and stared intently inside. Lights from the parking lot didn't inhibit my view as much on this side. I made out a pair of jean-clad legs. From the twisting motion of her legs, I inferred she was bound both hands and feet, I deduced from the grunts of her efforts to move her body from that position she was also gagged.

Tapping on the glass stopped her writhing. I was about to smash the glass with my bar when she spluttered *No!* through her gag. It stopped me cold.

"Alarm . . . door," she gasped out.

Each moment of indecision was an agony to endure for us both. I clung to the side mirror for balance and couldn't see her face in the darkened area.

"I'll get help," I said, as loudly as I dared.

"Wait, no... wait!"

"The cops," I hissed into the glass. "I'll bring cops."

I'm arguing with a kidnap victim about saving her from thugs. Whether prostitution or dope were behind her reaction, it didn't matter. Logy from hours of driving and lack of sleep, dull-witted from the greasy slop I'd ingested, I sensed my life careening into the surreal.

Leaving her slobbering an anguished cry of protest, I tossed the bar to the ground and raced back to the diner. Walking past that booth, feeling their eyes on me, I summoned a discipline I didn't feel to portray a confused customer looking for the restroom but heading toward the kitchen doors right beside the men's room—bad *feng shui*. I was grateful to the architect for not minding their proximity to each other. It made my "mistake' look less suspicious, although I felt Russell's eyes boring through my back as I walked through the kitchen double doors.

A fry cook dumping a basket of potatoes cut for French fries looked up as I approached.

"A woman, there's a woman held prisoner in one of those trucks outside! Call the Sheriff's! Get somebody here right now!"

He stared at me.

He thinks I'm a lunatic...

"Did you hear me? Call nine-one-one!"

He bolted past me.

I stood there breathing in the pungent odors of cooking and frying. I was pondering what I'd say, how I'd say it, when the police arrived—even looking beyond my Good Samaritan deed to the next phase of my life's unraveling. I intended to wait outside rather than endure the truckers' stares one more time. My hand pushed the aluminum door a few inches open. I glimpsed the cook talking to the three truckers, gesturing with a limp arm toward the very door I cowered behind. I imagined three heads swiveling as one.

The fight-or-flight alarm in my head made its decision. Running was all I ever did. Right down to running into a cushy academic career. I looked around, caught the glint of knives on the cutting table under fluorescent lights, and decided. I grabbed a butcher knife, and unclamped an industrial-sized can opener from the end of the table. Tucked it under my arm like a football, I ran to the back door.

A goggle-eyed Sherri came around the corner just then carrying a tray of dishes from the other side of the diner. She jumped back, screaming, threw the tray to the side. I heard the horrendous crash of broken glass and spilled plates and utensils.

I flew past the dumpsters, skidded to a stop to get my bearings. I had 70 yards to cover back to the Freightliner. I tucked the knife into the back of my belt.

Years of indolence and sedentary living came home to roost. On a dead sprint, my thigh muscles burned in protest, my lungs wheezed painfully, and my body moved in a clumsy, herky-jerky fashion. With one arm pumping and the other cradling my theft from the kitchen, the tractor-trailer loomed larger in slow increments of time as I ran. My brain told me they'd search for me in the kitchen—until I realized Sherri would simply point to the door I fled out of.

In-sane, in-sane... the word beat time in my head along with my rhythm of my pounding feet on the asphalt. Stopping in front of the passenger side door, I flung the can opener through the window, leapt to the step, and thrust my arm inside to open the door. I nearly knocked myself to the ground instead. Clinging to it while it swung open, I kicked my legs out, fumbling above ground, finally managed to get my right foot on the metal door step and swing the door closed with me on the inside.

She sat in the dark on the edge of the tiny slab of cot, watching my Buster Keaton farce. Her soggy cloth gag hung under her chin; she'd finally worked it loose.

I pulled the knife from my belt and moved toward

her. She reared back about to scream.

Precious seconds lost hushing and reassuring her. When she understood, she turned her body sideways so that I could get at the bindings. In that cramped space meant for one, not two, bodies, the nylon cuffs were tough to cut through at that angle without scoring her flesh. I sliced through the ankle cuffs more easily.

"Out!" I screamed at her. "Let's go!"

I retrieved my tire-changing bar to have a second weapon. She didn't follow right away. Like someone boxing a compass, she turned in all four directions until she realized I was the best bet under the circumstances. I should have anticipated her hesitation, but where else was she going to go?

In those chaotic moments, there was no time to think long. Voices, shouting, men running in our direction. The semi stood between us and our pursuers.

"My Jeep," I said, running a slow and fast as I could manage. Sheer dumb luck that the walk to the diner allowed me to get the kinks out of my aching back muscles and my legs, the reason not to park in front of the diner.

They were already at the semi. My Jeep, a dozen yards off.

"Get down," I told her.

Dropping to the ground, I rolled under the trailer of the closest truck. She duplicated my move, our bodies touching.

"Scooch over," she hissed in my face.

I wriggled to let her get farther in. A stab of anguish swept over me when she spooned right into me, a habit Julia had before she finally fell asleep.

Boots in my line of sight, the exposed diamond-shaped tip of an ugly combat knife carried loose in one hand. More boots, talking.

A voice, the deeper basso-profundo that becalmed the irate Russell back in the diner: "The fucking fuck they at, Russell?"

"Fuck do I know. I look like a goddamn psycho?"

The third trucker: "Cocksucker threw a fuckin' can opener through the window, you believe that shit? I'll gut that motherfucker I find him."

Russell meant *psychic*, of course. More absurdity in a night already full of it. Only this time, threaded with terror. Like a kid in church with the giggles, I wanted to laugh at Russell's dim-witted remark. I was verging on convulsions of laughter despite my hand covering my mouth. Sensing danger, she clamped her hand over mine, yanked her face into mine inches away. The fear and anger comingled in her look sobered me at once. I'd seen Julia irritated with me dozens of times. I'd never seen *that look* before on any person's face.

"Keep looking!" The alpha male trucker again.

After what felt like hours, not minutes, they moved away, walking down the line of trucks away from us, still much too close to my Wrangler to risk leaving our position.

"Who are you?" I asked.

"We can git acquainted later, ya'll," she said. All I saw were small, close-set eyes. One front tooth bent inward. Her breath was sour in my face from spitting and yelling into the rag over her mouth.

I had the better view. "They'll see us when they come back this way," I said. "My Jeep's just beyond that last truck. I'll get it, come back for you. You wait here."

"Fuck that, Jack," she replied, spit flecks hitting my face. "We're both goin' or ain't none of us goin'."

"Get ready, then."

"Wait! Hear that?"

Low, rumbling thunder in the distance. No, not

thunder—motorcycles, big bikes from the sound waves coming closer, booming off the metal trailers.

"They're turning in."

"Who?"

"The Bandidos."

Two truckers started walking toward them as they lined up out front of the diner. More searchers, I figured, once they knew what they were about to hear from the barrel-chested Russell bearing down on them.

"Now," I told her. "Follow me."

I rolled out—ten feet behind the other trucker who stayed behind to keep looking for us. He carried a big wrench and was bending low to look behind the cab where the wiring harness and pigtail delivered electricity to the trailer lights. I covered the distance fast but not fast enough; he straightened up when he saw me and raised an arm when he saw my own arm raised to strike him. Adrenalin put force behind the swing; the sound of the metal catching him across the temple was satisfying and sickening simultaneously.

"Hit 'im again," her voice said behind me. "Don't stand there lookin' at 'im, for Chrissake!"

No need to. He dropped where he stood, the wrench beat him to the ground by a fraction of a second.

Sprinting ahead, fishing in my pocket for my keys, I glanced back to see her keeping pace with me. She gripped a small satchel in one hand. I never noticed it before.

I got in, started the engine. She landed in the seat beside me, agile as a monkey. I did a three-point turn and avoided squealing of rubber going through the gears to draw attention. My car could outrun a slow-moving tractor-trailer but not those bikes with the ape-hanger bars capable of catching up to me in minutes even with a good head start.

"I'm going north. Does the John Kilpatrick Turnpike mean anything to you?"

"Nope."

"You couldn't leave your purse behind?"

"It ain't a purse."

"That last highway sign," I said, my knuckles white on the steering wheel, "it said Overholser Road. That mean anything to you?"

"Fugg, no. Just keep goin', man!"

"Shit."

"What?"

"Warning light came on ten miles before I stopped for gas back there."

I meant to get gas right after my meal. Now what? I could make a run for Oklahoma City and hope I made it inside the city lines--enough to see houses, traffic, signs of civilization before the gas tank emptied and we got caught from behind.

"Does that Lake Overholser sign mean anything to you?"

"Quit askin' me for directions, dammit. I look like I was born and raised around here?"

"You're welcome," I said.

"Welcome? For what?"

"You're welcome—for saving you back there. You might show a little gratitude or is that too much to ask?"

"So I'll give you a blowjob later," she said. "That do?"

"I'm taking the next road in after the campground," I said. "The park isn't open for another hour. We can't outrun those bikes on an open highway."

"What's it look like on your side?" I asked her.

"Sketchy."

"Sketchy?"

"You asked."

I was reacting like a creature of my class. Middle-class

envy. That must mean big lake houses, private security, a safe haven.

"Where's a cop when you need one, huh?"

"For someone kidnapped by truckers, lying bound and gagged, you're taking this pretty well."

"I been in some tough scrapes in my life."

"That bag in your lap. I'll bet it doesn't contain your overnight clothes."

"You never mind what's in it, mister."

"What's your name—or is that too much of an imposition, considering we haven't been introduced?"

"I figger you're a Yankee from that shitty accent. My name is Champagne."

"Cham—did you say 'Champagne'?"

"What of it?"

"Nothing."

I waited for her to ask me my name. She didn't. She sat there staring through the windshield as calmly as though I'd picked up a hitchhiker. This was the first time I had a good look at her until then. I put her age somewhere between 25 and 40, mousy brown hair. Sharp features, an aquiline nose pressed between dark brown eyes suggested a bird. Not a yardbird, more a predatory bird, one small and fast like a tercel. The gas tank was down to vapors. I'd never run my Jeep so far past the red line before. I used to scold Julia for riding around on an eighth of a tank.

Another sign: Lake Overholser Dam 3 mi. ahead.

"Cabins!"

She punched my arm and pointed off to the left where a curved gravel road led down to a row of cabins. The shingled roofs were barely visible.

"What good's that going to do? It's five-forty-five in the morning—"

The coughing chug of the Wrangler's engine going

dry interrupted me.

"We're empty," I said.

"No shit, Captain Obvious."

I turned to look at her. "You know the expression 'If looks could kill'?"

"T'hell with your expressions. You hear them bikes? Turn!"

It made as much sense as anything at that point. If nothing else, I could coast down the hill and try to park out of sight near the edge of a thin tree line. Enough gas to get close to the bottom. I parked several cabins from the last one below the sightline of the road leading to the dam.

She hopped out and took off. I debated a long second about going in another direction. It felt wrong like reading half a book and slamming it shut for no reason.

She was wriggling through a screen on the far side of the last cabin at the bottom of the hill near the North Canadian River. Her legs disappeared the instant I caught the scissoring motion. Had I turned a second later, I'd never have seen her.

The window was chest height. The bottom of the screen hung loose where she'd ripped it out to crawl through. I hoisted myself up and see-sawed my body until gravity did the rest. It wasn't a graceful fall and I barely avoided a face-plant. I let my eyes adjust.

I stood, rubbing the shoulder that took the brunt of the impact. She was peeking out a crack in the door.

"Thanks for your help."

"Tarnation, man, you couldn't find your own cabin?"

"You're just about the most ungrateful—"

"Shut up! Hear that?"

Harleys throttling down to take the turn at the crest of the hill would have been heard across the river to the reservoir.

"You think they'll search the cabins for us?"

"Pope shit in the woods? Hellfire, yes, they'll search."

"I take it they'd like the contents of that bag returned forthwith."

"Prolly so. But they ain't gettin' it. It's mine now."

"Those truckers, the ones who had you talked about a 'package.' I assume they meant dope or money."

"Well, you'd be assumin' wrong. I'm the package they's supposed to deliver."

Before I could utter another word, the bike engines changed to that staccato thrumming of mighty horsepower reigned in for cruising speed. Looking as they drove. Voices, a command voice taking over, giving directions for searching the brush, the walking trails near the river, and every cabin. Once they noticed that loose screen—

Champagne realized it before I did. She took quick steps to the window and pulled it tight against the aluminum frame. I had enough light to see her expression; she mouthed: *Help*.

The cabins were minimal; stairs led to a tiny loft. A kitchenette and a bathroom stall with a latrine and shower to the right. Nothing lying in sight, no utensils. I went to the bathroom, saw a soap-on-a-rope hanging from the shower head.

When I made it to Champagne's side, she was flattened against the wall, one hand gripping the end of the screen flap taut. She saw the bar of soap in my hand. I had no experience with sign language or reading lips but anyone could have read *What the Fuck*.

I rubbed the soap in an L-shaped motion along the window frame. Taking it from her as carefully as though it were a Fabergé egg, I pressed the edges of the screen into the soaped wood and hoped it would dry to form a seal. I avoided looking at Champagne the whole time; she took the soap from me and rubbed one side vigorously as I had done to the bottom of the frame.

We moved away from the window as voices approached.

"You check all the doors this side?"

"Locked," said a surprisingly high-pitched voice that could have been a male falsetto.

Champagne's expression said *Will it work?* I raised my eyebrows: *No idea.*

They moved to the back and then the side window where we'd done our makeshift work with the bar of soap.

"You see anything in there?" The voice rough, deep.

If you can stop your heartbeat by an act of will, I did mine for long seconds while that biker gazed through the screen, one hand over his forehead. Shaggy beard, bald-headed. Champagne's hand squeezed my forearm, her nails digging into my flesh. The voices moved off.

It was light enough for me to see the blood running down my arm as red, not black.

"Close one, huh? Think they're gone?"

"They've seen the Jeep," I replied. "They know we're here somewhere. How badly do they want you?"

"I'm just somethin' to do right now. They'll get bored and move off soon."

I wanted to take comfort in her words, but I couldn't. The place where she stood a moment ago revealed a small yellow puddle of urine.

"We should stay here," I said tactfully. "Wait until dark before leaving and hope nobody rents this cabin out."

"Yeah, rest up," Champagne replied.

She left for the bathroom. My teeth were on edge the entire time the shower ran.

She came out dripping wet and naked as a jaybird, holding her jeans in front of her.

"Ain't any towels in the whole fuckin' place."

She stopped to stare at me. "What are you gittin' your panties in a twist over? Never seen a girl naked before?"

"I'm getting used to a lot of things I never expected to deal with."

I picked up the table and pulled it close to the tiny kitchen out of sight of the window.

"Ya'll married?"

"Yes—no."

"Well, which is it?"

"I was," I replied. "I'm not now."

"You want that blowjob now?"

I stared at her. "I can't believe you."

She shrugged. "You was complaining all to hell back there about me bein' a ungrateful bitch."

"I never said that."

"Whatever. Ah, fuck it, let's try to git along on account of we're cornered like rats here."

"Suits me fine."

By early afternoon, the small cabin was stuffy. I itched with boredom and wanted a change of clothes, but showering with men hunting us outside stopped me. The water from the kitchen faucet was tepid and foul-tasting, adding to my discomfort. My mental distress was off the charts. Cars passed us, going up and down. Hikers chatted walking near the riverfront. Champagne slept next to the kitchenette, using her satchel as a pillow. Her adenoidal snore made me yearn for my bed at home—until my mind put Julia in it with her boyfriend rampant.

"Gawd-damn," Champagne yawned. "Anything to eat in this place?"

"Welcome back to the world, Sleeping Beauty," I said, envious of her long nap. "Don't worry about those armed killers out there scouring for us. Let's have some Ritz crackers, maybe some peanut butter to go with them."

"Whooee, who put a bug up your ass, Jack?"

"My name's not Jack."

"It'll do. I don't want to know your name anyway."

"It's Frank, you cheap barroom tart. Okie trash slut."

For a second, I thought she was going to make a run at me, her long nails extended like a cat.

"I was beginning to wonder what it took to get your goat."

"My goat's got, I assure you. As soon as I can put some distance between me, you, and those lowlife bikers, the better."

"Reckon it might be safe now."

My temper tantrum passed. I didn't apologize. Instead, I told her I'd been checking the door and window every ten minutes while she slept. It looked like what it was supposed to be: people going by with picnic baskets, fishing poles, camping gear. All that summer festivity belied by the horror of sex-trafficking psychopaths on steel horses. Real Mongols on the Oklahoma plains.

"I'm going to check on the Jeep as soon as the sun clears those treetops."

"Keerful," she said.

"Keer—oh, *careful*. Yes, I'll be careful." Her rapid-fire, mumbled Oklahoma accent made it hard for me to understand.

"That's how people talk in Chickasha. Plus, I got me a little Cherokee blood."

"The Trail of Tears."

"Yeah, that. I ain't heard it called in a long time. Trail of Tears. Story of my fuckin' life."

I didn't want to hear the story of her "fuckin' life." I wanted a way out, somewhere else to go. But she had a captive audience, and truth be told, the sound of her voice—

slushy accent and all—was a way to pass time and relieve anxiety. Hers was a sordid catastrophe, for sure. An unwanted infant, state-raised, sexually abused by foster parents, a runaway at seventeen, a heroin addict at eighteen, abusive boyfriends and two husbands, one a drunk, one a meth head; she had that proverbial snowball's chance in hell. Yet there she was, more or less intact, feisty and foul-mouthed with her ill-gotten swag tucked into her lap like a child's safety blanket.

"We must be the only two people in this state without a cell phone right now," she said.

"I left mine at home."

"That was plenty dumb now, wasn't it? I mean, when you actually think about it, could you have done anything dumber? I mean shit, hell, fuck. Shit on a stick, Frank."

At least, she remembered my name. By midafternoon, I couldn't wait any longer. The fear of the sun going down and night falling added more than a dollop of terror to the waiting.

I slipped out the door and stayed as close to the cabins as I could without alarming the occupants of the ones nearby who showed since daylight. Families and kids with dogs. Maybe that's what drove off the bikers: normal people on vacation. My ears so attuned to the sound of revving motorcycles, a backfire close by hit me with an adrenalin jolt that nauseated me. A few more cabins up the hill, I saw the corner of my ragtop and the fire-engine-red gate peeking from between the cabins.

They trashed it. All tires, including the spare, flat with a long gashes. The vinyl top and sides ripped from front to back. If I could find gas, I could still drive it. That hope was dashed when I looked inside: the gear shift had been snapped off. Somebody tossed a dead racoon into the back, a biker's calling card.

The voice in my head said: *Keep walking, find the manager's cabin, thumb a ride, flag down a driver to call the cops for you—she'll be fine. Cats always land on their feet.*

Cursing myself for a fool, I turned around to go back. It all seemed like a bad dream ending; the chirping birds and insects were wiping the last twelve hours from my mind in the sanitizing force of sunlight.

Lost in a reverie, I almost stumbled into a nightmarish tableau: a white panel truck in the driveway of the cabin, a man smoking inside on his cell phone—the alpha trucker. Russell and the trucker I'd conked in the parking lot with a plaster bandage on his scalp were hustling Champagne out the door between them. Tiny between the two big men, her feet didn't touch the ground. Russell had a hand clamped over her mouth. Still, she fought, kicking and flailing her arms. By the time I was a dozen feet from them, running hard, on the far side of the road, I had a baseball-sized branch from a fallen limb beside the road in my hands.

When the van driver looked up to see me flying past the front of his van, he couldn't react in time. He hit the horn at the same time Champagne bit Russell's palm before he hustled her into the van's side door. He yelped and coldcocked her with a punch to the jaw that didn't travel twelve inches. She dropped to the ground. By then, I was on top of them with my branch coming down on Russell's head. The other trucker leapt backward and went to the ground. I slammed the club down on his kneecap, rendering him *hors de combat*.

The driver flung open the door—a bull-sized man. I pivoted from the two on the ground, stepped into him like a batter at home plate swinging for the upper decks. I put my hips into it and caught him on the underside of the jaw. His momentum propelled him forward, and he landed on top of me, although he was out cold.

That red mist people see in a sudden collision? I saw it. I had to roll his bulk off me. Acting with no input from my neocortex—it was all paleocortex, lizard-brain instinct and impulse—I stooped low and swept Champagne off the ground like a bundle of clothes somebody dropped from a basket on the grass. I threw her so hard into the van past the driver's seat that she smacked her head on the passenger side door and lay crumpled, half her body on the seat, the other half on the floor.

Hopping in, I punched the van's accelerator to the floorboard; we barreled up that hill to the main access road and swerved onto the grass going in the opposite direction from the dam. I was afraid to check the gas gauge until we were miles out of the park altogether—a tad under full.

Thank you, shithead, for filling it up…

I drove flat-out to the interstate junction and hit I-44 going north. No state troopers behind me, no Bandidos, Cossacks, or Mongols roaring up in the rearview mirrors.

She groaned, sat up in the seat holding her head in both hands. By the time we passed the Tulsa interchange, she was still groggy but coherent.

"Ow, fuck. That bastard musta bit me on the head, too. I got a lump the size of a possum egg back there."

"The opossum doesn't lay eggs."

"I know it, smartie. It's jist an Okie sayin'. Ow. Bet you didn't know a possum kin eat through a dead body's asshole. Core you like a friggin' apple."

"You're a living, breathing *Wikipedia*," I said, "You know all about possum habits, dope-dealing and sex-trafficking by outlaw bikers, truck-stop prostitution—"

"Whoah, just you hang on there, Jack! That's your Momma you're talkin' about, with that truck-stop whore bullshit!"

"You're welcome, by the way."

"Fuck you!"

"'How sharper than a serpent's tooth it is to have an ungrateful child.'"

"There you go, funny talkin' again with your pinhead bullshit. Got-damn it anyhow. My head hurts like a motherfucker."

"Maybe silence is the best response."

"How's about I put my foot up your ass—ya know, might could bring you down a peg. I knowed it was you that threw me into that door and banged up my head."

"If even half what you told me about your trail of tears, Champagne, as you so eloquently put it, is true, then I suspect you can spare a few more brain cells. You sound like a retired NFL linebacker who says that last tackle gave him CTE."

"CT—what? Oh, I ain't listenin' to any more of your garbage, Mister Dumas."

"*Dumas*—I get it. Despite your thick Okie accent too. Mister *Dumb-Ass*. Aren't you the clever one."

"You know that blowjob I promised you?"

"I do."

"Forget it."

I smiled—then I broke out into a laugh—a wonderful, cleansing belly laugh. Tears of joy streamed down my cheeks. I sobbed at the end, exhausted.

"You don't know what you're missing. I give real slurpy—"

Worse and worse. The laughter that welled up from deep in my guts this time had me swerving from one lane to the other until she tucked herself in the seat, afraid I was going to slam the van into a guardrail.

"I'm OK," I assured her. "I'll be *keer*ful."

"Fuckin' better be, Jack."

After an hour's driving, she said, "Where the holy

hell we goin'?"

"*We* aren't going anywhere," I replied. "You're going to drop me off at the Greyhound bus station in Fort Smith. I'm going home. You keep the van. I was waiting to surprise you. They put the bag in the back there. Good luck with it—and all the rest."

"And all the rest," she clucked, flying between the seats to get in back to check.

"Happy now?"

"Fuckin'-A, I'm happy. Better'n deep-fried bull testicles at the county fair."

"I'll take your word for it."

***

The long ride north to Toledo with squalling kids, foul smells, and constant chatter all around me was a descent into one of Dante's lower circles—but not the lowest. I'd stepped into it and come out to live to tell the tale.

It's been six months since I've been back. Julia and I are still working on it, and there are moments where I see her measuring my neck over something said, done wrong, or undone. But we're both getting there. I'm glad. The highways aren't me. There's a different America out there I had a glimpse of, and I'm grateful to be out of it.

Maybe someday I'll tell her about my road trip girl with the Oklahoma accent.

Kiss of Death

"Fifty-five dollars."

Gracie looked at me with that expression that made me want to crack him on the jaw. His eyes popped and that stupid, hound-dog expression appeared again for the fifth time that night. It wasn't the first time I regretted taking on a loser of a partner. That last misjudgment cost me five years in Dannemora when the getaway driver fingered me and Mac Kennedy for a jewelry store heist in Rochester that netted a lot of costume jewelry and garbage we couldn't fence or sell. Mac gave some to his girlfriend, a meth head, who traded us in for a get-out-of-jail card.

"Huh, what'd you say, boss?"

I repeated it, walking away before I did clout him a good one across his stupid face:

"You told me they had thousands on them when they came back from the casino."

I grabbed a beer from the fridge. "'Thousands stashed in the house,' blah-blah, bullshit. Just lying around in wadded bundles, you said. Remember that, Gracie? Just bend over and pick them up. I should have known you meant bend over and take it in the ass."

"I said they *probably* had money stashed somewhere in the house. I'm tellin' you, man. I seen this same couple walk away from the teller's window with more cash than they could carry!"

The hound-dog look came back with an added, curled lip that made me really want to bang his head against the coffee table and walk the fuck out of this mess. I was sick of him, sick of everything going wrong for too long. It was like somebody somewhere had a voodoo doll of me and was jabbing pins into it non-stop. After Dannemora, everything turned to shit. The only people I could connect with were amateur jerks like Bill Gracie. I was at the age when all the good guys I used to run with had long numbers attached to their file photos in some warden's office.

He mumbled it again, walking away from me. The way he emphasized *probably* like a lawyer made a red curtain drop down over my eyes. My hands twitched. That was the moment—the exact moment—I knew I should start walking out of that house while the beef was still a home invasion with intent to rob. Gracie was a boat anchor to that notion. If I left then, dragging him out of there by the scruff of his neck, I knew he'd be tracked right back to the casino. The couple knew him, must have seen him around the place. He'd squawk two minutes into his interrogation and the police artist wouldn't need to draw my face. Gracie would point me out on the casino's CCTV tapes like a kid asked to watch his favorite cartoon.

The couple on the kitchen floor with their hands and ankles cuffed heard everything we said. They strained their heads to look despite the gags and zip ties. They reminded me of a pair of turtles I had as a kid. Gracie refused to look at them; stepped around them as though they were a pair of Fabergé eggs.

That was the other thing that told me my partner was as useless as tits on a dump truck. "Go in fast," I repeated. "Once that door is cracked open, it's blitz time. They'll mistrust strangers at the door. Who the fuck doesn't nowadays? But they'll buy the story about the neighbor's car for sale. Go in fast, like I said. Take them both down to the floor."

Instead he froze on the doorstep like somebody drove ten-penny nails through his shoes. The old guy fought, swung at me on the way down, while his wife stood there with her mouth opening and closing. Gracie pissing his pants on the front stoop, me trying to get hubby's hands cuffed while he's scratching face trying to claw my eyes out. Then the little prick has the gall to tell me he pulled a charley horse trying to get past me to the old lady.

All for nothing. Worse, it cost me half my stash to get to their house. Two days on the road, money for gas, and food—lousy food, too. Truck drivers and their keen sense for the best highway restaurants. I learned years ago that was bullshit. Most of them don't reach sixty and have hearts the size of canned hams from eating all that greasy slop on the road. I had stomach bloating and cramps from the food where we pulled off to eat.

"Fuck eating," Gracie said when I took the exit ramp to get food. "Let's keep going, man! We're right here!"

"Armies travel on their bellies," I told him, repeating an old con's lesson to me.

"That con of yours, he's so smart. How come he got caught."

I answered with a look and said, "Myron got jugged because he worked with an amateur who ratted him out."

No reaction, just a smirk. By then, I knew I could pile comments like that around Gracie's ankles up to his neck all day long and he wouldn't get it.

The one thing Gracie was right about was how easy it was to get inside their house. The 4-Sale sign on their camper in the driveway was all it took. As soon as I spotted it coming down the road, I told him to forget the neighbor's car. This was our way inside. *"Hello there, sir. I was passing by and saw your sale sign in the back window of that camper…"*

He cut his eyes from me and my happy-assed smile to Gracie, who looked every bit the nervous creep you do not ever open your door to. Then it was bumrush time: Shit, meet fan.

So there we were. Stuck in Mr. and Mrs. Normal's house, watching them slobber through their gags, hoping for mercy, while knucklehead and I ransacked their entire house top to bottom looking for cash that wasn't there. Bet they weren't thinking about selling the camper now. They were thinking how everything in life they thought was so urgent or important could mean jack-shit now.

I was sick of watching their heads wag together, straining at the cuffs, no longer in shock. Just intensely interested in the moment-by-moment words and gestures of two violent strangers who destroyed their peace of mind for good. Another festering black mark against my newest partner in crime, that. Gracie holding the gun on them while I zip-tied them side-by-side. Gracie staring the whole time, holding the gun so the barrel was pointing right at me half the time, the moron.

I wasn't looking to score that much. Just a stake for a job in San Diego my former cellie called me about. The Mountaineer Casino's slots and horses had cleaned me out. That made me vulnerable to Gracie's pitch. After dropping my $500 at the blackjack table, a pimply-faced guy with slick hair and a Hello-My-Name-Is-Billy plastic tag on his vest followed me out the door. In five minutes, I had everything from him about the "rich" couple and their secret stash.

"You in?"

He was homelier when he tried to smile.

"Give me a cigarette," I said.

He looked surprised by the request, expecting me to jump in with both feet, no questions asked. "Sure."

He walked me to my car with me. I gestured toward the closed-circuit camera lens above the entrance doors with my cigarette. The lightbulb went off.

"Oh, yeah, right! So where do we meet up to discuss my project?"

Project. Jesus on a pogo stick.

I named a place away from lights, people, and cameras.

He met me after his shift. I had everything from him in five minutes—all but the important facts. Namely, that his couple were shit-lucky just that one time he spotted them leaving. They had no stash, no safe in the bedroom closet. When I took the gags off after they'd calmed down, they both told me the same thing; the fifty-thousand was spent on a new bathroom and a sectional couch. The rest went into a trust fund for their only grandkid.

Gracie, working his shift on the night they scored, let his imagination run away with him when he picked up scuttlebutt how much the couple made at the blackjack tables and slots. He was a car thief by trade, and a lousy one, apparently.

But I stopped to listen. My error. You know those crime shows where a husband or a wife desperate to be rid of a spouse goes around town asking everybody and his dog if he knows someone who'll kill the spouse for a few bucks? That was young Bill Gracie to a tee. He convinced himself they had a safe in their bedroom. He didn't even know that casinos report big earnings at the payout window. Uncle Sam, the biggest thief of all, gets his cut first.

"The money's here somewhere, I know it," he said for the twentieth time, although we'd both stopped searching a half-hour ago. I was only waiting to make up my mind.

"You check the cookie jar?"

"Ha-ha, funny."

"The money went into their bank account the day after they got back," I said to him. "It's gone."

"I don't believe them," he snarled.

He wasn't leaving without the money. His kind of stubbornness got guys caught or killed.

"Are you blind, kid? If they had it, they'd give it up by now."

"Let me try."

"Go for it."

I haven't been back to prison in ten years because I got better at it since I started doing crime in my juvie days in gladiator school. Trouble was, I'd read young Gracie right in a first impression. I just didn't act on it. Prison hospital wards are packed with old men who got sloppy.

He leaned over to scream in the man's ear; then the clown kicked the husband in the temple.

Where is it! Where is it at, you motherfucker! I swear to God I'll kill you!

Stupid TV shit. The TV I'd turned on in case any neighbors were out walking their dogs, I wanted them to see the television set glowing inside. For the first time, I paid attention. An old black-and-white gangster film was playing. I'd seen it in the rec room at Dannemora. I recognized Richard Widmark's goofy leer as Tommy Udo in *Kiss of Death*.

"Gimme the gun!" Gracie spluttered. He ran up to me, demanding I hand it to him.

"I'll make the motherfucker talk!"

"No."

He had tunnel vision, the kind an adrenalin jolt gives you. No matter how weak your partner is, if he thinks you're slipping, he'll look for a chance to put the shiv in. More guys get jumped in the chow line than the yard when they get careless about the pack. What's that saying: "If you run with wolves, don't trip"?

His eyes cut to my gun hand. He thought about snatching the Glock. Instead, I handed it to him. He looked like a kid with a new Christmas toy.

He whipped around to go back to the couple on the

floor. I dropped him before he went five feet with a kick to the back of his left knee. I stepped around fast and my arm came up. I squeezed off a round from the .22 Beretta Jetfire I carried in the back of my belt. Gracie's head snapped back. He dropped straight down to the floor like a puppet with its strings cut.

Arms and legs splayed, the look on his face didn't register shock or surprise or the anger I'd seen a moment ago. Just nothing at all. An older con who'd bounced around the prison system took pity on me when I first got to Riker's. He told me the Greeks had a myth about three sisters who snipped those strings holding you upright. Bill Gracie, a lifeless puppet on the floor.

The husband made gurgling sounds in his throat from the kick Gracie delivered. His eyes wobbled between his half-closed eyelids. The wife lasered me with her stare now. She squeezed them shut when she realized what was about to happen. I did her first so she wouldn't have to wait those seconds, watching me execute her husband. The bullet punched through skull bone, bounced around in the brain, churned it to mush. The Glock would alert the insomniacs in the neighborhood and the slug might have plowed through her head before burying itself in the floor.

Hubby was semi-conscious when I shot him through the top of his head. His carotid said he was already gone. Widmark's cackling laughter in the background made me jump up and turn around.

I've always kept a light, pocket gun handy since my twenties. None of that .44 magnum, Clint Eastwood nonsense. Or young, dumb gangbangers with their niners blasting away. If you need a gun, and a 4-shot Derringer or .22 won't do the trick, you're not in a scrape, you're in a shitstorm.

This fuck-up of a job made me angry and tired at the

same time. San Diego was a thousand miles away. I'd make a thermos of coffee, pack a couple sandwiches, and hit the road after a catnap on the couple's nice new couch. It looked cozy. This was a nice house, warm colors. I wanted a smoke, but these people didn't and I wasn't going to add to the catastrophe by leaving more DNA around with the dead bodies.

The Glock came from a pawn shop in North Dakota. It couldn't be traced back to me. I dragged Gracie over to the couple. I rubbed my hands on Gracie's. Enough gunshot residue particles would be picked up in the test they'd do when they printed him in the morgue. The shot in his head was too far back to make them think suicide. I couldn't do anything about the skin cells or hairs I'd left behind in the rooms I'd searched. Maybe the cops in this small town weren't good at homicide. Chances were they'd trace him to his casino and watch videotape. I didn't believe him when he said he was never arrested for boosting cars. They'd see me cadge a cigarette on the steps, chat with him for a couple minutes, then go our separate ways. No one could put us together. Even if a nosy neighbor saw the two of us going up to the door, I made sure Gracie blocked me from a good view from the nearby houses.

The blood from their wounds had spread wider, seeping into the cracks in the grout. When it turned a rust-brown at the edges of the pool, I'd leave for California. If it turns black, and I'm still here napping on this nice couch, I waited too long and I'm not going anywhere. I'm probably sitting on that couch with the gun in my lap waiting to decide if I get up to leave before the blood turns black. They say poets and philosophers are the ones who contemplate life's meaninglessness. Maybe they should consider giving aging criminals an invite to the club. Either way, I'm nearing the end of my string. The kiss of death will be waiting for me out in that golden state, that cesspool of greed and beautiful people. Maybe it's right there on the couch. By dawn's early light, as the song goes, I'll know for sure.

Fish Out of Water

Eugene Frady joked to his buddies at the bar that he didn't drink water unless it came with a whiskey chaser, which wasn't always a joke, and which also helped explain a lifelong pattern of restlessness and traveling from state to state. Born in Mobile, Alabama, where his mother bartended near the Navy shipyards, he never knew his sperm-donor father stationed there, which was just long enough to impregnate Eugene's mother before shipping out to the Philippines.

Eugene dropped out of high school his sophomore year, bragging he never read a single book in his entire time, which was also true. By then, he'd racked up a dozen suspensions for insubordination, unexcused absences, and fighting that it was a matter of time before one of two things happened, the first being expulsion; the second and more likely was incarceration in the juvie facility on Costarides Street. Eugene was big for his age. A solid 210 pounds by the end of his freshman year, the school hoped football might discipline him; that hope evaporated like smoke when he told his JV coach "to kiss his ass" after one practice and walked off the field. His size and notoriety prompted bigger varsity players to confront him in the halls. Most ended in verbal altercations, after-school detentions, and a few memorable fights. Eugene won most until the team's star linebacker, a recruiting prospect of the Crimson Tide, showed up with the kid Eugene was supposed to fight. Bigger than Eugene by twenty pounds and agile as a cat, he broke three ribs and cracked Eugene's jaw.

Eugene's mother in those days was rarely home, often shacked up with her new man or, when she was home, too drunk, stoned, or hung over to care what her only son was up to. Eugene himself couldn't write the letter, owing to his limited reading skill and impoverished vocabulary, although he could easily forge her loopy signature in a letter attesting to her "approval to allow my son to quit school."

Getting a classmate who lived nearby to write it was no problem; Eugene merely stood in his yard leaning against an oak until he did it. Keeping his mother sober, and arranging a meeting with the principal were bigger problems. The principal and the superintendent were both happy to abet the swindle, however, as neither wanted more of Eugene Frady, and so a phony "suitable work program" was agreed to by all. Once everyone's ass was covered with a document, Eugene threw some clothes into a duffel bag stolen from Dick's Sporting Goods and made his way into the world three months before his sixteenth birthday.

He hated water, didn't like fishing, and never learned to swim. But water seemed to be in his destiny. By eighteen, he was operating rig floor mud buckets offshore near New Iberia, Louisiana. From there, he went on to work as a deckhand for barges on the Mississippi—until his phony Ordinary Seaman's license was revoked and he skipped town. By the time he was thirty, he was living in Milwaukee. A sailor in a bar sold his Able Seaman's license. He taught him half-hitch and bowline knots. In time, with the help of his doctored license, he found berths on self-unloading freighters as a conveyorman, the dirtiest job on the Great Lakes, spending hours in the bowels of bulk carriers, emerging from the cargo holds at the ends of shift where coal, crushed stone, and taconite pellets are stored. It took repeated showering to remove grit and coal dust from his pores. After a quick shower, he'd hit the bars in port, receive fishy looks from the regulars, amused by the gray patina of his skin and his dusky eye shadow from coal dust. If anyone made a comment on his "creepy mascara," it either resulted in a quick apology from the offender or a fight behind the bar. Eugene's full size topped six feet and he weighed 250 or 260 pounds, depending on how much beer he'd consumed that week.

In a cement-block bar in Northtown, another grubby, rust-belt port-of-call at the end of the sailing season, a tall man with long, stringy black hair, almost blue-black, made a comment about Eugene's appearance from his end of the bar. Not twenty minutes before, Eugene had hauled ass down the gangway ladder as soon as the last of the iron ore was shoveled onto the belt; he hit the first bar he came to before closing. The man who called him "a drag queen" happened to be a member of the Sioux tribe in town visiting a cousin. He also happened to be a professional MMA fighter.

The fight didn't last long. Eugene left his unfinished beer on the bar and limped back to his ore boat. In the morning, his limbs ached with fierce, stabbing pains, and he had trouble getting out of his bunk. Bruises, one eyebrow puffed and split with a zigzag gash. The back pain during his first watch forced him to throw down the shovel and climb up the cargo hold ladder, no easy feat when the rungs were caked with dust or gravel and he was lightheaded from pain; it was a long way down to the steel-plated, foot-thick deck, and he knew he wouldn't bounce. A dockside taxi took him to the emergency room of Northtown's hospital. The first mate told him they were casting off bow lines just after dawn.

The MRI diagnosis was "severe stenosis of the fifth and sixth vertebrae." Eugene recalled the leg sweep that took him down hard and the arm brace on his neck seconds later. "Like fightin' an octopus," he bragged later in bars. Steroid-heavy prescriptions for Tramadol, Tizanidine, Meloxicam, and Gabapentin added to his irritability. He remembered the triple-horn blast of his vessel, the *Col. James Pickands*, leaving port under the tug boat's escort and wondered what came next.

His sailing days over, Eugene's stash dwindled fast over his idle time in Northtown despite the high salary seamen made. But his gambling, drinking, and lap dances in bars up and down the Great Lakes from Duluth to Buffalo and he was lucky to cover his rent deposit on the apartment on Bridge Street in the harbor district.

Eugene hadn't improved intellectually since his liberation from school. By dint of enforced confinement, sailors, like prison inmates, read voraciously. Eugene maintained his record of never having read a book. Standing in a cold, damp wind in a strange town, he knew one thing only: he was done with boats, done with water.

A week of picking up scuttlebutt in bars led him to the Eagle's Nest, Freddy Persico's bar.

"Persico" meant "perch" in Italian. In his fifties, bald and fat, he talked a blue streak, a trait Eugene despised in men and women alike. He tolerated it in women because he wanted something from them, and by allowing them to bleat their sob stories about treacherous ex-husbands or boyfriends, he knew it would pay dividends later when they'd drunk too much and wanted sex as much as he did. With men, however, he had no patience. They reminded him of those teachers in his youth who never shut their "friggin' pie holes," never saying anything interesting.

Exhausting his stock of small talk, Eugene waited for the man to get around to it, and he finally did, after much lamentation over how casinos, racinos (which Eugene never heard of), and the whole *puttana* state with its new legalizing gambling had all but destroyed his "business."

"*Madrone*," he wailed, "you got grandmas buying lotto tickets in grocery stores, factory guys going online to bet their paychecks, couples going to the Hard Rock and Jack in Cleveland dropping thousands. Me, I get the short stick—a couple college kids and retirees putting a few bucks on the Guardians or the Brownies. Don't get me started on the horse races in West Virginia or Pittsburgh, a few hours' drive down the interstate."

Eugene thought "the Guardians" was some kind of Indian casino like the one in the U.P. of Michigan or resort towns—boxy, cube-shaped structures with colorful rugs and murals on the walls inscribed with symbols to beguile gamblers and tourists, as though they were in a sacred museum instead of a temple to Mammon. He envisioned "Brownies" to be a racial slur at first; he thought of a battle royal pitting African-Americans against one another, like those old-fashioned smokers he heard of back home. Persico generally referred to black people as *moolies*, a term he'd never heard. When he realized what it meant, he thought of that long-ago, red-faced coach screaming at him through the veins in his neck.

"So what do ya'll want me to do?"

"Just let them know I want my money soon," Persico replied.

Eugene didn't trust a man who couldn't talk in one voice. Persico's voice went up and down the register like a Hollywood actor. The man was worse than his old teachers who, if he had to give them credit for something, managed not to stray from one topic to another like this clown.

"How big are you, Gene?"

"Eugene, Mister Persico, I'm big enough for this kind of work."

"They see you standing there, big as a house, they're gonna get that money out of the sock drawer or wherever they're hiding it from Uncle Sam or the old lady, and hand it to you on a platter, saying, 'Pretty please, won't you bring it to Mister Persico for me?'"

Shee-yit, collecting money from deadbeats for this lardass. What am I doing?

"How much?"

"How much what, Gene?"

"How much do I get, Mister Persico?"

"Ah, I see. Your cut. How's ten percent suit you?"

"Twenty-five."

"Fuck that, Gene. Ten. Take it or leave it."

They bargained down to fifteen. With nothing else on the horizon, Eugene agreed, shook the short, squat man's hand. Like Persico's forehead always with a sheen of perspiration, his palm was clammy like touching a fish's belly.

He wasn't surprised Persico's book comprised more than a few college kids and retirees. Northtown's citizenry had a gambling addiction that didn't get sated by the many forms of legalized gambling Persico said Ohio offered its people. Despite the slew of TV commercials featuring celebrities and athletes warning of excessive gambling, to play responsibly, which had all the impact of the "drink responsibly" tag on every six-pack of beer, many regulars in the Eagle's Nest were deep into some kind of addiction. Some wept as they coughed up the money owed, and he had to ignore the pleas and the sight of dirty dishes and filthy children in homes that couldn't afford to gamble. Persico told Eugene the town was full of depressed people recovering from the lockdowns and social isolation of the pandemic.

"Gene, they need more than scratch-off lottery tickets around here. I'm a public service."

Eugene doubted that, but he knew a goldmine when he was standing inside one.

Persico was right about another thing: people paid *pronto* when he showed up at the door. Some men grumbled, a few got lippy, especially the older women. Some of them tried to bribe him with sex. He told them: "Why buy the cow when the milk is free?"

He didn't let the misery or the wrath provoke him. He weathered the stony looks and harsh comments of their wives while the hubbies left for the hidden cash or the checkbook to make good on their debts without a word. Eugene never answered anyone's questions with more than a word or two, sometimes a grunt. He never threatened. One woman begged him to leave her husband alone, stop taking their household money.

"We've already lost one house because of his gambling," she openly cried.

"Ain't my problem, lady," he replied.

Some tried to act nonchalant about it, as though they were just on their way to see Persico when Eugene happened to roll up their driveways. When a college-aged youth shoved a wad of bills at his chest, told him to "go fuck himself," Eugene barely moved a muscle. He covered the boy's hand with his own big paw with the knuckles whitened to diamond points from years of brawling and bent back the punk's index finger to the breaking point. The boy's eyes watered, and he pleaded for release.

"Be nice, ya'll hear?"

Eugene released the finger, picked up the bills from the floor and walked out.

One gambler Eugene saw much of at his residence or factory parking lot where plastic parts were made from molds weighed about one-seventy, and was saved for last. Eugene didn't like him, and wasn't even sure of his name: McGinty or McDuffy, he couldn't tell because of Persico's shitty handwriting. When he collected at the man's house, he was left standing in the foyer for longer than it took to run up the stairs and fetch the money. Eugene let him play his game and when the big-screen TV in the next room was on, watched parts of programs until the man returned to pay up.

That week was different. Eugene's street instincts told him something was up this time. When the man came downstairs and approached him, Eugene knew his walk was different. Eugene stuck his hand out to take the money he expected to be handed. Instead, the guy's arm whipped up and he pointed a small silver gun at Eugene's head, told him to "fuck off" and "tell his dago boss" he'd get paid next week when he got his own paycheck.

"Don't show up again, white trash, or I'll blow your fucking head off."

Eugene recognized the gun, a 4-shot Derringer, because he'd lost a job on an oil rig when one was discovered in his locker. Eugene still hated the man who ratted him out to the boss because the prick owed him $500 from a Texas Hold 'em two nights before. Eugene shuffled backwards, held up his hands in mock fear, and said he'd "relay the message and was sorry about that, he was just the delivery boy," all of which was the most he'd said at one time in weeks.

McGinty or McDuffy seemed satisfied. Big mistake. Instead of retreating, Eugene stepped between the man's legs and threw a short punch that traveled less than a foot before connecting with the man's jaw. He flew backwards into the banister and went down in a heap, unconscious. Eugene took a watch on the kitchen counter, a cold beer from the fridge. On his way past the man's slumped body, he kicked him in the ribs.

Eugene drank in the Eagle's Nest for free, although Persico grumbled what it cost him.

"Think you can get it down to a gallon a day, Eugene? I'm going broke keeping you in booze."

"Sure thing, Mister Persico."

"Don't talk back to me, Calhoun."

"I ain't talkin' back, boss."

Persico nicknamed him that for his accent. He knew men grew uncomfortable when he sat next to them on the stools; couples in booths whispered when they saw him enter. Some women liked the aura of violence he gave off. They openly flirted with him despite their squirming boyfriends or husbands. *That's Persico's debt collector,* they said. *Better watch out!* He overheard Persico use his nickname in heated phone conversations with men who got behind. Once, he snarled into his cell phone: "I'll send my big dumb hillbilly out there!"

His reputation paid off in the sack. He preferred married women—fewer complications, less bullshit after the rockets went off. At the time, he was switching off two women, both married, one in her forties. He compared them to each other and tried to goad them into outdoing whatever he said the other had done. Marylee, the older woman, was obsessed with her looks, her "sagging boobs," as she said, although Eugene loved their size and heft.

It fell apart one night when both women were in the bar with their husbands. Marylee's rival, Mary Sue, stumbled back to her booth from the ladies' room; she'd been drinking Russian Mules. Marylee complained Mary Sue couldn't hold her liquor. One thing led to another, and by the end of the night, the two women were fighting in the parking lot, pulling hair, scratching with nails, and screaming accusations at each other. Eugene was bit on the hand trying to separate them and found himself in the middle of a brawl with two drunken husbands.

The following day Eugene showed up at the bar for his list of names and addresses. Persico told him he was fired.

"Them people, they all hate your guts. Marylee and her husband are splitting up. I know Bill and her for ten years."

"So what?"

"So you can't keep it in your pants is so what, asshole. I told you not to mess with the customers."

"By my reckoning, I made you a ton of money."

"Get out of my bar, or—"

He stopped in mid-sentence when Eugene raised up from his stool and stared into Persico's face. The bar counter was all that separated the men.

"You'll call the cops?"

Eugene knew the cops turned a blind eye; some of them gambled, too.

Persico must have realized what he had in front of him. He softened his tone and told Eugene he was adding a couple fifties to Eugene's "severance pay," although Eugene was always paid off the books.

"Make me a boilermaker before I go, boss."

"Fuck you."

Eugene vaulted the bar and chest-bumped Persico backwards into the shelves of liquor bottles. Eugene stepped around him, reached for the Johnny Walker Black Persico kept for show and poured a tumbler full. He drank it while Persico watched, unmoving. Eugene finished the drink, threw the bottle at the glass bubble of the jukebox, shattering it, and handed Persico the empty tumbler.

"Thanks for the drink."

"Don't let the door hit you in the ass, motherfu—"

Eugene on his way to the door stopped, turned around, stared at him.

Persico hadn't moved from his position behind the bar. His face was red and the sheen of sweat on his brow glistened. Eugene walked out to the parking lot. He regretted it didn't happen last week when Persico's five biggest gamblers took a pounding on the NCAA basketball tournament games. Tiny Butler U. in Indianapolis upset powerhouse North Carolina and covered the spread. The vigorish Persico charged on his regulars was enough to make a Brooklyn *mafioso* weep.

Eugene had two targets to hit before he blew the dust of this shithole town off his boots. One was an 85-year-old, retired ophthalmologist who lived in Jefferson ten miles away; the other was a Taco Bell franchise owner off Main Street. Both had mean gambling addictions and went big on their bets every week.

Taco Man was closer. He lived in his office, hiring and firing teenagers all day long when he wasn't training new hires. He offered Eugene a free taco or chalupa every time he came to collect.

He ignored the hostile looks of the counter servers and Taco Man's manager.

"Hey, Eugene, what up."

"Collecting," Eugene said.

Taco Man smiled. "I don't owe Persico shit. He owes me, man! You miss the fuckin' score? Wake Forest one-oh-one, Michigan ninety-six."

Eugene figured he had better than fifty-fifty odds, knowing Taco Man's habit of backing a losing streak with heavier bets. If his bluff worked, he's let him sort it out with Persico after he left town.

Eugene didn't expect resistance from this friendly, slender black man with the geometric hair style and pencil moustache. Taco Man lived in a gated community, supported a daughter at Howard University. The gun he was holding and pointing at Eugene's heart was a real surprise.

"Get your cracker ass the fuck out of my store, or I'll put a hole in your chest you can reach into and pull your wallet out of your back pocket."

Eugene knew when to call a bluff. He walked out without saying a word.

His gut told him what he'd find before he saw it with his eyes: the broken window, the missing duffel bag containing his $15,000 fuck-you money, all banded in wads of denominations.

He sat in silence for a long minute until the nausea passed. *Can't win for losing… can't win for losing…* His mother's expression rolled through his mind like a mantra.

"Get a grip, Eugene," he told himself.

He knew Taco Man was on the phone to Persico while he brooded in the parking lot. His scheme's upside was based on the fact an illegal bookie couldn't call the cops. Now he was the one ripped off who couldn't report it. Eugene had an intuitive sense of irony. But the cramp in his stomach. *Lost, done, fucked…*

The drive to Jefferson would take a half-hour if he stayed at the speed limit. Long enough for Persico to call everyone on the list to warn them of Eugene's scam. Seconds counted. *Run for it or go for it…* If a statie nailed him for speeding, he'd smile, sign the ticket, and wipe his ass with it as soon as the trooper's back was turned. He had to beat Persico's call to the old man.

Roaring down the gravel road turnoff, Eugene's car slewed from side to side, stones rattling under the chassis. He skidded across the doctor's lawn narrowly missing a raised circular flowerbed of red mulch, chewing up turf like a miniature seismic crumpling of land masses shoved together by tectonic plates.

He hammered on the door. Out here in the quiet country, it reverberated in the chilly air of a frigid Northern spring.

The doctor's wife opened the door, a woman with coiffed silver hair and brittle eyes, stared at him briefly, scowled, and shut the door in his face. That was routine: the old bitch opened the door, told husband "your bag man is here" and Doc appeared, flashed a razor-slit smile and forked over the cash in a manila envelope.

He looked at the big red maple in the yard. Some kind of bird with a treble-note song was calling from high up in the branches. He thought about the mockingbird outside his window when he was nine years old, lying in pain from a broken wrist, afraid to tell his mother. He jumped from a tree limb and missed the branch, smashing his wrist against a limb below—

The man himself standing there, interrupting his childhood reverie.

Older than water, a face crisscrossed by a thousand wrinkles, his wispy hair in tufts at the back of his head. He smiled, revealing stained yellow teeth. *Enough to gag a maggot.*

The doctor invited him in. He hoped it wasn't a sob story coming up. If so, he'd grab him by his scrawny, wrinkled neck and choke him like a chicken until he paid.

Fuckin'-A, Eugene thought; *the geezer's hiding the envelope behind his back. He don't want the old gal to see…*

Only it wasn't the envelope stuffed with cash; it was a flash of steel arcing toward Eugene's head, missing him by inches. Eugene stepped backward in plenty of time to let the head of the club swing harmlessly past. The old man's feet weren't planted to support the lunge, and he toppled past Eugene like a wind-bent, rotten tree. The doctor stayed down on the floor, moaning.

Eugene picked up the golf club. He'd never held one in his hands before. It had an open-faced, canted metal head. He didn't know what the writing on it meant, the letters and numbers. Eugene couldn't distinguish a putter from a sand wedge, but he knew from the engineered heft of its steel alloy that it would have hurt badly if the old man connected. Eugene wasn't angry; he was sad. He leaned the club against the wall, meat end up.

Eugene would think on the drive back to Northtown why he did it. He admired the moxie it took for a decrepit codger like Doc with his puny, matchstick arms to swing at him.

He almost left. His hand was touching the doorknob when that gnawing in his belly stopped him, made him turn around to see the doctor on all fours struggling to get to his feet. Wobbly, arms and legs akimbo, like a giant insect in a bathrobe.

He picked up the club, as though thinking but not actually, then—mindful of the distance between the walls—swung it at an angle downward in an oblique arc at the old man's head. The effect was instant, tragicomical in the *whoof* of air exploding from the doctor's lungs simultaneously with the crackling sound of gas being passed from his nether end.

After that, he made no sound on the floor; his right hand twitched once, ceased moving. Eugene didn't want him to suffer if he were still alive, so he measured the distance and gave him a second blow on the crown of his head with maximum force.

A high-pitched keening sound erupted from nearby. Eugene thought an alarm clock somewhere had gone off until he spied the doctor's wife lurching drunkenly around the corner. She'd seen it happen.

"I seen you fixin' to spit nails ever' fuckin' time I come over heah," Eugene said. "I reckon you won't mind my muddy boot prints on your carpet, ma'am."

She kept backing away from him, her hands fluttered in front of her like a pair of giant white cabbage moths dancing in the air. She made another, single-note keening sound.

Eugene covered the distance between them in two rapid steps. He delivered a two-handed, behind-the-head blow that left a portion of the club head stuck. Amazingly, she didn't fall right away. Her eyes rolled back and she went straight down to the floor, as though the brain required that extra millisecond to convey its dismal, fatal message to the rest of her body.

Like hittin' a couple rotten cantaloupes, he thought on his way to the car.

***

Battleship-gray waves came in regular phalanxes like a disciplined army on the march, smashing into the massive granite boulders of Northtown harbor's mile-long breakwall. Sailing gave Eugene a knowledge of winds no book could give. He knew in his bones how the sweeping winds from fast-moving, low-pressure system, an Alberta Clipper, could do to the Midwest in winter and make the world look like one frozen tundra. Add Lake Erie's snow machine to that and you had whiteout conditions even in late spring.

Eugene wore Levi's and a windbreaker over a black tee-shirt, not much protection from the biting northwest wind. He shivered and resisted the urge to stomp his feet. *No point in warming up.* The water breaking over the rocks in front of him was warmer than the air.

He had a vague understanding of hypothermia because a man he'd sailed with lost his father who went duck hunting when a snow squall kicked up, a rarity in Tennessee, and he died trying to find his way back to his truck.

Hands and feet go first. Muscle spasms, teeth chatter, shivering—all the usual shit to be expected. Then all your blood rushed to the trunk and you felt warm. Then sleepy. *What the fuck was it he said? Naked when they found him… Thought he was burning up and tore off all his clothes.*

Eugene sat down on the big slab of rock chiseled smooth by a century of wind and ice, the boots of fishermen.

Spray soaked him to his crotch. *That should help*, he thought. He didn't know how long he had. He tried thinking about God—but nothing happened. Waves of shivers overtook him and he bit off the tip of his tongue from his chattering teeth. The blood was warm in his mouth and tasted coppery.

Gawd fuckin' god-damn shitpissfuck and motherfuck.

He hoped he didn't shit his pants when they found him.

He was having trouble focusing on the waves coming at him in relentless columns as far as the horizon where far-off whitecaps dotted the intersection of lake and sky like a child's attempt at drawing a straight line. Massive pewter clouds with ragged bellies hung overhead. A sleety rain began falling, soon the pelting sting of icy rain turned into thick globs of half-frozen drops like frozen spit.

Time warped, passed, slowed to a molasses crawl. His brain recorded dots of flashing white light.

Eugene Frady from Alabama spoke his final three words sitting upright on that cold rock: "Fuckin' water anyhow."

A Perfect Stranger

The guy at the end of the bar looked like a lush and kept staring his way. Johnny Lomack was in no mood for chitchat with a stranger in a strange bar in a strange city. He despised what little he'd seen of this burgh since he arrived just before dawn: streets of grimy box houses, men walking around like glass-eyed zombies, some pushing shopping carts full of aluminum siding and pop cans, chemical plants belching smoke.

He hoped the guy wasn't eyeballing him to hit on him. He just wanted to knock back a few and exit this rustbelt town. Johnny was pissed off. He felt like suing the city for false advertising. He'd left everything behind in Joplin to drive through the night to get in line for what he thought was going to be a sure-fire job, one he'd read about in the *St. Louis Gazette*. A new iron-ore smelting plant was being built here. "Hundreds of high-paying jobs," the paper said.

Instead of a line of people looking to put in applications, he found a pot-bellied security guard in the gatehouse at the docks who told him plant construction was put on hold.

"What do you mean put on hold?"

"Something about the EPA. Nobody's hiring."

"You're shitting me."

"I ain't shitting you, Jack. You got fucked, buddy," the tubby guard said, "by whoever told you that."

Fucked and double-fucked, Johnny thought.

He'd cashed out every dollar he had left in his credit union and his bank account—that is, what Sharon didn't already empty out first. *Some conversation*, Johnny thought:

"You tell me you want a divorce, OK, I get it, things have been shitty, but you cleaned out our savings and checking first thing I noticed."

"My lawyer told me to do that…"

The conversation nosedived south after that. Johnny wasn't shocked by the divorce. He saw it coming like a haymaker in a barroom brawl. But he'd sold his hunting rifles and camping equipment, the quad bike, the Wrangler he'd just accessorized with high-lift jack points and fourteen-hundred dollar off-road bumpers, his street bike—good riddance to that piece-of-shit for tearing up his meniscus. He'd have a hitch in his step for the rest of his life, not to mention arthritis that already throbbed in damp weather. The worst of it was trying to increase his stash with an online bet on a Cardinals doubleheader. The Phillies swept the Cards.

The guy gave him another look, smiled, and raised his beer glass in Johnny's direction. Johnny wondered if he'd found the only gay bar in town—except that no self-respecting gay male he knew would come within ten yards of this dump with its stupid nautical name on the front. Inside was worse: a yellowing, cracked mirror with a sports posters taped to it, a few ugly chairs and tables and booths along the brick wall.

The big bartender who eyefucked him when he walked in looked like one of the Aiken brothers back home—slathered with tattoos, bragging about their Aryan Brotherhood connections, and always on somebody's shit list or on the run from a warrant. This guy was bald like Kenny Aiken and had loop earrings like brother Jerry as well as blue neck glyphs. Johnny couldn't tell whether they were Polynesian or Chinese from the distorted reflection in the mirror.

Fuck me, he'll be getting up to take the stool next to me in a minute. Sure as shit, here he comes—

Johnny intended to wave the barfly off when he got within earshot; he'd shoot him a look that would warn anybody not plastered to fuck off. But just as Johnny opened his mouth, the guy opened his hand to reveal a playing card. With nimble fingers like a blackjack dealer, the card sailed from the man's palm onto the bar top and skidded into Johnny's draft beer.

"What do you think you're doing, buddy?"

"Turn it over."

Johnny did, taking his glare off the stranger only long enough to flip the card over.

Not a playing card. A woman in her twenties posing, imitating a *Playboy* glam shot in a lace teddy. Her pouty duck lips resembled those selfie poses every teenager on *Instagram* imitated.

"So you've got a porno deck of cards. Big deal," Johnny said.

He'd had enough of this bullshit act. The man held up his hands in front of his chest in mock surrender, saying, "Easy, partner. I'm only asking if you've seen her."

"Seen a half-naked girl in this shithole? Are you out of your fucking mind?"

The beefy bartender at the other end raised his head and looked at them.

"Take it easy, hey. I'm just—she was supposed to meet me in here, see? I've been waiting for her ever since Nicky opened."

Nicky being the surly beefcake at the other end of the bar. The girl on the laminated card looked too classy and too young for the man standing there.

"How the hell could I see her before you did? You were here when I walked in."

Johnny's blood was up. This clown was drawing to

himself Johnny's bitterness over the phony job. The man gave his forehead a theatrical slap and said, "Dumbass me, you're right! Guess I've had one too many."

"You think? Look, man. I'm not looking for company, so do yourself a big favor and go back where you came from."

"We got a problem down there?" The bartender sounded bored.

"We're good but bring us both a shot-'n-beer."

He turned back to Johnny. "Look, I'll get out of your hair, but would you please just take a look at the photo?"

"I'm new in town. I don't know a single soul here."

The guy looked harmless: on the downslope of forty. Hazel eyes. Two-ten but not somebody who looked like he could handle himself in a fight. He just stood there staring at Johnny with a dopey expression. Johnny didn't hobnob with country club types in the bars he frequented at home, but this guy had *that look* about him somehow. Like the kind of look a prick salesman who used words too easily gives you before he stabs you in the back.

"I'll look."

Johnny held the card up in the bad lighting for a closer look.

"Nope."

The bartender took Johnny's beer glass away to refill it for the chaser.

She was pretty. No doubt about it. *Too good-looking for you, pal*. Maybe the guy cleaned up better than he looked in this shabby place or maybe he had the bucks to afford a younger girlfriend. *Probably married with five kids cheating on his old lady*, Johnny thought. Up close, the man lacked the belly and sallow complexion of the true drunkard. Johnny Lomack had spent enough time in bars to recognize the type. "*You're turning into one of those drunk you're always making fun of,*" Sharon would say just to get his goat.

He handed him back the card.

"I appreciate it," the man said. "Name's Freddie."

The handshake was firm, not the wet fish he expected.

Johnny reciprocated with his own name, suppressing a groan.

Truth be told, he didn't relish the long drive back so soon. He'd planned on a bed-and-breakfast after the "interview" for the job.

Bar protocol demanded he drink with the man until he could make his escape.

The man talked about his girl. He didn't slur, which Johnny thought odd since he looked blitzed when Johnny first walked in and sat down. In Johnny's experience, drunks glommed on to any bartender or customer willing to listen to their sob stories.

It became obvious the guy was educated because he picked his words carefully, not with a drunk's struggle to think and didn't use slangy obscenities like most men in bars, especially when it came to bragging about their women. Johnny winced at the memory of doing this to strangers when he first met Sharon.

"I don't understand it," Freddie lamented. "Jeanette said she'd meet me here."

"I'm sure she'll be along."

Johnny was indifferent to whether she did or didn't show. The long, boring drive back to Joplin was weighing him down. Every minute in this turd of a bar was adding to his depression.

"I'm sorry," Freddie said, interrupting another anecdote of his wonderful girl. "I'm boring you. Bartender!"

He did that finger-snapping thing over his head bartenders hated. Back home, you'd draw back a bloody stump at some of Johnny's taverns.

"Two more boilermakers if you're not too busy with your other two hundred customers."

"Fuck you."

"Top shelf this time, my good man. None of that Four Roses filth you've been pouring out."

"Go fuck yourself."

The bartender stopped midway down the bar, did a glide and slow turn like a ballet dancer; his pivot told Johnny the bartender wasn't one of those weightlifting lunks. He was light on his feet like a linebacker.

"That guy isn't very friendly," Johnny commented.

"Ah, Nick's a good guy. Known him for years."

The bartender carried the shot glasses and beer bottles between his fingers. He set the whiskey in front of them and the beers down by the necks.

"See what I said?" Freddie said, barking out a laugh. "Look at the paws on him. Didn't spill a drop."

Johnny grunted.

"What brings you to our fair town, John Lomack?"

Part of his mind had already fashioned a response that wouldn't make him look like a loser.

"On my way to Michigan to see a friend."

Think I'm gonna admit to being a bonehead to you? I just sold everything I own, sold it all cut-rate, and here I am in this place after a nine-hundred-mile drive for nothing.

"I heard a new plant is going up around here," Johnny said, hoping to probe a little more for any reason to hope.

"Ah, yes," Freddie said, nodding his head. "That turned sour."

Johnny would have said *clusterfuck* from his point of view.

"Part of Northtown doesn't want to see another

Love Canal."

Johnny thought that was some sitcom on TV. Sharon loved shit like that.

"Some folks salivated at the big paychecks," Freddie continued; "our local politicians were the most disappointed. Their ears lay flat against their heads and their eyes widened to cue balls at the thought of all that tax revenue flooding in."

"No plan to restart construction?"

"In time," Freddie replied. "Like building the Great Pyramid of Giza, I suspect."

"Shit, fuck, piss."

"Sorry to be the bearer of bad tidings, my friend. Were you hoping to land a job here? Somebody should have told you."

"Somebody did."

"Maybe I can help," Freddie said. "You say you're from Montana—"

"Missouri."

"A great state. You can't possibly be thinking of driving back so soon."

"Why not?"

"Nothing personal, John. Your eyes are a little bloodshot right now. I imagine you're sleep-deprived, too. Need I point out what a boilermaker rattling around in your bloodstream would mean if one of our fine state troopers pulled you over to ask you to blow into a breathalyzer?"

"I'll chance it."

Freddie's precise diction was a surprise. From sloppy drunk to one of Sharon's hoity-toity Lutheran preachers at the lectern explaining to the unwashed congregation one of Paul's letters. He'd known a few boozers who got wittier the drunker they got. This Freddie character was in a class by himself.

"Let me propose something," Freddie said, leaning closer to Johnny's shoulder as though Nick at the end of the bar might be eavesdropping.

"I'm going over to my girl's apartment on the other side of town. Stay a few hours in my place, catch up on your sleep. It'll save you the cost of a motel."

"Thanks but no thanks," Johnny said. "I'll hit the road soon's I fish—finish this drink."

"See what I mean?" Freddie laughed, putting a friendly hand on Johnny's shoulder.

"My condo is right on the lake. A mere mile from where we're warming these stools."

He pointed at the plate-glass windows. "Just out the door, up that street, one turn left, one turn right—and you're there."

"No, thanks."

"Nonsense! I insist! Here's the key. Stay as long as you like. I'm spending the weekend at Jeanette's."

Like that card magician trick he opened with, Freddie slipped the key into Johnny's right hand with the speed of one of those drug transactions on TV done in the blink of an eye. Johnny felt the cold metal in the palm of his hand.

"No, no," Johnny protested too late. "That's right decent of you—"

"*Right decent*, ha, I love the colloquialisms of our Midwest."

"No, man, I can't—"

"Take it, I beg you," Freddie urged. "Look, I'll put the directions on this elegant bar napkin."

With that same sleight of hand, he produced a pen and began scribbling; he handed it to Johnny and slipped the pen back to its invisible hiding place.

Johnny's booze intake clouded his judgment but not his vision. Two napkins were involved in the transaction.

Freddie handed him one that wasn't the one he wrote on.

Exhausted from the drive, a night without sleep, the booze, this stranger's razzle dazzle, Johnny was outmatched. Part of his surrender resulted from his bruised ego after Sharon and her lawyer had picked him clean in court. It was flattering to know a stranger trusted him like this. A complete stranger, no less. Johnny asked himself whether he'd ever do this. *Hell no*, came the immediate reply from his neocortex.

"I'll grab a few winks on your couch, stay an hour, two. Then I'm gone."

Another hearty back slap. This time, Nick looked up from his paper.

"Great, my man," Freddie blurted. "Help yourself to anything in the fridge. That goes for the beer and booze, too. Clean sheets and towels in the bathroom closet."

"I do 'preciate this," Johnny said.

"Pay it forward someday when you're flush, John," Freddie said.

He swigged the dregs of his drink and eased himself off his seat. "I must run. Jeanette will kill me if I'm late."

"Thought she was late," Johnny said. "Supposed to meet you here."

"She sent me a text message while I was in the can," Freddie said. "Last-second change of plans. Ha, you know women."

"I thought I did."

Another back clap, harder than the previous ones. "Take care, John Lomack."

"You, too."

On his way out, Freddie slapped a hand on the bar in front of him. "For you, barkeep."

Whatever the denomination of the bill under Freddie's hand, it impressed the bartender. He cut his eyes to the bill, back up to Freddie's face, then back to the bill.

He scooped it up and tucked it into his jeans.

Johnny unfolded the napkin to read the directions and noticed how much more writing Freddie would have had to do. Two boxes for the bar and the condo building, both joined by broken lines accompanied by compass directions and arrows.

Johnny finished his drink and headed to the door. He stopped near the bartender, "You know Freddie well?"

"Never saw him before this morning."

"You're kidding me, right?"

"I don't kid and I don't talk about customers," Nick said. His deltoids bunched as he leaned over the bar. "Anything else you want to know, buddy?"

"No."

"Good."

Johnny mumbled "fucking prick" on his way out the door.

"Don't let that door hit you in the ass," the bartender growled at his back.

Outside in the glare of the midday sun, Johnny knew without the slightest doubt he was hammered. White-hot sunshine hit him in the eyes like a fist.

Many pedestrians were out and about. Streams of cars on Bridge Street were a sharp contrast to the dreary ghost town he'd entered hours ago.

Crossing the street, Johnny was almost hit by a car coming from the opposite direction. The driver honked, swerved to avoid him. He kept his eyes averted from the shop windows he passed, knowing the shopkeepers were drawn to the spectacle of a drunk stumbling into traffic.

He passed a vape shop, a chocolate shop, some kind of vintage clothing store, a florist's and another bar before he realized he'd gone the wrong way. His pickup was parked in front of a private-investigator's window expressed in florid typeface. He quickly walked back the other way and passed another bar with a Mohawk Indian outlined in a decal on the plate-glass. The caricature made Johnny giggle. Too late, he noticed a mother holding a toddler's hand scowling at him.

He drifted too close to the curb a few times and was aware of more people looking at him. Trouble ahead: he saw two delivery trucks had his pickup sandwiched between them.

He got in fast, slammed the door. He needed a smoke. He grabbed his Marlboros off the dashboard and reached into his shirt pocket for his lighter, felt nothing, and wondered if he had dropped it back there somewhere. He started the engine, over-cranking it. Pulling out too fast in front of a red Nissan coming up behind him, Johnny heard the squeal of brakes. The horn blast was an exclamation point to the driver's rage.

Halfway up Bridge Street, Johnny blinked away sweat burning his eyes. The driver behind him was on his cell phone. *Maybe calling the cops on me...*

Johnny's damp palm sweated a hole in the napkin. He made out the blue arrow directing him to his second turn at the top of Walnut Beach hill.

Exactly a mile on Lake Road, as Freddie indicated, was the white-stone condominium. Beyond the entrance were a park leading to a baseball field and a pavilion with picnic tables. Close by was a playground in shiny blue and yellow colors.

He parked in the third row of the parking lot and got out. Trying to lock his door, he dropped the keys and reached down too fast to pick up the keys. Losing his balance, he slammed his head into the side of the door, skidding his forehead along the metal side as he went down to the asphalt.

"Are you OK, sir?"

Some guy in a khaki uniform stared at him from a panel truck.

"You're bleeding."

"Yesh—yeah, no, I'm fine, I'm good," Johnny blurted out in a word-slurry. *Christ, you're fucking smashed*, his brain retorted.

He scissor-walked to get away from the man, aiming for the center of the building like an errant missile with a faulty gyroscope; he couldn't stop weaving. Once inside, he passed mailboxes and potted plants, dimly aware of the stainless steel façade beyond the lobby. He prayed to the gods of drink to let it signify elevators. They responded by giving him an elevator car all to himself. He shot upwards to the twelfth floor with his stomach failing to keep up, holding itself a floor behind.

He reached Freddie's number just in time before his stomach revolted. He had a blurry image of whiteness—walls, furniture, eggshell-white carpeting—before he vomited through his fingers at the bathroom door.

Fuck, fuck, oh fuck, fuckfuck—

He ejected the remainder into the toilet bowl before he retched up nothing but sour-smelling Ohio air. Bouts of severe stomach spasms doubled him up and sent him to the tile floor. He crawled to the toilet bowl, hugged it with both hands, his face pressed against the cool ceramic until the pain came in manageable waves.

Johnny drank water, checked the fridge, and found a six-pack. He popped the tab and guzzled, waited a moment to see if more projectile vomiting were on the program. Gaseous, loud burps. *Good.* But he knew he was safe for the time being.

He staggered over to the couch facing a pair of french doors opening onto a tiny balcony and a spectacular view of Lake Erie's tranquil blue waters.

Johnny fumbled with the drapes, failed to shut them completely to block the sun's shafts of light pounding his skull behind his eyes. His throat felt as though he'd swallowed a pack of razor blades.

He grabbed a decorative shawl over the back of the couch, wrapped it around his head and shoulders and fell into a twitchy sleep full of nauseous dreams, grating sounds, and wicked thoughts.

He woke at sundown. He could tell from the slant of the shadows beneath the drapes. He sat up, still nauseated but past the vomiting stage, and—*good news at last*—hungry as a wolf.

"Let's check out your refrigerator, Freddie boy," he said with a fake jollity.

Food there was. Plenty of it. Some of it was still wrapped in the restaurant's packaging. He took out three styrofoam boxes and set them on the small table in the kitchen nook. Pasta, a salad not yet wilted, a bowl of chili—*better not risk it*—a casserole or goulash made of potatoes, onions, and some kind of meat.

He saw the microwave on the counter top but decided to eat everything cold. Joyless eating. He didn't care. He was coming back to life. He wasn't sleeping it off in the drunk tank of this shitty town. He'd shower, pack up some leftovers, take some bottled water, write a note thanking Freddie.

He downed three headache tablets from the bathroom cabinet with a can of beer, his tried-and-true remedy. Sharon always laughed at his faith in the hair-of-the-dog.

He pulled back the drapes and watched gulls wheeling in their spirals like inverted cones over the lake. The blue water took on a gunmetal tinge near the horizon. With the shawl wrapped around his shoulders again, he sat on the couch and nodded off.

It was dusk when he woke again. Out over the water, a lakeboat freighter cruised past, its starboard lights piercing the surrounding dark around it. He turned on a lamp to scope out the room for the first time. Bland, lots of gewgaws on shelves, ceramic stuff. Sharon would have approved. No photos anywhere, which was odd. No magazines or books. The flat screen on the wall was a smart TV, 65-inch. The remote looked like something NASA designed.

He wandered over to the stereo. Bose speakers, expensive. The stack of CDs contained lots of John Mayer, female vocalists like Taylor Swift, Lady Gaga, Shakira. Except for Zeppelin's *Lighter Than Air*, he didn't recognize many. Not a single country western. *Freddie listened to this crap?*

The slight buzzing in his ears told him the hangover wasn't bad enough to keep him from driving. He showered and felt better. Something nagged at him like a mosquito he couldn't kill. *What's that cop expression—JDLR? Just Doesn't Look Right…*

He went down the carpeted hallway to take a peek into the bedroom.

The door was shut. He opened it and looked inside. More beige and white. Clothes on the floor. More ceramic knick-knacks. Cluttered night stands beside the unmade bed. Medicine bottles, mostly. *Maybe old Freddie was a prescription drug freak.*

Who uses more than sheets in hot weather? The bed had a ruffled chenille bedspread. Too feminine. Nothing a man would choose. The bed wasn't just unmade; it had a tangle of sheets and coverlets rucked into a twisted pile.

He stepped closer, his heart hammering. All his sensory apparatus dulled by booze kicked back into action. He grabbed a corner of the mattress cover and tugged; it didn't give much. He used both hands and pulled it free.

She lay there nude in the fetal position he'd briefly disturbed.

Johnny cursed and stepped back as though he'd exposed a spitting cobra in the middle of the bed. He didn't know what to do. His brain screamed *Run, motherfucker!* But he stood there rooted to the floor looking at a dead woman's nude body.

She wasn't the young beauty Johnny had seen on Freddie's card. This was an older woman, maybe older than Freddie by a decade. She was slender to the point of boniness. Tiny blue veins stippled the whiteness of her skin, whiter than the carpeting he'd been walking on. Three dark splotches on her hip and lower backside showed where blood had begun pooling. He felt sad when he saw the protuberance of a bowel movement and the exposed pudenda with its unruly pubic ruff.

When Johnny whipped the sheets off her, he'd partially covered her face. He gently pulled the bed sheet away to see her eyes half-opened. She looked as though she'd fallen asleep and didn't wake up—except that she hadn't died in her sleep. The striations across her neck showed a crisscross of livid marks where she'd been throttled by something wrapped tight around her neck.

Fuck this, Johnny whispered. *Sorry, lady, whoever you are, but I'm outta here—*

He thought about covering her up the way he found her, changed his mind, and bolted for the door. He swatted the light switch on his way past.

You dumb fuck, Johnny Lomack.

Johnny's inner voice stopped him halfway down the hallway. His lifelong habit of talking to himself in his own voice sounded like him until lately when it acquired more of the tone and pitch Sharon's voice had when she scolded him about some fuck-up of his. By the time their marriage crashed and burned, his "nagging" voice, as he called it, was all Sharon's.

You've been set up from the git-go...

"I knew it," Johnny said to the empty hallway and walked slowly back into the room. He knew what he'd find on the night stand before he picked it up: his own cigarette lighter with his initials. Sharon's gift to him last Christmas.

Those quick hands back at the bar, Johnny remembered. *Card dealer's hands... pickpocket's hands. Jesus Jumping Christ.*

Like a lab rat in a maze, he ran from one end of the apartment to the other wiping down everywhere he thought he'd touched something. He found the handmade wire garrot under the bed.

His mind raced trying to reconstruct his conversation with Freddie. The clues were everywhere. He was led by a judas goat to slaughter.

Sharon, avid fan of crime shows, mocked him the entire time: *Your DNA is all over the place, you dummy. You slept here, ate food, drank beer, smoked cigarettes. You think they won't lift the floor drain, too? Or not find the blood drops from that cut on your forehead? They'll find something, Johnny. You're a cooked goose.*

You bitch. "I was in the bar when Freddie—or whatever that sick fuck's name is—was killing her! That bartender is a witness!"

You think so? That bartender's a moron like you.

"...never saw him before this morning—"

You're both patsies. He only saw you looking at Freddie's photo? He saw Freddie being friendly with you. You were hostile. For all he knows, Freddie was showing you his wife's photo. He'll say Freddie was waiting for her. He doesn't know time of her death from his dick. The prosecuting attorney will say you killed your friend's wife and tried to alibi yourself in a bar with him...

"Shut up, Sharon!"

Johnny ceased his frenetic scrambling on his hands and knees looking for more places to wipe down.

"Christ, look at me," he mumbled. "I'm arguing with my ex-wife."

But Sharon wouldn't shut up: *They'll say you were angry about the job and you went to that man's condo because he took pity on you. You were too drunk to drive but instead of sleeping, you tried to rape his sick wife…*

"No, no! I didn't do it!"

Run, Johnny, run!

Sharon's voice, his voice—he couldn't tell any longer. He ran.

He thumbed the elevator button in front of an elderly couple who looked on in fear. He saw the wife lean toward her husband to whisper. He heard "dope fiend" and turned around to snarl at them. When the elevator arrived and the doors clacked open, he jumped in while they stood back, terrified of getting in the same compartment with a madman.

In the lobby, he collided with an old man and knocked him to the floor. He started to help the old man up when he noticed a gaggle of onlookers approaching. He fled immediately, running for the parking lot.

He was yards from his pickup when he spotted a cop with a flashlight checking license plates in his row.

He raced back to the lobby in a stone-cold panic, a dog returning to his vomit. He shoved a couple aside to get into the elevator alone and punched the 12 button. The last image he had before the doors closed was the look of horror on their faces.

He still had Freddie's key in his pocket. He opened the door and put his back to it, panting. His breath came in great gulps, but he couldn't seem to get into his lungs. His mind a pinwheel, his heart a bongo.

The balcony. *Some fresh air, got to think*. Instead of fresh air, he smoked. Sirens caterwauled in the distance, their Doppler effect proving by wave refraction the police were getting closer. The nearest balcony was twenty feet away. With two good legs, he couldn't make it. He waited until the cruisers roared into the parking lot.

You can try talking to them, John. Freddie's voice now, another dog in the pack at his heels.

"I've got a better idea, fucker," he said.

He climbed to the top of the railing. He didn't look down. It was too black to see anything below anyway. He stared out over the water where a crescent of moon revealed a lighter shade above the cobalt blue, and then the blackness of the water and sky all around.

Tottering high in the black air, Johnny felt the cool breeze on his brow. "God damn it, Sharon. What happened? Well, here goes nothing," he said.

Johnny Lomack, twenty-nine years old, let go of gravity's hand.

I Remember

WEEK ONE: FRANK MEETS THE SHRINK

I had more concussions from my old man punching me in the head than I ever got playing football. I said that to the new prison shrink. He scribbled in his notepad.

Being in SHU in a max-con unit meant we couldn't meet inside my cell without ninja turtles on standby—the extraction team in full riot gear, hats and bats. He asked if I minded talking to him about my past. I still wonder if he thought I was going to blurt out the sordid catastrophes of my life and blame my parents for not potty training me right—a man of delicate sensibilities.

Talking's never been my problem. It's doing—rather, doing and getting caught while doing. I knew he was keen to get to it. If you're going to do crime for a living, you need to persuade like-minded people to follow you. I have my methods, depending on the one I'm drawing in. I'm not bragging. The people I know tend to jump in with both feet and ask questions later. I didn't feel the need to explain this to the earnest young headshrinker in the bow tie outside my bean chute.

He had moxie to make it this far after being peppered with abuse by the cons in the next tier below. He must have heard a lot about his wife's sexual appetite and how cute he'd look with his hair grown out and his name changed to Mary. The monkeymouths here aren't the worst, considering the places I've been detained, but I'd rank them high.

We talked through the reinforced glass above the food port, our voices out of sync like those chop-socky movies the lowbrows clamor for in every rec room in every Graybar Hotel I've spent half of my fifty-two years in.

So I talked, he listened, asked a few questions, wrote down words. I read writing upside-down, and I'm good at lip-reading cons with a mirror—you know, when you need to use the old-fashioned "kites" of the "convict telegraph," meaning a three-cornered, folded note attached to a long string tossed to another con down the row.

I made out some words from his hand movements in the notebook. One was "glib." I suppressed a smile when I detected two letters of the acronym "NPD," classic shrink jargon for "narcissistic personality disorder." Amused, not offended, by his rapid-fire diagnosis. If you spend enough time in lockup, the only two books you need to get acquainted with are the latest edition of the *DSM* and a legal dictionary.

On the first day, I flattered him, told him how "easy" it was to talk about my past. I opened up like a spigot and he drank with both hands like an Indian cup.

"Tell me more about high school," he said, scribbling fast. "You mentioned your problems started there."

"It was Monday before the big game, I remember—you know, the state quarterfinals. I played offense and defense. Second-team, all-state running back my junior year. Coach kept me out of practice because he could tell I wasn't right in the *cabeza*. I got into it the night before with my old man, who clocked me a good one in the temple. I was concussed the next day, still screwing off in classes, as usual. Coach looked in my eyes, said, 'You're sitting out practice today, Frankie'…' One of my boys must have mentioned the fight."

Any chance I had of getting out of that shithole neighborhood ended when my parents died within six weeks of each other. First, my junkie mother passed out at the kitchen table with a needle sticking out of her arm and a lethal dose of fentanyl in her bloodstream. The EMTs with the Narcan got there too late. My father cooked meth, dealt H, weed, pills, fenced stolen merch from the Norfolk & Southern yards. He was sent to Lucasville, the worst place to go to try out your alpha-male bullshit out by bumpin' titties in the yard. The Aryan Brotherhood sent somebody to dish out some "hard candy," as they called punishment back then. My father could scrap. He knocked four teeth out of that Brand enforcer's head. Six guys jumped him a week later, cracked his skull. The gang unit officer called me to deliver the news. He said my old man didn't make it easy—put two of them in the hospital. *I'm sorry to tell you this, son, but your father succumbed to his wounds yesterday.*

'Do you know the names of the men who killed him?' I asked.

'We're still investigating.

'When you find out, send me their names so I can send them all thank-you cards."

'He gasped over the phone. I laughed and thumbed off the connection.'"

I couldn't tell if Doc bought the revised version of my oh-so-sad upbringing.

"We've covered a lot today, Frank," he finally said.

"Did we make progress, Doc?"

"You're the only one who can answer that, Frank."

His insipid remark made me want to quote Freud: *In all ideation, there is aggression…*

He said we were at the beginning of "my road to recovery" and stammered something about "next week." Most convicts who run hustles are subhuman, but they know how to end a conversation unlike Doctor Bow Tie.

"See you next week, Doc."

He loped off to the next cell, slapping his notebook against his leg, pleased with his conquest of a convicted murderer. He must have tried talking to the con in the next cell through the bean chute again because I heard the guard escorting him say, "That's a good way to get your face sprayed with piss."

Actually, my next-door neighbor Jerome was more likely to jam a wad of feces-smeared Kleenex into Doc's face. From the symptoms I gleaned in my short time up on the SHU ward, from his spastic behavior and garbled speech, I guessed Friedreich's Ataxia. It became more apparent from Jerome's jitteriness and mental confusion that a diagnosis of Hashimoto's Encephalopathy would be more apt.

I wasted no time, hitting the floor for calisthenics by hooking my feet under the metal lip of my bunk for crunches. As Mike Tyson said after a loss, "Guess I'll just fade into Bolivion."

WEEK TWO: THE SHRINK OPENS UP TO FRANK

All week, Doc's pending visit tickled my brain cells. I had hope. He taught at a community college and wanted to interview inmates to understand how bad decision-making led to incarceration.

I pried out the fact he was married and had a three-year-old at home. He seemed vaguely threatened by a personal admission, although I didn't care if he was a bigamist with three wives and six kids in different states. The boogeyman scenario played out in his mind: *Convict Breaks Free, Attacks Psychologist Who Only Wanted to Help.*

I understand self-interest and didn't judge him. He wanted tenure at his silo college and an article on the wayward thinking of inmates would help him achieve that end. He'd dress it up for academic consumption for *The Journal of Abnormal Psychology* with something like: "The Lethal Mentality in the Incarcerated Individual." Maybe knock off a similar piece for popular consumption in *Psychology Today*: "How to Spot a Narcissist."

"I don't know, Frank," he lied. "Most refereed

journals aren't interested in the correlation between childhood violence and incarceration rates. It's been done."

"I could help on something like non-lethal assault on prisoner-on-prisoner violence."

He appreciated how I picked up on his jargon fetish. "I've seen my share over the years. Even in minimum-security joints, guys need a tough convict veneer to keep other cons at bay."

"'Veneer.' That's an interesting word choice, Frank. You told me you graduated high school with a 'Social Promotion' diploma because they were afraid to fail you."

I relished his condescension. "Me and about twenty-seven other thugs the size of NFL linemen they didn't want to see glaring at them from the back rows of classrooms. I must have picked that word up from some jailhouse lawyer."

"Tell me about your last…crime. Would you be willing to expand on it?"

"Doc, whatever you want. It'll help pass the time…"

I gave him another abridged version. The one I'd give to a parole board without the pity-me interruptions and head lowered in shame, which of course was moot. I'll see a parole board when I see pigs eating my brother, as Marlon Brando said to Dick Cavett.

The real version without flowery details was simple enough: The signs were in place it was going to turn to shit, yet I ignored them because I was hell-bent on that score ever since I heard from my source there was an inside man in the armored car depot. It was supposed to be my *adiós* to crime and my hello to paradise. Most cons tape up photos of their women in lingerie. I kept a raggedy-assed poster of Key West in my cell of a tiki bar beneath blue skies and turquoise waters.

Key West was a symbol of paradise. I'd have settled for any Key on US 1 past Miami. Weary of the cold, weary of stumbling from one caper to another, I was growing sick of the rollercoaster of getting money, blowing it on bar whores and gambling, always on the lookout for the next heist as soon as the booze fog lifted. Time and memory loss were wearing me down. I was worried about blood in my stool when I went to see the prison doctor. He ordered an MRI for a perforated ulcer, but it showed clear. I mentioned my memory lapses, joked about finding things misplaced in my cell. He ordered a Pet scan. Then that diagnosis. I was in bigger trouble than a duodenal ulcer.

Getting out of tight situations with my fists or my feet, with a gun on the outside, wasn't going to work with a rapidly rotting brain from whitish plaque overwhelming both hemispheres—every day a little more gone, every day a little less to remember.

It started fine. November, colder than a witch's teat. I drove north for Scotty, my former cellmate from Green Bay. He was living in a men's shelter in downtown Duluth, according to the hatchet-faced woman who answered the door of his double-wide. He laughed. "That's my fourth one."

"Why do you marry them? You know it won't work."

"I like being married."

Scotty wasn't the type to stay up late thinking about the dangers of orbiting space junk or wandering black holes. He liked my plan, didn't moan and piss about details like the McGuire brothers, Mickey and Tom. Before I knew it, that feeling I used to love before a job—feeling light on my feet as a jungle cat—was gone. Instead, I was walking around with an anvil in my arms trying to avoid trap doors.

The brothers were ex-cons from the U.P. who did time with another cellmate of mine. Tom, the smarter one, was his cellmate at Jackson when he did time on an armed robbery beef. My guy said the brothers were "cowboys," but you could count on them. They agreed to a quarter-share each, which Scotty was getting.

"Fucking-A," Mickey concurred. "You say the money's that good. Hell fuckin' yes, we're in."

Only nothing's easy. Triple that when it comes to a takedown of a money depot with armed guards inside.

Let me paint it for you the way my mind filmed in the aftermath without the day-to-day surveillance and dress rehearsals. I made them understand this could only work between the short interlude of the last two trucks arriving. My inside man was firm on that point: "They'll swarm you like flies on shit if that last truck gets inside. Three guys, assault rifles. Remember that…"

Gun-pointing a bank with a women tellers is nothing. They're making minimum wage and no one will risk her life; they're told to give it up, plant a dye pack only if they think they can get away with it. Most don't have burglar bars or automatic security windows. Maybe there's a manager willing to resist for a commendation from a grateful CEO. No wonder druggies off the street do it. It's another thing to loot three million with anywhere from six to eight guards milling around, drivers bringing in deposits, trucks leaving in timed sequences. Armed staff sorting cash in the counting room with state-of-the-art monitoring, all hi-def cameras everywhere except in the shitters—and maybe there, too. Protocols that kicked in if someone sneezed wrong. Like a unionized steel mill: two supervisors watching another supervisor watching one worker doing the scutwork. And there's a guarantee you'll find one Rambo willing to engage in a shootout to get his face in the paper.

I had one other advantage: That final week in November was scheduled to be the last time that place was being used. The entire operation was being shipped to a newly built site west of Chattanooga that looked like a mock version of the *Führerbunker*, only more protected.

That night, protocols were slightly relaxed for the big move. A skeleton crew was left in the depot; the rest of the staff were watching PowerPoints at the new site.

What started well ended in a bloodbath. Three dead bodies on the floor, Scotty slumped against a table with his brains leaking from his nose, dropped by friendly fire from one of the trigger-happy brothers. Three guards shot to rags in a fusillade of gunfire. I'd just left the counting house where two more guards lay bound in flex cuffs. I walked into a shitstorm.

A dying female guard blew a gout of blood coughed up on my legs as I ran past, gun out, heart thumping like a bongo, my eyes boxing the room. Mickey and Tom were firing in every direction, two guards I never saw before that moment firing back—fierce ricochets off metal lockers, shouting like the pandemonium of hell breaking loose in one small room.

The chaos lasted seconds, seemed like minutes. Then we were running for our lives with garbage bags of cash. I remember the sound of the Doppler effect of sirens screaming toward us. Seconds to flee, not minutes. The three million I'd planned for dwindled to whatever the McGuires had bolted with. I was empty-handed and Scotty's bag of money lay at his feet as though he were cuddling with it.

A slug fired by a wounded guard sizzled past my ear. I kept running, glanced over my shoulder to see the door jamb we'd just run through explode in splinters from the semi-auto rifle Mickey was firing. He was crazy and fearless. Tom screamed for his brother to run.

By the time I risked a second look back, the first cruisers were roaring up, and cops jumped out to fire from behind their cruisers. Mickey was surrounded. The paper said he died of "multiple gunshots" with his garbage bag of money beside him.

The van with the window-washing service logo I'd applied that morning sat where I left it. By the time I reached it, I was sucking air. An all-out sprint left me shaking by the time I got into the driver's seat and started the engine. I picked up Tom who'd cut down an alley behind the depot when the cops cut him off behind me.

He hopped in when I swung the van to the curb. Sobbing, panting, he wanted me to go back for his brother.

"Mickey's dead," I said. "There's no going back, Tom. It's all fucked up."

"Your fucking plan," he said. "You fucked up, Frank."

Our staging area was the last two rooms of an L-shaped, run-down motel with letters missing in the sign out front and triple X's for the films offered.

Tom threw the half-filled bag of money on one bed and went into the bathroom where we had a six-pack chilling in ice from the machine next to the lobby. It was supposed to be for the celebration when we divvied up the swag before going our separate ways.

Tom guzzled a can, crushed the empty in his fist, and threw it angrily at the wastebasket.

"What the hell happened, Frank?"

"The last truck before the weekend pickups," I said. "They carry an extra man. He must have seen the shit going down and tripped the silent alarm. Hell, he could have called the cops from inside the truck."

"Fuck me, you think?"

I had it all memorized. Or so I thought. That one big detail got past me, like an eye floater you see and then blink, it's gone forever. My inside man, that disgruntled employee everyone knows somewhere, told me to be damn sure the night I met him in Shenanigan's. *The last truck, be gone before it reaches the depot*...I was taking care of him out of my share. The others didn't need to know about him.

"You fucked up, Frank, you really did. My bro's dead because of you, fucker!"

"I'm sorry about Mickey. I truly am. But I don't see you shedding tears for putting a bullet in Scotty's head."

"He jumped in front of Mickey's gun, I don't know! You couldn't see with all the shooting going on in that room."

"How is it you two didn't neutralize the third guard when he walked in behind the driver and the other guard?"

I wanted Tom on the defensive. I didn't want him to make the connection that it was entirely my responsibility, not his.

"I was holding them three on the floor. He came in from another room. By the time I saw him, the bastard was shooting at us with an AR-Fifteen."

"The sonofabitch must have come in through a secret door," I said. "Not your fault, man. Nobody's fault."

"You're goddamned right it's not our fault!"

"Look, you take Mickey's share," I said, pointing at the bag of money. "Leave me a third of whatever's there. You take the van."

Both our cars were stashed in another parking lot a couple blocks away. Tom walked between the beds to fetch the bag.

"The cops will have this place on their radar. We better move out soon," I said.

Before I had my gun out from behind my belt, Tom shot through the garbage bag and hit me in the chest. The surgeon told me when I came out of anesthesia that the bullet missed the aorta by seven millimeters.

It felt like getting hit with a Louisville slugger. I remember lying on my back on that filthy carpet looking up at a ceiling marked with water stains in the shape of Africa. Tom looked down at me; the bore of the barrel was aimed between my eyes for the *coup de grâce* that never came. He must have decided not to risk the noise of a second shot.

Thus endeth chapter and verse of my clusterfuck heist. *Sayonara*, the good life.

The shrink seemed dissatisfied with the short version. He asked me if I regretted it. Would I have killed Tom McGuire if I shot first?

"No and yes."

"May I ask why?"

"No mystery, Doc. The McGuires were lowlifes the world is better off without. It's called beneficial population adjustment. If they'd gotten out with the millions and left those people dead on the floor doing it, I'd have split a beer with them, kept my part of the deal, paid them off, and gone my separate way after the split."

He penciled furiously in his notebook. The tip snapped; he dropped the notebook to the floor.

I laughed. He wrote so hard I could read *SPD* backwards and upside down in a glance when he stooped to pick it up: *Sociopathic Personality Disorder*.

WEEK THREE: FRANK WAITS FOR THE DOC TO SHOW

I was returning to general population soon. I was looking forward to the Doc's next visit and wondered how I could convince him to appeal to the assistant warden to let us continue. He was fifteen minutes late.

While I waited, pacing, rehearsing what I planned to say and how to say it, Marcus, the escort, appeared at my window. He mouthed: "You can stop pacing. Your tubby boyfriend in the bow tie called. He ain't coming today."

He called me two days later. Marcus grumbled, escorting me in shackles all the way to the phone.

"Hello, Frank. I have a question. You planned to steal somewhere in the neighborhood of three million you said. Yet you say you aren't greedy?"

"The money had a purpose," I replied. "To get me to Florida."

"Where? Why Florida?"

"At the time, I was still debating among Largo, Islamorada, and Key West."

"Yet you grabbed no money on your way out the door."

"Doc, do you have any idea how heavy a bag of money is? You can carry a million in both arms but you'll be defenseless from a shot in the back and you'll become exhausted before you can run far if it's two million. Nobody runs like a jackrabbit weighted down with sixty, seventy pounds of money."

"In the movies, they pack a million in a suitcase."

"Yes, in the movies. If I'd stayed ten seconds longer, I'd have been shot to rags with Mickey. The result would have been the same. I wouldn't have had enough to live off. Shooting it out with cops and escaping is another one for the movies."

"I'll see you soon. I've got something to propose to you."

Being entombed in a narrow cell, free to read, eat, shit, shower, and shave with a couple hours rec time in an outside isolation cage. It's more restrictive than being a dangerous animal confined in a zoo where workers can move an animal from one shift cage to another to reach their outside enclosures.

WEEK FOUR: THE SHRINK GETS TOUGH WITH FRANK

"Have you ever considered making an honest living?"

"Is that what you wanted to ask me on the phone?

The answer's yes."

"And?"

"You see me, right?"

"I'm curious. You could have done any number of things. I've seen your Beta and Wais tests on file."

As lousy as my grades were, I'd always hoped to do a bait-and-switch on college recruiters when they scoped that hilarious Social Promotion Diploma. "I'd flash them my IQ test, proving 149, a borderline genius, and plead: *I can and will apply myself, sir, if your school gives me half a chance…*"

"So why crime—and spare me the usual convict sob story."

"Wow, this is a switch. That acerbic tone tells me you've chatted with some people who don't like me much."

"'Acerbic'? Another Frank word trotted out to impress, huh? To be…no pun intended, *frank*—I have discussed you with the warden, and the prosecuting attorney who convicted you. I even spoke to your cellmate from McAlester."

"How is old Jason?"

"Still doing time there—thanks to you, he says."

"And what pray tell do they say about me, these confidants of my reckless youth?"

"They say you're a callous, manipulative person to know. They say you're dangerous. You throw people away as soon as you've gotten what you want out of them. One used the term 'murderous.'"

"Let me guess. That would be Schmitt, the prosecutor. He dinned that word in the jury's ear so many times I suspected half of them went sleepwalking in their homes muttering 'Frank Carstairs is a murderous fiend… Frank Carstairs is a murderous fiend.' You know the expression 'obnoxious as a jury foreman?' That was Herr Schmitt and his jury foreman to a tee."

"We say 'foreperson' now."

"Apologies for my inbred male chauvinism. I'm unreformed. Prison doesn't expose one to a more genteel social circle. These guys, they say 'fucking' in every sentence, like 'Pass the fucking butter.'"

"You're digressing. Well, are you, Frank? Are you murderous?"

"Schmitt must have told you he failed to convict me of any murder charge on the bill, right."

"He said they failed to match a ballistics test to the gun they found in the motel. That doesn't mean you didn't kill one or more of those guards."

"True, guilt by association," I replied. "Co-conspirators in felony murder in this state are just as guilty as the ones pulling the trigger. I pled to agg armed robbery, conspiracy to murder, and three counts of felony manslaughter. I got fifty-five-to-life. They couldn't pin four dead guards on me like Schmitt wanted to get me the stainless steel ride."

"What about your cellmate in Oklahoma?"

"My former cellie is a pathological liar. I met him in a shitkicker bar in New Mexico with a name like Lobo Wolf or something as grim-sounding—you know, miles and miles of busted oil derricks, barbed-wire fences, and clapped-out trailers you wouldn't keep a dog in. He had this scheme to make money in Oklahoma selling speedkittens and snowcones to high schoolers."

"What?"

"Meth and ketamine. Crushed amphetamines mixed in blunts."

The rest of our time didn't go as planned. The well was poisoned by whatever *kaffeeklatsch* he and my enemies put together to discuss me. You get used to setbacks in my chosen profession. As football coaches everywhere loved to say, 'It's how you get back up that counts.'

WEEK 5: FRANK RETURNS TO GENERAL POPULATION
You watch yourself back in the pod because eyes are on you everywhere from the chow line to the work assignment to lights out. Who talks to you, who doesn't. It adds up to your profile, the one the cons keep, not the suits in administration.

"Doc, you know what a rat king is?"

"Sounds like a Disney cartoon."

"It's a bunch of squeaking, snarling rats in a burrow fighting over food. Their sticky tails get entangled. It makes for one giant swirling rat, a rat king."

"What's your point, Frank?"

"My point is I'm in a burrow with a lot of bad rats with sharp teeth. I want to talk to you but we need to find a way to do it without the other rats listening in."

"I'm working on something. Talk to you soon."

WEEK SIX: FRANK GETS HIS WISH
The hook was baited. He chomped down hard. He had a sabbatical lined up, and a proposal accepted. He wanted to do a book. The subject of it, he said, beaming like a man who'd just gotten his rocks off, was me.

"I'm not sure I have anything that important to contribute, although I'm sure it's important."

"Don't be modest, Frank. You're ideal for it."

Lethal Narcissism, Referential Thinking, and Aberrant Response in the Convicted Felon. A mouthful. I asked him what it meant; he dodged the question, threw me a tossed word salad of gobbledygook.

"Will you be doing anything on treatments?"

I don't have a winsome face. Too many tomcat scars and a bent nose, so I mimed humility.

"Of course! A whole chapter. This study can really

help you, Frank."

A beaded string of lies couched in psycho-babble. I worked my face muscles so as not to betray my contempt. The only thing helped by his study was to secure tenure, and maybe a charming female grad student worshiping at his knees—or, more likely, on her knees.

"That's wonderful, Doc."

"And the best part? I've arranged with the warden to allow us to meet in the lawyer conference room…"

Bliss. He was so enamored with his project that he missed the effort it took me to suppress my glee. Privacy, soundproofed walls, one window slat for the guard to peek into every twenty minutes—but no CCTV cameras by law. The only place in a prison other than the showers and your cell shitter with or without the jackoff curtain. One guard to escort him in, one behind the glass to buzz him out.

Dee-Dee made the money transactions last week. It was only this last piece of the puzzle.

"That's a nice sport coat, Doc. You celebrating tenure prematurely?"

"Ha, no. My wife bought it. A size 44, it's big in the shoulders."

"No, it's not. It's perfect."

"I've been putting on weight. You know, the sedentary life of an academic."

"Tell me about it."

Week Seven: The Shrink Asks Frank to Be Totally Honest for the Record

"They feeding you OK in here, Frank? You look like you've lost weight."

"Prisons are supposed to fatten you up with all that starch they serve. Exercising in my cell a lot to help with the insomnia. All the clanging metal and shrieks going on at night."

"Let's get started. I have to make the condition that you won't hold anything back."

"I won't hold back. I promise you."

"Good. Let's begin. I'd like the book to have something catchy, an attention-grabber as they say in publishing, so I'd like to start at the end. That is, when you came to on the floor of that motel with a bullet in your chest, what was the first thing you thought of?"

"I thought: 'Frank, you idiot, you should have been quicker on the draw.'"

"Quicker? And why do you keep scratching your legs? Does this place have bedbugs?"

"Tons of them," I said. I inserted the custom-made key into my ankle lock and twisted. He couldn't see below the edge of the table. "I meant to kill Tom with the combat dagger I'd hidden between the mattress and the box springs. If all three, including Scotty, made it back, I planned to shoot them all as soon as they were toasting our success. The gun they found, the Glock Nineteen that hadn't been used, was right beside that punch dagger. One bullet for each. A nice red herring to keep the cops busy while I scooted."

"My God, that's cold, Frank."

"Not as cold as you think, Doc. You see, when I learned my brain was going bad fast, I knew I had to hustle if I wanted to die in a warm place, drooling on my shirt front or not."

"Frank, wait a second…"

"I didn't waste time in the counting room. I had wads of big denominations tucked into pouches Dee-Dee sewed into my clothing—backup in case things went sideways. Once the gunfire started, we ran to see what was going on. That's when Scotty caught the slug from those fool McGuire brothers."

"They never found any money."

"That's because I shoved it inside the ductwork before I collapsed for good. Dee-Dee told me the motel's scheduled for demolition, so I've been on a timeclock with all the other pressures."

"Who's Dee-Dee? What pressures? You're losing me here."

"So many things to prepare for, Doc. Take my weight loss. That forty-four jacket you're wearing. It'll be a tight fit."

"My jacket—what? I'm confused. What are you saying?"

"That money I stashed in the motel after I picked myself off the floor with a bullet in my chest. Ever since that first day, it's been going to people I trust on the outside to do right by me. Men I've done jobs with. The one person you should have talked to is my girl Dee-Dee."

"She's…the one who gave you a character reference at sentencing?"

"We've been corresponding for years. You should have chosen a study on why women are attracted to incarcerated men. God knows, there are plenty of them. Maybe something about knowing a man is where you want him to be. Some will do anything you ask."

"You're scaring me now."

I lifted my shackled arms from the table. "Look, you're safe, Doc. I'm getting to the good parts."

He looked as though he'd swallowed a large and nasty spider. His eyes were pinned to my face.

"Dee-Dee's been sending that money here and there at my direction. For necessary services."

"Necessary services?"

"Like money put into certain cons' commissary accounts here. Men with certain skills to do certain jobs."

"I think we're done here."

"Dee-Dee sews. She made me what I'm wearing underneath. All I need is your suit jacket. Your badge will get me out the doors where she's waiting by the front gate."

"Whoah—"

"Every guard except that clown behind the glass has been paid a princely sum. Not one of them saw you before so they'll have a fifty-fifty chance of keeping their lousy jobs afterward during the investigation. That guy operating the doors from the cube, he'll be distracted by the two guys mopping the floor in front of him. Once they start fighting, he won't notice that the chubby psychology teacher he buzzed out doesn't altogether resemble the one he buzzed in forty minutes ago."

"It hasn't been forty minutes—"

"I'm allowing for the twenty minutes between peeks by the guard checking in at the window. I'll need time to make the change of clothes, slap on that silly moustache Dee-Dee made."

"You're out of your mind," he whispered. "You're shackled to that eye bolt in the wall."

"Five thousand dollars says I can. That's what the key made in shop cost me. I palmed it before they took me down to this room. If I can't palm something so small as a key in nineteen years of being locked up with all that time on my hands, I don't deserve to escape."

"*Escape*... you're bluffing."

"There's his mug in the window slat now. What a dough-faced loser. Probably goes home at night, gets shitfaced on Jim Beam, and thumps the old lady around the trailer."

"*I'm leaving now...*"

He didn't bother to scoop his recorder or papers into the attaché case he brought in. His blanched face, the razor-slit expression on his jowly, overfed mug—I savored the moment. He fumbled at the man-down looped around his neck to alert the prison.

"Too bad, Doc. I sent five-hundred to a guy's wife in Pigeon Fork to have that one made and given to you. Keep thumbing the button, maybe it'll work."

He whimpered, pressed the button even as I approached.

"Doc, didn't Freud say doing the same thing and getting the same result was the definition of insanity?"

I had him from behind the neck in an arm bar. I strengthened my forearms with hours of resistance training in my cell. Sometimes I'd tell Henry my cellmate to sit on my back while I did pushups.

The wrist shackles came off the minute after I gave Doc a demonstration of my "helplessness."

I couldn't see his eyes bulge—but I imagined it. It made me stiff. He did a light, two-step shuffle step in his loafers as I tipped him backwards. A few spasms, then his bowels released. A puddle of urine at his feet. I held my grip for a full minute longer than needed. "I'm going to set you down over here just out of sight, shitpants," I said, dragging him to a corner of the room.

You can look for me in the Keys. I'm sure the Marshals Service is blanketing every one of them by now. They won't find me. I set that up years ago, like the ratty-looking poster I taped to my cell. I'm nowhere near Florida. There are thousands of warm places to go. I never told anyone about my paradise, not even Dee-Dee. I hope she's sent to a minimum-security joint where she can use her sewing skills.

I wanted a few good years before my brain caves in and all my memories go with it. As they say, money isn't everything. *Sayonara*, motherfuckers.

Gone Fishing

Going fishing with Marty Kincaid had as much appeal as a choice between a Brazilian butt lift and a hot-lead enema. Marty plus fishing was going to add up to one shitty Saturday.

"C'mon, don't be a dick. The walleye are sticking the hooks in their own mouths and climbing into the boat. I gotta club 'em to keep from capsizing."

"Water looks rough today, Marty."

"Did you say something? Sounded like 'my pussy hurts.'"

Erie in autumn is a risk. The big ore boats still going up and down the Great Lakes, but bouncing through chop in Marty's crappy bass boat wasn't the same thing. Marty, his wife Beth, and I used to run across Flat Rocks on our way to the lighthouse as teenagers. This shithole town hadn't changed, but we're not the same except for Marty. Our high-school football star still thought he could hear the cheers from the stands. Even fishing for yellow perch or walleye was a blood sport. Beth and I, we let go of our dreams. Maybe that's why we hooked up after Marty thumped her around once too often.

The risks we took to meet were stupid, and she had to be super-cautious. Marty wasn't just violent, he was possessive about her and everything in his sphere of influence. *Wikipedia* has his name under the definition of "control freak."

Beth's dad and my old man worked in the same chemical plant. After high school, Marty and I played on the same fast-pitch softball team until I threw my shoulder out permanently. Marty said that was a good thing because I whiffed too much. Hitting a 90-m.p.h. fastball isn't as easy as it looked. He was used to being spotlighted in the *Herald Tribune* as star center fielder for the Northtown Stealth Fighters, which ridiculous name went back to Northtown's glory days as the producer of titanium for America's stealth fighters. Now it produces cancer. Half the night-shift crew Beth's father and my dad worked died of weird cancers after retirement. This town is the poster child for the superfund sites, although lawyers made off with most of that government money long ago.

My injury drew Beth and me closer. We sat in the stands cheering on the team. At the state championship in Columbus last year, we planned to stay overnight after the game, hit a few bars on Front Street near the OSU campus and return in the morning. I waited in my room for them to call; hours passed, the phone rang: Beth said Marty wasn't feeling well and canceled out. He waved the bat at tricky fastballs at the plate three times with men on. The Stealth Fighters lost 7-6. Saying Marty was a bad loser was like saying rain was wet.

She knocked on my door around one in the morning, the left side of her face swollen.

"He finally passed out," she said.

I went into the bathroom to get a towel to wrap some ice in it. "Dumb idea," I said to my reflection. Twenty minutes later, Beth was grinding down on my cock, and I was holding both her breasts in my hands.

Marty wore dark glasses and slept in the back seat on the ride home. Beth rode up front, but we didn't speak the entire time. Once she reached over and squeezed my hand.

Two weeks passed before we spoke again. Marty was working nights.

"Can I come over?"

"Are you sure about this?"

By the time I thumbed off the connection, most of the blood in my body was surging south of the beltline.

Weeks passed before she'd call again. We told ourselves we were being careful, so the call to go fishing that Saturday wasn't unusual—except for that shiver in the neocortex that nature planted back when human beings were painting their faces blue and barking at trees. I should have paid more attention to it than to the worry Marty might become suspicious if I refused to go.

"What's a good lure?"

"Spoons, crankbaits, jigs, poppers, gliders—"

"Twenty minutes."

"…paddle tails, bottom bouncers—I've got these shaky-head, soft-craw baits guaranteed to—"

"I said I'm coming."

I convinced myself Marty's ego would never let him see me as competition.

He yapped all the way to public access ramp at Lake Shore Park, still bragging about his touchdowns or walk-off homeruns in the long ago. I hummed "Glory Days" until he got the point, cursed me, and laughed.

"What did you do to your hand?" A flesh-colored bandage covered the palm of his right hand to his knuckles. I didn't even see it until I noticed it while he maneuvered the tiller slantwise through the waves. He deliberately took a couple big waves at a bad angle so I'd get the brunt of the spray in my face. Clouds with gray, ragged shreds under their bellies were moving in from the northwest. One of those strange weather days when your skin prickled from the crazy mix of alternating warm and cold bands of air.

"Sheepshead fin stuck me as I was pulling out the hook. Got infected."

"Bet you bashed in his head for that stunt."

"Fuckin'-A, hillbilly."

Hillbilly. The insult and phony Appalachian dialect were for my benefit. When we first met on the playground of elementary school, he mocked my West Virginia accent. We'd just moved up North when my dad's coal mine closed. We fought after school that day. I lost, was left a bloody mess on the asphalt, but somehow I earned his respect. I caught him looking at me out of the corner of my eye. When someone knew you well, you found it hard to believe that person didn't have your best interests in mind.

"We ought to stay near the harbor," I said.

"You were a deckhand on the Great Lakes, right? You're worried about a few ripples on the lake? Have a can of liquid courage, loser."

He tossed me a beer from the stern.

Pulling his ballcap low, he gave the outboard full throttle, heading for open water past the lighthouse. His 16-footer had a 40 hp outboard—too much thrust for an aluminum boat meant for weed-filled coves. We plowed into the teeth of wind-driven waves. He liked to see how close he could come to tipping the hull to the sky and sinking the boat motor first.

"I know this sweet little spot near the cliffs."

I tucked my hands under me on the folding seat for warmth. Canada lay 50 nautical miles off to port. In four or five weeks, Alberta Clippers would be hammering the northern Midwest states with Arctic cold and whiteout squalls.

A loose tarp in the bow flapped as we bucked along. A bat handle poked out.

"You're using your softball bat to brain your catch? Overkill there, Marty."

I shouted to make myself heard above the engine whine and the rhythmic thud of waves slapping the boat's metal. I reached over and pulled the bat free. Not just any softball bat—Marty's pride and joy, the Easton Ghost, the same bat he'd taken to the state championship playoff. A fastpitch softball bat's 2¼ inch barrel diameter and width-to-length ratio varies as much as minus 13. Marty's was barely regulation: 34-inch length and "heavy"—as heavy as regulation league play permitted. The humiliation of his strikeouts must have galled him to hate it. Just like Marty, a bully and a braggart, to blame his bat. Why else demote a custom-made $500 bat to a fish billy? Now pocked and dented, it looked like something from a shelf at Goodwill's.

"Almost there... Almost... there."

I read his lips; it seemed more like a prayer. Marty normally spewed out obscenities like a fiend. The boat swung hard to starboard, and I almost fell off my seat.

The lake had been high for years; new littorals were carved out of the shoreline by the pounding waves. It seemed unlikely deep-water game fish clung to the shoreline to feed—especially in these murky swells. When I was fifteen, a rogue wave, a rare Lake Erie seiche, came out of nowhere on a sunny day and knocked me off the breakwall while I fished for carp with my bamboo pole. I flew backwards over the massive granite boulders and landed in a stagnant pool. Coughing up dirty, sandy water, my lungs became infected. I spent a week in the hospital with bronchial pneumonia. Even sailing the ore boats, I was leery of deep water. Marty, on the other hand, bragged that he'd squeezed more water out of his socks than I sailed over.

"Better than working near the vats, right? Wearing that heavy gear."

He meant our former union jobs that paid $30 an hour. Overtime up the ass with the Department of Defense contracts. Take a 90-degree day, a hot night, protective gear that included steel-toed boots, ear plugs, face masks with respirators, heavy firemen's coveralls, add a steel kettle full of molten steel you couldn't work by more than fifteen minutes at a time, and you earned every cent. Our classmate fell off a catwalk into a molten vat and lived an hour, brain-dead but breathing through a respirator. I blocked my mind from thinking how he suffered from that 450-degree swim.

"You ever think it would turn to shit like this?"

"You did all right, Marty."

"Yeah, I suppose. Better than you, ridge runner. Unloading trucks from Walmart like some brain-dead lackey—with a bum shoulder, too."

No disputing that. My shoulder throbbed so much by the end of shift I drove home one-armed.

"That CBD oil work?"

"You know, I might have been born in West Virginia. That doesn't make me a junkie."

"I was you, hillbilly, I'd get me some Oxy. They call it *Hillbilly* heroin, right? Made for your kind. Put a snootful up your when you clock in."

"My doctor doesn't believe in drugs for pain management." We both knew that was a lie. I spent three years walking around Northtown in a drug-induced stupor. Lost two decent jobs and wound up working alongside a neo-Nazi, two alcoholics, and six college kids who sat together in the break room, ignoring us three "old-timers," talking about the latest violent video game. I didn't blame them.

"I like a little reasonable weed now and then," Marty said. "Beth likes to fuck when she's high."

"We gonna fish or jawbone all day?"

The sky had darkened more since we left the boat ramp. Blue-black skies at the horizon with a slim belt of turquoise that reminded me of warm Caribbean waters in travel brochures—except you'd be lucky to last three hours this time of year if you went over the side. I recalled the emerald-green waters of Lake Superior from my sailing days. One third mate told me of a boating accident offshore Thunder Bay: "Pulled a couple men out treadin' water. They died of heart attacks, lay there on the deck floppin' like fish," he said. "Boy, that water's too cold to survive even in summer."

Marty swung the boat into the waves and told me to toss the anchor. We were so close to shore I could see the tops of the bluffs and benches put there to watch sunsets in summer.

"No fish is going for bait this close. The water's too roiled up."

"Fish hang at the bottom, dummy. Toss your line and shut the fuck up. If I wanted someone to nag me, I'd have brought Beth."

We fished awhile in silence. I felt Marty's eyes on me the whole time.

That thought he might *know* was like a chunk of ice stuck in my esophagus—*out here alone with a betrayed husband, no one in sight*—

But that thought didn't jibe with Marty bragging about his one-night stands, arranged for his out-of-town games with a hook-up app on his cell phone. Marty kept me around like the sidekick in a buddy movie, although I wasn't chubby or shy. I was there, like Beth, to sing his praises. It swept over me like a foul aftertaste that I was assuming Marty would act like a sane, normal husband if he discovered his wife was cheating on him with his friend—and that was far worse under present circumstances.

"Fuck this, I'm changing lures," he said.

"Give 'em something brighter to see," he said, interrupting my unpleasant reverie. "Where's my tackle box? Hand me the bat, Steve, in case I get lucky."

Nature gave us reptile brains for a reason. I was slow

to use mine. My dad, for example, was a family joke because he was colorblind. Seeing him with unmatched socks was typical. But he had an uncanny ability to detect a dozen shades of beige or tan where normal-sighted people saw just one—a useful skill for primitive man hunting wild game in tall grass. The prickly sensation on my neck told me I had made one huge mistake coming out here with Marty this Saturday morning.

Swiveling my neck at the right moment, I glimpsed Marty with the bat upraised looming right over me. Trying to keep his feet steady in the rolling boat cost him a valuable second that saved my life. His face became a mask of pure rage, nothing I'd ever seen before, eyes bulged to pig size, body tensed for a swing that would have split my skull open.

The meat end of the bat clipped the reel in my hands sending metal pieces flying. I had no time to worry about the pain shooting through my hands and arms because Marty's spit-flecked rage hadn't subsided with a single swing.

"Moth-er-FUCK-ing TRAI-tor!"

Nearly flat on my back with my head almost hitting the underside of the transom doubler, his second strike slammed into the metal bridge where the painter bow eye was attached. The force of the blow dented it in half, cutting me in the forehead with a sliver of metal, opening a geyser of blood pouring into my eyes.

"You know I'm going to kill you, don't you?"

Hovering over me while I was pinned to the hull bottom, he measured me for the killing blow. Pure adrenalin saved me. I bucked up from the floor as he took a small step closer, like a boxer trying to plant his front foot between his opponent's, all to add torque to the coming blow.

Before he could level the bat, I planted both feet into his solar plexus and sent him stumbling backward, flopping onto the seat, but still holding the bat despite a hand that must have rung like bells from striking the metal stanchion instead of my head.

That Marty grin, like rictus—Marty going into combat, the big game on the line, entering the batter's box. Enjoying the moment before the kill. Me, the helpless prey.

"You shouldn't have fucked her—"

"Marty, Marty—wait! Think what you're fucking doing!"

"Motherfucker, I'm going to beat your brains into pulp, you white-trash fuck!"

I didn't waste another second trying to talk him down. I heaved myself up and went over the side. The ice-cold water was a brutal shock to every nerve in my body.

Years ago, I'd gone into the drink fully clothed. I stole a raft from a boat being scrapped in the harbor in the middle of the river on a sunny day. I nearly drowned. My clothes—just shorts, a tee shirt, and tennis shoes—dragged me down into the murky green water. This was worse, as though I had ankle and wrist weights attached.

Finally breaking the surface before my lungs burst, I started to swim for shore but seemed stuck in place, unmoving despite the strokes. Twisting my head behind to see where he was, it looked as though Marty were floating above the crests of the waves, magically walking over the waves, owing to the boat's invisibility from my angle. I bobbed like a cork. Intestinal-twisting fear motivated me to ignore the pain in my shoulder and keep muscling through the cold, dense water.

Behind me, the engine started with a sputtering roar. Waves pushed me under whenever I tried to turn my head to see where the boat was. Weighted down by heavy clothing and shoes, rolling waves pushed frothy water into my mouth every time I opened it to suck in air. I didn't have much time; it was drown or die from the churning propeller blades.

Kicking as hard as I could, I grabbed the water with cupped hands, still unable to make progress like one of those nightmares where you flee what's pursuing you but it's like running on a treadmill. Marty loomed closer, bigger than ever, every detail in his face exposed to my tunnel vision—his ugly grimace. Marty at the plate—my head the ball.

I dove under just as the boat bore down on me. Now, I couldn't go down fast enough. A bubbled, green rectangle appeared over my head an instant later. A green vortex of rotating blades that missed me by inches, meant to churn my face to spaghetti.

With the air left in my lungs, I swam underwater, kicking toward the shoreline. I followed the frothy spume of crashing waves guiding me. Every time I stroked for the surface to gulp air, Marty found me and aimed the boat at my head. He lost me circling—no reprieve, however. Finally, near exhaustion, I dog-paddled the rest of the way in, hoping the waves kept me from being spotted.

Closer to the pounding surf, I couldn't hear the engine until the boat was almost on top of me. Under once more, my hands clawed at the resistant water, pushing myself down, down.

I came up a final time to see the stern of the boat cutting a swathe, making another circle. Out of strength by that point, I was tempted to let the waters close over me—better that than getting run down by the propeller blades or having my head caved in by Marty's bat. I drifted into the surf where Marty wouldn't be able to negotiate the shallows without capsizing.

When I felt sandbar under my feet, I knew I was safe. The waves and gravity did the rest; the turbulent water pushed me the last few feet before the receding water could drag me backward. My eyes stung, my throat felt as if I'd swallowed fire, but the sound of waves breaking over the stones like BBs shot from a fire hose was the sweetest sound I heard in my life.

I lay panting, helpless as a rag doll, sobbing from exhaustion. West Virginians have a saying: A wounded dog is the most dangerous dog. I crawled for shelter in a patch of cattails at the base of the cliff. Their waving fronds beckoned like flags. I flopped on my belly and curled up, out of Marty's reach, breathing hard and gathering strength.

My limbs shook. My teeth started to chatter. Both bad signs: hypothermia. The blood rushed to my trunk. Getting to my feet, tormented by muscle fatigue in every limb, was the hardest thing I ever did.

No going up those sheer bluffs, a hundred feet straight up, no handholds even if I had strength to climb. The clay and siltstone of those cliffs would have crumbled like crackers in my fingers.

No choice but to follow the shoreline, one foot in front of the other. Some of the trek would require walking on sandy beach, some through knee- or waist-deep ice water. My legs felt as though lead weights had been attached.

To my left, a pitch-black terrain. People in the big houses overlooking the water couldn't see me if they looked over their decks. Lake Erie's crashing surf ensured my yelling couldn't be heard. I couldn't see a path through the foliage. The crescent moon appeared above the lip of the crimson Belt of Venus, my only light. No guiding stars. I walked, stumbled, fell to my knees, got up, put one foot in front of the other. Full night descended, the temperature dropped ten more degrees from what started as a chilly day. I stumbled on in my waterlogged shoes and wet clothes.

I barely traveled a half-mile in that condition. I thought I'd been walking all night and dawn would arrive any second. The feeling in my fingers and toes was long gone. I talked to myself, mainly to curse Marty. I noticed a firefly making small patterns in the blackness. Not a firefly, not this time of year—a tiny crimson light. Not a light: a cigarette tip. A smoker.

That smoker turned out to be a dancer. She'd just finished her set at Northtown's sleazy strip club and was enjoying a quick smoke in the parking lot when she spotted what she thought was an animal on all fours coming toward her from the beach below. She flicked her cigarette at the beast, went inside, told the manager and some customers. Two men—brothers, both drunk—decided to get their 30.06 deer rifles from the gun racks in their pickups and bag themselves a coyote.

A cop later told me later that one of the men had already sighted on me before his brother shoved the barrel up. "Ain't no fuckin' coyote, bro," he said; "that's a *got-damn* human *be-an*."

That quote got cleaned up in the *Herald-Tribune* the day after to this: "I said to Jim. 'Jimmy Don, hold your fire! I think that is a person out there.'" The brothers Sizemore testified at my trial—for the prosecution.

My bad luck with Marty was offset by, of all things, that dancer whose double-D bra size was much touted by the bar's patrons and which brought in three times the number of customers. If she hadn't seen me, or I her, I might have kept stumbling along the shoreline until I dropped. She might have been the draw that night, but when the brothers Sizemore dragged me through the front doors, each with an arm around my shoulder, I beat her for sheer eyeball attention.

My memory is still cloudy to this day. I picture being surrounded by drinkers and a trio of bottled-dye blondes in orange and yellow thongs, citrusy perfume wafting in my nostrils, and The Tubes' *She's a Beauty* blaring from scratchy wall speakers at ear-bleed decibels.

Someone inside the bar knew how to treat hypothermia, and I wasn't damaged by various arguments to the contrary proposed by a few drunks. After the ministering of my hands and feet, I was patched together, shoved into dry clothes that appeared from nowhere. I remember a dancer, not Miss Double Dee, coming into assist my numb fingers in the dancers' dressing room.

One of the Sizemore brothers greeted me when I walked out. "Ha, lucky you them girls cain't see your shriveled dick from that icy lake, bro, or you'd never get pussy again." When my speech returned without that slurry, lockjawed numbness, I asked them for a ride into town.

"Better have you a drink first, bud."

Someone poured me a shot, which I coughed up once the fiery liquid hit my gullet. Jimmy Don escorted me to his vehicle, gripping me by the triceps muscle as if I were blind instead of half-frozen. I rode "bitch"—little brother's expression—in a dinged-up, Ford dually truck littered with empties and wadded packs of Marlboros. By then, I was coherent enough to add a few details to my story of having gone fishing alone in skiff and got overturned when the motor stalled.

The brothers took the soggy twenties I handed them, and roared off. I stood in the street looking at Marty's house. His Dodge Challenger sat in the driveway behind Beth's Celica.

I looked in the windows but couldn't see anything. I rang the bell and knocked—nothing. Their neighbors would know I didn't belong by sight. Checking out the back of the house seemed as risky as what I decided to do. I picked up a decorative bench with a potted plant and tossed it through a porch window. I crawled through, calling out her name. No response—a quiet house, an immaculate house—not a dirty dish in the sink.

Going up the carpeted stairs to the upper floor, I headed down the hallway to the bedrooms.

Slapping at the wall for the light switch, I smelled it immediately—a coppery stench mixed with other, sharper odors. The light bloomed everything in that room into focus at once, searing the image into my brain. A room of red horror that'll remain stuck in my neocortex until I die.

What was left of Beth lay across the bed, although distinguishing legs from arms wasn't easy at first. Beth's face in the carnage couldn't be recognized. My brain struggled to make sense of what I was seeing. The amount of gore brought a sob into my throat. She was carved up. The walls and floor were spattered. Even the ceiling plaster was speckled with comets of cast-off blood where the weapon had been raised and plunged over and over. A clump of intestines tangled in a swirl of bed sheets was the final, hideous insult, and it sent me into the master bathroom to vomit up the whiskey I'd consumed. Wherever blood had pooled, it turned rusty at the perimeter. Marty killed her long before he picked me up. I thought of the bandage across his hand.

In a daze, I picked up the bloody filleting knife from the floor. I was still holding it in my hand, babbling nonsense, when the cops burst in, guns pointed, and threw me to the floor.

The pathologist was quoted as saying Beth had been almost "eviscerated"; he counted over 250 wounds, most post-mortem punctures but some slashes so deep they left jagged rips that exposed bones, ligaments, and tendons. At least twenty, he said, had penetrated through the body into the mattress.

Marty left me a message in the headboard: a Valentine's Day heart with an arrow bisecting it. Beth's and my initials carved inside.

Marty never came back. Investigators speculated I killed him, hid the body. Gossips who believed my version said he was out there living in hiding or else he died on Lake Erie.

I know better. Marty aimed his small boat toward Canada, knowing he couldn't make the trip across even if he survived the big waves. When his engine died, he'd have sat there alone in the cold black night thinking about what he'd done and what he'd failed to do.

Of all the things Marty was not known one for, "regret" tops the list. He weighed his options while the boat pitched near the shoreline where he tried to kill me. He understood he'd failed in the same way he understood he failed at the plate that day during the softball tournament, striking out at the plate—and probably with the same moral indifference. Then he calmly stepped over the side.

Cops wanted to arrest me for a double homicide. In the end, they had to settle for the stronger case and charged me with Beth's murder. Charges were added and dropped one by one as the evidence to convict came up short. I spent five months in the county jail until they released me because the D.A. finally admitted he didn't have enough evidence to convict in Beth's case, either. Just like TV, I was told not to leave town when they escorted me out the door to do a second perp walk for the cameras.

***

Northtown is still divided on my guilt. Marty had powerful friends who refuse to believe he could do something so vicious. Social media never stopped discussing it. I quit reading their posts as soon as I realized that people who had never spoken two words to me were psychoanalyzing me: "He envied Marty his wife" or "Marty befriended him, the white-trash scumbag." Strangers in public said they'll "fuck me up" if they ever saw me in public. Death threats online and in the mails haven't stopped. My car's been vandalized so often the police told me to "deal with it."

I keep my mouth shut, my head down, and don't leave the apartment much. I stopped drinking in the bars on Bridge Street because Marty's friends, and even some of Beth's relatives, are supposed to be waiting for an opportunity to jump me. It would be easier all around if I knocked back a few boilermakers and stepped out the door some dark night and let it happen. I miss Beth. My dreams are terrifying and last past the point of waking.

Deep down, I knew there was a collision coming between Marty and me. Maybe my guilt wanted it to happen. Could I have saved Beth? I still don't have an answer to the question Marty asked me that day in the boat: *When did it all go to shit?*

I doubt if I'll ever know.

Kettle Blowing

I once got into a lengthy argument at work over which of the Jurovat twins was worse. The loading dock boss I was talking to at the time said Tony, not Terry, could ride in the Shit-for-Brains parade every year. "They should name it for him," he told me. Sam Hathaway supervised both brothers for a month before they were transferred to the nightly cleaning crew where I work. He added, "Terry definitely belongs in there, but Tony, hell, he's the undisputed Grand Marshal." Anywhere else, those two Neanderthals would have been fired except for one outstanding fact: their uncle, Martin Jurovat, owned the plant.

I belong in that losers' parade myself. I've been arrested twice for narcotics possession, three times for DUI, and was sentenced by one of our more creative criminal court judges to stand on the busiest corner downtown on Main Street and Park for two weeks one summer holding up a sign that proclaimed to the world: *Sign Holder Lives in Thrall to Narcotics*, which I thought was just poetically vague enough to confuse some of my fellow citizens. Turned out, I was right: many passersby gave me an approving nod or a thumb's-up.

But it finally took one OD to make me see the error of my ways. When I came out of the stupor, a paramedic was leaning over me holding a syringe in one latex hand and a Naloxone kit in the other, not to mention six of my rubbernecking neighbors gawking at me as I lay nude in my driveway. Maybe it takes a druggie to understand another druggie's impulse to do Whack, tear off your clothes, and then decide taking a bag of garbage out of the kitchen is a great idea. The whole time, my downstairs neighbor and fellow druggie, Jerry Hollobeck, nodded off at the kitchen table. Jerry's a diehard "tipsy-flipper," all about Ecstasy and booze, a much safer routine than mine, which was combining fentanyl-laced heroin and PCP. It was time to quit, finally and forever, as we rehabilitated addicts love to say at our Nar-Anon meetings.

Fourteen weeks clean, taking it a day at a time, as alkies' love to say, I applied for work all over Northtown. I have a degree in journalism; however, nobody is hiring people with my record, so I took a shift at one of the few plastics factories still operating: Jurovat Plastics. Mine's the graveyard shift, the domain of the unskilled laboring class. The days when these factories worked three shifts and had sweetheart deals with the big automakers in Detroit are long gone. I make a dollar over minimum plus an extra dime per hour because it's the night shift.

Working nights blew up my daily routines as well as my body clock, that circadian rhythm that keeps body and mind in sync. After the second week on the job, I was stumbling around my tiny upstairs apartment on Tivision Avenue like a drunk in traffic mentally exhausted from sleep deprivation; simple tasks became difficult and little frustrations at work sent me over the edge. Drugs destroyed that peaceful world I used to live in. Now, trying to regain some sanity and order, I found myself entering a new phase of hell. What I thought would be a short stroll in sunlight turned into a long slog up a steep hill. But the day I sucker-punched one of the Jurovat twins, however, was the day I entered a new hell.

My take on Terry stems from the brief time he was told by a foreman to shadow me to learn how to "blow the kettle" at the correct times twice during our shift. The kettle is a massive, stainless-steel boiler filled with a powerful cleansing solution made with diluted hydrochloric acid. It sits on an iron deck of metal grating two stories above the factory floor, and when it's cooked to a specific temperature, I throw the lever that releases it in a gushing roar into sluices that carry it to a ductwork of channels that feed into pipes where residual chemicals can interfere with production and undermine the molding of large parts formed in huge open vats. Then workers wash out and hand-polish them. It guarantees we're maintaining a level of purity the automakers' engineers require for stress-testing and durability.

It wouldn't matter to me if we were making tacos and that hot, boiling shit was designed to clean out ovens. The thing is, you have to give the workers below a loud warning on the bell so they can scoot to the safety lines marked on the floor before that roiling cloud of burning steam heads their way.

Terry thought it would be fun to watch the workers below run like scalded sewer rats when he threw the switch to release the acid solution. I tried to stop him, but he said I'd "pull back a bloody stump" if I tried to reach for the warning bell.

I remember Terry holding on to the rail, laughing so hard he was doubled over. I glanced over the side in time to catch several workers running, all assholes and elbows, to get away from that dangerous cloud of hissing steam. High-pitched screams, roars, plenty of curses were directed upward at my station when everyone had made it to safety beyond the yellow lines painted on the floor.

The report said the bell's pull rope had rotted from the acid mist and the disconnected alarm failed for that reason. When I checked, I noticed scratch marks from a knife, not acid. Two of the crew missed days because their boots were soaked, which resulted in third-degree burns.

The twins found out a daytime shift supervisor was

going to rat them off, so they arranged an accident for him. That night, I overheard Tony say something about a jammed fan belt and walk off with an arm around the supervisor's shoulder. Ten minutes later, that very supervisor came into the breakroom where I was drinking a coffee. The man's eyes were glazed like a dead bird's. When he passed me, I saw why: his severed hand was clutched in his fist against the stump of his wrist.

Besides drag-racing fun with forklifts, the brothers harassed workers on the dayshift and tried to start fights with a few who thought they were taking on one brother, not two. They ogled and groped female workers, sent them crying into the lavatory, and often showed up drunk and stoned.

Their biggest caper should have alerted management to their darker intentions. The week Uncle Marty left for a vacation, the twins jimmied the lock on his house and set up a scene to fool the manager of the bank where the company did business. Tony wrapped his face and head in Ace bandages to disguise himself. Terry covered him under sheets so only his head peeked out. Terry called the banker and said his uncle had been in a terrible car accident and needed to transfer Jurovat's power of attorney, as well as its bank accounts, to his nephews.

As bizarre as it sounded, it almost worked. The manager made an appointment the following day and was met at the uncle's door by Terry in a pinstriped navy-blue suit and tie. The manager knew something wasn't right when "Uncle Marty" reached for the papers and exposed his arm. Tony had a sleeve tattoo that began with skeleton knuckle bones and extended with various designs and symbols to his bicep. Tony, being a natural southpaw, reached out with the wrong arm. By the time Uncle Marty returned from Hawaii, the twins had a story prepared—a harmless "prank," they claimed.

The way they ganged up reminded me of the raptors in *Jurassic Park:* all muscle mass, reptile cunning, and the same walnut-sized brains.

Evil has its own way of finding you out like water seeking its equilibrium. The brothers had never paid me much attention, other than a "Hey, you," or a "What the fuck're you lookin' at, fag?" A fact for which I was grateful. I was already tagged an ex-doper.

Eventually, though, it came to that point where it was heading all along. One night, I was at my worst—frazzled, worn down by insomnia, and diarrhea—and Tony stuck out a boot and tripped me as I walked past. I hit the deck hard. Normally, I'd have picked myself up and slunk off like a sheep. This time, I got up, turned around, and swung at his jaw.

Miracle of miracles, I missed the jaw, but my gloved fist struck him in the temple; he toppled sideways. I stood there gaping at him. Tony was an ugly streetfighter who bragged about his battles in shitkicker bars and parking lots all over the county. He and Terry couldn't drink at the same time in half of them because Tony was banned from the premises for his fighting.

What have I done? I thought.

I expected Terry to come blazing around the corner and kick the living shit out of me. Instead, he and a couple workers rushed over when they spotted Tony on the concrete.

"What the fuck happened here?" Terry roared.

"I don't know," I replied. "He just looked pale and suddenly fell over."

That was true. I omitted the part about throwing a punch.

"Get the fuck out of my way! You, call Nine-One-One! You stupid motherfuckers, don't just stand there!"

The ambulance came. Paramedics questioned Terry about a possible overdose which, given their sideline hobby, was a likely possibility. In the end, they decided not to use Narcan and whisked him off on a gurney and loaded him into the ambulance.

I was living on borrowed time.

I counted on a twenty-four-hour "grace period" before the twins struck. That seemed to be their *modus operandi* in past revenges. It wasn't much time, but it was enough to set things in motion.

I picked a time to act out my plan: morning shift change—no one paid attention to anyone else for the most part. I jumped on a tow motor and picked up a pallet of styrene barrels—*Nothing to see here, folks*—and drove it over to Building One near the loading dock. The plant safety meeting, a fifteen-minute mandatory farce, was scheduled for all workers that morning on the far side of Building Two. Some OSHA lackey would drone on, we'd all pretend to give a rat's ass about our fellow worker's safety, and we'd go back to our jobs with the same corner-cutting, me-first, fuck-you-too attitude as ever. So far, sweated labor was not living up to its promise of changing my life for the better. I was like everyone else waiting for the Grim Reaper in the form of cancer to harvest me. I'd be replaced by the next drone in line and leave as much of a memory behind as sticking my finger in a bucket of water and pulling it out. People wondered why I did drugs. I did drugs because it's fun compared to a piece-of-shit life.

Three minutes, Lord, I prayed. That was all I needed to remove one barrel from the pallet, swing it over to Jerry's pickup borrowed the night before and backed into the loading bay. I didn't even bother to tie the fucker down. I just had to get out of sight fast before the meeting broke up or some nosey-nellie foreman cruised by looking for some underling to holler at or ask what the fuck I'm doing with that barrel.

It rattled and banged around back there, but my luck held out because no cop spotted me driving with an unsecured load. I pulled into my driveway, drove around to the back of the two-story apartment to get out of sight in case the landlord swung by as was his custom. Knowing of my drug convictions, he made up one excuse after another to drop by to ensure I wasn't trashing his place in some drug-addled frenzy.

Sore and tired from work, I needed a shower, some chow, some sleep, but fear pumped adrenalin into me and jazzed me up too much to do anything but work on my plan. I drove to Walmart's and cleaned out their shelves on drinking glasses, metal and plastic buckets. Any kind, any size or color, whatever goofy slogans written on them—it didn't matter providing they could hold liquid.

The barrel wasn't going out of the pickup anytime soon, so I had to use my own vehicle. I packed the trunk, back seat, passenger seat, and every available space of my Jeep. I barely had room to shift gears and heard several glasses breaking inside the cardboard boxes on the way back.

I couldn't afford to be sloppy. I knew what the diluted solution I used in the big kettle could do. I just had to look at the raised bumps of scar tissue running down the insides of my arms like crisscrossing white worms if I needed a reminder. This, however, was the real McCoy: hydrochloric acid, undiluted.

It took hours, as I knew it would. When the barrel was empty enough to work it to the edge of the truck bed's gate, I woke Jerry up from his dope nod and asked him to help me lift it to the ground. We dragged it behind the garage out of sight. I'd deal with it later. I was panting like a dog, half-moons of sweat under my arms, my face perspiring, and my hands shaking with tremors. An image of powerful Tony lowering and raising a full barrel by his fingers alone sent an icy ripple of fear up my spine.

"What the fuck are you snorting, man?" Jerry asked me.

"Nothing, man, I swear," I replied.

"Yeah, right. Pull this leg," he said; "it's got the bells on it."

I gave him a twenty for the loan of his pickup and a hundred to "fuck off" for the night.

"Where am I supposed to go?"

"Trust me, buddy," I said. "You do not want to be in your apartment on this night."

He rode off, convinced I wasn't sharing my stash. He said he needed to take a piss and then left in his truck. He was convinced I wasn't just back to using, I must be cooking up there in one of those quickie Beavis-and-Butthead methods where the cooks blow themselves to smithereens or die from the gas fumes.

So be it. It was my life I was concerned about, not my ragtag reputation.

It was already late afternoon. I had to clean up, eat, get some sleep, and get ready for my night visitors, those twin terrors who were out there somewhere like a pair of nomad lions on the prowl in the Serengeti.

The expression "sleeping with one eye open" isn't a joke. It doesn't permit much sleep, either, although I managed a few winks. Every strange noise jolted me upright in bed, anxious, heart thumping. *Them—the twins… coming—*

The best time, I reckoned, would be close to shift change. They'd have a ready-made alibi: *We were at work, Officer, my brother'n me…*

One of my own crew mates would be strong-armed into supporting their alibi.

I checked my wristwatch a few dozen times, waiting in the dark, all the windows open for ventilation and to hear cars approaching from my end of Harbor Avenue. Fifteen minutes before I'd normally be leaving the apartment and heading down the steps out back, I heard the first sound. A step board groaned under someone's weight. I had visitors. Three more times, the slightest *creak* told me I was right. *They're coming*, I told myself. *Get ready*.

It seemed an hour passed but it could have been minutes. I was aware of the door opening by the lighter shade against the outside blackness. I'd been hunched at the end of the hallway dressed in gale-proof black raingear from the Army-Navy store downtown, a mountaineer's oxygen bottle and mask to keep the fumes from searing my lungs, and a pullover head mask with eyeholes. I was wrapped tight with masking tape at the wrists and ankles and clutching a Louisville slugger against my chest. I was cramped, frightened, my hearing pitched to hear a dog whistle.

Then another sound. A hand brushed the wall: one of them reaching for the light switch. The click was audible, loud as a pistol shot to my rarefied hearing.

An urgent whisper, one brother saying something to the other. It sounded like hisses. They'd seen my car in the driveway: I had to be inside.

I'd intentionally left a clear path between hallway and kitchen, three feet wide leading straight to me. I'd cut the power to my apartment hours ago. If they brought flashlights, they'd see everything, but I was counting on these morons swaggering right into my bedroom and jumping me while I lay prone in bed, helpless and unable to fight back.

This was the moment I needed discipline. I had trained myself to wait from my kettle job. Delay too long and the risk of explosion was increased. The top would blow off and I'd be spattered with hot acid solution. Throw the switch before the needle in the gauge was halfway into the red, and I'd send down an ineffective cleansing that wouldn't do the job. I'd be responsible for ruining an entire shift's work.

Come on, you lunks, I prayed in silence. *Keep coming.*

I sensed them before I saw them. They were creeping toward me, dressed in ninja black, only the whites of their eyeballs visible; their faces were smeared in night-black camo paint, and they lingered in the threshold separating the kitchen from the single-room living space of my apartment. Two big cats taking their bearings, sniffing out prey—me. From my vantage, the brothers looked like a single creature, a two-headed beast with four eyes; it was looking straight at me. My stomach heaved at the apparition.

One more step… one more step. I sent my telepathic message into the darkness and waited.

One of them, I don't know which brother, made the necessary step and tripped the wire I'd strung across the doorway; that stumble upended the two tin buckets on either side of the doorway and set everything into chaos.

"What the fuck's this shit?"

It would be cold like ice water—then it would burn like fire.

"Holy fuckin' Jesus, I'm burning!"

The hydrochloric acid from the buckets sloshed their pantlegs. I knew they'd most likely be wearing their steel-toe work boots, so it was crucial the buckets were triggered to set off the panic.

"Put the light on! Put the light on!"

Noises, stumbling, grunts—the panic part was happening as planned.

"I'll fuckin' kill… fucking burns! Terry, help me!"

Gotcha, Tony.

In seconds, Tony first and then Terry had moved away from "the acid-free zone," when I set up every glass, one at a time all around the apartment. Hundreds of glasses filled to the brim with deadly hydrochloric acid about six inches apart. Two men stomping around in the dark kicking over glass after glass, getting it on their clothes first, and then their bare hands, any exposed skin, was the ultimate goal. I heard something clatter to the floor—a knife from the sound of it.

How's it feel, boys, when the skin of your face melts, sloughing off like a month-old dead body dumped and decomposing in a river?

Screams that would shatter glass erupted—music to my ears—how can I describe the joy of witnessing through my imagination what was happening in the dark of my apartment?

Tony and Terry were doing the acid shuffle just feet away, running into each other like bulls, slamming their bodies into walls, both desperate to escape the fires consuming them, breaking even more glasses of acid in their terror.

It must have dawned on one of them what I'd done, the trap I'd set. The words *fuck* and *kill* were bellowed over and over in a sick kind of counterpoint to the other brother's cries, a wailing, howling symphony of pain. I shivered when the sound of acid being splashed around by kicking limbs on the floor reached my ears.

***

I can say now that I was satisfied with the plan I'd created. I remember standing, hefting the meat end of the slugger in my hands, thinking whether I should go after them and club them senseless, bash their brains in until they fell to the floor in a widening pool of spilled acid. Then, I'd restore the power to watch the acid eat their faces away.

In the end, I didn't have the stomach for the full

revenge. They slipped and slid on the acid-greased linoleum of my kitchen, still colliding into each other to get out the doorway like two clowns out of a circus Volkswagen. One or both fell down the steps. More howls like deranged wolves from the bottom of the steps. Curses, hurled back in the darkness, a car's engine starting—Terry's rebuilt Trans Am—and a final sound of gravel from the driveway rattling under the chassis as they sped off into the night.

  They made it to the hospital, somehow, half-blinded. Both brothers were air-flighted by a medical chopper to the burn unit at the Cleveland Clinic. They're still there. They'll be there for a long time, I'm told. The county prosecutor keeps my lawyer informed. Many reconstructive surgeries and skin grafts will be required. Years of pain lie ahead for both. Uncle Marty will be writing checks for a long time, too, I figure, but then, he had the opportunity to corral these monsters long ago and failed to do it. He bears as much responsibility as I do for their transformation into a pair of crippled, hideous freaks.

  I'm out on bail, a very lenient one considering the damage done to the apartment, which amounted to thousands in damage as the entire upper floor had to be ripped out and replaced. Jerry's pissed at me because his apartment was damaged. "My kitchen looks like a set from the fuckin' *Alien* movie when the acid blood dripped through the spaceship."

  My lawyer says the photos they took at the hospital will garner sympathy despite the fact the brothers are well known in Northtown. Not to worry, he says, because they've hurt too many people and done, as he says, dropping the legal jargon, "way too much negative shit." That gives me encouragement. The trial's a long way off, not on the docket until September, and they'll have time to upgrade the charges to attempted voluntary manslaughter if they choose. My lawyer's worried about the judge changing venue after *voir dire* if the publicity works against us.

I'm not worried about that, however. I'm at peace with myself. Revenge, as they say, is sweet. I'm jobless and on welfare but I'm making a few bucks under the table doing construction work and odd jobs around town. People know me differently now.

I've rediscovered my early zeal for journalism. I sold the story of the twins for twenty dollars under the *nom de plume* Freddie Bardamu to a website that publishes "gruesome tales of revenge."

I've picked up a new bad habit lately: vaping. That scented smoke reminds me of the steam billowing from the kettle when I pulled the release valve. That's where I got my idea for revenge, in that glimpse of legs running from a cloud of acid smoke, Terry beside me howling like a baboon. The piss tests don't scare as they did when I was using. I've learned something about myself. Neanderthal DNA is inside my cells, too. You can't go back from that.

A Civilized Man

What is a civilized man? A friend of mine told me it's someone who steps out the shower to take a piss. Maybe that's all there is to it.

When I think of the polite "warfare" of chess, I think of my dead fiancée's words. They ring in my head like a smoke alarm going off in the middle of the night.

She won all the time. Our ritual before my inevitable checkmate was for her to pause and say, "I'll kill you for that move" or "You know I'm going to kill you now, right?" Or "I'm gonna kill you for that, babe."

Her spatial sense was a gift. I loved the game for her sake, watching her mentally focus, see the board in her head and then zero in on my weak attack or defense like an owl plunging from a branch onto a field mouse. Those expressions she polished me off with rarely varied and were never said with malice.

That last time we played, I tried the London opening for the first time. That was when she complained of the headache. But I might as well have opened with Fool's Mate because she clobbered me in six moves and then got up, saying she was going to run down to the pharmacy for some aspirin and would be back in "a few minutes."

Why didn't I go for her? Was I sulking because I thought I had half a chance since she had a headache or because I studied some online gambits?

It wasn't that late. That pharmacy was a mile from my house close to a busy intersection we call Five Points in Northtown. Two males abducted her in the parking lot when she came out. CCTV cameras caught them in a blitz-attack before she could get into her car. The tape was grainy, and they wore bandannas over the faces with ballcaps pulled low. One black, one white according to Det. Sgt. Joe Hawley, the lead detective. Both young, twenties to early thirties, both slender despite the baggy clothing they wore to disguise themselves. Cops found the plastic, single-use bag with the aspirin and the receipt still inside around dawn. Everything, even the plastic bag, was dusted for prints but came up empty.

I had wasted an hour in the precinct talking to a desk sergeant on duty who told me to come back in the morning to file a "missing persons" report. He said my wife was an adult; adults in America are entitled to go missing if they so choose. The smirk told me he'd heard similar stories of missing spouses and girlfriends before—a wife skipping off to a late-night liaison with a lover.

"If she doesn't turn up in a couple hours," he said; "come back and we'll get right on it."

My stomach was so full of acid that I nearly heaved in the police station lot.

She did turn up—two weeks later. She was beaten, stabbed, and strangled to death.

Her killers had dumped her in some weeds near a jogging trail off Tannery Hill Road less than a mile from the pharmacy. At first, I tried to block the awful images from my head: me, a bewildered look on my face, wandering around under the lights of the pharmacy parking lot, feeling sick and hopeless, looking at streams of cars speeding past from the row of traffic lights.

Normal life, a calm evening in late spring. People living their normal lives. Just me left to wonder what happened—*where could María Victoria have gone that she would not come right home?*

The cops worked the case but had no leads. Any clues at "the crime scene" were obliterated by the heat and the thunderstorms since. Her body was in an advanced state of decomposition. Animals had been at her. The flesh of her face was chewed away. An opossum family had burrowed into the intestinal tract. Any DNA under her fingernails was too degenerated for testing. The skin was either "soapy" or blackened. Bone nicks on her scapula and ribs told me she had died fighting hard. I insisted on seeing the report despite the detective's warning.

The case went cold. Nine months passed. My messages to the homicide bureau were passed on to Det. Hawley, but his return calls grew less frequent over time. He told me to wait for the "anniversary" of her murder and call the crime-beat reporter at the *North Coast Tribune* to do a story.

"It might generate some leads," he said.

I had a better idea.

I depleted my savings and checking accounts. I sold the second car, a vacation camper along with most of my camping and hunting gear. In two weeks, I had $60,000 to spread around.

The fact that the males were a mixed race gave me hope.

We have three areas in Northtown that could politely be described as "disadvantaged." Most residents would call them something less kind or politically correct. I laid out a grid for all three and determined how I would approach them. The first thing I did was purchase billboard space at east-west ends of the Five Points junction with a blow-up of an engagement photo of María Victoria and the $30,000 reward for finding her killer or killers right under it across the bottom.

I systematically canvassed three streets in the harbor that had been on the decline for a generation. I let it be known that an "arrest and conviction" would be "ideal," but

I would be satisfied with two names and "reasonable proof of guilt." I spoke to welfare mothers, idle males, teenagers with earbuds and cell phones, crackheads, and grandmothers left to raise small children when their mothers and fathers went off to prison. A young woman with a nose ring and purple hair stood in the doorway of her porch from which a sour effluvium of smells wafted out. She asked me if I'd be interested in buying "tango," Carfentanil—every zombie's drug of choice at the time. A powerful analgesic used on bears and elephants.

My next grid search took me to a blighted area downtown off Main Street near the low-income high rises where men and women of all ages were housed with the terrified elderly. These were citizens no employer would ever hire. That yielded several names, but nothing panned out. Everywhere I went, I paid for information, even when I suspected I was being scammed.

The final section was situated at the west end of Northtown and was by far the worst of the three. All these streets bore the names of presidents. More weeks of knocking on doors, sleeping in my car, alert for a black and white male duo. I learned where the party and dope houses were among those desolate streets where abandoned houses were planked over from drug raids and the graffiti of taggers declared gang allegiance, war on cops, whites, dissed one another's masculinity, mocked girls' names as "hoes" or advocated some kind of witless rebellion against life.

Around three a.m. on a Saturday night, a dented Toyota Avalon with a loud exhaust and missing hubcaps drove down Monroe, the worst street in a neighborhood where rapes, child murder, and domestic violence were common. The driver parked opposite me. I slunk low in the seat to avoid being seen. Two males—a light-skinned African-American and a bearded white male with a shaved head—got out and headed up the steps of a house where loud rap music was blaring through the walls. I had been to that house, too. At that time, I spoke to a tall black male with tattoos and a shaved head. He frowned when I handed him one of the cards I'd made up with my name cell phone number and the $30,000 figure on it.

With flashlight in hand, I walked across the street, avoiding the cone of light from the lone streetlight at this end that still worked. I headed for their vehicle. Most of the houses were dark except for the one the two men entered and one next door. The sedan wasn't locked. I slipped into the back seat and flashed the beam low all around. I don't know what I was searching for or what I expected to find. Common sense said to note the car's tags, give it along with a description of the males and the address of the house to Det. Hawley.

The back was littered with fast-food wrappers and empty cans of beer and plastic water bottles. It smelt bad: a reek of sweat and cologne, other odors like spoiled onions or unwashed clothing. My light's beam bounced off it at once where it lay under the driver's seat. My eyes flooded with tears as soon as I held it in my hand. Her engagement ring. We'd met in college. She was studying physics, and I'd given it to her in the Philippines on the day I asked her parents for their daughter's hand in marriage. She'd managed to remove it in the struggle and either shove it or kick under the seat before being subdued. I placed the ring in my pocket and got out, crouching behind the rear wheel, trying to decide my next move.

A door slammed. I peered through the windshield to see them coming out at a trot. They must have been told inside about my visit—or maybe they'd seen the card I'd left with the reward and decided they'd better become scarce. Money goes far in the ghetto despite all those "Bless you, young man" and "good luck" farewells from the devout grandmothers. My reward money talked louder.

My titanium flashlight was purchased in a specialty outfitter store for mountaineers and hikers in Melbourne. It's also a club. The black male hopped in the front passenger seat. As soon as the white male went around to the driver's side, I moved up from the curbside behind the fender and swung at his head just as his hand reached for the door latch.

His companion didn't hear anything because he was too busy fiddling with the radio. Moving low, I raced around to his side and waited for him to get out. Time stretched absurdly. I had tunnel vision. I was a Neanderthal with a club waiting for my prey to move from its hiding place. Fragments of guttural rap poured out of the vehicle and into the calm night air; the words *fuck, bitch,* and *kill* crescendoing around me.

His head out the window. "Yo, Jess… Jess! Where da fuck you at, man? C'mon, motherfucker, let's go!"

The door opened, and he got out. Before he straightened up to his full height, I pounced and swung my flashlight. His reflexes deflected the blow. Instead of cracking him across the temple where I aimed, my swing hit him in the face. He howled, fell back inside the car, his nose a spouting geyser of blood. He tried to scramble backward to the driver's side. I slammed the flashlight on his kneecap. By then, adrenalin was surging through both of us. He grunted, growling animal sounds and tried to evade my next swing, his head well out of range.

Instinctively, I grabbed the fabric of his pants at the crotch and squeezed my hand into a fist. I jerked him out of the car, and he flopped on his back on the lawn. He raised his arms to ward off my swings. I clubbed at his hands and forearms, battering my way clear to a head shot. He ignored the pain. I missed and kept missing while he twisted away from my blows. Finally, I clipped him on the chin with enough force to knock him out cold.

Lights were coming on in the party house and the one next door. I heard a door opening. Shouts, unintelligible words coming from both directions. I concentrated on one thing: sprinting to my car, swinging parallel to theirs, hauling the dead weight of two unconscious males into my trunk, all the while panting and wheezing. As I used my shoulder to pile one body on top of the other, a bullet sizzled the air next to my right ear. Another *thunk*ed into the fender. I never heard the shots.

With the lid flipped open, I hopped in and gunned it up the street, stopping only for a few seconds at the intersection of Monroe and Main to get out to shove in a leg of one and an arm of another to close the trunk—a clownish spectacle, if anyone had witnessed. I was conscious of myself but thoughtless at the same time, my brain on autopilot.

I drove down to the gulf near the jogging path where my beloved was brutally assaulted and murdered. In the dark, I had to guess where the spot was. The crime-scene tape was long gone. I parked in a dense thicket of stunted weeds and tall grasses oblivious to the likelihood of being stuck.

Groaning from the trunk. With my "club" raised, I opened it.

Grabbing the black male first under the shoulders, I lifted him out and laid him on the grass. I heaved and pulled at the white male, whose body seemed to be part-concrete, part-elastic. I wasn't sure I'd killed him with that one vicious blow. Whatever part of my reptile brain I'd activated, I hadn't come all the way around to abandoning the civilized part.

Wiping the flashlight free of blood and sweat, I positioned myself above each man's head. I struck down with a measured blow. Then again. Before I knew it, I rained blows on each man's head, spouting a rant of insane gibberish, vile obscenities discharged like mucous from my mouth, filthy expressions I had never used in my life, putrid and ugly words that spewed out of my mouth. I clubbed and kept swinging, the thwack of the blows created a hideous rhythm of its own. Obscenities interspersed with the sound of human heads being destroyed until nothing was left but pulp. My arm ached, but I kept swinging. I pounded teeth out of jaws and split mandibles apart. No one, not their mothers, or whatever women they fornicated with could recognize them. A shotgun in their mouths would have done less damage.

Exhausted, sobbing, I fell down into the grass, my sodden flashlight still gripped in my hand despite the bits of bone and flesh adhering to it.

The three-corner turn must have been done with that lower part of the human brain, the one beneath the neocortex because I don't remember getting in, starting the car, or driving home other than blurred images of streets and familiar buildings I passed.

My bruised hands and sore fingers peeled off the clothes as I walked up the steps of my house to shower off the blood. I crawled into bed and fell asleep for two days.

I was vacuuming the carpets, looking for blood stains, when Detective Hawley called to tell me two bodies were found in the gulf near María Victoria's crime scene.

He wanted me to come down to the precinct. I told him to go fuck himself. I'd never said that to anyone in my life—at least not without holding a weaponized flashlight in my hand.

The cops know I did it. They're building a case. It's been weeks. The crime-beat reporter for the *Tribune* called for an interview. He wouldn't say how he got my name or why he wanted to talk to me about the two "unsolved crimes in the gulf." He got the same message as Det. Hawley.

My passport hasn't been blocked, although I'm noted as "a person of interest." Maybe I'll stay and see it through. María Victoria would want me to. It's odd that I feel no guilt or shame.

Quite the opposite. I feel... *pleased*, if that's the right word.

Would I still consider myself a civilized man? That depends on your definition of "civilized," doesn't it?

Home for the Funeral

The semi-lit reception room of the funeral home was standard Victorian-era décor down to the lamps with frilled borders on the side tables—a time warp, John thought. He hadn't worn a suit in decades. Some mourners he remembered, most he didn't. Murmurs of greetings or condolences erupted in pockets around the room. Not much mourning going on, John thought, which was no surprise either, considering who lay in the casket.

"Said hello to our stepmom yet?"

His sister, creeping up from behind, just as she used to when they were teens.

"You're funny as a rubber crutch, Miriam."

"She's looking at you now—see her? She's wondering what the prodigal son is doing at her husband's wake."

"Let her wonder, the pig."

"My, my," Miriam said. "I didn't know you carried grudges this long. You haven't been back in—"

"Can it, Miriam," John replied. "You don't like me, I don't like you. Neither of us likes that lap-dancing tart he married."

Miriam ignored the rebuke, nodding. "You'd think she'd find something less revealing to wear. After all, this is supposed to be a solemn ceremony—*boo-hoo*. So why *are* you here, John, as if I didn't know?"

"Tell me, has that lazy slob you married found work yet or are you still supporting him?"

Miriam shrugged, a reply unworthy of rebuttal. John didn't care.

"Look at her, she can't keep her eyes off you. Maybe

she's looking for her next ex-husband," Miriam said.

A heavy-set woman behind them made distressing noise in her throat. John turned and received a scowl from her; she wore a navy-blue shawl wrapped around her throat like an Elizabethan ruff.

"Who's she?"

"Dad's lawyer's wife. You don't remember? God, they came over to the house every Wednesdays for bridge for years."

"She put on weight," John said. "I almost didn't recognize *you*."

"I told the children their Uncle John was dead, rotting in some Brazilian jungle chasing after diamonds."

"Not diamonds. Tourmalines. You have kids?"

"You're totally disgusting," Miriam said. "You plan on coming to the house after? Nikki and her brood are living there now. She moved in after the divorce before Mom got sick. You couldn't dynamite her out of there now."

"Where's the rest of it, Miriam?"

Miriam snorted. "You come right to the point, don't you?"

"Some hidden drawer in an antique desk, somewhere."

"You heard of safety-deposit boxes, right?"

"No way," John said, "not him. He wouldn't have wanted her to have them. He hid them somewhere."

"Her being… Mom?" …

"No, idiot. That dyed-blonde tart in black with the boobs hanging to her knees."

"If that's the case, Nikki has them by now. Don't you think she'd have torn the house apart after Mom died?"

"Nikki could find her ass with both hands and a mirror. See you around, Sis."

"God, I hope not. Go back to your jungle, loser."

***

When you hate someone as much as John did, you learn everything about that person. He studied his father up close and from afar the way Nelson Mandela studied Afrikaans on Robben Island. You want to defeat your enemy, you learn his language. John's father's language was money—money in every denomination from dollars to the Ugandan shilling. He could recite the values of the world's currencies to the dollar in an eye blink. John tested his father with the Thai Bhat. His father responded with a figure involving three numbers after the decimal point. John told him he was wrong—"off by point-oh-two percentage points."

"That was yesterday's number," his father had replied. *"Check the forex tables for today."*

His father was correct.

But by the time he was seventeen, his life went up in smoke—literally. By his eighteenth birthday, his father kicked him out of the house for smoking weed. By then, he was crashing on friends' couches and selling "candy blunts"—marijuana blunts dipped in cough syrup—to high schoolers to support himself. He never went home again—not until the funeral.

John heard from the executor when he was in São Paulo trading in his tourmalines from months in the field. His finds always kept him supplied for another expedition, but he never hit the motherlode because the big mining outfits squeezed out solo adventurers from the prime digging locations where the rarest of Paraiba's neon-blue tourmalines were to be found.

"I'm done impersonating a mole," he told the lawyer. His lungs were clogged with the white dust from digging in unsafe conditions.

"How much is my cut?"

"Nothing," the lawyer said. "Your father was very specific."

John figured out what his siblings had been left. He knew his father had shilled them all, especially the ex-lap dancer wife. His father's wealth was easily six times what the will stated.

Once his father's favorite, "a chip off the old block," as everyone said who saw them together, John knew his dad's thinking inside and out. His dad's wrath was aimed at his drug use, not him, and when John refused to accept a dime for college tuition and went sailing as a deckhand on the Great Lakes, his father cut off all contact with him.

He drove to the cement-block bar outside the township where his stepmother used to dance. The sign out front proclaimed DANC RS EV RY NITE, its missing letters like his stepmother's mouth until the old man paid for a fancy set of new choppers.

He drank rum-and-Cokes, one after the other, and thought it out. At twenty past two in the morning, as the bulked-up, tattooed bartender brought him another drink, saying, "Last one, we're closing," John finally *knew*.

His father left a message only he understood when he left him out of the will. The money was *there*, by God, there and waiting—if he had the guts to get it.

"You're drunk, man," the bartender said. He leaned toward John, deltoids bunched. "Hit the road."

John flew off the bar stool. He drove fast to the cemetery and used a tire iron to pop the latch on the tool shed.

With a full moon to assist, John trotted to the fresh grave using the cover of a stand of birch trees.

Digging through fresh dirt was easier than what he'd been doing in Paraiba looking for gems; after a couple hours, filthy and sweating through his clothes, he jammed the shovel's blade into the lip of the coffin. Pressing with his weight, he popped it open at the seam.

His father's face was bathed in the moon's saffron light; it transformed his dead expression into a knowing grimace. John knew the look well—his old man's expression every time he studied the financial section of the newspapers.

John braced himself for the task ahead. He felt all around his father's body, starting from his shoulders and moving down. Embalming fluid had converted soft flesh into hard planking. Then his fingers touched something at the small of his father's lower back beneath the fabric of the burial suit.

He flipped his father over and pulled up the split suitcoat, ripped the back of the shirt open and found it—a synthetic sheet wrapped to conform to the body like the neoprene of a wet suit. The white edge of folded papers caught his eye in the moonlight. Delicately, like a surgeon removing a tumor, John removed them from their protective covering.

Too dark to read but he knew exactly what they were. He counted ten bearer bonds. Better than cash. He rapidly calculated their value based on what was left to the family.

Without turning his father's corpse back over or shutting the coffin lid, he reburied the grave.

Thought you'd take it with you, huh?

***

He passed the last sign heading out of town. John relaxed, feeling like a knight errant who'd passed his test—slain the dragon, saved the damsel in distress, conquered his enemy. The dawn breeze streamed over him. He smiled, thinking: *The books got it wrong. You can go home again.*

Easy Money

Stevie Malone and I grew up across the Hudson from New York City. We used to drive out dates down to De la Torma Park by the river, watch the New York skyline glittering like millions of fireflies in the dark and brag about the things we'd do after high school. His bedroom walls had foldouts of porn stars from *Juggs* and *Score*. My walls were decorated with sports cars — Lamborghinis everywhere: the Miura, the Murcielago, the Diablo, and my all-time favorite, the Countach Periscopo. Another wall of Ferraris: the 250 GTO, the F40 with its elegant Bizzarrini-designed bodywork, the 365 GT4 BB, the "Berlinetta Boxer."

    I went to work for a meat-packing plant that made deliveries into Manhattan. He forgot the things we said back then. I never did. The straight-and-narrow had no appeal to me. I helped myself to cargo which led to a felony conviction that sent me to Torture Island, better known as Riker's.

    Thanks to the Coronavirus, overcrowding, and my non-violent offense, I was given an early release. I took my experiences, including a five-inch scar around my neck from some guy's sharpened toothbrush, and a determination never to return, no matter if they did vote to close the place.

    Petey Gaetano called me the day after I got out and asked me to meet him in Soho.

"This your place, Spider?"

"This my place? Naw, a guy lets me borrow it when he's out of town. I feed his cats. Nobody's called me that in a long time."

    He got the nickname because he seemed to have eight eyes in his head, always looking around, nervous, never focusing on one thing at a time. I met Spider at an Irish wake in the Bowery years ago. He never did crime but he knew *beaucoup* criminals in and out of slammers all over the five boroughs.

I didn't ask if the drinks were provided by the friend. That first whiskey and beer chaser after years of no booze and starchy food tasted like an angel pissing on my tongue. A Dixie cup of pruno might cost two weeks' worth of snacks back on the island. The first swallow scorched a path down my esophagus.

Gaetano began talking. An old story. He knew someone who knew someone—that old story. The long and short was that a Latin Kings shotcaller was doing a bid for manslaughter and looking at serious time. He had contacts all over the city doing scores. "Dude's a regular clearinghouse for crimeys like you," Gaetano said. "He's looking for ex-cons willing to put in work for the LK."

"Steve Malone said you were doing OK, babe."

Gaetano called everyone "babe."

"You know the saying, 'Do the time, don't let the time do you.'"

"'Don't let the time…' Good old convict wisdom, huh, Sonny? I meant, you know, this."

Gaetano repeated everything you said, a human parrot. He mimed taking a drink.

"So why are we here, Petey?"

"Catching up on old times, maybe do business."

"What kind of business?"—as if I couldn't guess.

"What kind? The kind that puts money in your pocket, laddie."

"What's your cut?"

"No wasting time, huh? I like that."

He collected a "finder's fee" for recruiting; a percentage of the take was parceled out to addresses around

Brooklyn. These "associates" of gang members would funnel money where ordered and dribble a few bucks into the shotcaller's commissary account.

Fine by me, I told him. When my time got short, word got out in the yard to give me space. The shotcaller was grooming me, I figured, because cons will try to screw up your release date when you're doing "the short and shitty"—what it's called because you get jumpy during those last days, nerves get frayed, and diarrhea is one of the symptoms. Getting chalked up for dumb infractions prolongs your time. A con's idea of a joke, in other words.

"No strongarm," I told Petey; "I don't do gunpointing, no banks, no cowboy stuff."

He looked at me as if I'd asked if his grandmother was still into cannibalism.

"No way, babe! A child could do it," he said. "Easy-peasy."

I thought of all the guys back in Rikers, packed in like sardines, telling lies in the chow hall about how "easy" their crime should have been if it weren't for some rat, some unexpected glitch they didn't plan for. Nobody stays up after lights out in Rikers worrying about quark entanglement.

"You used to drive for Nolan Meats, the Bronx."

"Queens," I said.

That was before I sold frozen turkeys to an undercover cop.

"But you know how to drive big rigs, right?"

"A delivery truck."

"Whatever, same thing."

I'd always dreamed of gearing down a Porsche Carrera at my age.

He outlined it while he poured me a double shot of single malt.

"A truck heist," I repeated.

"Easy-peasy."

"I'll get you details. Meet me here Wednesday."

"Should I ask what's in it?"

"Fifty-five gallon drums of ammonia nitrate pellets," Petey replied. "A fertilizer bomb."

"You asshole."

Petey's idea of humor.

"You don't gotta know. Don't worry about it, neither. The driver's in on it. He's gonna leave it idling. You just climb in, shift the gears"—adding in a noise like worn-out brake pads for effect.

Then he mimicked hand-washing. "Done, like that. Five thou. Easy money, babe."

Everything's easy to guys who never do it. Besides "fuck you," "easy money" are the two most common words you'll hear at Rikers.

They say you lose ten-thousand brain cells with every sip of alcohol. Dwelling in that mystical cloud of booze fog where everything is all right with the world, I felt invincible.

"I'm in."

"Good," Petey said. He gave me a reassuring clap on the back. "You won't regret it."

That might be the other most common expression heard around Rikers.

***

Learning to shift an 18-speed transmission is like building an airplane while you're flying it. All standard shifting follows an H-pattern. If I could get it out of low without grinding the transmission, I'd be OK. New York streets were deserted. Tumbleweeds blew down Times Square.

No matter what the cargo, it was a guaranteed trip back to the island. Skip MCC—a bad enough hellhole with mold on the walls, bugs in the cells, and feces in the shower stalls—go straight to Rikers.

***

Five people on the bus to Soho wearing homemade facemasks. Petey had the shot glass ready for me when I knocked. I demanded a couple hundred front money. He told me the pick-up and drop-off spots.

"Why a shithole like Hunt's Point?"

"Who cares, Sonny?"

I was familiar with that section of the Bronx; it's all abandoned warehouses, a place full of street hookers and meth addicts before the virus, now as deserted as Manhattan.

"They got the precinct patrols timed out in that section," Petey told me, "so be on time. One more thing."

"Yeah?"

"Go easy on the booze, huh?"

I smiled with convict sincerity. "One day at a time, Petey, like they say."

Another cliché that never panned out when you were up against it.

The driver met me in front of my old house in Corona—the name a cruel reminder of some of the virus' worst damage since the lockdown. Kids, parents, and grandparents packed together in one house just like when I was a kid. Migrants who used to have low-paying jobs in the city moped around with panicky looks in their eyes. Food lines stretched around the block. I told the cabbie to take the Roosevelt Expressway and get off at the Broadway exit.

New York's streets deserted at rush hour—surreal.

I walked past the place and found an alleyway off 82nd Street where I could keep an eye on the back lot from the opposite end. A pint of Jim Beam kept me company. Some homeless people living under cardboard midway down the alley made snorting noises every now and then.

Gaetano could kiss my ass. I carried a go-bag with tools, including a pair of bolt cutters, and a map with my escape route highlighted. I wasn't going where he expected.

From my vantage, I could see the back lot where the eighteen-wheeler was sitting behind a fenced-off parking lot surrounded by apartment high-rises and a yellow-brick three-story with a loading dock.

I passed the time drinking, enjoying my buzz. Ten o'clock, a full moon—if you could see it—and I was half-blitzed. I hadn't eaten. Every time I popped my head out, I saw the same man on the loading dock. He could be an employee or he could be security.

I was close enough to hear the big diesel running. I'd made it to the cyclone fencing and snipped through the links to crawl under it.

Hours passed. When I didn't show at the drop-off spot in the Bronx, calls would be made.

I was warm from the booze but my limbs were cramping up in the night air. I couldn't see worth a tinker's damn. I watched the glow of a cigarette at the top of the arc as he inhaled. More minutes passed. Then the butt traced a crimson zigzag as he flicked it off the dock.

The go-bag slung over my shoulder, I broke from cover to the fencing and worked my way along it to the section I'd cut. I jammed my bag under and belly-crawled after it.

The lot's overhead lights made me visible to anyone standing on the dock. I ran to the cab, opened the door and flung my bag in. My legs gave out just as I hoisted myself up, lost my footing trying to get all the way in, and went down hard ass over teacup to the concrete. The air was knocked from my lungs. I wheezed, struggled to my feet. Red spots appeared in my vision. Too late to regret the whiskey, and too terrified to go back, I reached for the handle, adrenalin pumping.

A shout from behind: "Hey!"

I vaulted inside this time. My hand reached for the gear knob and I slammed it into what I hoped was first. A hellish noise, the truck lunged—and stalled out. All tunnel vision now, I turned the key, the semi bucked again, stalled out again. Sweating, I started the motor again, slammed the clutch to the floorboard and worked the shift until I felt it slip sideways in neutral.

Voices, more shouting. The side mirror showed people running toward me.

I slammed the gear shift into what was either going to be a low gear or the end of me when the gears meshed and the semi moved forward. I eased off the clutch and gave it gas. The noise and the shouting directed at me was pure pandemonium. I risked another gear and there was more speed. I almost took out an unmanned gatehouse and nearly sideswiped a row of parked cars.

Getting the feel of it, I gained speed with less grinding of gears. My heart hammered in my chest. Having room on the empty streets helped my confidence—that and the hour spent checking out online big-rig driving lessons. I held it to a steady speed, my knuckles white on the steering wheel and my eyes darting to the side mirrors for cops.

I knew from the second Gaetano gave me the Hunt's Point location, I was being set up. Toll booths have cameras. No way off an island without hitting one. The goods, whatever was in the back, would be my fuck-you money.

My route took me to the southeast of Queens down Lafayette to an abandoned textile factory where I planned to unload the cargo, a place I'd used before my Manhattan pinch. I'd done a recon before I met Gaetano on Wednesday;

it was exactly as I remembered it years ago. I'd unload, wipe down the cab, leave the semi close to the Bed-Stuy projects, and move the goods at leisure. Furs and hi-def TVs were easy. If what was behind me wasn't packed with cartons of pizza shells, I could start dreaming of owning a Lamborghini again.

The high-beams showed me the old cinder path beyond a cement-block foundation half-obscured in dockweed. I drove around to the back out of sight and reversed into the sloped loading bay. I cut the lights and engine, and sat back against the seat. My head pounded with tension and the onset of a hangover. My breathing slowed and the circulation in my aching hands returned to normal. I remembered Norwegian rats the size of housecats scampering about, their red eyes glowing at me in my flashlight beam.

Grabbing the flashlight and bolt cutters from my bag, I hopped out and went around to the back.

It took more time with the bolt cutters than I expected, and I was almost sobbing when I cut through the padlock. The door handle didn't open; it had a separate locking mechanism.

What the hell. I swung my beam over the floor of the factory and spotted broken chunks of concrete block with rebar sticking out. I smashed a couple blocks together and jerked the rebar free. I used it to pry the entire handle off.

Flinging the single panel door wide, a wave of chilled air hit me in the face. Please be high-end furs, not sides of beef or crates of lettuce…

My flashlight swept over racks of elongated objects crammed floor to ceiling all the way back. Maybe it was the headache, the dullness after so much anxiety, the booze fog still lingering. I wasn't thinking clearly and I couldn't see well enough to determine what the cargo was.

I worked my way down the center aisle between the stacks. Leather was also shipped in cold storage vans. Not like furs but less risk and much easier to unload to a fence.

Halfway down the truck, I stooped over one pile of these tarp bags and rubbed my hands along its surface trying to feel what was contained inside. My mind raced with possibilities—all but the obvious one.

My fingers touched metal—a zipper. Instinctively, still not registering, I tugged the zipper.

A white human face stared back up at me. Lower jaw wide open in rigor, milky eyes unseeing, yet staring into my flashlight.

The odor walloped me like a kick to the nuts, blasting up my nostrils into my brain. I doubled over, spewing the contents of my stomach, mostly undigested liquor, all of it adding to the reek.

Body bags—a morgue truck. I stole a hospital morgue truck full of corpses—

The shock made me reel backwards in horror. I dropped my flashlight and stumbled against a metal framework attached to one side and collapsed it, body bags tumbled off the rack, one hitting me in the shoulder and propelling me forward into the opened body bag.

In the blackness, I flung my hand out and did the very thing I tried to avoid: my hand slammed into the dead face, raking my fingers over the teeth, slicing a long gash along the palm, accompanied by the sound of a twig snapping—my wrist.

I grabbed my wounded hand tight against my chest, blood flowing down my shirt, and picked myself up. Dizzy, nauseated, I made my way toward the door. My mind was shutting down, terror oozed from every pore.

Coronavirus... dead bodies... infection—

I groped toward the door feeling my way like a blind

man at the bottom of a mine shaft. My foot banged into the door. I felt around for an inside handle—nothing. I got down on all fours and felt for the hold-back designed to keep swinging doors from closing shut. I found the door's hold-back and its protection plate lying on the floor, snapped off at the welding joint.

Sick with panic, I slapped at the door, screaming with all my might: "Out! Let me out!"

Exhausted, I fell back. It was as if a switch had been thrown in my brain. I remembered nothing, seeing only blackness in front of my own unseeing eyes.

***

They told me later I was trapped in there with 38 Covid-19 victims for twenty-six hours. Some taggers with spray cans heard moaning inside. They said I was slumped against it, gibbering through cracked lips like a lunatic.

Six fingers and four toes had to be amputated. I woke up from surgery long enough to see I was bandaged and restrained to the bed rails. An exhausted surgeon in protective garb and face shield stopped by to tell me I was positive for Covid-19 and would remain in quarantine until I recovered—or not, he said, disgust in his voice, and went on with his rounds.

When I woke up again, a chubby detective in full-body PPE sat beside my bed. He looked gleeful behind the plastic shield.

"You're a big joke at the Two-Five," he said, the smile widening. "Doc out there says them little Coronaviruses can infect either lobe of your brain, some mumbo-jumbo about a half-life of decay. Depends, he says, where the viruses landed while youse in that truck wrestling around with dead bodies for two days—not that you have much of a brain to lose, I told him. My, my, Sonny. What the hell were you thinking?"

He laughed. A puff of condensation misted over the plastic hole where his mouth was.

"How much does a corpse go for nowadays, I wonder."

Too groggy from the anesthetic to tell him where to put his jokes.

"Youse s'posed to grab the semi in the next parking lot over, dummy. Some hedge-fund manager on the Eastside bought himself a couple pricey sportscars. A McLaren FL—never heard of it, did you? Thing tops out at 240, they say. The other's a Testarossa F50. Candy-apple red, got these nostrils and wings, a real Italian beauty…"

His Bronx honk is a fingernail swiped down a blackboard. My lungs are filling with more fluid by the hour, slowly suffocating me. That TV image of the Coronavirus with its spiky red tendrils is burned into my brain where I see them roaming, replicating. I imagine them clamped onto my lung and brain cells like climbers wearing crampons. The cop drones on, adding to my torture, relishing my suffering. I'd give anything right now to be back in my cell on Rikers…

I close my eyes, seeing swollen body bags bursting in the darkness, covering me with slime. One bag looks out with my own face, stares with my own dead eyes.

A nurse beckons him from the window and points at her wrist: time to go. The cop stares down at me, thrusts home the *coup de grâce*: "Yeah, real classics, those babies in that other semi, worth about five million each…"

Barn Find

I'm a railroad cargo pilferage specialist by trade. That's not what you might think. I tell people that to stop them from getting too curious about the source of my cash. To be blunt, I steal from railroads, in fact, which is no big deal because anybody with bolt cutters, a crowbar, and a little testosterone can do it. It ain't rocket science, trust me. I've been doing it a long time.

But a little good luck never hurts anybody. I've cracked open more boxcars loaded with generic dog food and cases of ketchup than Nintendo Wii stations or plasma TVs I can fence in a hurry.

My union steward gave me the news I was laid off and not likely to be hired on again. Somebody dug into my record and discovered a conviction for possession of weed shortly after I turned eighteen. I was screwed from a union job from then on. You can say I let my bitterness get the best of me to go stealing from my former employer.

Shortly after I lost my job, my girlfriend Carla dumped me for a sugar daddy. But she let me know she wouldn't be opposed to an occasional afternoon quickie while he was out as long as I was discreet.

"Baby, you know me," I told her, already stiffening. "You'll find my name next to *discreet* in the dictionary."

Two days later, she called me up and then immediately called me back to cancel. I was curious, so I drove over to her apartments and sat in the parking lot. *Maybe she had a better offer*, I thought. I'd met Carla in a country-western bar on Johnnycake Road. The night I picked her up, the bartender who brought over the drink I bought her winked at me on the way back down the bar. He might as well have shouted "sure thing" in my ear. I found out later Carla wasn't famous for fidelity.

Sitting there like a sleazy gumshoe, I wondered what I was doing. People came and went from the glass doors. Oldsters with Q-tip hair shuffled along with canes and walkers as if they were trying to stay a step ahead of the Grim Reaper. Very few looked to be Carla's age but every person who passed by me looked to have money. The lot was jammed with expensive SUVs.

I was just about to call off my surveillance and go home when I saw her step out with her new man. I wanted to laugh. He was a dumpy, pot-bellied, middle-aged man with silver hair in an expensive suit.

She giggled and slapped his hand away playfully when he put it on her rump. They got into a pearl Infiniti and drove off. Call me bored, horny, or simply curious, I followed the lovebirds.

They jumped on Interstate 90 going at a fast clip and merged with the stream of traffic heading for downtown Cleveland twenty miles west. Instead of heading downtown on East Ninth Street, the Infiniti stayed in the fast lane around Dead Man's Curve and headed past the ball park where the Guardians was playing a doubleheader with the Tigers. When they took the right lane for Interstate 71, I figured they were heading to the airport. Following a dozen cars behind, going an easy 60 m.p.h., I knew Carla could smell money the way a piranha knows blood is in the water. She was honest enough to tell me she'd made a mistake with me. I happened to be flush from a big score when we met, wearing my best suit at the bar. She assumed I was loaded.

Away from the big city, we hit a patch of countryside where developers hadn't taken over with strip malls and housing developments. A few derelict farms and wind-stunted apple trees in abandoned orchards separated the soybean fields that replaced the small farms of yesteryear.

They surprised me when they took the exit several miles from the airport. I stayed behind and watched as the Infiniti took a chewed-up asphalt road. They turned in at a modest Craftsman opposite some crappy farmhouses and a derelict trailer with plastic riding toys scattered about the front yard. I drove past the driveway, it being much too isolated out here to follow close. I took the next right a couple hundred yards ahead down a gravel road.

Pulling off to the side, I fetched my clothing and the hiker's boots. I keep an extra set of clothes and boots in a duffel bag in my trunk for emergencies—meaning idling boxcars stuck at a lonely siding. Say a sheriff's deputy swings past and wonders what I'm up to. I keep a bird book, field glasses, and a ledger with bird sightings handy. I've even memorized a dozen rare bird species in case I have to talk about my bird-watching hobby: *See, Officer, my Audubon Society alert mentioned a Louisiana waterthrush sighting here last week…*

I came out somewhere close to the backyard of the Craftsman where the grass required a brush hog to mow. Big, hump-backed old barn behind the house—good for cover. I made it in a fast trot. The boards were black with age. I moved a couple slats to peek inside, but the light was too dim.

Decision time. I'd been in tight situations in the Conrail yards before, once getting my truck stuck in mud after a bollixed three-corner turn with a load of microwaves in the bed.

Slipping inside was easy. The barn smelled of rotted hay and warm pigeon dung. Holes in the roof provided shafts of light. Rusted farm tools and old bikes hung from pegs on the walls. Other pieces of farming gear that had lost even antique value in the passing years.

My thief's instinct whispered to me because I sensed

it rather than saw it: a dusty tarp between stacked bales of hay. I climbed over and yanked a corner of the tarp. Insects I'd disturbed scurried off in all directions.

Holy Mother of God... She was gorgeous. Just sitting there waiting. Waiting for someone to find her—

A goddess waiting to be reborn. Red beneath a patina of dust. Wheels dry-rotted to the floor. Nonetheless, a big, gorgeous GTO.

I had to see the rest. I whipped off the tarp. The flurry of dust rose into the columns of sunlight streaming down. The sheer beauty lurking in that filthy barn made me speechless. I nodded with glee at that gorgeous "Coke-bottle" design and the kicked-up rear fenders. The owner had chosen well: a pillared coupe, the XS option of a factory Ram Air set-up, and the high-lift cam. I couldn't believe my eyes. Just a few dozen had ever been factory originals — and this was one.

Jumping Jesus... even the Strato bucket seats were intact, unaffected by time—

My eyes burned with the filth stirred into the air. I was on the verge of a mighty sneeze when I heard the barn door being jimmied. Shocked out of my trance, I threw the tarp over the car. No time to flee.

The loft ladder saved me. I scrambled up, my hands paying the price with dozens of wood slivers. I flattened my body to the floorboards and hoped my weight wouldn't come crashing down on the GTO. Luckily, they came inside talking among themselves: Sugar Daddy, Carla, and a woman I assumed to be the owner of the vehicle.

I lay unmoving for the entire hour they stood negotiating below. Insects found crevices and folds in my body. The itching was pure torture! I risked a peek at Carla looking bored. She held her arms across her chest, loathing the dirty surroundings, no doubt, and kicked at the straw with her calf-length boots. Her cleavage on display was my sole reward for lying so still. If she'd looked up, she'd have been staring right into my eyes peering at her. It took every ounce of my will power to hold that sneeze at bay.

From what I gleaned of their conversation, the woman was the sister of the original owner, a brother killed in the Afghan conflict. Carla's man had a gruff, overbearing voice in contrast to the woman's. I heard her say *cancer*. His barbered, silver head shone in that gloomy barn. I heard him say "agreed." Out came his checkbook.

When I heard the price, I almost gave myself away: $9,700.

For that diamond of a GTO classic… You thieving cocksucker, I thought. *You're worse than me.*

Watching him hand her that measly check, I made up my mind to steal that car.

El Cheapskate told her he'd arrange for a tow "tomorrow morning." That gave me little time. Four hours, max. One hour to get home, another to arrange my own transport, a third to get back here and a final hour to haul away "Princess." Tighter than a tick's ass.

They were no sooner out of earshot, heading back to the house, than Carla's old man started making small talk, knowing he'd just ripped off a woman with cancer.

I climbed down the ladder and sprinted through the weeds, running full tilt straight back to my own wheels.

I didn't stop to change and to hell with cops—

I hit the freeway, nearly spun out on the shoulder, and only slowed for a notorious three-mile stretch near Linndale where cops spot speeders like hyenas spot hamstrings. I have the position of every robot speed trap camera in this part of the state memorized. It's called "doing your homework" if you want to stay out of jail.

I made it back to the Craftsman twelve minutes

ahead of schedule with a rented tow truck. In fact, I was only just in time to see Sugar Daddy supervise the removal of Princess.

The gods can be cruel. *What happened to 'tomorrow morning, earliest,' you scumbag?*

My rental tow truck was parked on a parallel road where I could observe. Chunks and flaps of decayed rubber fell from the wheels as my poor baby was pulled an inch at a time up the ramp. It made the acid churn in my stomach. It was like watching a magnificent iridescent marlin caught with a grappling hook.

Don't damage it, you white-trash imbeciles…

***

Carla showed up at La Taverna on Johnnycake Road the next night. She came in unaccompanied by her dapper-haired welfare hump. I moved on her before some quiffhound moved on her. She saw me and smiled. Or maybe smirked. I almost hated her then. She walked with a jaunty stride, making the breasts sway and the blood of every male on the line of stools surge south of the beltline.

"Hey, you," Carla said, rubbing my arm.

"Hey, babe, what's up?"

"Not much."

She cast a meaningful look at my crotch.

Truth was, I didn't want sex. I wanted to know what Sugar Daddy was up to with his shiny new toy.

She didn't mention him for a long time despite my attempts to get her to talk.

Then she surprised me. Her pretty oval face transformed into what she thought was a gloomy expression by scrunching her facial muscles into a pose.

"He thinks I'm cheating on him."

"So what? He's married. He has no claim on you."

I took a sip of bourbon, hope welling in my chest.

"You don't know him."

"What don't I know, Carla?"

"He's capable of—"

"Capable of... what?"

"He's capable of... doing things."

Ye gods, forty-thousand years of the English language, twelve years of public school education and this was all she could manage.

When I began thieving, I reduced life to two basic points. Point number one being me in poverty. Point two being me lolling in a hammock, piña colada in hand, watching the sunset from an overwater bungalow in Bora Bora or somewhere just as fine. Working for a living on the docks in Cleveland got my old man dead at fifty-seven from bleeding ulcers.

We spoke of trivial things and drank but my mind constantly raced ahead, planning the next stage of liberating Princess from the grip of her swinish lover.

"You can't have real dreams here," she said.

"Where, sweetie?"

I was barely listening.

"This crappy state, 'the heart of America'—what a laugh," Carla said.

"That's because the brain is somewhere else."

Me, the tavern wit.

"How about a blow job?"

A few heads swiveled our way.

Decision time. Sex now could be risky, especially if Carla was being followed, which she seemed to think her aged boy-toy arranged whenever he was out of town. I decided to let Dickie and the Boys make the call.

She drove us to a cheap motel off Route 20 across

from one those endless strip malls that remind me you could be in any small town in America.

"What's wrong?" This after the rockets had gone off.

"Yesterday he threatened to kill me if I cheated on him." Her voice husky from fear, child-like, nothing like the shrieks and yelps she made during sex.

Thanks for telling me that now, I thought.

"Has he hit you?"

"No, no, he's never done that," she said "but—"

"—but what, Carla?"

"Never mind. What do you care anyway? Why don't you just fuck off!"

"Carla, you dumped me, as I clearly recall."

Women… Jesus H. Christ. Busting into freight cars is child's play compared to figuring them out.

We met again at La Taverna the next night. Carla was in a better mood. She told me "a muscle car from some shithole barn" was all her man wanted to talk about, how he was going to take her for a ride as soon as he had it fixed up.

Despite her happier mood, her eyes were big with fear. I'd already noticed the grab marks on her triceps. She'd troweled makeup on under one eye where the bruising showed through.

I should have been more sympathetic, but I had another woman in mind; I had eyes only for my Princess.

"Did he put new tires on it?"

I sipped my Tom Collins, holding my breath while I waited for her response.

"Those tires cost him a month's rent at my condo. He was on eBay all afternoon."

Music to my ears…

"Where is it now, the muscle car?"

"Some storage warehouse in the Flats."

We spent the night chatting about one thing or

another. She'd taken an Uber to the bar because Cheapo hadn't delivered on his promise to buy her a car. When I pulled into the parking lot of Carla's condo, she ducked her head into my lap, making me think Happy Time again. "Get us out of here NOW!"

"Carla, what the fuck?"

The dark blue SUV parked near the condo's entrance panicked her.

"That's Vinnie. He works for him!"

"Vinnie, huh?"

I wanted to laugh. That sounded like some old-time Collinwood hood from the Danny Greene-John Nardi days when Cleveland *mafioso* blew one another up in car bombs.

"If he sees you with me—"

I didn't have time for this jealous-boyfriend horseshit. I had to liberate my goddess, and it was going to be a busy day tomorrow. I was ditching Carla and my old life both, all of it going in the rearview mirror. I was Chicago-bound with Princess, just the two us.

Driving around just to humor her, I killed time. An hour later, I dropped her off at her condo.

Yeah, I'm a shitheel...

"You care about me, don't you, Roy?" From raving slut to frightened little girl in a split-second.

Like most men—*stupid* men—I assumed it was about the sex. I reached my hand between her legs to fondle the vertical smile with her nub of clitoris big as a baby's thumb.

"Things'll work out. You'll see."

You'll see me gone was what I thought.

Sugar Daddy's GTO was going to change ownership in less than a day.

***

By then, I knew Daddy-O's name, address, place of business, his warehouse's location, and even his wife's pet name for her Shar Pei. I called their house midmorning and said I was the assistant CFO from her husband's office and needed to contact him right away about "the Boyer contract." She said he was in Sandusky all day.

Let me be immodest here. I stole that GTO as easily as tying my shoes. Once I'd hotwired Princess, I savored the subdued rumble from her throat, then had her on the ramp and tied down in ten minutes flat.

Nothing to be done about my exposure to the CCTV cameras—my disguise would have to do, the bulky clothing, shades, and the facial hair disguise.

I drove us—Princess and me—to my apartment, patted her gleaming hood, covered her with a plastic tarp and told her I'd be right back. I took an Uber to the tow truck and paid off the rental fee, using one of my fake IDs. I'd already transferred my funds to a Chicago bank and packed what I planned to take.

Holding my speed to five miles under the limit, I reveled in the stares from passing cars.

Go ahead, stare, you mopes, I thought. *She's all mine.*

I found a place in a gentrified section downtown near the Magnificent Mile where all the action was and near all the action and couldn't wait to hit the club scene. I'm a fiend for deep house music spiced with a little Ex.

Life couldn't be better…

***

I was in such a hurry to get a key made for Princess that I postponed a thorough cleaning. A few days passed before I noticed a sweet, pungent odor coming from the vents. Maybe a field mouse or chipmunk had burrowed inside and died there.

Decomposition, all right—but not rodent.

Carla was quietly rotting away in several pieces wrapped in brown butcher's paper.

She had lain in the trunk the whole time I drove around Chicago. The key man, a couple coworkers, and several customers strolled over to eyeball the GTO. When I popped the trunk, Carla's head with milky, dead eyes stared into mine. My eyes took in the severed, maggot-infested limbs. I buckled at the knees, my hands gripping the edge of the trunk.

Someone called the cops. People hovered around taking videos and aiming their cell phones.

I could have run for it, but what would have been the point?

Fast-forward to my trial. I accepted the Alford plea my lawyer suggested. He told me the evidence was "compelling."

So there you have it: guilty but innocent.

They had me as the last person to see her alive on closed-circuit TV at the motel and gunning the engine at the parking lot of her condominium. The prosecutor sent the tape off to NASA where they developed the pixels to such accuracy you can see Carla's open mouth in what looks like a scream. My lawyer's investigator could not trace a "Vinnie" in any database.

Carla's old man was never indicted. At my trial, my lawyer used the old SODDI defense they teach in law school—you know, Some Other Dude Did It. He was exposed as a cheating spouse—that's all. The man had a trio of hot-shot trial lawyers on call just in case.

The best touch was my fingerprints on the crowbar used to batter Carla's brains out. If I had listened to what she was telling me about him, I might have seen it coming in time to save us both.

I should be grateful I'm not going to do my time in Joliet, where I'd be as helpless as a double-wide in Tornado Alley. I'm cooling my heels for the next fifteen years in a medium-security prison. Take away the razor wire and it looks like a college campus in a pasture. *A lover's quarrel, a jealous rage, they said. Sickening but happens all the time—*

My first parole hearing will arrive ten years into my sentence, and my lawyer said not to expect probation first time out. He assures me I'll be out in fifteen years. Fifteen years in Joliet Correctional.

"Think of it this way," he said; "you got away with a lot of stolen stuff over the years. Consider this payback."

Being a railroad thief doesn't carry weight in a penitentiary where your manhood is measured by violence. Being convicted for butchering a girl, on the other hand, opens me up to chin-checks in the yard and chow line. Only the "chomos"—child molesters— have it worse.

Last week I received a packet of photos mailed from a shipping address. Each one showed Princess gleaming in her full glory with a dozen coats of candy-apple-red paint. The engine and pipes were a shiny chrome luster that winked in the spotlight. She was polished to a high gloss and photographed under lights that showed her off to every advantage like some giraffe-legged Parisian model.

The one that hit me in the solar plexus was the last one in the pack. The trunk was featured in a close-up that brought out a tattoo designed under several layers of new paint and then more paint to bring it out under lighting. Carla's name in fluorescent, gothic lettering. Beneath that, a black rose dripped a single drop of crimson blood.

It's a gypsy tattoo. It curses the first one who sees it.

The One Who Saves You

Hughie Brown stared at the rat; the rat stared back at him. Each occupied a corner of the same dumpster. Hughie thought rats were supposed to have red eyes because of something he read in a book a long time back in college, long before his *Juris Doctor* degree. Maybe that was at night when they fluoresced like a cat's. This rat had matte-black eyes and whiskers that filtered the air continuously while it poked its nose into the surrounding trash. Hughie wondered how the rat made it into the dumpster because he'd been forced to dive through the open lid, scraping both thighs and tearing the tender flesh of his palms from a steel burr on the rim.

Fear gave him wings; he flew down that alley once his botched holdup became clear. Despite the fear of lockjaw (assuming he made it out of the dumpster without being cuffed by screaming cops), it was the only thing he'd done right that day since he handed the teller the note he'd labored on for an hour, crafting each block letter. He'd torn up a dozen drafts in fear that someone might identify his handwriting—*Yeah, that's exactly how Hubert Brown used to do his letter S's, some long-forgotten classmate said to the phantom cop…* His hand shook as he formed the wiggly block letters demanding "all the cash," even adding a hasty postscript: NO DYE PACKS OR ELSE!!!

The tripling of exclamation points pleased him. Both exclamatory and immature, his clever red herring. No self-respecting writer of lawyer briefs would ever use one, let alone three. As soon as the teller's eyes cut to the message he handed her, Hughie planned to flip open the flannel shirt to show the butt of the gun. With its pink-tipped barrel out of sight in his pants, as per law for all toy guns, she'd have only time to glance, not enough to tell it was a water pistol.

Instead of forking over the money, she calmly gazed at him and swiveled off her chair. Hughie watched her, his mouth agape, brain firing off a cascade of crackles. "Hey!" he shouted—except that came out in a choking gurgle. Amazingly, she returned with the manager beside her. Hughie noticed how the light picked up amber highlights in her hair.

"What is this about, sir?" the manager asked.

Hughie stared at the wavy pattern in his tie—and bolted for the door. His plan was to head for the parking lot where his battered Honda sat out of range of the bank's CCTV cameras.

Instead, he turned left, toward Capitol Hill, where he'd been hanging out with the rest of the street people, that sorry parade of *les misérables* looking to score drugs or cadge money from the few passersby foolish enough to wander Seattle's worst high-crime area.

Knowing he was too far to make it without being spotted by a passing cruiser, he turned into an alley separating a paperback bookstore and an out-of-business furniture store. As soon as he spotted the dumpster with two lids flipped open, he amazed himself with a one-handed vault. With the rat for company, he sat in an adrenalin-drained stupor amid the stench of rotten food, contemplating this disaster in his life.

It wasn't as though he robbed banks for a living. Hughie Brown did nothing for a living. As soon as he could con a friendly-looking caseworker into believing his story of "severe stenosis of the lower vertebrae," handing her the doctored MRI he'd bought in South Park from a junkie, he allowed the working taxpayers of Seattle to pick up the tab for his living expenses. Subsistence living wasn't what he'd planned, though. He also hadn't planned on a drug habit that sent him spiraling downward to join the masses of falling-down addicts and mentally deranged homeless existing between Pike and Pine Streets.

What cost Hughie his first real job at a reputable law firm six months ago was a joke—just a lousy, ill-timed joke at the office Halloween party. Two of his peers talked him into wearing a papier-mâché "toilet suit." Jake Roethlisberger from Wills & Estates and Donnie Coltrane from Torts, both aspiring partners, talked him into wearing it as a gag. His face daubed with pancake makeup and disguised behind a tower of toilet tissue rolls, he hunched down in one of the stalls in the women's lavatory waiting until his knees cramped. He nixed Donnie's plan to wear a Go-Pro headband to capture the moment, arguing he just got hired and didn't plan to wind up in a lawsuit.

"Stop wiggling," Jake commanded. "That plaster of Paris shit crumbles every time you move."

Hughie thought his knees would crack if he had to wait one more minute when he heard the restroom door open and footsteps cross the tile floor. The door to his stall opened and he heard a shuffling sound, clothing being pulled down. Before he knew it, he had a belowdecks view of Shirley Beamis, the office manager's broad, orange-skin-pitted ass cheeks and hairy cleft looming toward him. As soon as her nether quarters felt Hughie's lap, detected the seismic shift beneath her buttocks, she leapt to her feet, screaming, her cotton panties ripping apart in her haste to pull them up. Hughie, encumbered by his ridiculous costume, pieces half-stuck to various body parts as he emerged from the restroom, walked in grim silence down a gauntlet of withering scorn from the staff—Donnie and Jake predictably absent—as plaster lumps of his fake toilet dropped from him. Down the hall, he punched the elevator buttons in a fervor to escape, flee. He spent the weekend on his apology to Shirley and the entire firm, a wasted effort because his termination was hand-delivered in certified mail just as he left his apartment on Monday.

Ergo, his short-lived, second career as an impoverished and desperate stickup artist.

By around ten o'clock that evening, fatigued and famished but not wearing leg irons or doing a perp walk for the cameras as a disgraced former lawyer, he poked his head above the rim to see if hordes of police were poised to take him down. Just the pervasive stench of the alley. By then he was nose blind to the stench from the dumpster itself; his companion in ignominy long gone to wherever rats go when they've had their fill.

***

More desperate days later, he roamed about Capitol Hill when a pleasant-faced, young male in his mid-twenties with tattoos and a buzzcut asked him if he'd like to make a hundred bucks.

"I'm not gay," he replied.

He wasn't upset or even surprised by the man's offer. He'd had several bizarre offers before in this stretch between Pike and Pine Streets.

"A hundred bucks to fight this guy, an old bum."

The thought of money to buy food alerted his stomach juices; the man heard the gurgle from where he stood.

"Why me? You fight him."

"Ever heard of *Bum Fights*? A hundred busks cash to take a few swipes at this other bum—this other guy."

"How do you know I'm a citizen in distress?"

"You smell like dogshit. Your eyes are pissholes. I figure you can use the money."

THE ONE WHO SAVES YOU

"What's in it for you?"

"Clicks and eyeballs, homey. I video it with my smartphone, upload it to my *YouTube* channel."

The other guy — "a stoner, a geezer half your size and twice your age" — was waiting for them behind the Cal Anderson pool that night in a semi-circle of a dozen young men, all college-aged, none looking like the street people he'd jostled shoulders with since his abortive bank job. The old timer was everything the YouTuber said, and Hughie was starting to feel shame and pity for the decrepit old man until someone near him handed him a bill and shoved him out of the crowd's inner circle.

Another man stepped forward from behind the crowd. He looked fierce, and the sneer on his face said he couldn't wait to get the mayhem started.

Hughie looked around for the YouTuber, but he was nowhere to be seen, and Hughie himself was dazed by the hazy glare of so many cell phone lights shoved in his face. He noted the illuminated makeshift ring where the battle with the big man was to occur. The man's face expressed a sneer of contempt, waiting for the action to commence.

A Beretta Jetfire isn't a noisy gun, but when it goes off close by, the effect is as good as large-caliber weapon. The crowd dispersed in all directions. The last to run were the YouTuber and the ringer meant to beat Hughie to a bloody pulp for the sake of "clicks and eyeballs."

"Take off, motherfuckers!" the shrill voice shouted, "or I'll give you something real good to film!"

They left in the same direction, the bigger man making a show of taking his time.

The one who saved him was a girl—slim, dark clothing, tattoo sleeves, wild, unkempt hair.

"Come with me before those assholes change their minds."

"Do you know them?"

"Yeah," she said. "They look for stupid assholes like you. That guy, Rory. One of his bum fights left this homeless guy brain-dead. At least the guy's out of the weather and getting fed—from a tube."

"Gee, he said he does it for *YouTube*."

"You're dumber than a bag of dicks if you believed him. You might could put one on for a day, maybe two. He uploads all kinds of that gruesome shit to the dark web."

"Why don't the cops do something?"

"Are you out of your fucking mind? Seattle cops don't investigate *rapes* nowadays."

***

Her name was Jordan. She took him to her "home," a tent in a homeless encampment the cops left alone because it was out of sight of street traffic.

She brought him food. She found—stole, more likely, Hughie believed—a tube of Bactrim ointment for his infected hand. They ate soup together—some food pantry giveaways of outdated stock. She asked him for nothing and expected nothing back. She kept the .22 Jetfire on her all the time except when she slept, and then, it was tucked for easy reach under the sofa cushion she used for a pillow.

Jordan was an abused child abandoned to the streets by a junkie mother. She remembered a house in San Diego, but that was too many years back, she said. She never knew her father. Once they had to hightail it deeper into the brushy undergrowth when a camera crew with the KOMO News logo approached, looking for yet another sob story of the wasted lives of the residents of the encampment.

When he felt they'd shared enough confidences, he asked her how she survived. "What do you do for money?"

They were eating cold chicken soup out of cans.

"Anal sex," Jordan replied calmly.

Hughie sputtered, slobbered his soup.

"What's wrong?"

"Oh nothing," he said. *A few weeks ago, I was a newly minted lawyer. Now I'm talking to a street whore about anal sex…*

Little by little, she revealed that a clutch of pederasts met at certain places in the South Park district looking for male prostitutes. She charged fifty dollars apiece, dropped her pants and bent over.

"Doesn't it… hurt?"

"Hell, what these losers stick in there isn't as big as what comes out. I walked around with a banana up there when I decided to make money that way. That bother you, bank robber?"

The simpering way she called him that told him his attempt to make himself sound less like the halfwit amateur she thought he was sound like a reckless act of bravado had failed miserably. She used the computers at the public library and showed him the Xeroxed article captioned "Bank Heist Failed" in a small paragraph on page seven of the *Times*.

"Cops still lookin' for you?"

"I suppose," Hughie responded glumly, his embarrassment aggravated by the knowledge that the F.B.I. had jurisdiction over bank robberies, not an understaffed city police force—and they never forgot. If he wanted, he could have recited the criminal statute to her and the penalty, which started at twenty years in a federal prison, no "good time" or extra-day weekend like the state's penal system.

"You can always go back to law practice," she said. "Me, I got nothin'."

"I'm disbarred," he reminded her.

He flashed to Shirley Beamis' broad ass, the dimpled skin, the whispering sound of her cotton panties tearing in her attempt to flee the human toilet. Donnie and Jake both called him within a day of his termination being announced *sub rosa* to the firm's legal staff. Donnie told him Shirley was given a hefty "bonus" and asked to sign a non-disclosure agreement. "You fuckers ought to go down with me!" Hughie shouted to each one. Donnie wept and begged him "for the sake of my wife and children" to keep *stumm* about his own involvement. Jake was more stoic on the phone, but Hughie knew he'd just gotten engaged to a society girl, and the knowledge he'd been involved in this "sexualized prank," as one senior associate delicately put it, would wreck his pending marriage as well as his career. In the end, he agreed "to take one for the team," but he told Jake that, if he ever saw him or Donnie at a bar, he'd take his $400 Easton Ghost softball bat to his head.

Weeks passed. Hughie stopped thinking about his family at the apple farm in Western Washington. He slept all day sometimes, walking around the downtown at night, lost in the jumble of hustling addicts and nodding junkies asleep in front of stores or urinating in the street.

Jordan gave him a butterfly knife she admitted to stealing from an Army-Navy store. He tried to refuse it, but she became furious and threatened to gut him with it if he didn't keep it on him when he left their tent. Jarred from his usual state of numbed indifference, he finally agreed.

She cares about me…

That disturbed him throughout his rambling sojourn about the city that night and for a long while afterward.

A few days after that incident, Hughie contemplated how he was going to break the news to her. He found the only pay phone in the city that hadn't been removed or trashed. He called a distant cousin in Phoenix, who agreed to fetch him. He sobbed on the phone to a relative he barely knew.

"You've got to save me," he begged the man, who agreed to meet him that Friday near the Space Needle.

By the time he returned to the encampment, he found her delirious and spitting up blood. He picked her up; she weighed nothing. He ran with her two blocks to the place she called the Barf Hotel, dodging a man with a knife at one point. He set her down fast on the sidewalk and drew his own knife to ward the man off.

When no cars stopped or paid attention to him, he jumped off the curb in front of a car with an Uber sign in the windshield.

He threw a wad of bills at the driver she kept hidden in a slit in her pillow. The Uber driver was a Sikh who mumbled prayers *en route* to the hospital. He dropped them off in the semicircular emergency room entrance. Hughie was so nerve shot and covered in Jordan's bloody spray in his lap that he heard only the last of the driver's words—something about *kasaya* and "dirt" or "evil."

He spent nights and days in the lobby of the emergency room silently watching the parade of beaten-down humanity come and go. EMT's shoved gurneys with dying or wounded through doors meant to crash open to deposit their cargo and head back out to scoop up more of the city's beleaguered and unlucky.

Friday came and went; he gave it no more thought than to note the day. He watched insipid daytime programs on the communal TV and waited for daily updates on Jordan's condition.

"It's end-stage TB," the physician told him.

Every time the doctor spoke to Hughie, a look of annoyance passed over his pink, close-shaved features. He cut his eyes from Hughie's face down to his hands to his shoes as though he were summarizing him in sections.

"When will she be released?"

"Didn't you hear me? It's final-stage. He's not coming out. We're transferring him to the county facility in the morning. Hospice will look after your friend."

"You said 'him.'"

"I must be stuttering today." The doctor's smooth forehead wrinkled briefly. "Yes, he, your friend—"

"*Her* name is Jordan."

"The patient you brought in is male. I didn't need a diploma from a medical school to distinguish between male and female anatomy."

Hughie was stunned to silence.

The doctor wasn't inclined to sympathy, but he put a hand on Hughie's shoulder. "You didn't know. Maybe he had a good reason to assume a female gender…"

Hughie stumbled out of the emergency room and blinked into the cold sunshine. The rainy season was coming fast. The St. Martin De Porres Shelter would take him in but would close before he could make it.

Lighter by thirty pounds, tanned to leather, always hungry, he walked back to their place and found it ransacked of everything of value, including Jordan's money. *Res ipsa loquitur*, a phrase from tort law rang in his head: "The thing speaks for itself."

He walked in the direction of the shelter under a torrential rain, unhurried, mindlessly humming a Puccini aria he remembered from an opera his parents had taken him to and which he hated at the time. Those twin sisters, Sorrow and Shame, yanked at his spirit as he walked through the rain that both cleansed his tears and drowned his sobs.

Boosting for the Devil

I started stealing cars at fifteen. My parents were decent people, solid working class, but I've always had an urge to walk on the wild side. It's something you can't explain to other people. It's like an itch you can't scratch or satisfy, following everybody's rules.

My parents wanted to take me to a shrink by the time I was seventeen. They'd had enough of their wayward son, the numerous juvie court appearances, the lawyer fees, and my phony excuses. They washed their hands of me. Three weeks before my eighteenth birthday, I found a calendar shoved under my bedroom door with my birthday circled in red. Newspaper clippings from the Help Wanted section were scotch-taped taped to the back.

I took the hint. I stuffed some clothes into a backpack and left in the middle of the night while they slept. On my way out, I stole the family emergency cash from a not-so-secret drawer in my grandmother's roll-top secretary desk. I took the ice-cream cake out of the freezer they bought for me and set it on the table to melt.

My destination: Miami. My career: boosting cars—what else? Where else but Miami and a few other cities can you walk up to an intersection and spot a Lamborghini, a Bugatti, and a Ferrari all sitting at a stoplight? Kids taped posters of rock stars and bikini-clad beauties to their bedroom walls. My walls had glossy posters of a black Huracán, a yellow Murcielago with gull-wing doors, and a red-over-black Veneno.

Boosting sedans in Ohio was easy as pie. I took them from the mall and drove them out of town where I lifted the catalytic converter out and sold the car to a guy who ran a crooked garage. TV makes hot-wiring a car look easy. *YouTube* teaches teenaged jackers how to steal a Kia in ten seconds. I put as many hours into my skill as any Vegas magician with card tricks.

I practiced one skill to perfection: reading a key by holding it in my hand for a few seconds. My special technique was to check out the classifieds for car sales, dress in a clean shirt, show up at the seller's house, all smiles and ask for a test run to help me decide. We'd drive around the block. Once back in the driveway, I'd act indecisive while letting my hand memorize the key's peaks and valleys. Then I'd toss the key back and tell him or her I'd "think about it." Off to the nearest hardware store to get a duplicate made to that precise specification. As I always promised the owner, I'd be back—and usually in the wee hours to steal the car.

Miami, however, wasn't panning out as I'd thought. Those postcard images of the Gold Coast—the white sandy beaches and aquamarine waters lapping the delicate ankles of the beautiful people—pictures in my head I entertained myself with on the long bus ride—well, that's for tourists. I wasted some cash to get my feet in the water and I stood there as obvious as a booger on a white linen tablecloth that I didn't belong. My age, my clothes, my face—all wrong. The only thing I had going for me as camouflage was the pallor of my skin like the middle-aged snowbirds on the blankets, retirees with pot bellies and cellulite thighs, lolling in the February sunshine. I wound up in Little Havana looking even more out of place. Finally, half-starved, I bought a greasy "danger dog," a bacon-wrapped, deep-fried hot dog, from a street vendor and took an Uber to Liberty City where I found a motel. I was down to $65 and fast becoming disenchanted with my dream.

The room stank of disinfectant. A patch of mold on the ceiling shaped like Brazil made me even more depressed.

Sandwiched between a prostitute's hangout and a party pad for junkies, I had to listen to the action on both sides, which went on all night. That and the screaming ambulance and police sirens, the gunshots at two a.m., and drunks screaming at other drunks made me lose sleep. Those gorgeous Lambos and Bugatti Chirons parked outside the trendy clubs of South Beach might as well have been parked on the moon. What made me think I could pop down here and start ripping off cars like that?

By the second day, I knew better than to wander the streets. Gangs had watchers posted on their turf so that any pedestrian got a hard look. One thing about serious stealing is that you learn to up your situational awareness if you want to stay in business. I found a piece of rebar and took it back to my room. It was four in the morning when I heard shouts in the parking lot. My sleep was ragged at best, so I hopped out, grabbed the bar, and cracked the door.

Some guy was getting jumped by three young guys. I mean, they were stomping the hell out of him with kicks and punches. I closed the door—none of my business.

But something told me I had nothing to lose at that point. Going back home to frigid Ohio was worse than failure. Rebar in hand, I bolted for the parking lot.

They never heard me coming up behind them. I cracked one across the base of the skull and didn't pause to watch him drop. The second guy saw me but had no time to react before the bar caught him across the forearm he raised before it connected with his jaw. Guy number three took one look at the madman swinging what could have been a machete for all he knew and took off like he had a rocket strapped to his buttocks. The one I'd coldcocked lay on the ground moaning. The other one, bent over from the pain of a broken bone, spat curses and limped off like a wounded animal.

I grabbed their victim beneath the armpit, dragging him to my room. I'd had plenty of bruises and scrapes from my own nighttime prowls and knew enough to do a half-assed nursing job. I ripped up a tee and bandaged him as best I could. He asked for water, so I gave him some from a Dixie cup in the bathroom. He swallowed three more as if I were handing him ambrosia from the gods. His face was puffed and he had an eye squinting to see out of, yet he seemed to be OK. I wondered if the guy was used to finding himself in dodgy circumstances, a phrase some judge used on me once.

"You're concussed," I said; "you're going to look like roadkill tomorrow."

"Who are you—some Good Samaritan or a cop?"

He spat a gob of blood onto the floor and felt around the inside of his mouth checking for loose teeth.

"Just a tourist checking out some of Miami's finer night spots."

"I notice you ain't said nothing about what was happening out there in the parking lot."

"Not my business," I replied.

"You done any time?"

"Why?"

"You got that look, kid. You took a big chance out there. Those guys are New Moneii. Better pack your shit up and get out of that motel because they'll be back with their friends."

"They looked about fourteen."

"Fourteen going on forty, man. They're rat-packing on their cell phones right now. You said you were new to Miami but are you stupid, too? Ouch, God damn it, don't make me talk so much."

I had my stuff jammed into the backpack in a minute, and we left together at a fast clip out of the motel lot and headed down Hyacinth. A crimson dawn was just breaking over the abandoned factories.

"Where are we going?" I asked.

"I don't park around here. I don't want to come back to a burnt-out hulk."

"So I'm also guessing you're repaying me by giving me a lift to better digs."

We were just then passing a vacant lot. Somebody had attached a homemade sign to the cyclone fence:

Guns Down! Bibles Up!
Say yes to God! Say No to the Devil!
Say Yes to Love! Say No to Hate!

"I'll do better than that," he said, looking over his shoulder.

In the light, I saw he was about thirty, maybe older, and whatever had gotten him in trouble with those violent punks wasn't something he was going to tell me about. I already knew there were two kinds of people in the world; the kind who blurt everything onto social media and the other kind, the ones who don't use ten words when none will do.

His LaCrosse was parked at a diner on Riviera. I'd stolen one just like it not two months ago. He gave me a name and a phone number on a piece of paper when he dropped me off.

"Call this number. He'll find you work."

"Who's 'he' and why should I do that?"

"You need me to tell you that, shithead?"

He drove off. *OK*, I thought, *I acted on impulse that time. Let's see where this goes.*

In a world of cell phones, locating a pay phone not busted up and slathered with obscene graffiti was a minor miracle, but I found one on Calaveras Avenue in front of an all-night pharmacy.

I punched in the numbers while a homeless woman

watched me as if I'd just painted my face blue and sprouted wings. Morning traffic was picking up, mostly black and brown faces behind the windshields.

"Who's this?"

An unfriendly voice, gruff.

"Morning to you, too, sweetheart," I said.

I was still feeling cocky from clobbering three skinny teens with an iron bar and getting away scot-free.

"How'd you get this number?"

I told him the name of my source—if that was even the guy's real name. An exceptionally long pause.

"You there?"

"Yeah."

"By the way," I said, still riding the crest of my adrenalin wave, "who am I talking to?"

"Russell," the gruff voice replied. "Hang on."

I held the receiver so long my palm left a damp imprint on it. Feeling dumber by the minute, convinced I'd been had by that guy I rescued, I was just about to hang up when a different voice came on the line.

"Hello," it said. "What's your name again?"

I told him and gave him an abridged version of how I'd met his contact.

He gave me an address and told me to be there at two o'clock "precisely." If a voice can be suave on the phone, his was. He reminded me of a Spanish teacher I had in high school who enunciated every syllable with that kind of exaggeration. The class always made fun of him.

Curbing my newfound hope wasn't easy. I played the wide-eyed tourist gawking in store windows. Lindor's Garage was a dumpy-looking place off 7th Avenue that reminded me of Greasy George back home, the man who ran the chop shop. I'd sold him dozens of radios, GPS trackers, and everything else dumbass people leave in their cars.

Everything from cell phones to a portable TV, once, outside a dentist's office. My expectations crashed when I walked inside at two p.m. on the dot.

"You're on time," the second phone voice said just behind me. "I take it you've met Russell, my associate."

He was slim, middle-aged, possessed silver hair, carefully styled. Clean shaven, of medium height and much too well dressed to be the owner of the place.

"Come into my office," he said. "Let me introduce you to Russell. I'm Fernando, by the way. Everyone calls me Nando."

That was how I met the Devil and his chief henchman.

His "associate" Russell was a craggy-faced man of indeterminate age, very tall, balding, with spotted skin. His hand was clammy when we shook. I resisted wiping my hand on my pantleg.

Nando sat behind a beat-up desk in a swivel chair that looked like every office in every garage I've ever stepped inside: stacks of invoices on spikes, yellowed sales brochures, an array of papers, pencils, Bic pens scattered across the chipped surface of a desk you wouldn't donate to Goodwill.

"I'm going to ask you some questions first," Nando said.

His smile was friendly but it didn't go all the way up to his eyes. Under the crappy fluorescent lighting, his face was so closely shaved that the lighting made him look sallow, cadaverous.

"Shoot."

The questions came fast and were edged with an undertone of skepticism. He evaluated me on my knowledge of car thievery. Though younger than most car thieves, I was considered an equal by men far more experienced. Nando grilled me like a pro. He scoffed at some of my responses, calling me a mere "opportunity thief." I bit back my anger, kept my poise, and responded politely to his every question. He asked me about how to steal high-end cars through a "relay attack," that is, getting past the keyless entry system.

I told him what I'd do.

"But you've never done it, have you? You see a mounting device for a cell phone or a GPS and you decide to target a vehicle?"

"It's as good an indication as any."

Russell laughed, aping his boss. "This guy, he breaks the windows with a rock."

I felt heat rising in my face but I stayed calm.

"Now, Russell, be kind. We allow for that when it's about the parts, not the vehicle."

His smile never left me the whole time.

Russell interjected: "So you crack the window, brush aside the broken glass, and drive off?"

"I prefer a slim jim," I replied. "Or maybe you think walking up to the door and asking for the key fob from the owner works better."

A chuckle from Nando at that. My slim jim was the same kind used by cops and repo men, not your DIY version. I described my uses of "shaved keys" cut to new configurations and my own "palming technique" of memorizing valleys and peaks in seconds. That seemed to impress Nando. He allowed Russell to grill me on hotwiring and disabling alarms. Russell snorted once when I said that ripping out wires was the fastest way.

"What do you think, Russell?"

Russell looked at his master and curled his lip. I was about to get my "grade."

"We have problems," Russell replied in his gruff voice. "He steals old cars. He don't know jack about passive anti-theft systems."

Which was mainly true. I could crack a steering column, identify the starter and power wires with a pen flashlight stuck in my mouth, and I'd be off in fifteen seconds flat. You didn't find many Maseratis cruising around the shitburg where I grew up. I boosted an Escalade once and a Dodge Challenger HEMI, my biggest scores.

Russell was right about my ignorance of the passive anti-theft system. I had to give many late-model Fords a pass for that reason. You have to know how to crack the encryption on an RFID chip and use a transmitter to open the car. They don't teach that in shop classes.

Nando took no time at all to "draw a picture" for me. He wanted me to bring him certain makes and models of car for his "business." He called his method of obtaining these vehicles without the owners' permission his "pre-planned attacks." No more amateur hour walking past parked cars at night looking for identifying alarm stickers or tapping the glass to see if one goes off," he said, sarcasm dripping from his voice at my "limited expertise."

That was my crude interpretation of his eloquent description of his "business." I would deal exclusively with Russell, who would supply me the models he wanted and drive me to the sites.

My verbal exam completed, I then had to pass a "field test," according to Nando. He shook my hand and wished me "good luck."

"When do I go?"

"Tonight," he replied. "Russell will give you the details."

I was dismissed. Russell walked me out through a bay door and gave me the name of a street corner to meet him at four-thirty that afternoon.

"Bring your tools," he growled. "Don't wear black like some idiot ninja on TV—and don't be late."

I had time to kill and my nerves were frayed after the interrogation in Lindor's. Russell didn't faze me. He was a stooge, a nobody. But Nando exuded something I'd never experienced. Just being in his presence, I felt his power. Other feelings too, ones not easily described but the kind of gut-roiling nausea that happens when you're confronted with a menace so unnatural it seems inhuman. My desire for wealth blocked out everything. I knew I had that one chance everybody yearns for and few ever realize.

I also knew I wasn't going to be stealing a Honda Civic. This was big-time, Grand Theft Auto—only not the video game where you can run over pedestrians after a carjacking in Los Santos. I had to worry about the likelihood of LoJack or an engine immobilizer. Rich people don't use the guy at the mall to install their theft systems; they use professionals who think about putting it where a thief wouldn't expect it and they use alarms that alert you when the car is moved. Unlike my hometown folk, they never put valuables in plain sight or hide a second set of keys on the car in case they get locked out.

No longer so cocky, I was going from the minors to the majors and not much time to prepare. I had no idea where Russell would bring me, but I was sure it wasn't going to be anywhere near my motel up in Liberty City. I bought maps and started studying streets, checking for escape routes as I did in Ohio. I doubted Russell was going to make anything easy for me.

Lingering at the intersection of Cielo and Chapultepec, I was fifteen-minutes early. Russell was late. No apologies, however.

"You bring your stuff?"

"Don't worry about it."

"Hey, kid, it won't be me doing three years in South Bay Correctional if you screw up. They like cute boys up there. They make them grow out their hair and wear dresses."

"You're funny, Russell. Why don't you cut the shit and tell me what I'm going after."

"You'll see."

I nudged a paper grocery sack sitting between us on the console.

"What's in the bag?"

"You'll find out."

We drove on in silence. The longer and further we went, the more expensive the homes and the landscaping looked. I was in Money Town. But when I read the street sign, my stomach lurched. Oceanside Drive was one of America's most expensive patches of real estate, never mind the state of Florida.

"What's my target?"

"An easy one. He gave me a crooked smile and licked his lips, worse than his normal expression. "This being your first time. We're going past it in a few minutes. You'll get one look."

The houses were all multi-million-dollar here. More concrete in the driveways than in half the buildings in my hometown. I concentrated on the cars in the driveway and ignored the spacious mansion. Three vehicles: an IROC with black racing stripes, the Beemer, and a 2018 Gran Turismo at the location. *Mucho dinero…*

He drove down the black and pulled up to a curb.

"You going to tell me or do I have to guess?"

"The BMW."

"Good, we're making progress, Russ. Now tell me, what's in the bag of tricks."

I was hoping he'd pull something sophisticated out like a specialized lock pick, or some decoding tool that would enable me to spoof or clone the car's internal communication system and bypass the security.

"Look inside," he said.

A khaki shirt, work gloves, and a small shovel.

"Is this a joke?"

"In the front pocket, a piece of paper with an address. That's where we meet up later."

"You motherf—"

He snapped a punch at my jaw that stunned me. He reached across me, opened the door, and pushed me out. He tossed the bag out after, spilling the contents. A key fob was the last item to roll out.

Merciful Jesus, be what I think it is...

I watched him drive off, flipping him the bird. I've never felt so alone and naked in my life. The hair on my neck prickled. My imagination made me think I was being watched by a dozen pair of eyes, fingers ready to hit 9-1-1.

The house was a hundred yards away. I had two choices: go back or go forward.

The money in my Levi's pocket was enough for rent for one last night at a cheap motel. I walked toward the house feeling like some crippled soldier on the Bataan Death March. *This isn't going to end well*, I recall thinking.

On the way, I slipped the shirt and gloves on; the shovel dangled at my side in one hand. *Trick-or-Treat, I'm a landscaper...*

The late-afternoon sun dappled Sabal palm fronds and trellises draped with tropical flowers. Hibiscus flowers as big as dinner plates glowed in several colors in the impressive yards I passed. The light turned from lemon to gold. I'd rarely stolen in daytime. I remember the sneer on Nando's face when he called me "an opportunity thief." This was my baptism by fire. *So be it—*

Approaching the target driveway, I let my gaze drift to the house's windows. No one in sight, no stirring behind the lace curtains, no sounds. Still, I felt those eyes burning holes in me.

The Beemer was an S-Class and I heaved a sigh of relief — easier to steal. From my vantage, I couldn't tell if the place had a Ring doorbell, but security placards dotted every other yard. *Smile for the cameras*, I told myself. *Sheer madness*.

As soon as I approached the BMW, I touched the door handle and pressed the repeater Russell had "forgotten" to mention he'd included in the bag. A repeater intercepts the UHF beam triggered by touching the door. It fools the system by sending a second UHF beam on a separate frequency to communicate with the authentication receiver inside the vehicle.

I was inside in a split-second. I hit the starter button and listened to the purr of the engine above my hammering heartbeat. I slipped the gear into reverse and backed out, one eye on the rearview, the other on the house. No outraged owner screaming bloody murder. No traffic in the street. I drove off at a normal speed.

At the designated meeting spot, I parked the car and leaned against the fender. My gardener's outfit and spade had gone into a dumpster three blocks back.

Russell drove up in a different older car this time. I was tempted to smash his face with a right cross, but I played it Mr. Cool-as-Ice, car thief extraordinaire.

"About time," I complained.

"I had to make sure no cops were tailing you," he said; he sounded bored as if the obvious explanation were a chore.

"Get in."

"What about the—"

"Leave it," he barked. "That's for someone else."

He dropped me off at a motel that was only a slight

improvement on my first because of the fewer number of derelicts randomly walking about.

"I'll call you in the morning. The room's paid for."

He tossed a burner phone at me. "Don't lose it."

"Why don't you kiss my—"

He burned rubber leaving the parking lot.

"—ass!"

That was the beginning of my apprenticeship with Nando. In the coming weeks, I stole three more cars including a Diablo in an underground parking lot in downtown Miami where every sound was magnified and security patrolled every fifteen minutes. I waved driving past the guard at the gate.

Nando told me the story of how that Lambo got its name. Some fierce bulldog owned by a nineteenth-century duke from someplace I never heard of defeated another fighting dog named *El Chicorro*.

"An epic battle," Nando said.

"Nice dog story," I said. "But the car's better."

I despised Russell the more I saw him. I kept my feelings hidden. Nando's preference for me was irking him. He'd heard me call him "Sourpuss" to Nando in conversation. I knew he'd relish an opportunity to see me fail. Except for the specifics of whatever caper I participated in, I never talked about "the business" to Russell or to Nando, especially. I guessed that the cars I stole were headed to Europe, but I was a small cog in a big machine.

"Do not concern yourself with anything outside your job," Nando warned me once. "Understand me?"

"Sure, Nando. No problem."

"Good. I want you to live a long time and prosper in our business."

A shiver ran up my back despite the friendly words. I knew he wouldn't hesitate to make me "disappear" if I proved troublesome or failed. My stealing was always called an "assignment" or a "mission." *Disappear* was a word that Nando used when it came to anything he called a problem.

I now had money to improve my lodgings. I stayed at the Radisson and shopped for clothes at Austin Burke's on 6th Avenue. I ate at Fiola Miami and Obra. I cultivated a taste for Cuban coffee and cuisine. I smiled thinking of my parents back home and their big weekly treat—a Whopper and fries at Burger King. I never asked what my percentage of the cars I stole was. I took the packet of bills Russell handed me every two weeks without a word and shoved it into my jacket. If Russell expected me to thank him, he was disappointed every time.

It's what happens to many professionals who get good at what they do. They overlook a small detail, thinking it can't hurt. That was my downfall. I got sloppy.

Russell was his usual obnoxious self and gave me the next assignment, which turned out to be located in Coconut Grove. The target car was a cobalt-blue Audi, a step down from what I'd been boosting lately. Nando's rules were to confirm any discrepancy at the site. I didn't feel like calling in and waiting twenty minutes before his callback. It took me less time to take the car instead.

Big mistake. Wrong Audi.

The car was a deep blue but the street lighting made it seem darker than it was. I ignore that tickle of doubt. I was never involved in the scouting part, so I didn't care who messed up that small detail—only it wasn't small. The Audi I took had an expensive and difficult anti-theft system, not to mention it alerted the owner's computer the second I started it. I was picked up by a passing cruiser and had to make a run for it with a wailing siren behind me for ten miles before I managed to ditch the car in a working-class neighborhood.

I raced through a couple back alleys, avoided a Dobermann by inches and cut my palms on a barbed-wire fence. Two hours later, I collapsed on my hotel bed, exhausted.

In the morning, I ate breakfast and headed to Lindor's, my fallback spot for any mission that didn't go as planned.

Heading to the office, the unshaven owner looked at me blankly. I didn't know how much of Nando's illegal business he was privy to.

Three hours passed. No one showed, no call. When I called Nando's number, a mechanical voice said that number was no longer in service.

OK, I thought, *just Nando being super careful. No big deal.*

I returned to my hotel and waited. By four o'clock, I was worried. I figured that ugly lout Russell was keeping me in suspense on purpose. I took the elevator down to the bar and had a few cold ones. The game on the set was boring so I finished my drink, left a twenty on the bar, and checked my watch: seven-thirty.

Something, however, was gnawing at me. I knew it as soon as I got in the elevator. I'd grown lazy with too much cash on hand. I thought I was invincible. Making a beeline to my room, I went right to the safe. I had something like fifteen thousand in there by this point.

My instincts proved right: empty. Nothing but dead air inside. My fake IDs were gone, too. I thought of the room boy who passed me in the lobby. *Was that a knowing grin on his face?*

Don't panic, I told myself. *Nothing that can't be fixed. Nando is a reasonable man. He'll understand…*

Finally, my phone trilled. I answered, wary of who might be on the other end.

Russell. He sounded different—almost pleased when

I tried to explain what happened with the Audi. He brushed me off.

"Never mind that," he barked. "Get your ass to the meeting at Lindor's tomorrow, ten o'clock sharp."

"I'm never—"

I wanted to say *late*, but he'd ended the connection.

Lindor's Garage was closed when I pulled up the next morning. I was driving a rental Jaguar, blowing money like a drunken sailor. I spotted Russell inside. He was standing there alone, staring back at me. He flicked his fingers waving me inside and turned around, heading to that shabby office.

All good thieves practice alertness; they have a saying: *Check your baseline normal.* See something odd about it? Time to haul ass.

I had signs all around me saying my own baseline normal was crooked as an epileptic pissing, yet I had ignored my instincts.

Too late.

Whatever hit me from behind knocked me senseless to the floor. I had a moment where I regained consciousness. I thought: *my expensive shirt is going to be ruined from the oily filth on this floor...* and then I passed out again.

I came to more slowly a third time. I was in a dark tunnel; then I realized it was just dark and I was confined in a small space. I was bound hand and foot with cuffs that bit into my flesh. As my senses dragged themselves together, the floating sensation, of being in an airplane going through turbulence, became clear. I was in the trunk of a car traveling at speed, probably on a major highway judging from the sounds beneath the chassis.

Then the motion slowed and I was jostled from side to side. My head told me we were slowing down, taking sharp curves. Then things came to a stop. I heard the engine shut off and the driver's side door open and close.

An old car, probably one of those junkers Russell drove. Did it come with the mandatory emergency trunk release or was it too old for that? I uttered the sincerest prayer since my altar boy days back at Our Lady of the Seven Sorrows in Northtown: *Please God, let it be one with an emergency trunk-release…*

I knew where it had to be if this car had one. I twisted and squirmed until I was able to raise my legs high enough to feel around the trunk with one foot. One of my shoes was missing. Something glittered as I moved around in the dark—a brief glimmer of light penetrated where the rubber seal was ripped or loose. It shone on a piece of aluminum attached to one edge of the trunk. My foot, bleeding from my effort to find the release lever, felt what the device was: someone had retrofitted the trunk with a release catch right there instead of the centerline where it would normally be.

With the heel of my foot, I kicked at it oblivious to the pain. It must have rusted over the years. With a furious effort to kick it loose, I activated it and the trunk sprang open.

It took all my remaining strength to wiggle my body to the lip of the trunk and use gravity to tip me over. The fall knocked what little breath I had right out of me. I lay on the cement, gagging. When I sat up against the fender, unable to rise, I was determined to die there with a bullet before I'd let anybody put me back inside that stinking coffin.

Groggy, dizzy but aware of people around, I knew I was at a rest stop. People came closer, seeing me slumped behind a vehicle, sobbing. Finally someone leaned over and spoke. The words were in Spanish. But I knew I was saved.

My nylon cuffs were cut by a state trooper called to the rest stop. I told him I'd been kidnapped—and that was all I said despite the lengthy interrogation I received at the barracks once my wounds were tended to. Of course, neither Russell nor the driver were ever found. They ran a check on me, but I was using a fake ID provided by Nando.

The police were suspicious but had nothing to hold me on. An officer drove me to my hotel. No one ever connected me to the abortive Audi jacking.

At a diner across the street, I called the Radisson and discovered all my possessions had been removed "at my own instructions." The clerk told me I'd presented identification "in person." The room bill had been paid in full. I suspected a few staff had been paid off, too.

I moved to a bedsit in Broward County and found a job as a busboy in an all-night café. My heart thumped against my ribs every time a customer came in who remotely resembled Nando.

Finally, I'd saved enough for the bus ride back North. I read an old copy of the *Miami Herald* a customer left behind on a table. A back-page article described how the body of an unidentified middle-aged man had been found floating in a mangrove swamp near the Everglades. The circumstances were "weird," according to the reporter. The victim was discovered nude inside a bass boat by two employees from the South Florida Wildlife Management Agency. They were hunting Burmese pythons with shotguns.

Holes had been cut by a welding torch for the victim's hands and feet to protrude. Russell's body was secured to the bottom of the boat in a prone position. His body was unrecognizable, almost devoured to the bone by insects. They had burrowed into every orifice of his body and eaten the soft organs and laid eggs. A police spokesperson consulted an anthropologist from South Florida U. who believed the man died by an ancient torture called "the Boats."

The victim is smeared with honey to draw flying

insects and then forced to ingest milk and honey, causing diarrhea, according to the scholar, and thus promoting "more insect life to gnaw and burrow." Set adrift, he died from a combination of insects and dehydration. "If a gator had gotten to him," the scholar concluded, "it would have been a mercy. The man would have been lucky to go insane first. He'd be aware of insects eating him alive the whole time."

Nando doesn't tolerate failure... one of the first things Russell said to me.

I'm back home now living with my parents. *The prodigal son returneth,* my father quipped. I had to eat a lot of humble pie to get back in their good graces.

I'm through boosting cars. I take a bus to the community college where I study mechanical engineering. I'll crawl on my knees through broken glass before I ever steal another car. At night in my dreams, Russell's ugly face is a technicolor horror show I can't turn my eyes from; his face contorted in agony. Sometimes I see that Devil Nando standing on the shoreline cold as any bull gator beneath the surface watching his former associate, taking sips of Russell's pain.

It terrifies me in those dreams when Nando turns to see me hiding in the swamp. He smiles—and then I wake in a cold sweat with a soundless scream forming in my throat.

The Defecator

Smiley Mondine hiked up his pants and smiled for the camera—the CCTV lens in the garage corner, that is. He knew he was on tape. That added to the pleasure, always had. Once he spotted "an opportunity," as he thought of them, he found a lightening in his chest and a bounce in his step.

He'd been taking a shit in people's houses, campers, and cars since he was fourteen. A stint in juvie and six months in the local caboose at eighteen didn't deter him. He was addicted; knew from his first fistfight in the schoolyard that he had nothing in common with other people. Even his nickname. Like a lot of monikers, his was the opposite of the truth; he never smiled—except for the cameras after he'd dropped a load on someone's dining room table or inside the toilet tank (not an easy feat when you think of it). Since his last incarceration for grand theft auto, he'd finessed his skills with more discretion. The first thing he did after a recon was to pick the right time, often in the small hours, and always do what many of those rich mutts failed to do: lock the car.

Getting inside a cyclone fenced area, like this one tonight, was child's play. Smiley boosted for a chop shop. Tonight was business. Heavy-duty bolt cutters to take care of the padlock; crowbar and leather gloves like the high-risk parkour kids wore for the razor wire in case the "goods" were stashed inside a fenced-in cage inside the warehouse. His bag of specialized lock picks and a decoder enabled him to spoof the car's internal security system. Exactly like this rich prick's Veneno Roadster, straight from Sant'Agata Bolognese to the docks with no stopover at the dealer's.

Smiley didn't know the man who ordered it and didn't care. He was obviously filthy rich like all the rest of them. Ever since his first break-in at the home next door, he felt that same thrill in his belly at what he was about to do. Sometimes the urge to crap was sexual and he felt Little Smiley stirring in anticipation. *Double the pleasure*, like the chewing gum commercial.

He'd stolen plenty of popular vehicles for chopping; the highbrow ones—the Lexuses, Infinitis, Escalades, including a Jaguar Spyder, and a Porsche—all destined for overseas delivery. Not your average Porsche, either. A Boxster manufactured for the high speeds attained on the Autobahn.

His second Lambo and his first for jacking. He parked his Toyota near a vacant lot and gathered his tools. As he approached the outer wire behind the storage facility, the excitement increased. The inner perimeter was jammed with high-end campers, which normally would have drawn him to choose one.

He knew the prize was inside the building, however, and he knew where thanks to one of the laborers who couldn't keep his mouth shut after a few boilermakers at that cement-block, shitkicker bar near the docks. Smiley had picked up good tips there in the past.

He popped the cheap padlock—another reason that cretin deserved what was going to happen to his prize. He tapped the metal doors with the crowbar and waited a few seconds just in case anyone was inside. Unlikely at this hour, but he wasn't interested in tangling assholes with some rent-a-cop that stevedore didn't mention. He dug the wood from behind the hasp and inserted the beveled edge of the bar. With less pressure than he'd need to open a pickle jar, the hasp burst free.

Inside, his eyes adjusted to the dark. He hoped the cameras inside were better than the last time. Smiley loved seeing his image on the nightly news channel and the articles asking the public for information about him. He kept his face covered with a pandemic mask until it was time to go; then he'd slip it off and flash a toothy smile at the lens swiveling to find him with its blinking red eye.

Jesus, what a moron! The driver's door was open. The gurgling in his intestines told him his body was getting ready, but the temptation to sit behind the wheel of this beauty before squatting and dropping off some brown friends was too great.

What's this? A cell phone on the passenger seat.

Smiley picked it up. When its ringtones chimed off, his surprise was so great the phone, a burner, flew out of his hands and landed on his crotch.

He picked it up with a thumping heart and thumbed the on key.

"Congratulations, asshole. You made it inside."

Smiley's eyes boxed the empty warehouse again—nothing.

"Who—who is this?"

"Remember that Aventador in the parking garage on Mayfield you took a shit on two months ago?"

Smiley couldn't forget it. His first Lambo. He was leery of cracking in because he didn't have the right device to bypass the internal communication system with a clone signal, so he hopped up on the hood and let loose a fusillade from his intestines all over the windshield.

"That wasn't me."

"Shut up and listen. I made my fortune with the Defense Department. We design UCAV's for the military."

The doors were locked automatically from a signal. His bag of heavy tools to bust through the windshield lay out of reach on the concrete floor.

The car started on its own. Someone, somewhere out of sight, punched the key fob. The metal folding doors rattled upward. He was being let out in the car.

Never look a gift horse in the mouth, his car thief mentor taught him. *If a dumbass leaves a car unlocked, fuckin' take it...*

Smiley blew out the open door of the building, scraping the roof. He gunned it for the gate and smashed through, already going seventy. The Lambo had wings.

He'd find somewhere safe, kick out the windshield, run like a motherfucker and not look back—

Then he remembered; ice filled his belly, not the tingly kind, either: UCAV meant Unmanned Combat Aerial Vehicle. Hunter-killer drones with a heavy-lift payload to blow any targeted jihadi skyward in a thousand tiny pieces, no meeting their seventy-two virgins with a hardon...

The burner phone chirped again.

"Wait! Wait!"

"Not to worry," that same laconic voice said. "The car's insured. I ordered a duplicate the same day I discovered who you were—"

Smiley slammed the phone into the console before the voice said another word.

Smiley was three blocks from the pier. He' could hide inside the massive warehouses. He aimed the big machine in that direction and floored it.

Blood pressure thrummed in his ears; the adrenalin jolt almost lifted him out of his seat before nauseating him. His tunnel vision confined to a single focus: the speedometer needle racing into the red. He kept the goal of slamming into the warehouse bay as fast as he could uppermost in his mind.

The whine of the engine turned into buzzing; he blanked out the noise and fixed his vision on the warehouses ahead, gaining in size as he careened from one side of the gravel road to the other at a suicidal clip.

Oh God, no...

Fear unleashed his intestines and a foul gush of diarrhea exploded from his sphincter, soaking his Levi's, enveloping him in a marsh-like vapor.

The drone struck in a blinding flash before the bubble in Smiley's esophagus materialized in an anguished, heart-breaking, final sob.

Wrong Place, Wrong Time

I drove my piece-of-shit car to Richard's shop as I'd been doing for the last two years.

There's no Richard despite the barely legible sign above the garage door, actually a converted barn. Bobby's over 350 pounds and bald. Fat rolls on his neck show dirt caked in the creases. I guessed his name from the tops of the tattooed letters peeking out of his grease-spotted wifebeater. Driving ten miles out into the countryside past a dozen in-town garages to this burgh just to let Bobby work on my car made no sense unless you understood how deeply I hate dealing with human beings. I tell him in a sentence or two what's wrong, he calls a day later and leaves a single word in my voicemail: "Done."

Sometimes I'd pass a scruffy-looking teenager or a dodgy-looking older male who'd eyefuck me on my way past the farmhouse to the barn. The stack of catalytic converters on a shelf told me Bobby did a sideline business. The longest conversation he and I had happened a week before this time. He was feeding his six pit bulls in big metal kennels behind the barn.

"What happens if you let them out at the same time?"

"They'll kill each other," he replied.

This time there was no sign of life at the place. Odd. I debated whether to knock on the door of his house when a couple men stepped out the door, stopped and stared at me. The gun coming up seemed to be in slow motion. I ran—but not far. The bullet slamming into my back felt like a red-hot spike pounded through it in one mighty swing.

When my brain snapped back into place, I was sprawled in the dirt on my belly. Playing possum seemed like a good idea. A heavy boot kicked me in the leg.

"Who is he?"

"Who gives a shit," a different voice said. "Put another one in him."

Playing possum wasn't so wise.

A different voice: "What if he ain't no citizen? We bring heat down on the club, our asses are next."

"Quit fuckin' the dog. Check his motherfucking wallet," the second voice said. "Then finish it, what the fuck."

At that point, one of those kids Bobby dealt with must have come stumbling up the driveway carrying another stolen converter. Apparently the mope had his earbuds in and didn't notice the two big guys standing over a third guy lying on the ground.

When he did figure it out, it was too late. Voices yelling, gunshots. A high-pitched scream loud enough to shatter crystal. Another gunshot. Risking a backward glance, I scrambled to my feet, absorbing the pain with an act of will and a dose of adrenalin.

Stumbling my way to the back of the barn to the cages, I flipped the latches, one by one. A slug caromed off metal missing my head by inches. I hurled myself inside an empty cage and curled into a ball, although the freed dog in the next cage refused to leave; it went berserk, slathering and pawing to get to me. The next slug ricocheted off the top of the cage.

Two strangers running aggressively toward them provided a better target.

The bigger of the two men braced himself for a shot

and hit the lead dog coming for him. His buddy decided discretion was the better part of valor. Three dogs hit the shooter like brindled missiles; he went down hard, flailing, screaming.

The running man never made it to the house. The dogs packed up, took him down like wolves on an elk, a dog on each limb. One tearing at the crotch. They eviscerated him, bloody jaws snapping. I watched one sniff the dead boy's face. One dog trotted into the barn looking for Bobby.

My bullet wound festered. Another half-day in that cage would have done it. While conscious, I watched the dogs roam and feed off the corpses.

A detective later told me they might need me in court someday. All I learned was that Bobby narced on his biker gang.

"You were just in the wrong place at the wrong time," he said.

Last Supper in New Zenith

I'd just gone down to the river to escape the old man for a couple hours. He was drinking heavier than ever now, and we were going to be stuck up north because of the bad weather. We'd be working our way south at this time of the year, but the money was short, the customers fewer at each stop, and winter here would be miserable for both of us. He'd drink himself into a stupor every night and I'd be trapped all day inside some cheap motel with nothing but old magazines to read. Dad didn't allow the TV. Devil's work, he said.

Traffic on the Ohio River was tapering off like everything else, just a few barges pushing crushed stone and fracking waste. The ferry from Sistersville making its last run of the night. I hoped the girl I'd noticed yesterday would be standing on the upper ferry deck tonight. I didn't get to see many girls. I wondered about the sin of lust. She appeared to be just a short deckhand working the bow lines until I spotted the twin yellow braids hanging from a skullcap pulled low over her forehead. Her quilted parka kept the bitter wind off and made me think she was a man. I knew she could see me here at the same spot near the "Long Reach" landing; this is where George Washington once camped on a surveying trip. I was thinking he'd have done me a big favor if he'd never marked this spot on a map and it stayed a wilderness. Foolish thoughts like that were all I had in my head because I was afraid to think of what was on my mind at that hopeless time. I was fourteen, not a kid, but too young to light out on my own—or so I said to cover my fear of running away.

Not that the old man beat me—he mostly ignored me unless we were working a place and then he would bark commands to do this, do that, go there. I'd get a bible quote if I didn't hustle—something to do with being ungrateful or lazy.

Before he was defrocked and kicked out of his church in Davenport, Iowa, he was a popular fire-and-brimstone preacher. Too popular with the wives of his congregation, I later discovered, as the cause of our being uprooted. After my mother left us, he fell deeper into the bottle, lost his faith, and came up with this brainstorm he could make money doing tent revivals. That worked for a while until property owners refused to allow him onto their land and vandals burned down the tent outside East Palestine. His next big idea was to buy a cattle hauler with the money left over and "promote awareness of the Seven Deadly Sins in everyday life."

A drunk father, sins, demons and hell—that seemed to be my fate in life, and I was feeling sorry for myself. I heard footsteps coming up behind me. For a split second, I was in a panic thinking the old man had come down to the river looking for me, and only a big to-do could pull that pint of Jim Beam from his lips.

But it was the girl from the ferry.

"Hey," she said, "what are you doing here?"

"Hey," I replied. I brushed a sleeve across my nose to wipe the snot away. "Nothing. What are you doing?"

"Nothing," she replied. She pointed to the cars driving down the ramp. "My dad's the pilot."

"That's nice," I said. I didn't want to tell her what my father was.

"You live here in Fly?"

"No," I said; "we've just arrived."

"Visiting, huh? Fly is a shithole. You related to any

of them crazy people?"

We'd been to Fly, Ohio three years ago. I remembered no crazy people there.

"What crazy people?"

"Them crazy religious freaks just outside Fly," she said. "New Zenith. They settled there after Jeffrey Lundgren killed that family."

"Who was Jeffrey Lundgren?" I asked her.

"A serial killer," she replied. "He killed five people in one family. He said he was a prophet and God talked to him."

"That seems odd God would tell him to kill a whole family," I replied.

Her eyes, like mine, watered from the cold wind but they were blue as the sky in Palestine in one of Dad's tracts; her face was leached of color except for the tip of her nose and her lips, which looked purple-red compared to the white skin of her face, like a clown's mouth pasted on a leper's face. I guessed her age as the same as mine.

"My dad lets me skip school to make the crossing with him," she said. "How come you're not in school?"

"I'm home-schooled."

I told people that if they asked. The only things my father taught me had to do with loading and unloading the cattle truck and breaking down the sets. When he was in a pleasant mood, he called them "dioramas," but they were just painted signboards some man in Gauley Bridge made for him. They illustrated "the pitfalls and temptations," he said, of each Deadly Sin. People who paid their money to enter laughed out loud when they saw them. The deeply religious customers didn't laugh; they all came from places with names like Raccoon, Pig, Hippo, Spider, Disco, Bitter End, Cucumber. Our last trip included places called Oddville and Bethlehem. I'd been up and down the hills of Tennessee, Kentucky, and West Virginia in the Appalachians so often I wondered if I'd ever see a straight road or a flat plain again. Fly, Ohio was as close to flatland as we'd been in months.

The ferry whistle blew a long and two short blasts. "I gotta go," she said suddenly. "That's my dad calling me."

"Hey, what's your name?" I wasn't sure she could hear me with the wind whipping about.

"Natty," she called back.

Her full name was Natalie Sue Thorvaldsdottir, a grand name. However, she insisted on being called "Natty."

Natty showed up the next afternoon after I'd set up the truck. I hadn't realized how much I wanted her to come back. Living on the road, I had few chances to speak to someone my age. I had told her how my father and I roamed the hills with our traveling "freak show," although my father had a fancier term; he called it "a mobile religious experience for the saving of souls." Natty asked me if my father was just a crook. I couldn't say he was for sure. He was a complicated man was how he described himself.

"He's haunted by God," I replied, unsure what I meant exactly by that. "I think this is his way of atoning for his 'great sin,' as he says."

"What about you?" she asked me.

"I just want out of it," I said. I didn't have to think hard about an answer.

"Then how come you carry that bible with you?"

"I have to take it," I said. "It's the only way I can get away if he thinks I'm off reading it. It's one of them Gideon bibles. He took it from this motel we was staying at in Coffee Creek. That was in Tennessee a couple years back."

"You should say 'were,' not 'was.' 'We were staying at.'"

"I thought that's what I said," I replied, confused.

"Your English isn't too good. Maybe you should go to a real school," she said.

It felt like being kicked in the stomach. I had learned

how to hide my feelings so I just shrugged my shoulders. "As soon as I get clear of this whole thing," I said, "I'm going to California."

"Lots of people say that," Natty said. "They never do go. I'd like to go to California."

We talked until the ferry whistle blew for her. She told me all about computers, cell phones, and the internet. I knew of them, of course, but it sounded like magic the way she talked about it.

"You mean there's this woman Siri who lives inside the web and she knows everything?"

"Jerome, honest to God, you're so ignorant for someone your age," Natty said.

I made her laugh when I described each sin we displayed on our truck. My father used some old fence boards to feature "sins in action." It was a way to put a "spotlight on the devil's work." His favorite verse, one he made me memorize when I was six, was from John: "And this is the condemnation, that the light has come into the world, and men loved darkness rather than light, because their deeds were evil."

Customers walked up a ramp from the rear of the semi just like cattle had when the truck was new; in fact, it still smelled of dung no matter how often I washed it out. The people would pass down a center walkway and look over a short fence on either side where the big sin "held court," in my father's words. "So, for example, Wrath," I explained. "You have to show the wickedness in violence." He had me fetch these old store mannequins from a landfill in Raccoon, Kentucky, we were passing through. The mannequin I named "Joe" had a plastic baseball bat he was about bring down on the head of his companion, who had a damaged face I couldn't clean up. They played cards, gambled, and drank, all illustrated by a deck of cards and empty booze bottles. My father liked to show sins working in combination with other sins; he called it "demonic synergy."

I explained all the sins in a mocking way, yet secretly proud of having helped to create them. Younger then, I believed wholly in my father's righteousness.

"One time," I told Natty, "we picked up this guy passing through a town called Gripe, I forget what state. Anyway, he was real fat, this guy named Ottis. He drank with my father. So when we got set up, my father gave him some money to pretend to be 'Gluttony-Come-Alive.' He would sit in his pen and pretend to eat from cans of SpaghettiOs with a spoon. I put empty cans on the floor all around him and his mouth was all red with sauce like a beard. People loved it—except he asked for more money because he said he was now 'the main attraction.' My father refused. He talked him into playing Sloth in the next couple of places we stopped at. He'd sit in this beat-up La-Z-Boy and scratch his stomach and pretend to watch TV, but it was just a busted-up one I found in a junkyard."

"What happened to him?"

"He got drunk in Lodi and never came back," I said.

Natty got up to leave and leaned toward me; she gave me a kiss on the cheek. I blushed. I didn't even remember my mother's kisses. She left when I was five.

"I feel sorry for you," she said. She squinted at me in that funny way that made her freckles jump. "We had to read a novel by Mark Twain for class. You remind me of that only you use a cattle hauler. The part where these phony guys come to this river town and advertise a play, but it's fake, and the people show up for the final performance with baskets of rotten tomatoes to throw at them."

"Never heard of him," I said. "My father doesn't believe in made-up stuff like that. He says it's idleness and takes us away from God."

We stayed silent for a long time, two kids sitting on the riverbank, but my heart was thumping. I wanted to kiss her on the lips, but I was too afraid. Again I thought about the sin of lust.

"I like when the sun sets on the river this way. It turns it into a glassy gold—so pretty."

"Pretty filthy, if you look at all the junk floating in it and what's below the surface."

I wished I hadn't said that. It ruined the mood.

"Listen, Jerome. Stay away from Fly tomorrow."

"You mean those crazy Amish, right?"

"I mean it, Jerome!"

"What's wrong?"

"They ain't—aren't Amish, dummy. I told you! They're like the ones that killed that family up north."

She meant the Jeffrey Lundgren murders of the family up in Kirtland on Lake Erie. Lundgren, self-proclaimed prophet of a Latter-Day Saints cult movement, was executed ten years ago in Lucasville, the state pen on this same Ohio River. Natalie obsessed over the murders.

"Them people over there, there's a secret cult nobody knows about a few miles past Fly. They pretend to be ordinary people, but they're all blood-related and they sacrifice to the Devil."

"Crazy talk," I told her, and, besides, being related in small towns was no big thing. "Seems like half the names on the mailboxes back in the hollows had the same name on 'em."

"It ain't—isn't no joke, I'm telling you!"

"What are you saying, Natty?"

"People talk about ceremonies in the woods yonder in New Zenith."

I laughed. "Listen, I been all over these old hills and there ain't no devil worshippers. That's what rich people say about us hillbillies. It don't mean a doggone thing."

Something in me loved to see her riled up. She was the first girl who ever paid attention to me. The thought of leaving her behind after we broke down the sets and headed out put a cold feeling in me. My father never consulted me on our comings and goings, especially when he was hungover or after a dismal turnout and we had little money from ticket sales. He placed a "donation box" at the exit ramp, right next to Pride, our fanciest sin where posters of expensive sports cars and beautiful women sporting jewels and wearing lavish evening gowns from a bygone era were pinned to the walls. Only once in a while did someone drop an extra bill into it.

"I'll be careful," I said. "Stop worrying."

Then I asked her the thing that was in my mind the whole time we sat together. "Natty, can we write each other when I leave town?"

"Nobody writes letters today, stupid. Everything's emails and texting. Oh, man, there's the whistle! Look, I have to run. So long, Jerome."

"Natty, wait!"

"My dad'll be angry if I make him wait. So long, you. Good luck with… your religious thing."

The words faded in the wind behind her. I was alone at the river's edge once more. It felt like ice water had been poured down my shirt in the freezing wind.

That night I dreamed of her. My father had told me about "nocturnal emissions" when I turned thirteen, but his half-drunken explanation with his fancy words confused me. He might have been describing light-minutes in astronomical units for all I understood.

We always avoided the bigger cities, the "Sodoms and Gomorrahs," but a rust-belt town was sometimes on our route when county fairs coincided with our travels. My father often cajoled the local minister into arranging a temporary berth near one of the exhibition barns. His wheedling reminded me of a deer tick that drops from a twig and burrows into your skin. More often than not, a local sheriff would drop by after complaints started about a "fraud," and we would be asked to remove ourselves. My father would argue and sometimes wangled an extra day from some embarrassed official, but he usually just huffed and puffed; then I'd be stuck loading up the gear, securing the ramps, and packing the displays.

As soon as I got back from the river, I saw how drunk he was. Weaving on his feet, the bottle hanging from his fingertips like an attachment he couldn't release if he tried.

"We're leaving," he said.

My heart hammered in my chest. I'd never find Natalie's address if we left, but what he said next relieved my anxiety.

"Up the road, place called New Zenith."

When we got to New Zenith it made Fly look like one of the more prosperous riverside towns. I didn't think people could find us out there in the sticks, but they did—dozens, all ages, men and women, older kids, too. They handed me their dollar bills and trudged up the ramp to the exhibits. My father's mood lightened and his bad temper evaporated with his hangover. Now and then, he'd glance over at me while he went through his set speech to the people, something he did less often unless a number of customers made it worthwhile. Then he'd transform into the preacher he once was. Mostly he sat in the cab and drank while I took the money and handled the questions—but never refunding the money, a mistake I made once in Tuttle, Kentucky when a man in hunter's camos threatened me into giving back his dollar.

Seeing the surprising turnout, my father was in a state of bliss. Money could do that when liquor wasn't controlling his brain.

They arrived and kept coming. Sometimes they'd gather around a certain sin and lean over the wooden slats like neighbors leaning over a fence. I couldn't hear what they were saying, but I felt nervous remembering what Natalie'd said about the "secret cult" and "human sacrifices" deep in the woods.

They looked normal—almost. There was something not right about them, seeing them all together. I couldn't explain it. Just a look in my direction now and then. You can't see what's behind a person's eyes, but I could sense something off about these people. They all wore dark clothing. No tennis shoes, tee-shirts or jackets with funny or obscene sayings on them like everywhere else we'd been. We'd encountered some strange types before like the ones hoping for the Apocalypse or the so-called "doomsday preppers." They reminded me of that.

Unlike other crowds, nobody laughed at our ramshackle set-up or the amateur drawings and outdated posters. You would think they were in a museum the way they all stared and kept their comments low among themselves. Not even the young ones laughed. They bothered me most of all because they didn't turn their gaze away when our eyes locked. I'd never been looked at that way before. When I turned eight, my father made me become Envy-in-Action; he placed me in the middle of one pen with a broken toy and pretending to stare longingly at a poster of a Christmas tree and a happy family opening presents on Christmas morning. At ten, I played Greed. Nobody believed me as a shriveled-up, aged miser with actor's paint bouncing a bag of coins sprayed gold on my knees.

Three white-haired men lurked near the exit ramp talking intently among themselves. I'd been in enough fly-speck villages to know the respect and power elders held in their communities. I didn't like the way they looked from one to another or cast backward glances at either me or my father, who was much too busy reveling in his success to notice anything going on. When the last of the people had exited the ramp, they milled about and talked among themselves. I was bolting the entrance ramp in place when my father approached. He had money stuffed in his pockets.

"What are you doing?"

"Packing up," I said. "It's dark. No one else is coming." My voice quavered. I couldn't say what I was afraid of. Natalie's words echoed in my head.

"They invited us for dinner," my father announced. "Let that go for now. Plenty of time in daylight."

"We're staying overnight?"

"Shut up, Jerome. Don't offend our guests. We've been invited to partake of a meal with these godly folk and that's what we're going to do," he said. My father brooked no argument, as he liked to say, whenever he had made up his mind on anything.

Dinner was in some farmer's hog barn. Tables had been smacked up against one another. All the adults sat together with their families, but I noticed the children were absent—not a good sign. The bread they passed around stuck in my throat. I could barely eat anything that night because of Natty's warning. The aromas of food had the big boars grunting and snorting in their pens.

My father was some distance from me; he sat with the three elders and talked religion. Now and then, I saw my father's face screw up or his eyes widen at what was being said to him by one of the men. Although my father was steeped in religion, none of it had ever taken with me, not deep down. He called me "a whited sepulcher." The angel Michael with his sword or the angel Moroni—what's the difference when it came to how human beings behaved? I went along with it to avoid trouble and be forced to abide his endless lectures about my many failings and horrid weaknesses as a Christian. God and the devil were things to scare kids with. I didn't know which one caused most of the suffering in the world but if I had to bet, I'd say God, hands down. He had the upper hand for the all-out, insane mischief inside people's heads. My father's face, half-hidden in shadow from the lanterns set out on the tables, spooked me. The lanterns provided little illumination and gave off an oily smoke that burned my eyes and irritated my nostrils.

If you've ever been in a car accident, you'll know what the feeling is. Just before you're about to be hit, time slows, reverses. The voices at the end of the last table where my father sat got louder. I heard the word "Antichrist" and then I saw my father's face sink and his whole body shrivel as if he'd been lashed by a whip. All heads swiveled toward that table. I turned my head opposite the way everyone else was looking at one of the hog pens on the opposite side of the barn.

I bolted before anyone could react. I jumped up from the table and crossed the barn in a sprint and hurdled the top rail and dove headfirst through the opened panel, fashioned like a pet door, leading to the corral. I went right through it into a slurry of mud, straw, and feces and came up with feet churning, slipping, and dodging hogs everywhere. The startled boars and sows ran off in every direction, but I was intent on escaping whatever was going to happen back there.

I leaped the last rail of the enclosure despite the filth clinging to my pants and shoes and headed past the barn into the open fields and woods beyond. I heard shouts behind me and halfway to the woods, I heard the baying of dogs. It only made me run harder. I kept an image of the river in my head and ran toward it. My terrified brain wasn't able to think of anything at that point but escaping some unimaginable horror. I ran and kept running. I ran all night.

My father found me walking like a zombie on the road to Fly at dawn. I was numb with cold and my teeth chattered. He had to help me inside. In the warmth of the cab's interior, the heat made my muscles shiver even more.

"You damn fool! What did you take off for like

that?"

I said nothing. My brain wouldn't work right, and no words came into my mouth. I couldn't tell him I thought he was dead, tortured, and murdered by those people back there in some bizarre ritual.

"Those were the kindest, most decent people I ever met, and you take off like some scared rabbit and make them search for you! Hard-working people who need their sleep! What the hell's wrong with you?"

That's when he struck me across the face with his fist. If it weren't for my exhausted condition, I might have sobbed. As it was, tears poured down my cheeks. I didn't wipe my face. I was ashamed at having run off like a coward.

He lectured me all the way to the Sistersville ferry. The names he called me were biblical, like "spawn of Beelzebub," but the one he favored most was "fool." The more he talked, the more I realized how wrong I was about everything I once thought I knew. We were a traveling freak show, the people who clumped up the ramp were also freaks. Freaks on the road showing freaks in towns how bad they were with stupid displays and painted mannequins. Being hit by my father taught me something else: violence wasn't always bad. I grew up after the blow.

After an hour or longer of his badgering, I said: "Why don't you shut the fuck up and quit your talking?"

That stunned him. I expected to get hit really hard for that—but nothing happened. We drove on in silence for the rest of the day.

We made more stops on our way south, the cold weather creeping up behind us. The truck broke down and he had to use some of the "Florida money" to repair it. The goal never changed: get enough money to sit out the winter in some RV camp in Georgia or Alabama until the spring. Then head back to the Appalachians in March.

I abandoned him once more, and for good, at a rest

stop in Dothan, Alabama on our way back north. I'd been waiting for the first opportunity and warm weather to chance it. A gruff-spoken long-haul trucker with a load of steel coil going to Louisiana gave me a ride when I told him a story about losing money for a Greyhound bus and having family in California.

All he wanted to do was talk about sexual things and rub himself. When I didn't respond to his questions about girls I had sex with, he changed the subject. He had a plastic statue of Jesus on his console and religious postcards taped above his head. One showed Jesus in white robes surrounded by people. The adults looked fearful, like animals approaching a campfire, but the children stood near him and gazed in rapture up at his face. Another one showed an Indian-looking man in a red shirt with frizzy black hair holding up his hands like a man about to be robbed. The caption read: "The grace of God is like insurance." It was signed Baba. The trucker never told me his name; we stopped for a meal in Baton Rouge at a truck stop, and I disappeared while he was browsing among the goods in the shop next to the restaurant.

Years later, I realized how dangerous what I did was. He might not have been a harmless pervert. I was learning so much so fast about the real world. My father's crazy ideas fell out of my head as fast as new things came into it.

I washed dishes and took out garbage in diners all the way down to New Orleans. I stayed with some street kids in abandoned houses. When the police came by to roust the squatters, we'd find another like cockroaches avoiding the light. I learned to panhandle and steal in those days, and which neighborhoods to avoid because of black gangsters. I seemed to be growing and stretching every day. I could never get enough food in me after living like a jungle animal without the nourishment my body needed. I never reached my full growth and still have problems with eating.

I made it to California when I was twenty-two, although I'm not sure if that was my correct age. I never saw my father or Natalie again. I thought of her constantly, especially at night when I was worried about something.

Little by little, I stopped thinking about my father. In my imagination, he would still be driving through those same Appalachian hills in the semi hauling around displays of the very sins he embodied. I used to wonder if he ever bothered to look for me; then somehow, I gave up thinking about that.

Today, I have a job. I have routines. I belong to the domain of unskilled labor, as Richard, one of my co-workers, describes it. He's a reformed meth addict and works in the freezer goods section mostly. He has all kinds of tattoos on his arms, stomach and chest. He showed me the one on his back from Thessalonians in gothic lettering: "Therefore let us not sleep as others do but let us watch and be sober." Richard or the tattooist got the number of the verse wrong, but I didn't tell him that. I read the bible an hour every day even though I still don't believe.

We unload delivery trucks for the big Walmart store on Route 17. I live in a small apartment a few blocks from the beach. When I'm not thinking of Natalie, I can hear the waves lapping on the shore, but I know that's not possible. I don't have friends; some people say hello to me at work. The shift supervisor was nice for a while until I told her about traveling around with my father. She told the others about me, so I keep to myself mostly. I don't want to lose this job. I'm afraid of drifting. Richard says it's the "forces of randomness" I'm afraid of. He says it's waiting out there in the dark. I don't know what he means most of the time.

I have bad dreams occasionally and wake soaked in sweat, sometimes yelling words I don't remember. I have a suspicion that's my past creeping back inside my head. The books from the Goodwill store sit on my nightstand and help me improve my English, as Natty once said on the shore of the Ohio. I read the Royal Nonesuch part in *Huckleberry Finn*. I saw my father and me as the two rascals romping onstage and escaping before they had rotten vegetables thrown at them. The guy who wrote the introduction called it "a farce comedy mixed with elements of tragedy." He must have meant the part with the feuding families where Buck got shot and killed.

It's almost Halloween. The store shelves are loaded up with cheap junk, bags of candy corn, costumes of witches and Hollywood celebrities. The toy gadgets resemble Frankenstein monsters, mummies, and movie characters like Jason Vorhees and Freddy Krueger with his razor glove. The Grim Reapers have blinking red eyes and there are thousands of plastic jack-o'-lanterns in all sizes. The day after Halloween, we'll be bringing out all the Thanksgiving stuff. Then Christmas the day after that. Most of it has already arrived and plenty more is on the way.

It's hard to recognize time when all the seasons blur into one another. Halloween is the best, the most honest. It's about us and the monsters and freaks we are when the masks come off.

Revenge of the Judas Goat

Ralphie Kendrew drank like a bladder fish. Yeah, sure, he was everybody's best drinking buddy—until the shit hit the fan. It wasn't his fault that Caltrans' so-called explosive expert couldn't hold his booze and vaporized himself against a panel truck, damaged two vans, a concrete mixer, and an asphalt pavement machine—what a dope! The investigation commission put the blame on his ass despite the fact that everybody from his crew was boozing at the Big Gulch Saloon off Highway 1. How was he supposed to know that tequila shots were half-price that Tuesday? Or that a troupe of lap dancers were called in to service a bunch of political bigwigs?

They abandoned him, those pricks—his so-called friends, guys he'd worked with for twenty-five years. Being supervisor meant he had to fall on his sword, even though Jake MacDonald and the powder monkey had their faces mashed into the twats of two strippers dancing on the bar top. Fired, all because he was the road crew supervisor. "You should have known better," this aged prick with double chin wattles scolded, wagging his finger at him, calling him a "lush" and a "Judas goat," whatever that was.

Humiliation was a new feeling for Ralphie. He didn't like it. Even more, he intended to have the last laugh from the minute he walked out of the municipal building—*Yessirree, Bob, laugh at me all you want, you backstabbing motherfuckers.*

Work on the Sumash Bridge above the Gabrielino

Gorge was all but completed by then. The steel gusset plates binding key parts of the structure were intact, signed off by the county building inspector. All except for one plate in the center of the bridge. In the chaos after the powder monkey's explosion, that section still had to be approved, because that walking turd of a civil engineer told him in his mumbo-jumbo, college-boy gibberish—something about "buckling loads" and steel plates. But work somehow shifted to removing the Type 80SW's, those ugly bridge railings that looked more like concrete tank traps, and only because the latte-sippers in Sacramento wanted to improve the view of California's oceanside scenery. They didn't give shit for the thousands of working stiffs piling into their crappy Honda Civics heading into the city for the morning shift jobs to work for the elites,

Ralphie hated them, hated every single one of those glamorous residents in the gated community overlooking the Pacific from the decks of their multi-million-dollar monster houses. Walking out of the disciplinary hearing where his union refused to support him, he found his inspiration in the form of a little boy playing with his plastic toy cars, squealing as he pushed his cars off a ramp of two-by-fours. *You want a more pleasing view of the canyon? OK, motherfuckers, I'll see what I can do about it…*

Two nights after he was told to clean out his locker, after the last guy packed up his gear in the bed of his pickup and drove off, he set to work on his plan. He worked all night with his Ford F-150 and a towing chain to remove the fastenings to the I-girders beneath the steel mesh where the plate sat. Just before dawn, he picked up the BRIDGE CLOSED signs, slapped his handmade stencil OPEN over CLOSED, slathered it with black spray paint, and replaced the signs, keeping the main highway access closed. He wasn't about to deal with traffic flow—certainly not cars of working moms and kids on their way to school.

Removing the heavy-duty saw horses blocking the bridge entrance, he took his position at the entrance and hoped no la-dee-da art critics *en route* to downtown L.A. would detect the slovenly paint job of his signs. Everything prepared, he awaited the first arrival of the morning commute.

Not a minute to lose, he thought, checking his watch. The members of that exclusive community would be finishing up their second mocha latte, nibbling a pastry from some *ooh-la-la* bakery on Santa Monica, more worried about their cereal-infused ice cream scoop for lunch than the bridge they were about to drive over with its view of the ocean, oblivious to that engineer's Martian lingo about "membrane compression."

Grabbing his neon-yellow traffic vest from the truck bed, Ralphie planted himself at the entrance of the gated community's only exit to the bridge. The first car approached at six-fifteen. He gulped and watched the sports car slowly approach.

He isn't sure, Ralphie thought. The paper said next week was the planned date to reopen.

The throaty purr of the big Porsche engine almost drowned out the driver's words. Ralphie took in the attaché case, the styled cut, expensive sunglasses, the bone-white shirt with gold cuffs, and thought: *Good, a lawyer*.

"Hey, I thought the bridge was closed for another week," the driver said.

Ralphie couldn't see his eyes, but the man looked annoyed. He had that classic "I-smell-excrement" look on his clean-shaven mug, a look aimed at lowlifes like Ralphie Kendrew.

"Fuck, I've been getting up an hour early for a month because of this goddamned detour."

"Well, your worries are over. We just opened it up last night."

"Why the fuck wasn't it mentioned on the radio? Just another Caltrans boondoggle to give you lazy union guys more unnecessary work."

Ralphie smiled. "That's right, sir. I like your sports car, by the way. Is it a Porsche?"

"Did you miss the shield with the black horse on the coat of arms on the hood? Right under your nose, pal."

"Gee, bet it costs a fortune. What model is it?"

"What the—it's a Carrera, one hundred thou before the goodies are toted up. You're an unskilled laborer. You and all your highway bozos working on your tans with your little traffic signs. Keep sucking on the public teat with your forty-dollar-an-hour job. Maybe you can get one someday."

"Wow, a bit testy this morning, aren't we, sir? Did your live-in cook substitute Folger's for the roasted beans from Costa Rica? Tsk-tsk."

"I'll humor you since I got up early for the detour. This is a Nine-One-One, just like the emergency number you'll be calling one of these days soon when that beer belly hanging over your pants gives you a heart attack."

Ralphie made a sad, pouty face and mimicked tears streaming down his cheek with his index finger. "Better get going or you'll be late for work. I imagine you have lots of clients waiting for you to bill them a hundred bucks an hour for your big lawyer words."

"Fuck you, you envious little *peon*. Loser!"

He roared off.

Ralphie's eyes were glued to the diminishing slope of the Porsche's rear as it accelerated, the distinctive targa bar and aluminum gills flashed in the dawn sunlight. He held his breath. The high-pitched whine became a low rumble as the Doppler effect kicked in, stringing out the sound waves behind the receding vehicle.

Close, close... there, right there, you're right there about... Now—

The driver's scream had a Doppler effect of its own. Ralphie stood nailed to the spot, all ears, as the man's yodeling cry dropped an octave-per-second along with his vehicle that seemed to match the 38 feet-per-second descent—a long, 800-foot plunge into the creek bed below.

Good riddance, you snob motherfucker!

Ralphie ran to check the damage to the bridge. *Perfect!* The 20-by-20 square hole was exactly what he hoped for when he removed the bracing struts and fasteners. But no time to relish the moment—another vehicle was fast approaching; he scurried back to his position.

Yet another foreign job. *What was it with rich people anyhow and their lust for everything not made in America?* Watching it swerve past the last hillside curve to the bridge entrance, Ralphie stood ready with his doctored sign.

The driver slowed to a stop just as the first one had. The window came down with a pneumatic *whoosh*, releasing an expensive cologne wafting upward to prickle Ralphie's nostrils.

"Redundant, isn't it?"

"Sorry, sir?"

"Your sign. It's redundant," the driver said. "Unnecessary. If the bridge is open, it's open. Why are you standing there with your sign proclaiming it to be open?"

Ralphie stammered. The man sounded logical, flustering him. He hadn't thought of that. He feared the man might have spotted the gap in the bridge's center coming around the hill.

"Hey, man, relax. Just jerking your chain. Glad to see the bridge fixed. That detour was costing me a ton. Any idea what it costs to fill this baby up?"

"No, sir."

The driver, a man in his early thirties broke into a laugh.

"A lot."

"I'll bet."

Ralphie scoped the interior of the Lamborghini, as much as he could see. He spotted a white lab coat and the disc-shaped resonator of what must be a stethoscope sticking out.

"Are you a doctor, sir?"

The man cut his eyes to where Ralphie was looking. "Naw, that stuff on the seat, that's just to pick up chicks."

Ralphie stared. The man burst into another laugh.

"Yes, I confess to the crime. I am a doctor. You need a boob implant, I'm your man."

"No, thanks, I'm good."

"I thought I had a droll sense of humor, but you have me beat."

"Uh-huh."

He winked at Ralphie. "Got a half-dozen pairs of tits to perk up before lunch. *Adiós, amigo.*"

"Have a…"

The Lamborghini sped down the bridge at a higher speed than the Porsche.

"…nice day."

This time, it wasn't a yodel but an ear-splitting crunch of metal and shattered glass. The Lambo had slammed into the other side before dropping into the gulch. Seconds later, he heard the echoing splashes of pieces of the sports car hitting the water.

Too bad, he seemed an OK guy," Ralphie thought.

He was thinking of choosing which drivers to send plummeting to their deaths when the van rolled up. Ralphie realized this wasn't from one of the hillside mansions; it must have bypassed the phony road signs he'd planted earlier.

The window came down. Ralphie noted five teenaged males crammed inside.

"...'fuck up, man?"

The driver, a buzzcut with neck glyphs and sleeve tatts, looked at him with a bored expression. The odor of weed escaping from the van was so strong Ralphie had to step backwards to keep from inhaling.

"What the fuck, Nico," the Eminem lookalike in the passenger seat said to the driver. "Quit wasting time with this motherfucker."

That set up a chorus of hoots from the backseat. They looked the same, each one tatted up, adorned with eyebrow studs, and clothing that looked like something from a Goodwill bin but even with gaping holes would cost more than he once made in a week.

"Just wanna ask the dude something, all right?"

Nico's expression was serious. "Where do you buy your shoes, man?"

Ralphie replied, "Steel-toe boots. Got 'em at Target."

Before the van peeled off with a chorus of yipping hyenas, the passengers engaged in crotch-grabbing and shouts, calling him "Target Man" accompanied by loud farts that sounded like marbles tossed into a bathtub. The van blasted away, swerving from side to side down the bridge, the driver having fun. A third of the way down, rap music blasted from the van, drowning out their howls. The thumping beat, a staccato mumble of slang directed at enemies and "bitches" trailed in the van's wake. The last thing Ralphie heard was something about "chewing on cocks" before the van disappeared, ass-over-teacup, into the hole.

So long, fellas. Have a nice day, ya jerkoffs...

The rapper's jovial obscenities played all the way

down to the bottom of the ravine before the impact. Ralphie wondered if the two sports cars before them took the brunt of the van's fall. He liked the idea, but he didn't have time to wonder because three more vehicles appeared around the last bend and headed toward the bridge. He held up his sign and waved them past, as though traffic were piling up.

Solo drivers, two women and one man. All three well-groomed, driving expensive cars—An Audi, a Saab, and a Benz. Two wore sunglasses in preparation for the drive downtown. At peak morning rush, the stream of cars, fender-to-fender, with the morning sun glittering off chrome would blind a driver sitting in traffic like that. The man was texting as he passed, both women were on their cell phones. He watched their mouths moving as they drove past, completely ignoring him.

Head-to-butt, like ants at a picnic, Ralphie thought, watching them go by. They picked up speed by the time they reached the middle of the bridge. The first two vehicles disappeared like a magic trick in a headlong dive into the abyss. The third driver sensed something just in time despite her distracted driving. She hit the brakes hard with a screech of burning rubber, the big Benz slewed, skidded the front portion leaning over the gap.

Ralphie trotted to it, panting from exertion. The Benz and driver hung over the lip, the updraft buffeting the chassis from below. Like a floundering ship in rough weather seeking its moment of righting against waves battering the hull, the car struggled against gravity's relentless tug. She tried slamming the car into reverse. The tires screamed with effort.

Ralphie jogged to the driver's side window. "Do something!" the woman screamed. He ran around to the rear and planted himself against the left back fender. Her eyes in the rearview were bugged with horror. He shoved hard. The acrid smell of burning rubber singed his nose hairs. He grunted with effort, the woman screaming and cursing him when she realized what he was doing.

Her window came down; he heard her piercing warble: "WHAT THE FUCK ARE YOU DOING, YOU ASS—"

The car took the plunge with a final heave, a big circus cat digging its claws into the sawdust—to no avail.

"...HOLE!"

He wanted to watch it fall all the way but a fear of heights kept him from getting too close to the edge.

In the next hour, the bridge's hungry maw would consume ten more vehicles, all driven by single men or women. He turned back three cars with children inside. Told them to take the detour. Two mothers and one dad cursed him and their luck but turned around. He stood happily watching them go. No more early birds like the first three or the van; the cars spaced themselves nicely, allowing for an occasional chat with a curious driver about his presence on the bridge.

He couldn't have calibrated "arrivals and departures" any better if he had a computer. He wondered if any of the free-falling residents of Condo Fucko or Paradisio-Kiss-My-Assio considered that the modern conveniences of air-conditioning, Bose sound systems, and cell phones all contributed to their untimely demise. *What was it those yoga freaks liked to say about paying attention in the moment?*

By eleven, it was steamy hot; the temperature rising into the mid-eighties. The shimmering mirage of heat waves assisted the deception, making the gap in the bridge invisible until a driver was right there about to go into it. Fewer brakes were applied now. An occasional horrified wail from the car's interior reached him, but mostly all he heard was the barely discernible sound of crunching metal in the muggy air.

No reader of books, Ralphie bragged to his crew that the only books he read in high school were all written by some guy named Cliff Notes. Yet, standing there at the entrance with his cheap sign, he felt like some character in one of those Greek myths. That made him recall his old English teacher with dyed hair like a skunk's tail. She bored his class with some long-assed poem about a lady god who turned dudes into animals. But her eyes sparkled when she told them about an ugly, club-footed god whose wife was a whore who kept screwing other gods. He couldn't remember how his teacher put it, but the wife-god was banging another god when her husband trapped them in a net so finely made it was invisible. When he showed the two tangled-up lovers to the chief god, the other gods laughed instead.

He felt like that crippled god, vindicated and cheated at the same time. The sun grew higher, he wiped a sheen of perspiration from his brow. More cars went past; he ignored them, even the ones flipping him off or tooting their horns.

The first Caltrans truck showed up at noon from other work sites; his ruse of misdirecting traffic finally discovered. Workers hopped out, started to approach him, but were shouted back by the new supervisor, his replacement—that mealy-mouthed bastard Billy Johnson.

By the time the first police cruiser pulled up with its siren screaming and light bar flashing a rhythmic turquoise and cherry, the last passengers into the abyss were taking the ride of their lives: a black Navigator, a teal Infiniti, a battleship-gray Escalade, and a silver Lexus. He guessed at their professions—a corporate big shot, a hedge-fund manager, a real-estate wheeler-dealer—and a lady he recognized from the TV news. Her lipstick was a glossy pink, her cleavage exposed in her half-bra as she drove past oblivious to him and to her fate. *Sheila something from Channel 7…*

The two officers approached with guns drawn, ordered him to get "the fuck down in the road." They had him walk backwards to them. He complied without resisting. They patted him down, cuffed him up, and bundled him into the back of a second cruiser.

When they reached the Bixel Street off-ramp of Interstate 110, he asked the cop, "Officer, what in the hell is a Judas goat anyway?"

About the Stories

"Roy Boone's Return" was first published in Ammar Habib's *Thriller Magazine* in Vol. 2, Issue 2 in 2019. 18-27. Print. Kettle Blowing" and "Gone Fishing" were published in *Close to the Bone Magazine*, the latter on May 30, 2022. "A Civilized Man" was also published in *Thriller* (Vol. 2, Issue 1) on July 5, 2019. 5-9. Kindle. "Home for the Funeral" went to *Underside Stories* on June 8, 2022. "Easy Money" was published in *The Raven Review* on Jan. 3, 2021. "Barn Find" went up on *Rock and a Hard Place*. Ed.-in-Chief Roger Nokes. Vol. 1. Issue 3. (Rock and a Hard Place Pub., 2020). 92-100. Print. "The One Who Saves You" went online in *Terror House Magazine* by Editor-in-Chief Matt Forney on Aug. 5, 2022. "Boosting for the Devil" was accepted by U.K.'s *K-Zine Magazine*'s editor for the May 2020 issue. "Wrong Place, Wrong Time" went up on *Down in the Dirt*'s online magazine and was printed in *Eclipsed* Vol. 80 (Scars Pub., 2021): 46-47. Print. Finally, "Revenge of the Judas Goat" went up on *Short-Story.Me* on Aug. 20, 2022.

About the Author

Robert (Terry) White lives in Northeastern Ohio and has published crime, noir, and hardboiled novels featuring private investigators Thomas Haftmann and Raimo Jarvi, whose third outing occurred in 2024 with *Northtown Angelus*. His stories have appeared in magazines like *Switchblade, Down & Out, Black Cat Mystery Magazine, Mystery Tribune,* and *Mystery Weekly*. Nominated for a Derringer for one crime story, he has had another story selected for *Best American Mystery Stories,* 2019 and the Bouchercon anthologies. *Murder, Mayhem & More* cited two of his thrillers as finalists for Best Crime Books in 2018 and 2019. *Thriller Magazine* cited *The Russian Heist* as Best Novel in 2020. Another crime novella, *Burning Girl*, earned 2nd Place in the Whodunit competition in 2020. The Independent Fiction Alliance selected his collection of revenge tales *Betray Me Not* as Truly Best Indie Book of 2022.

Printed in Great Britain
by Amazon